STARCRAFT®
EVOLUTION

StarCraft®

EVOLUTION

TIMOTHY ZAHN

DEL REY

NEW YORK

Copyright © 2016 by Blizzard Entertainment, Inc. All rights reserved.

Published in the United States by Del Rey, an imprint of Random House, a division of Penguin Random House LLC, New York.

DEL REY and the HOUSE colophon are registered trademarks of Penguin Random House LLC.

STARCRAFT and BLIZZARD ENTERTAINMENT are trademarks or registered trademarks of Blizzard Entertainment, Inc., in the U.S. and/or other countries.

ISBN 978-0-425-28473-5
Ebook ISBN 978-0-425-28474-2

Printed in the United States of America on acid-free paper

randomhousebooks.com

2   4   6   8   9   7   5   3   1

First Edition

Book design by Christopher M. Zucker

For Corwin, who first brought StarCraft *into my life*

CHAPTER ONE

The war was over.

The nightmares weren't.

Marine Sergeant Foster "Whist" Cray didn't mind the dreams so much. Hell, he'd survived five straight years of living nightmares while he was deployed. He ought to be used to fear and panic by now.

What got him about the damn things was the *monotony*.

The war had been hell on wheels, but at least it had offered occasional changes of scenery. His platoon had been deployed to desert, jungle, forest, grassland, city—they weren't so much cities as they were heaps of shattered masonry and twisted pipe by the time his platoon got there, but it still counted—and once even on a beach.

The enemy had been pretty diverse, too. He'd blasted away at zerglings, hydralisks, ravagers, and all the rest of the umpty-ump hell-spawned varieties of zerg. Sometimes the overlord or queen or whoever was running that particular assault sent in the nastier monsters, at which point the marines would grab some dirt while a viking or a Thor waded in to deal with them.

But even new enemies meant something different to look at. He'd seen a few protoss, too, usually on the far side of the battlefield where they weren't doing the Dominion forces a whole lot of good. Once or twice he'd even ended up taking a potshot at one of them when the big alien had been careless enough to get in the way.

But the nightmares were all annoyingly the same.

It was always zerglings and hydralisks. It was always him and Jesse and Lena, standing shoulder to shoulder against the onslaught.

And his damn C-14 gauss rifle never worked.

It fired just fine. It barked out the usual *thud* and mule-kicked against his combat suit's shoulder just like it was supposed to. But instead of the 8mm spikes blazing toward the charging monsters at hypersonic speeds, they just blooped out in a pathetic little arc that nose-dived them into the dirt a couple of meters in front of him. He would fire again and again, not accomplishing a damn thing except to make a collection of spikes in the ground. The zerg kept coming, and they were just opening their jaws for lunch when he woke up in a cold sweat.

He never knew what happened to Jesse and Lena. He often wondered if they survived the dream.

Probably not. They hadn't survived the war. No reason they should survive the dream, either.

Afterward he usually just lay alone in the dark, listening to his heart thudding as he waited to fall asleep again. Sometimes he slipped out of his room in the marines' new barracks in Augustgrad and took a cup of coffee up to the roof to clear his head in the cold night air.

But today was special. Today was the sixth anniversary of the end of the war, or at least his part of it. Today the nightmare, and the reminder of the sacrifices of Jesse and Lena and all the others, called for something more.

Usually the roof was deserted, because sane people who weren't on night duty were in bed at this hour. Tonight, though, someone else was already topside when Whist arrived. The man was short and thin and hunched over a little, leaning his elbows on the low parapet and gazing toward the outskirts of the city. "About time," he called as Whist stepped out of the stairway.

Hastily, Whist lowered the bottle he'd liberated from the Non-commissioned Officers' Club, hiding it behind his leg. Hard liquor wasn't supposed to be consumed outside the club's controlled environment. "Excuse me?" he called back.

The other man half turned, and in the reflected light from the central part of the city behind him Whist could see the all-too-familiar fusion of physical youth and crushing psychological age. A war vet, for sure. "Sorry," the kid said. "I thought you were someone else." He beckoned. "Come on—join the crowd. I see you brought the refreshments."

Whist wrinkled his nose. So much for keeping the bottle hidden. For a second he thought about turning around and making a run for it before he could be identified, then decided he really didn't give a damn. "You've got a whacked idea of good places to meet people," he commented, starting across the uneven roofing material.

"I'm here for the view, not the ambience," the other said, gesturing over the edge of the roof behind him. "A buddy and I were going to watch a night training session. He must have slept through his alarm."

Whist frowned past his shoulder. In the distance, above one of the collections of rubble that had once been a suburb, he could see ten muted glows buzzing around like unhappy hornets. "What are those?"

"What do you think?" the kid countered with a snort. "Who else except reapers gets dragged out for training in the middle of the night these days?"

"I thought reapers mostly just kangarooed over hills and off cliffs," Whist said. "When did they start zooming around in circles?"

"Oh, they used to do that all the time," the kid said. "When the reaper program started, they were given fully flight-capable jetpacks."

"Sounds like fun."

"I'm sure it was," the kid said. "Trouble was, the new recruits also had a tendency to crash. A lot."

"I heard the packs used to explode, too."

"More often than anyone liked," the kid conceded. "Anyway, after the war ended and they suddenly had enough time for proper training, they started phasing in the old equipment design, keeping some of the standard units the same while putting others in the new, improved packs and taking them back to the original mission statement."

"Minus the random explosions?"

"So we hope, yes."

"Well, floating around certainly makes them better targets," Whist commented, choosing his words carefully. *We,* the kid had said. So he was a reaper, too? Terrific.

Because if marines were the best of the best, reapers were the worst of the worst. Literally.

Or at least they used to be. During the war, under the reign of Emperor Arcturus Mengsk, the whole corps had supposedly been made up of hardened criminals whose antisocial tendencies couldn't be brain-panned away, and who had opted for crazy-ass military duty as an alternative to prison or worse. Marines might like the way reapers could swoop down out of nowhere onto a zerg attack front, but no one really trusted them.

The new emperor, Arcturus's son, Valerian, was purportedly changing all that. Personally, Whist would believe it when he saw it.

"Spoken like someone who's been one of those targets." The kid offered his hand. "Lieutenant Dennis Halkman, 122nd Reapers."

"Yes, *sir*," Whist said, stiffening to attention and throwing a salute. A reaper *and* an officer. This just got better and better.

And if Halkman had been in the 122nd, he'd almost certainly been in the war. Possibly for years.

Which made him a definite anomaly. Typical service lifetime for a reaper was six months. "Sergeant Foster Cray, 934th Marines," Whist continued, identifying himself.

"Nice to meet you, Sergeant," the kid said, making no effort to lower his hand or return the salute. "And I should have mentioned that's *former* lieutenant. I've been rotated into the reserves, and you probably hate officers anyway, so let's skip the *sir*s and saluting, okay? And call me Dizz."

"Yes, sir," Whist said, frowning. Definitely not the kind of officer interaction he was used to.

Of course, Dizz would have an entire pre-reaper criminal skill set tucked away. Maybe this folksy, aw-shucks approach to new people was something he'd developed to put them at their ease. Maybe he'd been a con man? "And you can call me Whist," he added, taking Dizz's hand and shaking it. Dizz had a good, strong grip, the kind that dripped confidence and trustworthiness. Definitely would fit a con man persona.

Then again, it would fit a lot of other criminal types, too, up to and including serial murderers.

Did the reapers accept serial murderers?

"Much better," Dizz said approvingly, a frown creasing his forehead. He was probably wondering if Whist was speculating about his past sins, a conversation Whist had no intention of getting into. Certainly not on a deserted rooftop when he wasn't even wearing his sidearm.

So, okay. The minute Dizz started steering the conversation that direction, Whist would make an excuse and head back to his quarters—

"The 934th, you say," Dizz continued. "Were you the unit sent to clean the zerg out of the Northwoods Forest on New Sydney?"

Whist blinked, disengaging his brain from his mental gymnastics. The Northwoods Forest . . . "We were there, yeah," he confirmed. "You were the reaper unit, right?"

"Oh, yeah, that was us," Dizz said, grinning suddenly. "So I'm guessing you had a front-row seat when Boff brushed one of the trees, bounced sideways, and nearly cannonballed into one of your guys?"

Whist snorted. "Front-row seat, hell," he said. There were few enough reasons to smile in battle, but that incident had been one such rare gem. "I was maybe three marines to his left when your boy started his pinwheel act. For a second I thought he was coming straight at *me*."

"The way he was flying, probably everyone in the unit thought that," Dizz said. "I remember being impressed as hell that none of you hit the dirt or even flinched."

"Trust me, we were flinching inside," Whist said. "Just wasn't time to actually do anything."

"Except swear," Dizz said. "That marine he tried to flatten—what was his name again?"

"Grounder."

"Right. I think Grounder swore for three minutes straight without ever repeating himself."

"I don't doubt it," Whist said. "I was too busy with a pair of zerglings right after that to pay much attention. But if you wanted an applied history of terran vulgar language, Grounder was your man. Never knew anyone with that depth of vocabulary."

"Well, he sure impressed us," Dizz said. "Though probably less about the language than about the fact he kept Boff speechless that long."

"I think he got in a *sorry, mate* once when Grounder stopped for breath," Whist offered. "But that was about it."

"Made for an interesting day, all right," Dizz said. "That, plus the fact we won."

Whist hissed between his teeth, the brief glow of humor from that day fading away into the rest of the bad memories. Yes, they'd won. But at a hell of a cost. "Yeah," he said. "What happened to Boff? Did he make it?"

"He made it through that particular battle, anyway," Dizz said. "He was transferred right afterward, and I never heard what happened to him. How about Grounder?"

"He lasted three more battles," Whist said, looking away. "Bought it in the fourth."

"Oh. Sorry."

"Yeah," Whist said. "Not like he was the only one."

"Not by a long shot," Dizz said grimly. "How do you think I got promoted to lieutenant this young?"

"Usually it's for ability or courage."

"Maybe that's how it is with the marines," Dizz said. "With reapers, it's for whoever lives the longest. Sort of a reverse consolation prize." He sighed. "Actually, I kind of hope Boff didn't make it. The guy was a three-time murderer. Hell of a debt to society to have to pay off."

"Yeah," Whist said through suddenly stiff lips. For a minute there he'd forgotten who he was talking to. "I suppose that kind of background might come in handy when you're shooting at zerg."

"Not as much as you'd think," Dizz said, turning to look over his shoulder at the reaper exercise still going on in the distance. "That's why they're trying to bring in a whole new crop of kinder and gentler . . . damn."

"What?" Whist asked, focusing on the floating lights. Nothing seemed different.

"They're greening," Dizz bit out. "Damn stupid—you got your comm?"

"Yeah," Whist said, popping it off his belt and holding it out.

"You want Reaper Sergeant Stilson Blumquist," Dizz said, making no move to take the device. "When he comes on, tell him his two southern flankers are greening."

"Okay," Whist said, punching for the base comm nexus and wondering what the hell *greening* was. The computer responded, and he fed in Blumquist's name. "Shouldn't you be the one to tell—?"

"Sergeant Blumquist," a terse voice snapped from the comm. "Who the hell is this?"

Again, Whist started to offer Dizz the comm. Again, Dizz waved it away. "I've been instructed to inform you that your two southern flankers are greening," Whist said.

"Really," Blumquist said. "And you'd know this how?"

"Because I can *see* them," Whist growled. "Just fix it, okay?"

He keyed off. "What the hell is greening?" he asked Dizz.

"Jealousy or envy," Dizz said, still focused on the distant lights. "In this case, a pair of hotdoggers trying to outdo each other with fancy and stupid maneuvers. Oh, and here they come."

Whist felt his eyes widen. "Here they *come*?"

"At least Blumquist knows how to do a needle search," Dizz commented. "You told him you could see him, and he pinpointed you. So not a *complete* incompetent."

"Good to know," Whist ground out. The lights were definitely on the move now, and definitely moving in their direction. "Should we, uh, make ourselves scarce?"

"Well, *I* should," Dizz said, brushing past Whist. "Oh, and I'll take this," he added, plucking the bottle deftly from Whist's hand.

Very deftly, in fact. Did that imply the man had been a pickpocket?

"Don't worry—you'll be fine," Dizz added over his shoulder as he strode swiftly toward the door. "Just tell him he can't talk to you that way."

Whist stared at the kid's back as he reached the door, his muscles tensed in fight-or-flight knots. Whatever was going on here, it had zero to do with him. The smart move would be to follow Dizz into the building, return to his bunk, and forget all this had happened.

But for the second time that evening, he suddenly decided he didn't give a damn. He'd done nothing wrong—for a change—and there was no way in the world he was going to run. And sidearm or no sidearm, if a bunch of wannabe reapers felt like making trouble, he would show them the marine definition of the word.

Ten seconds later they arrived.

Their technique was a little chaotic, he noted as they dropped out of the sky around him. Their timing was off, and a good half of them couldn't even stick their landings. But the encirclement itself was competent enough, and a lot of the sloppiness was probably just basic inexperience.

There was only one of the group who showed as even halfway competent. Whist made sure he was facing that one when he pounded onto the roof. "Sergeant Blumquist," he greeted the reaper. "Nice night for a flight."

"Can it, fekk-head," Blumquist spat, taking a long stride forward.

Evidently, he expected Whist to fall back as he approached. Whist didn't, forcing Blumquist to come to a hasty, awkward, and—to Whist, at least—rather comical stop.

Which did nothing to help the other's mood. "I want your name, rank, and what the hell you're doing up here," Blumquist snarled as he regained his balance. "After that you can report to the brig downstairs while I work up the charges against you."

Whist blinked. *Charges?* "Since when is standing on a roof a chargeable offense?"

"When it interferes with a night exercise," Blumquist said. "Since when does a stupid jarbrain have any idea what reapers do anyway?"

"I've seen plenty of competent reapers." Whist waved a hand at the ring of trainees around him. "These aren't them." He cocked his head. "And then there was the greening."

Blumquist's eyes narrowed. "Who the bloody *hell* are you to call down my squad?" he demanded, taking another step forward.

And in the lower edge of his vision, Whist saw the reaper's hands ball into fists.

Deliberately, Whist kept his own hands loose. At ten-to-one odds, the last thing he could afford was to let Blumquist goad him into throwing the first punch, or even looking like he was about to do so.

The problem was that with these odds, *not* taking out one or two of them right at the start pretty much guaranteed he would quickly be on the wrong end of a dogpile.

But he had no choice. He hadn't given Blumquist his name, but reaper heads-up goggles had a record feature, and all ten of them undoubtedly had his face by now. Even if Whist won the brawl, the entire marine food chain would quickly make its own dogpile. The only way he was going to get out of here was to let Blumquist attack first, and hope he could survive until the squad got tired of beating on him—

"Ten-*hut!*"

Blumquist spun around toward the rooftop door, stumbling a little as the weight of his jump pack threw his balance off. Striding toward them was Dizz, a dark expression on his face, a set of lieutenant's bars glittering on his collar.

Bars, Whist noted, that hadn't been there before. "Lieutenant Halkman, 122nd Reapers," Dizz announced tersely. "What the hell's going on here, Sergeant?"

"I—" Blumquist floundered for a second. "This man interfered in our exercise, sir," he managed, gesturing back to Whist. "He also refused to give his name—"

"He interfered?" Dizz cut in. "He *interfered*? From *here*?"

"He—he commed while I was trying to run a drill," Blumquist said. "Argued about my technique. Distracted me while—"

"If all it takes is a comm call to distract you, Sergeant, you have no business in the field," Dizz again cut in. "Was his criticism valid?"

"It—" Blumquist glanced sideways toward one of his troops. "It might have been, sir, yes."

"Then take it, act on it, and resolve it," Dizz said. "And get your butts back in the air. Now."

Blumquist stiffened to attention. "Yes, sir. Squad, return to training locus. By numbers: *execute.*"

In pairs, the trainees lifted off from the roof and headed back toward the patch of sky they'd been working earlier. Blumquist was the last to leave, still at attention as he lifted.

"Well, that was a lot of nothing," Whist commented as they watched the trainees drive away into the night.

"Don't you believe it," Dizz said grimly. "Once he realized he didn't have a leg to stand on, his only way to get out without looking foolish was to goad you into attacking him."

"Yeah, I got that," Whist said. "Thanks for coming back, by the way."

"Oh, that was always the plan," Dizz assured him. "I know Blumquist. I just wanted to wait until he'd dug himself in too deep to get out before cutting him off at the knees."

"To make him look foolish?"

"To make him look incompetent," Dizz said, an edge of bitterness in his voice. "I saw way too many good men and women die because of sergeants and lieutenants who charged in without thinking or observing. If we're lucky, idiots like Blumquist will have been put on desk duty by the time the next war starts."

"If there is one."

"There will be," Dizz said tiredly. "There always is." He nodded back behind him. "I left your bottle inside the door. I gather you were going to drink to Grounder?"

"To him and everyone else," Whist said. In all the excitement, he'd almost forgotten about the bottle.

"Let's go get it," Dizz said, gesturing toward the door. "And then head down to the Officers' Club. It's warmer, and they've got some nice couches. Perfect place to tie one on."

"I thought all the clubs were closed."

"Do I look like I care?"

"Not really," Whist admitted. So did expertise at getting past locks mean Dizz had been a robbery or breaking-and-entering specialist? "I'm game if you are."

"Good." Dizz grinned. "And who knows? You're obviously wondering what I did that landed me in the reapers. Get me drunk enough, maybe I'll tell you."

"Well, then, let's get started," Whist said, inclining his head. "After you. Sir."

CHAPTER TWO

The war was over.

It was time to move on.

Provided, Tanya Caulfield knew, she was willing to pay the price.

Lying awake in the darkness, she had to smile. *The price.* Those were usually words connected to warfare, not peacetime. Or so she'd always assumed.

But then, peacetime wasn't a phenomenon Tanya was really familiar with. What with the Guild Wars, the rebellion against the Confederacy, the establishment of the Dominion, and the zerg and the Amon invasions, most of her life had been spent against the backdrop of conflict and death.

Maybe now the peoples of the Koprulu sector finally had a chance.

But in the meantime . . .

Tanya Caulfield? Are you troubled?

She twitched at the sudden voice in her head. It was Ulavu, of course—the tone of a protoss mental contact was highly distinctive. Besides, even if one of the other telepaths in their wing had sensed her wakefulness, none would have cared enough to check on her. *I'm fine, Ulavu,* she thought back.

There was a short silence, and Tanya could sense him touching the other ghosts' minds in their temporary Augustgrad quarters. Probably reassuring himself that he wasn't alone. Ulavu didn't like being alone. *Is there any way in which I can assist you?*

There's no need for assistance, Tanya assured him again. *I'm fine.*

I accept your declaration, he thought back. *But there is an unusual tone to your thoughts tonight. That was why I was concerned.*

Tanya shook her head, taking care that the thought and accompanying emotion didn't make it to the surface where Ulavu could read them. Even two floors away, he was attuned enough to her that he could usually distinguish among her moods. *There's nothing to be concerned about. Go back to sleep, and I'll see you in the morning.*

Very well. Sleep deeply, my friend.

The contact faded, and Tanya sensed the subtle change as Ulavu's mind returned to its alien thought pattern.

But even though he'd withdrawn from all the terrans surrounding him, she could still feel his continued light touch against her mind. Rather like a cat nestling up beside its owner, she'd often thought.

Another thought and image she'd been *very* careful to keep locked away in a private section of her mind. Ulavu was as friendly and cooperative as any protoss she'd ever met, but two and a quarter meters of proud, noble, and telepathic alien was *not* someone you wanted to let think he was being laughed at. Especially a protoss who'd grown as close to Tanya as Ulavu had.

Therein, of course, was the rub. And the price.

Because when she left, he would have only the others. And none of them cared about him nearly as much as she did.

Carefully, she closed off her thought line against the cozy touch of Ulavu's mind and ran the memory of the letter she'd received late that afternoon.

From: Commandant, Ghost Academy
To: Agent X39562B
Re: Petition to resign from ghost program

As of 15:00 today, your petition has been approved by Dominion Military Command. Your resignation will be formally accepted ten days from this date at 13:00 in the office of Colonel Davis Hartwell.

Your service to the Dominion has been greatly appreciated and will be sorely missed. Should you wish to rescind your resignation, you may do so at Colonel Hartwell's office anytime before that date.

Best wishes for your future success,
Commandant Barris Schmidt

And that was it. One short letter, ten more days of sitting on her hands while the bureaucrats loaded the Dominion's computers with a little more useless datawork, and her life would change forever.

It was time. Past time, really. In her twenty years with the ghost program, despite the wording of Schmidt's obvious form letter, she'd never done a lick of service for either the program or the Dominion in general. In fact, she hadn't been deployed in so much as a single operation.

She'd never been completely sure how she felt about that. On the one hand, she certainly understood the logic behind it. She wasn't particularly powerful—her psi index was a fairly lackluster 5.1—but her gift was incredibly rare. Rare enough, or so she'd been told, that it made up for her barely there telepathic ability and her complete lack of the enhanced strength and stealth that were usually part of the ghost package. It only made sense to wait to spring her on the zerg at the most opportune moment.

Except that the moment had never come. When the Queen of Blades and her zerg Swarm began carving a deadly swath across both terran and protoss planets, Tanya was pulled out of the ghost headquarters on Ursa and sent to a remote location. Then had come Amon and his attack, and still Tanya had remained in hiding.

She didn't know why she hadn't been used in one or the other of those desperate situations. Her only guess was that she'd simply been forgotten, or else had fallen through the bureaucratic cracks.

At any rate, when the dust finally settled, she'd been brought back, with the understanding that when the next invasion came, she would be deployed against it.

Only that invasion hadn't happened. There were a lot of rumors about the ultimate fates of both the Queen of Blades and Amon, but there were supposedly only a small number of people who knew the truth, and they weren't talking.

So on the one hand, Tanya felt like she'd been wasted. On the other, given how many ghosts had been killed on the war's countless battlefields, she had to admit there was a quiet relief that she'd been kept out of it.

But her safety had come at a price. Every mission she hadn't been sent on was a mission someone else had had to take.

How many men and women, she wondered, had died in her place?

She felt a small stirring in the presence that was Ulavu. He'd probably noticed the shifting of her thoughts and was having his doubts as to whether she was really as okay as she'd claimed. A stray thought came on top of the presence, a sort of distant voice . . .

What the hell are you *doing here?*

Tanya stiffened, her drifting mind snapping to full wakefulness. Ulavu wasn't in his room at all.

He was running loose on the streets of Korhal.

And from the tone of the voice that had been filtered through the protoss's mind, it sounded like he'd wandered someplace where he was very much not wanted.

Ulavu, where are you? she thought at him as she grabbed her clothes, straining to pull something—*anything*—from his mind. But her telepathic power was too weak. He must have taken his psionic booster with him for his thoughts to be this clear.

Unfortunately, the presence of a psionic booster meant he could be halfway around the planet. *Ulavu, tell me where you are.*

It is an establishment for partaking of food and drink, the answer came. In the background of his connection, she had the sense of more voices, and their tone was growing steadily angrier.

Where's your guard? Are they there?

I wished to be alone tonight, he thought back. *I left without them.*

Tanya mouthed a curse. So he'd somehow slipped his military escort, the people who were supposed to keep this exact thing from happening. Terrific. *Did you see a sign in the window when you went in?* she asked, sealing her jumpsuit and scooping up her boots. Belatedly, she wondered if her ghost uniform might have been a better choice—air of authority and all that. But time was of the essence, and it was too late to change now. *Or above the door?*

There is a sign. The image on it is three concentric circles.

Are there any words?

Yes, two. Dante's Circle.

Tanya made a face. The good news was that at least he was still in Augustgrad. The bad news was that Dante's Circle was a low-rent tavern run by and catering to men and women who'd had relatives and friends on Chau Sara when the planet was incinerated by the protoss.

In other words, it was about the last place on Korhal where a protoss would be welcome.

Damn it all. She and others had warned Commandant Schmidt that moving the academy here from their usual base on Ursa, even temporarily, was a bad idea. Up there, they had Ulavu contained and controlled. Here, one simple back-door sneak-out, and he had a whole planet to wander around.

And unless she did something fast, there was likely to be a very serious incident.

Ulavu, you need to get out of there right now, she said, hopping awkwardly down the corridor on her right foot as she pulled on her left boot. *Can you do that?*

That would not be polite. I believe the owners and guests wish me to stay. Some have indicated they want to speak further with me.

I'll just bet they have, Tanya bit out, running quickly through her options. The obvious one was to alert the guards who were *supposed* to be riding herd on him. But under the circumstances, she wasn't feeling wildly confident of their abilities. She could try the police instead, but their response time wasn't great this late at night, and most of them wouldn't have the slightest idea what to do with a wayward protoss anyway. Ditto for the regular MPs.

Besides, no one on Korhal knew Ulavu as well as Tanya. The only way this would end well would be for her to do it herself.

Dante's Circle was a good klick and a half away from their temporary barracks. Luckily, Jeff Cristofer always left his hoverbike parked at the side door, and she'd long since sussed out the starter code. Two minutes and about twenty broken traffic regs later, she was there.

She'd never seen the inside of Dante's, but from its rep she'd always imagined it would be dark and gloomy, with a pervading vibe of anger and resentment and brooding. She'd also expected that the clientele would be a match for the décor, with big, angry men drinking to numb the distant pain of their loss.

She was right on all counts. The only thing she'd missed was the haze of drifting smoke from the open grill.

In fact, the thought struck her as she eased her way through the crowd, Dante's might very well be someone's reconstruction of what it would be like to sit in a bar on an incinerated planet.

A deliberate attempt to play to the customers' pain? Possibly. It probably didn't hurt the drink sales, either.

She'd half expected to find Ulavu in the middle of a full-bore melee. To her relief, he was standing calmly with his back to the bar, stiff and motionless, the top of his head just below the level of the exposed ceiling beams, faced by a triple semicircle of muttering men.

Muttering, but also motionless.

Tanya couldn't blame them. A protoss, even a calm, nonthreatening one, was a hell of an intimidating sight. Tall and slender, his eyes glittering from his long, noseless and mouthless head, Ulavu seemed to radiate the sheer presence and ancient dignity of his race. His hands, two-fingered with a pair of flanking opposable thumbs, could twist a terran arm out of its socket or crush a terran throat. His legs were bent slightly at the back-jointed knees, his large, three-toed feet planted in a stable stance like small trees. He was wearing his usual outfit of a long civilian tunic and leg wrappings, the slender cylinder that was his psionic booster hanging from his waist sash.

There was no threat there, nor even a hint of the fearsome warrior that most terrans visualized when they thought of protoss. But still the mob hesitated. They might not like protoss, but apparently no one was willing to throw the first punch against something that outweighed and outsized them by that much.

Yet the stalemate might be about to come to an end. Standing just inside the inner circle, visible in glimpses as the crowd shuffled back and forth, was a man who might well be big enough to take down even a protoss. And judging by the slurring of his curses, he was drunk enough to try.

Ghosts often worked the battlefield alone, with little need for formal command training. But Tanya had picked up a few pointers along the way. Time to see if they worked.

"All right, clear the way, clear the way," she called over the muttering and garbled curses, pitching her voice as deep as she could and biting out the words like a marine sergeant she'd once met. "What the *hell's* going on here?"

For a second she thought it was actually going to work. The two outer rings magically peeled back as she strode toward them, opening a path toward the confrontation.

But the inner ring was made up of men who were slower, were drunker, or had used those extra couple of moments of lead time to stifle the automatic obedience to authority that the late emperor Arcturus Mengsk had worked so hard to instill in his subjects. Tanya had to physically shoulder her way through that last line, which cost her several seconds, a fair amount of effort, and whatever edge of authority she'd managed to build.

Unfortunately, none of that erosion was lost on the big drunk. Even as she broke her way into the open area, he turned and gave her the hard-edged glare he'd just been giving Ulavu. "Who th' hell are *you*?" he demanded. "His keeper?" His lip twisted. "His pet?"

"I'm just a friend," Tanya said, keeping her voice calm. Even with her limited teep ability, it was clear that she and Ulavu were sitting on a powder keg. A single wrong word, a single wrong move, and the place could erupt. "I sympathize with your loss. I really do. But Ulavu had nothing to do with Chau Sara. He's an academician, a researcher of—"

"How th' hell you know wha' we lost?" the big man demanded. "You think jus' 'cause—?" He broke off, his red face going even redder. "Ah, *damn*. You a ghos'? You a bloody damn *ghos'*."

An unpleasant ripple went through the crowd, both verbal and mental, dark with fear and anger and resentment. The ghosts had been Emperor Arcturus's personal assassin corps, nearly mythic beings who hit their targets and then faded into the night.

Tanya sighed. So much for keeping a low profile.

"Watch it, Rylan," someone in the crowd warned.

"Yeah, like hell I will," Rylan growled back. "They don't walk 'round killin' anymore. Emperor Val says so."

"Yeah, but she can still read your mind."

"She read my min', she's gonna see a whole heap o' ugly," Rylan retorted, his eyes still hard on Tanya. "You readin' me, curve?"

"It doesn't take a ghost to know you're all here because you're mourning Chau Sara," Tanya said, fighting against the red haze of anger that had suddenly formed across her eyes. Curve? *Curve?* How *dare* these idiot hard-shells talk to her that way? How *dare* they blame her or Ulavu for something that had happened over a decade ago, especially something neither of them had been involved with?

"Like wha' you care about Chau Sara?" Rylan bit out. "Y'ugly pal burned it. He *burned* it."

The red haze in front of Tanya's eyes took on the appearance of tongues of fire. *You want to see something burn?* she thought viciously toward him. *How about you? You want to see* you *burn?*

Because she could do it. She could set him on fire where he stood, turn him into a blazing torch of screaming stupid. They wanted to wallow in bitterness here in this useless retrograde bar? Fine. This idiot could be part of it. Show them what the destruction of Chau Sara had *really* been like.

For that matter, why stop with him? There were a whole bunch of people here who had nothing to do but pick at the scabs of past memories. Maybe a little *real* danger and pain would snap them back to the real world, a world that the ghosts and the rest of the Dominion forces—and yes, the protoss, too—had fought and bled and died for to make everyone safer.

Tanya Caulfield. Ulavu's voice came into her mind, flowing over her fury like cool water. *Calmness.*

For some ghosts, Tanya knew, a cautioning word from a friend or colleague was like throwing a cutoff switch. For her, it was never like that. But even with her self-control wavering, she could recognize Ulavu's logic. More than that, she was freshly aware that someone whose judgment she valued was watching.

Taking a deep breath, she pressed a finger against the side of her head, a little bit of mental encouragement for the implant that was even now feverishly sifting out various brain chemicals from her bloodstream and rerouting neural flow patterns.

And then, to her relief, the haze faded away. She had control back and could once again think straight.

She looked around the crowd, no longer seeing them as potential targets for her power but as simple, ordinary people. Time to put frustration aside and start thinking tactically.

All right. Rylan was clearly the leader here. If she could talk him down, she should be able to defuse the situation.

If she couldn't talk him down, she would have to break him.

Tanya? Ulavu spoke again into her mind.

I'm all right, she assured him. *Trust me.* "Even those who didn't have loved ones on Chau Sara felt the shock and horror of that day," she said, a shiver running up her back.

"Easy t' say," Rylan said contemptuously.

"Easy to feel," Tanya bit back. "I've been there. I've seen the devastation. Cities reduced to ash. Mountains shattered. Lakes and rivers vaporized and their beds broken and half melted. Plains turned to glass. Even after all these years, the only life that's started to come back are a few lichens and some bits of moss."

"Yeah, I've seen it, too," Rylan said, his voice low, his gaze lowered to the floor.

Then, abruptly, his eyes came up and his finger jabbed accusingly toward Ulavu. "And it was his people who did it."

Tanya sighed. So much for talking him down. "His people did, yes," she said, searching her peripheral vision for inspiration. The psionic booster hanging at Ulavu's waist was heavy enough to throw, but delicate enough—and expensive enough—to be strictly a last-ditch weapon. There were no liquor bottles within easy reach, and even if there were, she didn't want to seriously harm anyone. At least, not anymore.

On the bar beside Ulavu was a glass stein half full of beer. It wasn't much, but it would have to do.

Slowly, casually, she drifted across the circle toward Ulavu and the stein. "But it was the protoss leadership who made that decision, and other protoss who carried it out. Ulavu wasn't part of either group. You're right—their response to the zerg infestation was absolutely inexcusable. But we've paid them back," she added, again sweeping her gaze around the crowd as she came to Ulavu's side. "Trust me—we've paid them back in full." She raised her hand toward Ulavu in emphasis. "And as I said, Ulavu wasn't even there. You're surely not going to hurt an innocent protoss for the crimes of his—"

"*Inn'cent?*" Rylan cut in. "Who th' hell says any o' th' damn fish-faces are *inn'cent*?" His hands, which had been opening and closing restlessly at his sides, abruptly bunched into fists. His center of mass leaned forward, one foot starting into a stride toward the hated alien standing in front of him—

Tanya grabbed the stein and hurled the contents straight at Rylan's face.

She had maybe a quarter second to make this work. But she'd already run the numbers and knew what she needed to do. The flash point of ethyl alcohol in this concentration should be around fifty degrees, while the temperature at which human flesh started to register first-degree burns was about forty-four. An uncomfortably narrow target zone, but she'd trained long and hard to fine-tune her pyrokinesis to that kind of precision. She flash-heated the beer in midflight, watched Rylan's eyes widen in disbelief as it splashed into his face—

An instant later the surprise turned to shock as the scalding liquid punched a faceful of pain straight through his liquor-soaked nerves.

He roared in agony, his bunched fists changing to flat palms slapped over his eyes, that first forward step collapsing into an off-balance stumble backward. Confused, disoriented, and hurting, Rylan—along with his big, bad, brave attack against the hated symbol of the whole protoss race—had screeched to a halt.

And everyone in Dante's knew it. In that same stunned pair of seconds, the mood of the crowd shifted as their chosen hero faltered.

Tanya gave it another second to sink in. Then she took Ulavu's arm and again sent her gaze across the crowd, pausing to catch the eyes of the biggest men in sight. A couple of them held her gaze, but most of them quickly looked away. Rylan was clearly a bigger force here than even she had realized. "I don't think Rylan's up to a fight tonight," she said calmly. "So we'll be leaving now." She hesitated. "And please believe me that we're as sorry about Chau Sara as you are."

No one disputed the point. No one said anything at all. With Ulavu in tow, she walked boldly toward the crowd. This time all three rings opened for her without resistance.

A minute later they were out in the chilly night air.

There was no great need for you to come to my aid, Tanya Caulfield. Ulavu's thought came as she steered him toward her borrowed hoverbike. *That terran would not have caused me harm.*

You sure about that? she countered sourly. *Because it damn well looked* like he was getting ready to cause you harm.

For a moment Ulavu seemed to ponder that, his thoughts swirling by too rapidly for Tanya to keep up with. *You used your gift in a public forum,* he said at last. *Will your superiors not be unhappy with you?*

Tanya winced. Yes, they would definitely be unhappy. She was the ghost program's secret weapon, and they'd gone to incredible lengths to keep her power under wraps. They'd be well past unhappy, more into furious territory.

But only if they knew.

I'm hoping they don't find out, she said. *All anyone in the bar saw was me throwing beer into a man's face. They'll think his reaction was just from getting alcohol in his eyes.*

There will be no burns?

Nothing obvious. I kept the heat below the flash point, and it wasn't in contact long enough for any serious reddening. A little, maybe, but nothing too visible.

Again, Ulavu pondered. *But the terran himself will know.*

The terran himself was roaring drunk, Tanya reminded him. *I'm guessing the memories will be so hazy that he won't remember exactly what stopped him.*

You are guessing? Or you are hoping?

A little of both, Tanya conceded. She fixed him with a stern gaze. *Let's talk about you, now. What were you* doing *in there?*

I am a researcher, he said, his mental tone going full-bore protoss pride. *I wished to see and understand the sense of those who had lost companions and family to protoss errors.*

Tanya grimaced. *Protoss errors.* Did they still think of the destruction of an entire planet full of innocent terrans as simply an error?

The anger was starting to flow again. Sternly, she forced it back. *And do you understand?*

He gave the mental equivalent of a sigh. *There remains much pain. Much anger.*

And none of us blames them a bit for that, Tanya said pointedly. *So do* not *try something like that again. You hear me? Because the next time, I might just let them show you what terran pain and anger look like.*

There is no need for that, Ulavu said, a grim edge to his mental voice. *As you said, we were paid back in full.*

Tanya nodded silently. The war had indeed exacted a terrible toll on the protoss. Many of them had fallen in battle. Their homeworld of Aiur had been devastated and abandoned. Their society had been ripped apart, some of the factions eventually coming back together, others turning away from the rest of their people.

And worst of all, the Khala, the mystic psionic connection that had bound the protoss in thought and purpose for centuries, had been destroyed. Years after that cataclysm, they were still struggling with what it now meant to be protoss.

Was that desperate cultural struggle the reason Ulavu had been abandoned by his people? Was their attention so turned inward that they had no energy to spend in bringing him back and integrating him into their slowly redeveloping society?

Or was it something darker? Had he done something specific that had turned them against him?

Because sometimes making enemies was easy to do. Sometimes it was painfully easy to do.

She closed her eyes briefly, the emotional scab momentarily peeling back. She hadn't meant to lose control that day four years ago. Hadn't meant to offend or anger the rest of the ghosts by ignoring their efforts to calm her down.

It had been Ulavu who'd gotten through to her, who'd snapped the spiral of anger and chaos long enough for her implant to get the upper hand. The incident had resolved, and everyone had escaped unscathed. Even the ghost who'd started it, who Tanya still believed richly deserved all the scathing anyone could give him.

But the resolution had come at a cost. The failure of the other ghosts to calm her had been bad enough, but the fact that an alien *had* succeeded had ultimately created a barrier of resentment that Tanya had never been able to penetrate or tear down. Ever since then, it had been her and Ulavu against the world. She still lived and worked among the ghosts, but she would never again truly be one of them.

And very soon, they wouldn't have even that much of her.

She sat down on the hoverbike's saddle, conscious of the frustration hovering just beyond the wall of self-control. Hopefully a stronger wall than had once been there.

The big question now was what would happen to that self-control when she left the program.

Under Emperor Arcturus such a thing would have been unthinkable. Ghosts were ghosts, and they were in the program until they died. Period.

But Emperor Valerian was a new kind of leader. He'd cut way back on the brain-panning for marines—some said he'd stopped it entirely, but no one really believed that—and he'd also decided that ghosts who wanted to leave the program could do so.

As far as Tanya knew, she was going to be the first to take advantage of that option. And it raised a whole new list of questions.

Would they leave the implant in place? Surely they wouldn't just take it out. Maybe they would give her a new one, something designed to let her live as a civilian without turning irritating people into Roman candles everywhere she went.

Surely they wouldn't take it out. Would they?

Rylan still concerns me, Ulavu said, his tone going thoughtful.

I already told you not to worry about him, Tanya said.

I am not worried, Ulavu assured her. *Merely curious. How did he know you were a ghost?*

Tanya frowned. In the heat of the moment, the oddness of that identification had breezed right past her.

But Ulavu was right. How *had* Rylan known? She hadn't identified herself, and she was wearing civilian clothing. *No idea,* she admitted. *Maybe someone from the barracks hangs out at Dante's Circle and talks about a protoss in the ghost program.*

Perhaps, Ulavu said. *That would not be a good thing.*

Tanya snorted. *You think?*

I do, Ulavu said seriously, apparently missing the sarcasm in her tone. *But since you speak of the barracks, should we not return there?*

Abruptly, Tanya realized she was sitting on the hoverbike, staring out at the city, while Ulavu waited patiently. *Absolutely,* she agreed, gesturing to the passenger seat. *Come on—I'll give you a ride. Try not to be conspicuous.*

He drew himself up to his full height. *Try not to be* conspicuous?

Tanya sighed. A conspicuous protoss. An equally conspicuous pyrokinetic. Both of them rejected by their people. They really did deserve each other. *Okay, forget inconspicuous,* she said. *Just try not to fall off.*

CHAPTER THREE

"I understand the Dominion's concerns, Emperor Valerian," Envoy Louise DuPre said, her pleasant alto voice in sharp contrast with the flinty look in her eyes. "But you must also understand ours. The Umojan Protectorate suffered greatly under your father's territorial ambitions. We're not really interested in giving you the foothold he was never able to extort from us."

Emperor Valerian Mengsk suppressed a sigh. He'd hoped that his six years of more enlightened rule would have at least diminished the long shadow of his father's brutal methods. Apparently, it hadn't. "I understand your concerns as well," he told DuPre, keeping his own voice as calm as hers. The slightest hint of aggression, or even mild irritation, and she would instantly label him as Arcturus Mengsk the Second, and any hope of putting a rapid-response base in the Umoja system would be gone.

But there was an even more pressing problem. Several Dominion planets had suffered massive destruction of their fields and croplands during the war, and were still having trouble recovering. The sheer cost of transporting food and other necessities to those worlds was straining Valerian's resources to the limit, and another war could push the whole Dominion over the edge into famine. The Umojan Protectorate's advanced biotech could go a long way toward helping move them away from that line.

Unfortunately, about the only thing the Dominion had to offer in exchange was protection from a resurgence of the zerg, and the Protectorate wasn't interested.

"Please be assured that my only intention is to guard the Protectorate and the Dominion's southern flank against attack. The last thing you want is an infestation taking root before we can get a counterstrike force in place."

"I think we'd be able to handle an infestation without your help," DuPre said.

"Really?" Valerian asked. "Because if you're counting on protoss assistance, I strongly suggest you don't. Hierarch Artanis has enough trouble of his own without borrowing any from the Protectorate."

DuPre smiled thinly. But something in her eyes told Valerian that this was *exactly* what she and the Protectorate were counting on. "And you know this from your vast experience with protoss?"

"I know this from my ability to read the undercurrents of culture, society, and politics," Valerian said. "It's painfully clear that they didn't come out of the war in any better shape than the rest of us did."

"Perhaps," DuPre said. "May I speak bluntly?"

Valerian gestured to her. "Please."

"The zerg are a *potential* threat," she said. "The Dominion is a *definite* threat. Perhaps not as great as when Arcturus Mengsk was emperor," she continued quickly before Valerian could respond. "But whether or not you yourself have territorial ambitions, the fact remains that many in your government still want to see the Umojan Protectorate as part of the Dominion."

"I don't know if I'd categorize it as *many*," Valerian said. "And rest assured that we're weeding them out of sensitive positions as quickly as we can find suitable replacements."

"I'm glad to hear that," DuPre said. "When you've succeeded in that effort, and perhaps offered further proof of the Dominion's commitment to its current borders, we'll be happy to speak again."

A muted light glowed on the throne's small armrest status board. Scowling, Valerian looked at the display. He'd given strict instructions that this meeting wasn't to be interrupted for anything less than the end of the world . . .

Single leviathan, repeat, single leviathan has entered the system. Appears to be on course for Korhal IV.

Valerian felt a muscle in his cheek twitch. Leviathans were the zerg transport of choice, massive spacefaring creatures that the Swarm had infested and subsequently transformed into armored carriers capable of both interplanetary travel and ground-to-orbit flight. Their huge interior chambers could house tens of thousands of combat-ready zerg.

And despite the emphasized words in the brief alert, in Valerian's experience leviathans never traveled alone. Never.

DuPre was still listing the conditions Valerian needed to meet before the Umojan Protectorate would be willing to sit down at the negotiating table. "Excuse me, Envoy DuPre," Valerian interrupted. "A situation has arisen, and I must leave." He stood up, locking his eyes onto hers. "A leviathan has just appeared in the Korhal system, heading this way."

He had the minor satisfaction of watching her face go pale. "The *zerg*?"

"I don't know anyone else in the Koprulu sector who uses leviathans," he said. "I'll leave orders to have your ship prepped immediately, assuming you wish to leave."

"I do," she said, her words coming out mechanically.

"I don't blame you." Valerian raised his eyebrows. "And when you get back to Umoja, perhaps you and the Ruling Council will want to revise your threat assessments. The ones where the zerg are only a *potential* threat."

He was out of the throne room before she could come up with a reply.

When Arcturus Mengsk named himself emperor of the newly declared Terran Dominion, he began work on a war room that he hoped would be impervious to any conceivable attack. Valerian wasn't sure he'd completely achieved that goal, but he had to admit his father had taken a highly impressive run at it.

The Bunker, as it was universally called inside the palace, was a hundred meters underground, surrounded by multiple layers of reinforced plascrete and lead supplemented by mu-metal and superconducting meshes. Its air and water were filtered down to the molecular level. Its exterior was grounded against electromagnetic pulses and charged particle radiation, and it was a good fifty meters deeper than any protoss planetary incineration anyone had ever seen. It had instant communications with the entire planet and every ship and orbiting station in the system, it was stocked with small-arms weapons and loyal men and women who knew how to use them, and it had living quarters, food, and water for a hundred people to wait out a ten-year siege.

So why, Valerian thought as he passed through the final door, did he still feel as exposed as if he were strolling through the palace's rooftop garden?

There were half a dozen men and women waiting in the Combat Information Center when Valerian arrived: the top people in Korhal's planetary defense system and the Dominion's war-making machine. Six of the nine comm displays that wrapped around the emperor's chair connected him with other senior officers elsewhere in the system.

The remaining three displays showed images of the incoming leviathan.

Valerian frowned as he seated himself. Common wisdom and experience said that leviathans never traveled alone. But if this one had friends, they were certainly taking their time about making an appearance. "Admiral Horner," he called with proper respect and protocol toward Screen One. "What's our situation?"

Admiral Matt Horner, who'd been half turned to talk to someone else on the *Hyperion*'s bridge, pivoted back to the comm camera. "Emperor Valerian," he said, greeting the emperor with equal formality. "Situation is . . . puzzling. The leviathan's been transmitting a message on three separate frequencies—the signal's a bit faint, but we've got a good scrub. Here it is."

He reached somewhere offscreen, and his face was replaced with that of a zerg queen.

All zerg had a definite nightmare quality about them, with bodies that seemed composed mainly of bony plates, spikes, and flesh-ripping claws. But terran brains were adept at seeing patterns that perhaps weren't really there, and most people tended to look at zerg in terms of familiar creatures: giant spiders, armored slugs, or huge, bat-winged wasps.

Queens were a special case, though. There, the almost universal reaction was that someone had taken a centaur out of Old Earth legend, replaced the human torso with a section of centipede, and replaced the lower, equine part with a giant, nightmarishly armored crab.

And with that image came the memories. All of them. The horrors of the war. The animalistic excesses of the zerg, the sometimes arrogant excesses of the protoss, and the brutal, uncaring excesses of the terrans themselves. All the death and destruction, all the pain and suffering, flowing through Valerian's mind like a river of acid.

The history books too often made it seem as if the suffering ended when the fighting stopped. Valerian knew better now. Between the slow, costly reconstruction of devastated planets and the lingering pain of lost friends and loved ones, the bitter aftermath went on for years after the guns and mechs fell silent.

The Terran Dominion was still a long way from digging itself out of the last war. If the zerg now proposed to start a new one . . .

"I am Mukav," a deep voice rasped.

Someone in the room gave a startled mutter, and even Valerian felt his eyes narrow. Zerg queens typically couldn't communicate verbally. Had someone been playing with queen genetics again?

"I bring a greeting. I bring a message. I bring an urgent request. I am Mukav. I bring a greeting. I bring a message. I bring an urgent request."

The display cleared, and Matt was back. "And that's it," he said. "It just keeps repeating."

"Transmit loop?"

"I don't think so," Matt said. "I've watched a few rounds, and there are slight changes in her face and stance. I think she's just sitting there, repeating the message and waiting for us to answer."

"Any idea how she's communicating with us?" Valerian asked.

"I'm not sure," Matt said. "The transmitter she's using is running the same protocols as the comm system from an old Valkyrie."

"Really," Valerian said. The United Earth Directorate's foray into the Koprulu sector years ago had not exactly gone according to their expectations. Between Kerrigan's zerg Swarm, the protoss, and the Dominion itself, none of the UED's forces had survived to report back to the motherland. Most of their prized Valkyrie space frigates had been destroyed, but a fair number had fallen into Dominion hands. "The zerg have never used tech before."

"They may not be doing it now, either," Matt said. "It's the same protocols, but it's not a Valkyrie system. Best guess is that they scavenged one, studied it, and then put together their own version. Along with a zerg psi-to-transmitter interface."

"Impressive," Valerian murmured. Still, the protoss had to be doing something similar with their own psionics in order to communicate with terrans over terran comm systems.

No one had yet figured out how that worked. Odds were, they wouldn't crack this new zerg system very quickly, either.

"But it gets better," Matt continued. "I had a couple of Wraiths do a flyby, and nearly all of the leviathan's surface chambers and passages are open to space."

Valerian frowned. "They're *open*? As in, there's nothing in those chambers?"

"That's how it looks," Matt said. "Though that doesn't take into account the interior spaces—there could be other zerg lurking in there. Mukav has to be in one of those, too, of course."

"Yes," Valerian said, eyeing the displays. Leviathans were huge things, bigger even than protoss motherships.

But the outer chambers were the key to quick troop deployment. If they were all open to space, that would seem to indicate Mukav wasn't part of an attack. Or at least not part of a quick attack.

"There could also be mutalisks in the open chambers," Valerian pointed out. "They should be able to take hard vacuum this long."

"Absolutely," Matt agreed. "Wraith sensors can't penetrate deep enough to see all the way inside."

Valerian pursed his lips. This whole thing *could* be a trick. But subtlety wasn't usually the zerg's strong suit. Their preferred approach was to throw in huge numbers and survive or perish as the fates of battle decided. "I suppose we ought to see what she wants," he said.

"We're ready to go," Matt said.

"Good." Valerian squared his shoulders. "Open transmission."

"Transmission open."

"This is Emperor Valerian Mengsk of the Terran Dominion," Valerian said, pitching his voice as regally as possible. He had no idea whether Mukav would even notice his tone, but it couldn't hurt. "Tell me your urgent request."

The zerg's verbal loop continued for a couple of words, then broke off. "The request is not mine," she said. "The request is from Zagara, Overqueen of the Swarm."

Valerian frowned. *Overqueen?* That was a new one.

"The Overqueen asks the aid of the Terran Dominion in protecting the planet Gystt from the protoss," Mukav continued. "The Overqueen offers peace to both protoss and terrans. The Swarm desires only to be left alone. Will you help us? What is your answer?"

"One moment," Valerian said, trying hard to maintain his regal tone. The surprises were coming way too fast today. "Mute, please, Admiral."

There was a quiet tone from the board. "Muted," Matt confirmed. "Your thoughts?"

"I wish I had some," Matt admitted, looking more bemused than Valerian had ever seen him. "A zerg, asking *us* for help? And against the *protoss*? Not exactly your everyday occurrence."

"Agreed," Valerian said. The war had ended with a three-way cease-fire. And after Zagara forcibly laid claim to the systems around Char, leaving everyone else wondering as to her future intentions, Valerian had assumed she would try to keep as low a profile as possible. Something very serious must be going on for her to come to the Dominion for help.

"Let's see if we can sift a little sense out of it," he suggested. "Starting with this planet *Gystt*. Has anyone ever heard of it?"

There was a short pause. Some of the men and women on the

displays shook their heads; others lowered their eyes as they focused on their respective computers or datapads.

"Emperor Valerian?" the woman on Screen Five finally said. Valerian didn't recognize her, but she was wearing the collar flashes of a major in the ghost program. "Our protoss expert tells me that Gystt was a planet they incinerated just after the cleansing of Chau Sara."

"That's *one* word for it." The barely audible voice came from somewhere in the group of officers in the Bunker.

"Comment?" Valerian asked, swiveling toward the officers. His eyes came to rest on Colonel Abram Cruikshank. "Colonel Cruikshank?"

Cruikshank's lip twitched. "My apologies, Emperor Valerian," he said. "I was merely wondering how reliable this data was."

"I think a protoss ought to know his own history," Valerian reminded him mildly.

"Wait a minute," Matt put in, frowning. "A *protoss*? You mean Ulavu? I thought he'd gone."

"No, he's still here," Valerian said firmly, putting an edge of warning in his voice.

Matt, at least, got the message. "I see," he said. "Okay, so Gystt's a burnt-off planet. We know anything else?"

"One major continent constitutes about half the total landmass," the major said. "Two smaller continents and islands make up the rest. Thirty-hour day. The main continent is equatorial, with two mountain ranges—"

"Yes, fine," Matt said, cutting her off. "Do we have anything that would suggest why Zagara might set up shop there?"

"Nothing Ulavu knows about," the major said. "Maybe she hoped everyone would assume the place was harmless and ignore it."

"Possibly," Valerian said. "The more immediate question is why she needs or wants protection." He gestured. "Put me back on."

"Go ahead, sir."

"Tell me about your problem with the protoss," Valerian said to Mukav. "What are you doing on Gystt that has them upset?"

"The Overqueen asks the aid of the Terran Dominion in protecting the planet Gystt from the protoss," Mukav said. "The Overqueen offers peace to both protoss and terrans. The Swarm desires only to be left alone. Will you help us? What is your answer?"

Valerian frowned. That was the same thing she'd just said. "Admiral?"

"Not reading any transmission problems at this end," Matt said, his forehead wrinkled, his eyes flicking back and forth across his displays. "Try it again—we'll try adjusting the slip-pattern a bit."

Valerian nodded. "What is Zagara doing on Gystt that has the protoss upset?"

"The Overqueen asks the aid of the Terran Dominion in protecting the planet Gystt from the protoss. The Overqueen offers peace to both protoss and terrans. The Swarm desires only to be left alone. Will you help us? What is your answer?"

"Terrific," Cruikshank muttered. "Zagara sent us a panbrain."

Valerian gestured, and the transmission went to mute. "Or deliberately sent someone with a limited response set so that we wouldn't waste time sitting around here discussing it," he said. "Rather heightens the urgency of the message."

"Or is designed to get us to jump without knowing how deep the water is," Matt warned. "This could be a trick to drag us out into the middle of nowhere."

"To what end?" Valerian countered. "We're certainly not going to leave the Dominion defenseless."

"Or be defenseless ourselves," Cruikshank put in. "I assume you'll be sending a full battle force, Emperor Valerian."

Valerian studied Mukav's image. Sitting motionless, alone, and supposedly helpless aboard an otherwise deserted leviathan, waiting for the Dominion's answer to Zagara's plea. If this was a trick, it was well outside the zerg norm.

But Zagara had been an apprentice of the Queen of Blades, once known as Sarah Kerrigan, who'd been a powerful and highly skilled terran ghost before she was infested by the zerg. Could Kerrigan have taught her this kind of advanced subtlety?

Or at least taught her the right words to get what she wanted?

He signaled for transmission. "Mukav, this is Emperor Mengsk," he said. "Who leads the protoss force that threatens you?"

"The Overqueen asks the aid of the Terran Dominion in protecting the planet Gystt from the protoss. The Overqueen offers peace to both protoss and terrans. The Swarm desires only to be left alone. Will you help us? What is your answer?" Mukav tilted her head, as if thinking. "The protoss force is led by Hierarch Artanis."

Matt whistled softly. "Artanis *himself* is leading the charge? Interesting."

"It is indeed," Valerian agreed. And with that, he realized there really was no decision to make.

He didn't trust the zerg Swarm. That went double for Zagara, who'd been Kerrigan's closest disciple and ally among the zerg. Even at her best, Kerrigan had been something of a maverick. At her worst, she'd been a traitor. If Zagara was running a game here, it was likely to be a nasty one.

But if following up on Mukav's invitation meant some quality time with Artanis, it would definitely be worth the risk.

The Dominion was hurting. There were food and housing shortages and untold numbers of permanently maimed and psychologically fractured veterans, and reconstructing the more seriously damaged worlds was putting heavy pressure on the rest.

But in their own way, the protoss were hurting just as badly. Their numbers had been devastated by the war. The Khala that had once psionically bound them together as a race had been shattered and lost, and at least one fringe protoss faction had rejected Artanis's attempts to reunify their species and had headed off on its own.

The protoss had a long and honorable history, plus technology that was in many ways far superior to the terran versions. On the other hand, the Dominion was no slouch in the tech department, either, and terrans furthermore had a long history of tenacious and creative problem-solving. Together, Valerian had no doubt, the Dominion and the protoss could come up with solutions to their respective problems.

But to do that—to even broach the subject—Valerian needed to at least make the offer to Artanis. And so far, Artanis had been too preoccupied to sit down for that sort of conversation.

Maybe the space above Gystt was where they would finally have the necessary time.

And if Artanis *wasn't* there, it would prove that Kerrigan had taught Zagara how to manipulate terrans in general and Valerian in particular.

He signaled again for mute. "Admiral, how fast can the *Hyperion* be ready to travel?"

"Two hours," Matt said promptly. He'd been a friend and ally of Valerian's far too long to have missed the signs that his emperor had come to a decision. "Maybe three, depending on what size ground force you want."

"We shouldn't need much of anything," Valerian said. "Whatever we end up doing, we'll be doing it from orbit."

"Forgive me, Emperor, but that's not a good idea," Cruikshank said. He had his datapad out and was typing rapidly on it. "Unknown situations are notorious for not playing out the way everyone expects."

"He's right," Matt seconded. "Even if we don't get planetside, we'll want some marines and a few heavier units that can be deployed at onboard choke points in the event of an orbital attack and breach. Colonel, what can you pull together in three hours?"

"A couple of platoons of the 934th Marines are available on short notice," Cruikshank said. "I can add in one of my goliath squads and maybe a few Warhounds. Reapers . . . nothing but a couple of raw training groups in the area. But I've got a double handful of reserves I can call up. That's the minimum force size I'd recommend."

"Very well," Valerian said. Preparing to defend against a breach seemed slightly paranoid. Still, Cruikshank had a point about unknown situations. "What kind of orbital force are we looking at?"

"The *Hyperion* is nearly ready," Matt reported. "*Phobos* and *Titan* are an hour behind us; *Fury, Circe,* and *Cerberus* are four."

"Good," Valerian said. "We'll head out in three hours; *Fury* and the others can catch up. You'll need to ask Mukav for Gystt's coordinates."

"She already sent them," Matt said. "Major Vitkauskas also sent me Ulavu's numbers, and they match."

"Good," Valerian said again. "Speaking of Ulavu, tell Major Vitkauskas I want him prepped to join us. We might need someone on our side with a protoss perspective on the Swarm."

Matt's eyes widened, just noticeably. "Ah . . . I'm not sure that would be a good idea," he said, lowering his voice as if there weren't already fifty other people listening in on the conversation. "If Hierarch Artanis is going to be there, it could be . . . awkward."

"It'll be all right," Valerian said firmly. Whatever Ulavu's problems with the rest of the protoss were, there was a mystery to unravel. Valerian had been a researcher himself long enough to know that vital information and insight could come from the most unexpected sources. "Three hours, ladies and gentlemen. Make them count."

Three hours later, with Mukav in her leviathan leading the way, the *Hyperion* and its escort ships made the jump to the Gystt system.

The protoss, as Mukav's message had hinted, were already there in force: three void rays, two carriers, a swarm of phoenixes, even a massive mothership.

The zerg had their own force in orbit as well: six more leviathans. So far, though, the leviathans were keeping their distance from the intruders, apparently content to watch and wait. The protoss likewise seemed to be in an observation or possibly siege array, perhaps waiting for the zerg to make the next move.

And as for the planet itself . . .

"Matt?" Valerian murmured as he stood beside the admiral on the *Hyperion*'s bridge. "Didn't Ulavu say the protoss incinerated this planet?"

"Over a decade ago, yes," Matt murmured back.

"Completely?"

"I've never known the protoss to go with half measures."

Valerian nodded, gazing at the huge bridge display.

The display that currently showed the planet's major continent covered with a patchwork of prairies, broad scrubland, and lush green-and-purple forests.

None of which could possibly exist.

Valerian took a deep breath. "Okay," he said briskly. "Get a signal to that mothership. Let's see if Hierarch Artanis is taking the Dominion's calls today.

"Maybe he can tell us what the hell is going on."

CHAPTER FOUR

"The satellites were placed over Gystt eight years ago," Artanis said, the words coming from the *Hyperion*'s bridge speakers in the terran-sounding voice that resulted when protoss psionics intersected with comm systems. "It was during the absence of the Queen of Blades, and we wished advance knowledge of where she might next take the Swarm."

"And they missed seeing"—Valerian gestured to the planet below them—"all *that*?"

"The satellites were small to avoid drawing attention," Artanis said. "Their scale necessarily imposed limits on their range. It was assumed that a large migration of zerg would include many levia-thans, some of which would surely come within detection distance. It was only when the satellites failed that we sent an appraiser to investigate."

"And found that an incinerated planet had become a primeval paradise," Valerian said, frowning. "You said *both* satellites failed? At the same time?"

"Indeed," Artanis confirmed. "In retrospect, we now believe it was sabotage. The zerg were planning to leave Gystt and wished us not to observe their movements."

"With all due respect," Matt put in from across the bridge, "if that was Zagara's plan, she dropped the ball."

Artanis's luminescent eyes turned toward him. "Explain, Admiral Matthew Horner."

Valerian looked sideways at Matt. Normal protoss were intimidating enough, with their piercing eyes and long, utterly unreadable faces. But Artanis was a step up even from that. His glittering crownlike headpiece and ceremonial armor sent small flashes of light across the display with every movement, reminding everyone watching that this was the leader of a race that had been traveling the stars for millennia.

And not just traveling, but also locating, identifying, and watching over other sentient races. Noble, proud, and powerful, the protoss had been the guardians of this part of the galaxy for a long, long time.

What path would human civilization have taken, Valerian had often wondered, if the protoss' travels had led them to Old Earth's arm of the galaxy? Despite the Dae'Uhl, the protoss' principle of noninterference, would the humans there have noticed the visitors? If so, would the simple knowledge that humanity wasn't alone have sparked a golden age among Earth's peoples?

Or would it have precipitated their utter destruction?

Matt was apparently too focused on the task at hand to feel intimidated by Artanis's glare or presence. "If she was trying to pull off a mass evacuation before you could get a force out here to stop her, why is she still here?" he asked.

"Can you state with full knowledge that she did not send large forces from Gystt while we were blinded?" Artanis countered.

Matt's lips puckered. "No, I guess I can't," he conceded. "I just assumed that someone who styles herself an Overqueen would want to lead whatever charge she'd planned. Or at least go wherever they were going so she could watch."

"There's a lot here we're all assuming, and a lot we don't know," Valerian said, coming to his rescue. "But you're here, Hierarch Artanis, and we're here, and it's entirely possible we're both here by invitation." He inclined his head. "Invitations of a sort," he amended. "Ours was certainly more formal than yours."

"Forcing the mobilization of a protoss war fleet is not a proper invitation," Artanis said stiffly. "Nor is it a wise strategy."

"Agreement on both points," Valerian said, shivering at the memory of the last time he'd seen a protoss war fleet in action. "But Zagara may not think the same way we do. At any rate, as I say, we're here. Shall we invite her to join in the conversation and perhaps clear up some of these questions?"

"Do you expect to learn any truth from a zerg?"

"Normally, no." Valerian again gestured toward the incredible greenery on the planet below. "But until a few hours ago I wouldn't have believed something like that could happen, either. I'm not suggesting we trust whatever she has to say. But let's at least hear her out."

Artanis hunched his shoulders. "As you wish, Emperor Valerian. You of the Terran Dominion received the more formal invitation. It rests upon you to begin communications."

"Thank you," Valerian said. "Admiral, you have a connection prepared?"

"Yes, sir," Matt said. "Under the assumption that Zagara's using the same protocols as Mukav, we're going to try that frequency and slip-pattern again."

"Any reason why Zagara couldn't be using something else?"

"Not a one," Matt conceded readily. "We just thought we'd start there."

"Good enough," Valerian said. "Open a transmission, and let's give it a try."

"Transmission open."

"Overqueen Zagara, this is Emperor Valerian Mengsk of the Terran Dominion," Valerian said. "Also in the speaking circle is Hierarch Artanis, leader of the united protoss. You asked for terran help. Tell me what you wish from us."

"Greetings to you, Emperor Valerian and Hierarch Artanis," a grating voice replied from the bridge speakers. Simultaneously, the bony image of a zerg queen appeared on the comm display.

But not an ordinary queen. Back when Kerrigan was ruling the Swarm as the Queen of Blades, Zagara had been transformed into a broodmother, which had drastically modified both her appearance and her capabilities.

And not in the direction of being gentler or less threatening, either. Quite the opposite. The usual queen cranial bone armor had been thickened and spread outward to both sides, creating an umbrella-like helmet that made her virtually unassailable from above. Along the center of the helmet, running from front to back, was a set of horns that would do an Old Earth rhinoceros proud. The upper-knee parts of her legs had been equipped with similar spikes, curving up and back. Her slender forearms seemed to have been made more dexterous, the clawed hands more nimble.

For a moment the camera lingered on a full-body shot, showing Zagara in all her horrific detail. Then the image zoomed in slowly to focus on the angled face and glittering eyes. Almost, Valerian thought grimly, as if Zagara had wanted to remind her visitors just what it was they were facing before moving on to conversation.

Not that either he or Artanis was likely to forget. The creature peering out at them held the Swarm at her command, an army that had slaughtered millions of terrans and protoss and laid waste to dozens of planets. All previous zerg leaders had been utterly ruthless creatures, willing to do whatever was necessary to achieve their goal of domination and absorption.

Had that goal changed? Valerian hoped so. But even in his most optimistic moment he conceded that there was no proof of it. For all he knew, this was nothing but a slightly subtler ploy than usual that Zagara was using to draw her enemies into an unfavorable position.

"I welcome you to Gystt," Zagara continued. "Thank you, especially, Emperor Valerian, for your unexpectedly but gratifyingly prompt response to my invitation."

"My pleasure, Overqueen," Valerian said. "The situation sounded important, as well as intriguing."

"I trust you will find it rewarding as well," Zagara said. "You have questions, both of you. Speak them, and I will endeavor to answer."

"Let's start with the obvious one," Valerian said. "Tell us what happened to Gystt."

"The zerg happened to Gystt," Zagara said. "For the zerg have changed, Emperor Valerian. The very soul of the zerg has changed. She who was once Sarah Kerrigan, then the Queen of Blades, then ascended to xel'naga, showed us the way."

Xel'Naga. Reflexively, Valerian sat up a bit straighter. The reports of what had happened to Kerrigan had been confusing and contradictory, but they'd all agreed that she had once again been transformed, this time into something even more alien than any of the Koprulu sector's other species.

And the rumor was indeed that she'd been changed—or raised, or ascended—to some form of xel'naga.

Valerian had no idea what that meant. The xel'naga had once been the protoss' patrons, watching over them from afar, protecting them just as the protoss themselves would one day play a watchman role over younger species. Somehow, it seemed, Kerrigan had been accepted into that position, or endowed with the title, or something equally nebulous.

Kerrigan had been a combination of terran and zerg at the time of her ascension. Had someone somehow replaced those genetics, and possibly her entire cellular structure, with the xel'naga equivalents?

No one knew. For that matter, no one even knew if the transformation had been an honor, the inevitable next stage in terran or zerg evolution, or a condemnation and punishment.

Given that Kerrigan had never been seen again, Valerian rather tended toward the latter explanation. "She showed you the way to what?" he asked.

"To peace," Zagara said. "Throughout our history, the zerg have always striven to seek perfection in ourselves. But that ideal was always beyond our reach. And so before she departed forever, the Queen of Blades gave us a final gift."

Valerian glanced at Artanis's image, wondering if the hierarch was going to join in on the conversation. Certainly the protoss had had their fair share of dealings with Kerrigan and her later avatars.

But Artanis made no such sign. "What gift was that?" Valerian asked, turning back to Zagara. "The power to create new life on a barren planet?"

"The zerg have always had the power to create," Zagara said. "We have always known how to take living beings and meld and mix and mold them to our desired image."

"Then what did Kerrigan give you?" Valerian persisted.

"That which the zerg have never had." Zagara spread her claws outward. "Choice."

The word seemed to hang in the air. "Choice," Valerian repeated.

"The choice of whether to continue the path of destruction in our endless quest for perfection, or to accept what we are and use our skills to nurture life," Zagara said. "We have made our decision. Here, on Gystt, you see the result."

Valerian threw a sideways look at Matt. No—that simply wasn't possible. Everything in the Swarm's long and bloody history screamed the impossibility of such a change of goal. The zerg were in the business of annihilating planets, infesting and absorbing every species they could use, and destroying everything they couldn't. They'd left a trail of destruction and death behind them, not just through the Koprulu sector but all the way back through the light-years and the centuries to their primal world of Zerus.

Terrans didn't change like that. Not that quickly. Certainly not that completely. Neither did protoss. How in the world could the zerg?

And yet . . .

He looked at the display, and the cloud-speckled landscape below. And yet, there was the evidence of his eyes. A devastated planet *had* been renewed. Renewed, re-formed, and filled with new life.

And he had to admit there was a certain logic to it. The zerg were masters of genetic manipulation. If anyone could resurrect life from the ashes of a protoss incineration, it would be them. "You say *we* have made this choice. Who exactly is with you on this?"

"The Swarm is with me."

"That is no answer." Artanis spoke up at last, his voice deep and black-edged with suspicion. "We know the zerg command pyramid. We know queens and broodmothers. We know they have their own levels of sentience and free will. Their own levels of choice. You speak of the Swarm, but the Swarm is no longer a single entity."

"I spoke to simplify," Zagara said. "Perhaps I simplified too much. All the broodmothers of note are mine to command. The others will submit."

"That's very comforting," Valerian said, trying not to sound too sarcastic. Maybe Zagara simply didn't see the logical dissonance of broodmothers having choice but at the same time being under her control. "There's no dissension among you?"

"I have already said there is none," Zagara said. "We are the future of the Swarm." Her mandibles twitched up and down, a facial move Valerian had never seen in a zerg before. An attempt at a smile? "It is odd, is it not?" she added. "Here we see the zerg Swarm in greater harmony than either the terrans or the protoss. Not since the Overmind has there been such unity."

"Yes, we appreciate the irony," Valerian said. First an almost-smile, and now an almost-sense-of-humor? In some ways, that was more shocking even than the explosion of life on the planet below.

Or maybe she was just being sarcastic and condescending. *That* he could completely believe coming from a zerg. "I trust you won't take offense if I say that we can't simply accept your word for all this."

"That was of course anticipated," Zagara said. "The many betrayals and reversals of the zerg are well known. Name your tests."

Valerian frowned. "Our tests?"

"She refers to the tests by which we will ascertain the truth," Artanis said.

"Ah," Valerian said. "Well, let's begin with something simple. We'd like a closer look at the new world you've built."

"I assumed that would be your response," Zagara said. "We have devised a structure specifically for this meeting among us. I will send the coordinates. You, Emperor Valerian, and you, Hierarch Artanis, will join me for clear and open conversations by which we will seek the future of the Koprulu sector."

"An intriguing suggestion," Valerian said cautiously. Matt, he saw, had moved over to the sensor station and was holding a quiet conversation with the officer there. "But there's no need for us to come to the surface. Can't we simply continue our conversation in this manner?"

"Is it not terran and protoss custom to meet face-to-face with potential allies?"

"Potential allies and potential enemies both," Valerian said. "The latter type of meeting is called *war*."

"War is what I sincerely hope to avoid," Zagara assured him. "That is why I wish to speak with you in person. Only in person can Hierarch Artanis confirm that I am indeed speaking truth."

"I have had experience with zerg *truth*," Artanis said. "I have no interest in studying the subject closer."

"A moment, Hierarch," Valerian said, frowning as a thought struck him. "I know you and other protoss had some communication with Kerrigan during the Amon crisis. Did you have enough of a psionic connection with her that you might be able to tell whether or not Zagara is speaking truth?"

"From this distance? There is no possibility."

"How about from closer?" Valerian persisted. "From inside this conference structure she mentioned, for example?"

Artanis's eyes seemed to glitter a little brighter. "You wish me to step into her trap?"

"Isn't this worth taking a chance on?" Valerian asked. "A peaceful zerg Swarm would be a ground-shaking event."

"So likewise would be zerg treachery and a renewed war," Artanis countered.

"Agreed," Valerian said. "But if it's not treachery, Hierarch Artanis, then it may indeed be hope. Not just for a cease-fire, but for genuine, cooperative peace. I think it's worth investigating closer. Don't you?"

For a moment Artanis seemed to study him. "The risk is great," he said. "Not only for us, but for our peoples. If we were to be eliminated, who then would lead the protoss and the Dominion?"

"I don't think the danger is that great," Valerian said. "Luring us down just so she can make our respective peoples leaderless seems way too subtle for the Swarm. Especially since she could hardly take us both without being killed in return, making the whole thing into a three-way decapitation. Regardless, I'm prepared to take the risk. I'll go alone if I must, but I believe it would send a stronger message if you or another high-ranking protoss were to accompany me."

He gestured to Matt. "Admiral, I presume you're checking out Zagara's conference structure?"

"Yes, sir, we are," Matt said. He sounded even less enthusiastic than Artanis. "It's unique among zerg constructions, I'll give it that. It looks to be built along the general lines of a hatchery, except that it's nonliving and the central cone is open to the sky. As far as we can tell, the interior seems to have been thoroughly sterilized of everything zerg."

"What's the exterior like? As tough as a normal hatchery?"

"At least that tough. Probably tougher."

"So that if something tried to break in, I'd have plenty of time to get in my dropship and get back up here?"

"Unless they had a few flights of mutalisks in hiding, ready to zoom in and swat you out of the sky," Matt pointed out darkly. "With all that foliage, you could hide a hundred of them within potential striking range."

"For what reason would I do such a thing?" Zagara asked. "I sit beneath protoss and terran battle fleets. If I betray you, I, too, will perish."

"You are the Swarm," Artanis countered. "Individual zerg do not matter to the Swarm. Only the end matters."

"We have renounced that goal."

"And what of your other goals?" Artanis persisted. "Once, you sought genetic perfection by infesting terrans and attempting the same with protoss. Were those to be a perfection of the zerg, or merely a destruction of protoss and terrans?"

"That was the past," Zagara said firmly. "The Overmind is gone. The Queen of Blades is gone. *I* am the present. *I* am the future. My vision for the Swarm is as day is from night."

"Why should we believe that you have changed your ways?" Artanis demanded.

"Because I will show you," Zagara said. She was starting to sound angry, Valerian noted uneasily. "Come to Gystt and I will show you everything. Wonders that will benefit all of us, zerg and protoss and terran alike."

"What sort of benefits are you talking about?" Valerian put in before Artanis could respond.

"Many protoss and terran planets were devastated by the war," Zagara said. "In some places, food for the terran survivors is scarce, is it not?"

Valerian grimaced. It was hardly a secret, but he hadn't expected the zerg to keep up on such things. "It is," he confirmed.

"You see before you a possible solution," Zagara said. "What the zerg have done on Gystt, we can do on your planets as well." Her head turned slightly, presumably to the display showing Artanis's face. "The protoss' situation is different," she continued. "But many of your planets were likewise devastated. We could help heal them."

"We have seen what zerg do when they gain a foothold on other planets," Artanis said. The hierarch's skin was starting to mottle with emotion. "After the near-genocide of the protoss on Aiur, do you believe we would permit you to return under any pretext?"

"I deeply regret the destruction on your homeworld, Hierarch Artanis," Zagara said. "But be assured the zerg would not need to come there or to any of your other planets. The necessary genetic work could be individualized here, and you could administer it yourselves."

"But you first require us to come to your structure and meet with you," Artanis said.

"I *ask* you to come meet with me," Zagara said. "I lay no trap before you, Hierarch Artanis, or you, Emperor Valerian. The Swarm desires only to be left alone to live in peace."

"Yes," Valerian said. Catching Matt's eye, he beckoned to the admiral. "A moment, Overqueen, if you please."

Matt stepped to his side, gesturing to the comm officer to mute the microphone. "I don't like it, Valerian," the admiral said quietly, his voice pitched too low for anyone else on the bridge to hear.

"I'm not surprised," Valerian murmured back. "Anything solid backing up that feeling?"

"Just a finely tuned gut that's had a long and painful history with zerg," Matt said. "The building looks secure enough, at least as far as we can tell from orbit. If there's a double cross in the works, we can *probably* get you out in time."

"And if not, assure mutual destruction?"

"Between us and the protoss, absolutely," Matt said. "You really think she's sincere?"

Valerian shrugged. "She certainly knows the right buttons to push. The big question is whether the food solution is an offer or just bait, and we won't know which without going down for a closer look."

Matt snorted. "Forgive my cynicism, but you're not going to learn anything useful on an official guided tour."

"Agreed," Valerian said, giving him a tight smile. "But *I'm* not the one who'll be looking. Unmute me, will you?"

"Okay," Matt said, frowning as he gestured again to the comm officer. "Go ahead."

Valerian turned back to the display. "Thank you, Overqueen, for your patience," he said. "I would be honored to accept your invitation. With one stipulation: while we're having our talks, I want to send a survey team to examine the new life and perhaps ascertain whether your techniques can be adapted to terran planets and crops."

"I would welcome your survey team," Zagara said without hesitation.

"And they would be allowed to go anywhere on the planet?"

"They may go where they will," Zagara confirmed. "The Swarm has no evil intent, nor has it dark secrets."

"Very well." Valerian shifted his attention to the other comm display. "Hierarch Artanis, we would be most appreciative if you would join us."

For a long moment Valerian was sure the protoss would refuse. Worse, that he might even order a preemptive attack. Then, slowly, the mottling faded from his skin and he inclined his head. "I will accompany you, Emperor Valerian," he said, his voice back to its original flatness. "But I urge that neither of us travels alone. I do not believe it would be prudent."

"No, it would not," Valerian agreed softly, looking back at Zagara. "Not in the slightest."

"There," Dr. Erin Wyland said, pointing to her latest composite false-color map. "Do you see it *now*?"

She looked up at the man standing over her cramped shipboard workstation. But Colonel Cruikshank just shook his head. "Not really," he said. "But I'll take your word for it."

Erin ground her teeth. She didn't *want* him to take her word for it. This was science, and science wasn't supposed to be run by popular vote. She had objective *evidence*, blast it, and she wanted him to see it.

She shifted her gaze to the woman standing on her other side. "Do *you* see it?" she asked.

"Of course," Dr. Talise Cogan said calmly. "I saw it three iterations ago." She gestured to Cruikshank. "But we're scientists. He's military. We see the universe. He just tries to blow it up."

"Cute," Cruikshank growled. "Try to remember that it's because of the military that you get to do your science stuff instead of eating rats and hiding in zerg-infested rubble. So, fine, it's there. What do you suggest we do about it?"

"Do about what?" a familiar voice said from behind Erin.

She spun around in her chair, her heart suddenly beating faster. Striding toward her from the hatchway was the Dominion fleet's commander, Admiral Matt Horner—

And beside him, Emperor Valerian Mengsk himself. The man who'd started life as a scientist before rising to rule the entire Terran Dominion. More than that, the man who'd brought genuine ethics to government.

"Emperor Valerian," Cruikshank said, stiffening to attention. "I believe you know Dr. Cogan?"

"I do," Valerian confirmed, exchanging nods with the older xeno-biologist. "And this is . . . ?"

"Dr. Erin Wyland," Cruikshank said. "She's been analyzing the vegetation down there, and she may have found something interesting." He gestured to Erin. "Doctor?"

Furiously, Erin tried to unfreeze her brain. Never in her strangest dreams had she envisioned herself speaking directly to the man who'd saved the Dominion, not just from the protoss and zerg but also from itself. "There appear to be three distinct focal points on the planet from which the rest of the vegetation radiates," she began, trying not to stutter. "The points are—"

"What do you mean, radiates?" Admiral Horner interrupted. "How does plant life *radiate*?"

Erin floundered, forcing herself to take the necessary half second to get her brain back on track before speaking again. "I don't know, sir," she said. "But the pattern is there." She pointed to the false-color map. "The points are *here*, and—"

"Wait," Valerian ordered.

Erin froze, her stiffened forefinger hanging in midair halfway to the second radial point. The emperor moved closer to the workstation, his piercing gray eyes steady on the display. He was right behind Erin now, close enough that she could feel the heat radiating from his body. He reached out a finger, paused, and moved it to hover over the second point. "Here . . ." The finger drifted slowly across the terrain. "And here?"

Erin felt a flood of relief. So it *wasn't* just imagination. The emperor could see it, too. "Yes, Emperor Valerian," she said. "Uh . . . a bit farther east on the third one, actually. But you *do* see it?"

"I do," Valerian confirmed. "Interesting. Those are hills, right? Or mesas?"

"Probably low mesas, yes."

"Any idea what's there?"

"Not really, Emperor," Erin said. "I don't see anything noteworthy on the top surfaces. There's a line of trees along one edge of each mesa, blocking the view, so it's possible that what we see is just an overhang, with whatever's of interest underneath it. But it could also be a vertical wall—I can't tell from these pictures. I'm sorry."

"No need to apologize," Valerian said, his eyes still on the map. "Important discoveries always begin with small steps." He turned to Admiral Horner. "And this small step has just given us our starting point. Admiral?"

"I agree, sir," the admiral said. "Any preference as to which one?"

"We'll leave that to Dr. Wyland," Valerian said. "She can choose where she wants to start."

"I suppose I'd—" Erin broke off as the full implications of that sentence belatedly penetrated. "Excuse me, Emperor? Where *I* want to start?"

"We're sending a team down to study the vegetation and take some samples," Valerian said. "I *was* planning to send Dr. Cogan with them, as our leading xenobiologist. But under the circumstances, I think you should go instead." He raised his eyebrows. "Any objections, Dr. Cogan?"

"None at all, Emperor," Dr. Cogan said without hesitation. "Dr. Wyland's far better with alien vegetation than I am. Besides, I'm a bit too old for fieldwork."

"You aren't, really," the emperor disagreed mildly. "But the rest of your logic is sound. Dr. Wyland, welcome to the survey team. Colonel, get her ready."

"Yes, Emperor," Cruikshank said.

"And good hunting, Doctor," the emperor said, giving Erin the same kind of nod he'd given Dr. Cogan earlier. He then turned and left the compartment, Admiral Horner at his side.

"All right," Cruikshank said briskly, giving Erin a speculative look. "Have you had any experience with powered combat suits?"

"Uh—" Erin floundered again. "I trained for a week with an SCV. They wanted all of us to be able to move heavy machinery—"

"A T-285?" Cruikshank cut her off.

"It, uh, I think it was a T-270. What did he mean, *good hunting*?"

"I'm sure he was speaking in a scientific sense," Dr. Cogan said. But there was a tension around her eyes that sent a chill up Erin's spine.

"Or in the military sense," Cruikshank said flatly. "So, a T-270. More like a vehicle than powered armor, but it's a start. All right, come with me—I'll have one of our sergeants start checking you out on a CMC-400."

Erin felt her eyes go wide. "A *what*?"

"You're going down to the surface," Cruikshank said with strained patience. "A surface covered in zerg. You want to walk to this magic radial point in your jumpsuit?"

"I heard that Zagara promised they wouldn't bother the team," Dr. Cogan put in.

"Yeah, she did," Cruikshank agreed. "You want to count on a zerg promise?" He gestured to Erin. "That question's to you, Doc. Unless you want to tell the emperor you're backing out."

Erin felt a stirring inside her. The last thing she would ever do was disappoint Emperor Valerian. "Fine," she said tersely. "Let's go get this CMC-whatever."

CHAPTER FIVE

For the past three hours the *Hyperion* had been the scene of quiet and controlled chaos. Tanya had kept mostly to the sidelines, but from her limited teep power and occasional snatches of overheard conversation as people hurried past, it had sounded like Emperor Valerian was going to the surface to meet with the zerg Overqueen, while a second team would be sent elsewhere on the planet to study the explosion of life that had inexplicably taken place down there.

Now, with Valerian talking to Ulavu bare meters away, all of that earlier speculation had been confirmed. The emperor was sending a team, and he was asking Ulavu to be a part of it.

It was strange and probably extremely dangerous. It also, Tanya had to admit, sounded interesting.

But whatever happened from now on, she wouldn't be included. Thirty minutes ago, right in the middle of all the conversations and preparations, her clock had run out and she'd ceased to be part of the ghost program.

Or so she assumed. She obviously hadn't shown up in Colonel Hartwell's office for the formal procedure, but the datawork had presumably gone through as scheduled. Whether anyone aboard the *Hyperion* knew that, of course, was a different question.

But she knew. And suddenly, everything had changed.

Nearly her entire life had been spent in the ghost program. Certainly all of her life that she could clearly remember. The barracks, the people, the training, the life routine, even the low-level pain as comrades and acquaintances left for war—all of it was abruptly gone. She was a private citizen now, or at least she would be once she returned to Korhal and was sent on her way.

What did private citizens do? How did they live? *Where* did they live? In houses and apartments and lodges, of course, but how did someone find such places and arrange to move in? Where would she get food? How was it prepared? Where would she get the money to buy the food in the first place?

Where would she even find someone to answer all these questions?

She looked away from Ulavu and the emperor, gazing at all the other activity around her, a hollow feeling deep in her soul. It was as if she were standing on the street, watching a bus take off with everyone and everything she'd ever known aboard. All her life had been aimed toward the goal of serving the Dominion. Now that goal was suddenly gone.

I wanted this, she reminded herself firmly. *I asked to leave the program.*

The pep talk didn't help. Or maybe she hadn't really thought it all the way through.

I would be honored to join the survey team. She heard Ulavu's thoughts as he communicated them to Valerian. *The Terran Dominion has been kind and generous to me over these past years. I would welcome a chance to do something useful for its people.*

"Thank you," Valerian said, inclining his head. "Your insights into both protoss and zerg cultures and behavior have been most valuable to us. I'm sure they'll prove equally useful here."

Tanya nodded to herself. So Ulavu would indeed be going down to the planet. She'd figured that he would accept Valerian's offer.

She just hoped he would be up to the challenge. As she'd often noted, Ulavu didn't always work and play well with others.

I thank you in turn, Ulavu said. *But this is a service far and above that of a simple scholar.* He paused and half turned, looking sideways at Tanya. *Perhaps it will also redeem my face among the leaders of my kind.*

Tanya suppressed a grimace, on both the physical and the psionic levels. Challenges within challenges within challenges. She didn't know why Hierarch Artanis had refused to take Ulavu back after the ghosts had found him wandering on that battlefield. As far as she had heard, no one knew. Certainly Ulavu himself never talked about it. But there was clearly some bad blood there.

Not that there weren't also some bad feelings on the terran side of the aisle. Tanya had noticed that Colonel Cruikshank was making most of the arrangements for the two expeditions to the surface, yet Valerian had chosen to approach Ulavu personally instead of letting Cruikshank do it. The Dominion and the protoss might be non-combatants at the moment, but as she'd seen in Dante's Circle, there was plenty of simmering resentment out there.

"We can hope that this will mend some fences," Valerian agreed. "Thank you for your willingness."

The honor is mine. For a moment the protoss's thoughts faded from Tanya's mind as Ulavu shifted his psionic communication to Valerian alone. Tanya frowned, wondering what the protoss had to say that he didn't want her hearing—

"I understand," Valerian said, his eyes flicking to Tanya. "And there was no problem with your request that I bring Ms. Caulfield aboard. But as of a short time ago she ceased to be a member of the Dominion ghost program. I therefore can't directly order her to do anything she doesn't want to do."

Tanya felt a sudden stirring in her stomach. So the emperor, at least, was aware of her new status. Did that mean everyone else was, too? Did all the people hurrying by think of her as little more than a deserter?

A second later the rest of Valerian's words caught up with her. *Your request that I bring Ms. Caulfield aboard . . . Can't directly order her to do anything.* Had Ulavu asked Emperor Valerian himself to bring her aboard the *Hyperion*?

And was he now also asking that she join the survey team?

Apparently, he was. "I've received a request and suggestion from Ulavu, Ms. Caulfield," Valerian said. "He thinks your talents could be useful on this mission. Accordingly, he's asked me to invite you onto the team."

Tanya looked at Ulavu, noting the lack of any surprise that she had resigned from the program. How long had he known?

More important, why was he asking that she come along? Did he really think she would be useful?

Or was he simply trying to give her one last chance to do something for the Dominion so that she wouldn't leave with the feeling that she'd totally wasted her life?

This is an important mission, Ulavu said into her hesitation. *I believe you could be useful. Will you come with me?*

Tanya sighed. *With me.* Not *with us.* An act of charity, all right.

Still, to finally get a chance to serve the Dominion and the ghost program . . .

She focused on Valerian, standing silent and strong and regal. *Ulavu* had asked that she be added to the team, not Valerian. In fact, it didn't sound as if the emperor had even considered the possibility until the protoss had brought up the subject. Was that simply because Tanya was technically not under Dominion command anymore?

Was it more of the same pattern that had governed her entire life? Was she really so valuable to the ghosts that she'd been continually saved for something special?

Or was she more like a piece of fine crystal, a goblet too valuable to simply throw away but too delicate to drink from lest it shatter?

Did the ghosts think she was useless? Did everyone in the military think she was useless?

Was she useless?

"Thank you, Emperor Valerian," she said, bowing to him. "I would be honored to join the team."

"Thank you, Ms. Caulfield," Valerian said. "The rest of your team is assembling in the amidships hangar deck. Do you know where that is?"

"I can find it, Emperor, thank you," Tanya said. "Come on, Ulavu."

And if she was very, very lucky, Tanya thought as she and Ulavu headed down the passageway, they would find that Zagara had lied about everything being safe down there. Maybe then Tanya would finally find out what she could do, in real combat against real enemies.

Even if her part was only to die in service to the Dominion.

You and I against the world, Tanya Caulfield? Ulavu asked.

Tanya had to smile. *Yes,* she agreed. *You and I against the world.*

Because for once, it could almost literally be true.

"Let me get this straight," Whist said, eyeing the dropship and the techs busily prepping it for flight. "*We* get a single dropship. *They* get a protoss shuttle with full phoenix escort."

"Privileges of rank," Colonel Cruikshank said sourly. "So-called. Personally, I'd take a Dominion dropship any day over riding a robot-controlled box with a bunch of trigger-happy protoss on my tail."

"Mm," Whist said noncommittally. Given the mission, he would choose a protoss shuttle and escort in a heartbeat.

But he knew better than to say so. Cruikshank's biases against protoss were well known, and it was never a good idea to deliberately annoy your mission commander.

Still, Cruikshank was right about the rank thing. Since the protoss had the best space-to-ground transports, Hierarch Artanis had offered to fly over from his mothership and pick up Emperor Valerian and his guard, after which the two leaders would make their joint way down to the planet and Zagara's conference building. The hierarch was standing outside the shuttle, waiting for his guest like a good host, eight other protoss at his side.

Whist had been a marine for a long, long time, with all the bitter and violent experience and memories that came with that history. But even so, the sight of Artanis and his escort sent a shiver up his back. These weren't just fellow soldiers, but representatives of an ancient, powerful, utterly alien race. Everything about Artanis, from his stance to his armor to the quiet but palpable vigilance of his guards, screamed that.

His guards. It was a little hard to tell from this distance, but it looked like four of them were standard Aiur high templar and the other four were some of the formerly renegade Nerazim, the so-called dark templar.

Whist had heard that Artanis was trying to bring the two factions back together. It looked like he was making progress, which was probably good news all around. Getting caught in the middle of protoss tribal disputes was generally a very unhealthy thing to do.

Of course, if the next military action turned out to be between the protoss and the terrans, Artanis's reconciliation program would mean less chance for the Dominion to turn the various protoss groups against one another.

Whist shook his head. Like the old saying said, every silver lining had a cloud.

Across the hangar, one of the hatches opened and Emperor Valerian appeared, dressed in full-press court finery, walking within a phalanx of four personal bodyguards and four combat-suited marines.

Whist studied the man as he strode toward the protoss shuttle, wondering what was under all those trappings. There'd been plenty of hype about how different Valerian was from his father, but so far Whist hadn't seen a lot of changes.

Of course, Whist was in the marines. Changes always percolated more slowly through military hierarchies than they did through the civilian ranks. More significantly, perhaps, Valerian hadn't had a war to run for a few years. In Whist's experience, war was what brought out either the best or the worst in a leader.

Maybe today would be the day that Valerian proved himself. One way or the other.

Admiral Horner was walking beside the emperor, the two of them in quiet conversation. The group headed toward the shuttle, Artanis and his guards turning to face the approaching terrans—

"So this is our bus?"

Whist turned. Four people had entered the hangar from another hatchway and were walking toward him and Cruikshank. One was Whist's erstwhile rooftop drinking buddy, Lieutenant Dizz Halkman. The second was a woman striding along in a ghost skinsuit, her hood thrown back over her shoulders, a combination visor/air-supply system tucked under one arm and a C-10 canister rifle slung over her back.

Whist grimaced. A ghost. Great.

Walking close beside the ghost was a protoss, dressed in a civilian-type outfit of a long tunic, heavy-duty leg wraps, and thick, elbow-length gardening-style gloves.

The nerve cords attached to the back of his skull had been cut short, sparking a brief flicker of combined nostalgia and annoyance. During the war, shortened cords had been a sure indicator that the protoss facing you was a dark templar. Now, with whatever was going on with Artanis's reorganization of protoss society, all the aliens had cut their cords that way.

Which was a genuine pity. Protoss looked enough alike that *anything* that helped a marine distinguish one from another was a bonus.

And finally, bringing up the rear was someone in a marine CMC-400 combat suit, clunking awkwardly along like he'd never worn it before.

"That is indeed your bus, Lieutenant," Cruikshank confirmed. "Sergeant Cray, this is your commanding officer, Lieutenant Halkman—"

"We've met," Dizz said, nodding to Whist. "How you doing, Whist?"

"Pretty good, Dizz," Whist replied. Out of the corner of his eye he could see that Cruikshank seemed surprised, and not happy, at the lack of proper rank respect going on here. Not just between Whist and Dizz, but also between Dizz and Cruikshank himself.

Whist suppressed a smile. Irritating ranking officers was a favorite pastime in the marines. Apparently, the Reaper Corps had its own version of the game. "So are the five of us the whole team?" he asked.

"So I gather," Dizz said. "This is Tanya Caulfield, ghost. That's Ulavu, technical adviser—"

"Technical adviser on what?"

"On whatever we need advising for, I guess," Dizz said. "The colonel here was a bit fuzzy on that. And this is our armored newbie, Dr. Erin Wyland, xenobiologist."

Whist wrinkled his nose. A ghost, a protoss, a civilian science type, and a felon in a reaper jump pack. And a lone marine to ride herd on them. This just got better and better. "Dr. Wyland's another adviser, I gather?"

"Well, she's sure not here to show us any dance moves," Dizz said, cocking his head as he ran a critical eye up and down her. "Though for her first day in armor, she's doing pretty well."

"Try my second *hour* in armor," the woman's muffled voice came.

"Outside speaker, Erin," Dizz called. "Switch inside your left gauntlet—lower right."

There was a pause. The armor teetered a moment—

"I said it was only my second *hour* in this thing," Erin said, her voice now much clearer.

Whist cocked an eyebrow, his opinion of her going up a notch or two. Most of the xenobiologists he'd run into over the years had been humorless stuffed shirts. This girl at least had spirit.

"In that case, you're doing great," Dizz assured her. "They told me my armor and jump pack were already inside?"

"Not yet," Whist said. "Neither is mine. Got a rack of C-14s and P-45s and plenty of replacement mags, though, so at least we've got firepower. Full set of grenades, too."

"What, no flamethrowers or nukes?"

"Actually, there *is* a Perdition junior flamethrower," Whist said. "But yes, no nukes."

"Maybe they're with our armor." Dizz raised his eyebrows at Cruikshank. "The armor *is* on its way, right?"

"Just waiting on the tech guys," Cruikshank assured him. "They've got a new gadget they wanted to install."

Whist felt his lip twist. Like Dominion combat suits didn't have enough gear crammed into them already. "I hope it's at least something useful."

"Well, *they* think it is," Cruikshank said, his eyes steady on Ulavu. "It's called a psi block, based off the UED's sigma-radiation-driven psi disruptors. Along with the original function of slowing zerg movement and reaction, this adaptation is supposed to disrupt local communications. The theory is that'll make it harder for them to coordinate attacks and send out any alerts about your presence."

"Okay, that could be useful," Dizz acknowledged. "I assume they've been tested?"

"On what?" Cruikshank countered. "We haven't had zerg around to fight for six years. I seriously doubt anyone's gone out hunting for test subjects."

It seemed to Whist that Tanya's lip might have twitched at that. "So we're the field test?" Dizz asked.

"Basically." Cruikshank nodded past Whist's shoulder. "There they are."

Whist turned. Two techs were trundling toward them with a rolling cart on which a CMC-400 and a reaper light-infantry getup were stacked.

"Go on, get aboard," Cruikshank said. "I'll make sure your armor is stowed, then call Control for clearance."

"I like to make sure myself that my armor is stowed," Dizz said.

"And what a great world it would be if we all got everything we wanted," Cruikshank said, jerking his head toward the dropship. "You're on the clock, Lieutenant. Get your sorry butt aboard and start your preflight."

For a second Whist thought Dizz was going to argue the point. But the reaper just shrugged. "You heard the man," he added over his shoulder as he headed toward the dropship. "Everyone mount up. Erin, you'll need to unsuit. I'll give you a hand if you need it."

"Why does she need to unsuit?" Whist asked.

"Because I'm flying, *I'm* unsuited, and I don't want a rookie in powered armor at my back," Dizz said.

Cruikshank muttered something under his breath. "Lieutenant—"

"That's all right, Colonel," Erin said quickly. "I can use the practice anyway."

"Fine," Cruikshank growled. "Get going."

The scientist, the ghost, and the protoss headed off after Dizz.

Whist let them get a few steps away, then moved closer to Cruik-shank. "So this is really it, sir?" he murmured. "Five of us is the whole damn team?"

"Turns out you and Halkman are the only ones aboard with forest and jungle combat experience," Cruikshank murmured back. "Besides, this isn't supposed to be a combat mission."

"Yeah, I've heard *that* before," Whist growled.

"Well, this time they say you can believe it," Cruikshank said. "But watch yourselves." He nodded toward Dizz as he disappeared into the dropship. "And watch *him,* too."

Whist looked at the empty dropship hatchway. "Any reason in particular?"

"He's a reaper," Cruikshank said. "Isn't that enough?"

"Not if you know something else about him," Whist said. "What crime he was tossed into the reapers for, maybe?"

Cruikshank snorted. "Look, Sarge, I don't even know his real *name.* Most of them get new ones when they go in, precisely so jar-brains like you don't waste time sniffing around. I mean, come on—a reaper with a name like *Halkman*? Right."

"Yeah, I noticed that," Whist said. "So why is he in command again?"

"Because he's the ranking officer." Cruikshank raised his eyebrows. "And don't forget *that,* either."

"Hey, Whist—you coming?" Dizz's voice echoed out through the dropship's hatch. "'Cause if you aren't, I'm calling dibs on your CMC."

"Good luck starting it," Whist called. He gave Cruikshank a final brisk nod before resuming his walk toward the dropship.

"Never assume, Sergeant," Dizz called back. "Come on, move your butt."

Whist frowned. So was Dizz saying he could start someone else's locked-down armor? Did that mean he'd been a vehicle thief or a lock breaker?

He paused at the door as a sudden thought struck him. "Colonel, you said these psi blocks disrupt zerg communications. What's it going to do to Ulavu?"

"I don't know," Cruikshank said. "And frankly, I don't care."

Whist nodded. "Got it."

This was going to be fun, all right. Absolutely.

The greeting protocol for a face-to-face with the protoss hierarch was complicated but reasonably straightforward. Valerian made it through without stumbling, and from the tone of Artanis's responses, he gathered he'd gotten it correct. Or at least close enough that the protoss was satisfied.

Then again, maybe everyone simply had more important matters on their minds than etiquette.

"You're clear on things up here?" Valerian murmured to Matt as the protoss warriors and marines began filing into the shuttle.

"Very clear," Matt assured him. "First sign of trouble, we drop a full screen of vikings and banshees to cover your withdrawal."

"Assuming Artanis agrees to leave."

"I don't think there's any question that he'll be ready to bug out whenever you are," Matt said grimly. "He trusts Zagara even less than you do."

"Who said I trusted her at all?"

Matt shrugged slightly, his gaze shifting over Valerian's shoulder. "Them, maybe," he said. "Or at least *her*."

Frowning, Valerian turned. The marine—Sergeant Cray—was just disappearing into the dropship as Cruikshank gestured loading orders to the techs with the marine and reaper armor. "Which her? Dr. Wyland?"

"I was thinking more of Tanya Caulfield," Matt said. "I was just noticing that you're sending one of the ghosts' most secret weapons straight into Zagara's hands."

"Not exactly *straight*," Valerian corrected. "You have a point?"

"My point is that if Zagara takes Caulfield alive—or even freshly dead—she and the zerg will have a brand-new chunk of terran genetics to play with," Matt said grimly. "We saw what they did with Kerrigan. And hydralisks with poisoned needle spines are bad enough. Imagine one that could create fire, too."

"Understood," Valerian said. "Understand in turn that with this much Dominion and protoss firepower arrayed against her, Zagara would be hard-pressed to escape if shooting started. Grabbing Caulfield would gain her nothing except to give the lie to her stated desire for peace." He turned back, to find that Matt was staring at him. "What?"

"Are you saying you're setting her up as *bait*?" Matt asked, sounding dumbfounded. "Valerian, that's—" He broke off.

"That's what?" Valerian demanded. "Strategically risky? Tactically unsound?"

"Something your father would have done," Matt said bluntly. "Using people for his own ends."

Valerian snorted. "Wake up, Matt. Using people is something military and political people like us do every day."

"In order to achieve victory," Matt countered. "We send some to their deaths so that others will live. But not this way. Not as bait. Not a—"

"Not a young and inexperienced woman?"

Matt's lips compressed. "Fine. Not a young and inexperienced woman. Especially not one who could be a vital military asset to the enemy."

Valerian sighed. "Look below you, Matt. Look at what the zerg have accomplished. If this is a trick—if they're preparing for another all-out war—they could roll over every planet in the sector with nothing to stop them. If Zagara is planning treachery, our only hope is to find out about it while the Swarm is still more or less localized."

"I know," Matt said quietly. "But there has to be another way."

"There isn't," Valerian said. "But now flip the situation over. The Dominion is vulnerable right now, with food and refugee issues. The protoss have their own vulnerabilities. Yet Zagara hasn't launched an attack on either of us. More than that, she's holding out the hope of helping us solve some of our problems. Add together the current risk and the future hope—and the fact that Caulfield is flanked by a tough pair of war veterans—and I think it's a chance worth taking."

"Emperor Valerian?"

Valerian turned to the shuttle. The last of his bodyguards was standing at the hatchway with one of the dark templar across from him, both waiting for their leaders to board. "Keep an eye on things, Matt," Valerian said, touching his friend on his shoulder. He then strode toward the protoss ship.

"I will," Matt called after him.

His arguments were sound, Valerian knew. The strategy was risky, but necessary.

And it *wasn't* the kind of coldhearted move his father, Arcturus, would have made. Not at all.

CHAPTER SIX

From high orbit, Valerian noted, the planet's new landscape had looked incredible. Skimming along the surface at barely a thousand meters above the ground, it looked utterly impossible.

It wasn't just the colors and greenery. It was the sheer range and variation involved. He'd seen plenty of ecosystems in his years as an archaeologist, and Gystt ranked up there with the most vibrant of them. Only in a handful of places could he still see the blackened scars left by the protoss incineration over a decade ago, and even those were in the process of being overwritten.

It was a far cry from the complete devastation of Chau Sara and the other planets that had been incinerated during the war. There, some sparse flora had started to return, but it was nothing like the aggressive plant life here.

Perhaps a bit *too* aggressive? Zagara had suggested that the zerg technique could be used to revitalize damaged terran cropland. But Valerian had seen what could happen when non-native plants and animals were introduced into an unprepared ecosystem. Generating enough wheat and corn to feed the Dominion would be a hollow victory if the rest of the plant life was devastated in the process.

Could that be what this was all about? The zerg had failed to overrun terran and protoss territory using faunal infestations. Had Zagara decided to try a floral approach this time around?

For that matter, was Zagara really as fully in command of the zerg as she claimed? The zerg leadership had been incredibly fluid—some would say slippery—over the years, and at the moment there was no proof that there wasn't someone off in the shadows pulling Zagara's strings.

I saw Ulavu aboard your ship.

Valerian blinked. All the glory of Gystt flowing past beneath them, all the darker questions about what the zerg were up to pressing in around them, and Artanis was bringing up Ulavu? "Yes, he was there," he confirmed. "I wanted him along for any special insights he might have about the zerg."

As well as insights he might have about the protoss?

"That as well," Valerian admitted, wondering uneasily if Artanis would take that the wrong way. After all, he'd known even before leaving Korhal that Artanis was gathering a protoss task force at Gystt. Theoretically, the hierarch should be able to offer any protoss insights that Valerian needed.

He has served you well?

"His work with us has been exemplary," Valerian said, feeling his forehead creasing. The last time Ulavu had even come up in conversation with the protoss was over three years ago, when one of Artanis's aides had flatly refused the Dominion's final offer to return the wayward researcher to his people. Valerian had never found out what Ulavu had done to warrant such antipathy, but it had been abundantly clear that something was going on beneath the surface.

This probably wasn't the time or place to go into those details. On the other hand, given that Artanis had brought up the subject, maybe it was.

"I'm distressed, though, that he seems to have been ostracized by his fellow protoss," Valerian continued. "I hope we aren't the cause of that rejection, either terrans in general or the Dominion in particular."

Do not concern yourself with Ulavu or his relationship with the protoss, Emperor Valerian, Artanis said. *He serves you. That is sufficient for the present.* There was a pause, and Valerian sensed the hierarch's mental communication being widened to everyone aboard the shuttle. *Are there indications of mutalisk or devourer presence nearby? Are there other signs of zerg betrayal?*

One by one, the negative responses came in: telepathic whispers from the protoss on the shuttle, louder verbal ones from the marines who'd been given spots at the various sensor displays, psi-boosted calls from the protoss manning the phoenix escort ships. *We must continue to be vigilant,* Artanis said.

"Agreed," Valerian said. Had the hierarch sounded disappointed just then? Was he hoping that Zagara had set a trap for them?

Maybe he was. Maybe he was hoping for an excuse to incinerate Gystt again. To kill every zerg down there.

Maybe, down deep, Valerian was hoping the same thing.

The communing structure has appeared ahead, one of the protoss reported.

Valerian frowned at the displays wrapped around his seat. There it was, just coming into view on the horizon. It towered over the surrounding landscape like a white volcano, its surface twisted and textured like everything else the zerg created.

Search for indications of zerg in the region, Artanis ordered.

The search is ongoing, Hierarch. There are no indications of zerg presence outside the communing structure.

"And with nothing bigger than short bushes in the area, it would be hard for Zagara to hide anything large," Valerian pointed out. "At least, nothing that wouldn't have to dig itself out of hiding before it attacked."

Scan the inside of the structure, Artanis ordered, not acknowledging Valerian's comment. Either he'd already reached that same conclusion or he didn't think the statement merited a reply.

Scanning is difficult, Hierarch Artanis. The carapace is thick and strong. There are no discoverable anomalies as of yet.

Understood. Continue.

"And make sure the readings you get match those we got from orbit," Valerian added.

Artanis turned to him. *You believe that the zerg can affect our eyes or our sensors?*

"Zagara was with Sarah Kerrigan when Kerrigan disappeared," Valerian reminded him. "She already told us Kerrigan gave the zerg the gift of choice. Who knows what other gifts or toys she might have given them?"

A fair question, Emperor Valerian Mengsk, Artanis conceded. *All protoss: be especially watchful for such effects.*

Two minutes later, they were there.

Measurements from orbit had indicated that the central cone opening was more than big enough to allow a shuttle and the phoenix escort to enter. But it was only as the protoss pilot began lowering them into the cone that Valerian realized how much bigger than the protoss craft it actually was. Not only did they have plenty of clearance, but even at the tightest spots they still had some maneuvering room.

There is evidence of forced erosion at the apex of the cone, one of the protoss reported.

Valerian frowned at his displays. Had Zagara, seeing the size of the vehicles her guests would be arriving in, quickly peeled away the top of the cone to make the opening larger?

Of course, it might not have been entirely for her visitors' benefit. With the newly enlarged opening, there was now also enough room for a mutalisk or even a huge devourer to enter, should Zagara have betrayal on her mind. Still, as Valerian had already noted, there were no hiding spots for anything that big within fifty kilometers of the structure. Before an attack could reach them, the ships monitoring the situation from orbit would have plenty of time to sound an alarm.

Danger! Hierarch Artanis, danger!

Valerian's eyes flicked across the displays, his stomach wrenching into a knot. What the *hell*—?

There are several clusters of infested flora arrayed around the edges of the structure's floor, the protoss continued. *There may be risk of contamination.*

"I don't think so," one of the marines said. "All the plants are in sealed display cases. Something organic, but it pings like steelglass."

There is no proof that the undersides of the cases are sealed, the protoss countered.

"Who puts something in a case and then leaves its butt hanging out?" the marine scoffed.

That is enough idle speculation, Artanis said, cutting off the budding argument. *Draw in air samples as we descend and analyze for signs of zerg hyperevolutionary virus. We will not disembark until we are assured the interior is sterile.* He turned to Valerian, and Valerian sensed him once again focusing his communication. *We do not wish to inhale plant spores, whether benign or otherwise.*

"Agreed," Valerian said grimly. A motion on one of the displays caught his eye. "Zagara's entering the main chamber."

And she wasn't alone. Walking a few steps behind her was another zerg, nearly as big as the Overqueen, with a flat face, several green eyes—at least four—and large glowing blisters along the sides of his head and neck. Along with the usual zerg manipulative claws were a pair of shorter arms with disturbingly human-looking hands.

The two of them were heading toward a section along the chamber rim that was devoid of the plant cases, and had instead been set up with several chairs and a couple of low tables. A touch on the zoom control revealed that the tables held flasks of various liquids and small cakelike squares.

As if Valerian were going to eat or drink anything offered by a zerg.

There is sufficient room for a landing, the pilot reported. *Shall I begin the descent?*

Begin the descent, Artanis confirmed.

It was an odd feeling to be inside a zerg structure, and Valerian felt a twinge of claustrophobia as the shuttle floated to the floor. But there was no attack; there were no spores or other zerg infestation agents in the air outside, and Matt's reports from orbit continued to confirm that the surrounding couple of hundred square kilometers were clear of threats. The only sizable zerg nearby was Mukav's leviathan, which had set down twenty kilometers away from the conference building, and it was far too big to get inside.

For a long moment after they landed, no one spoke. Valerian found himself holding his breath, waiting against all signs and logic for a last-minute attack.

But the attack didn't come. Zagara and the other zerg remained where they were; no zerglings or roaches or drones burst forth from hidden chambers, and the air analyzers remained a steady green.

Beside him, Artanis stirred. *Begin the disembarkation,* he ordered. *Let us see what Zagara wishes to show us.*

The high templar and dark templar went first, their psi blades and warp blades blazing out from the focusers on the backs of their gauntlets. The marines were next, followed by Valerian's bodyguards, their weapons likewise held high and ready. Valerian watched on the monitors as the mixed group of warriors arranged themselves in a double semicircle around the shuttle's base.

Through it all Zagara and the other zerg remained motionless at their chosen spot by the chairs and tables.

Artanis gave it another moment. Then, after gesturing to Valerian, he unstrapped and led the way out the hatchway and onto the hard floor. Side by side, they headed toward Zagara, their guards falling into flanking positions around them.

Zagara waited until the group reached the chairs. Then she slowly lifted her arms. *I greet you, Hierarch Artanis,* she said. *I greet you, Emperor Valerian Mengsk. May I present Abathur, evolution master of the Swarm?*

"Overqueen, Evolution Master," Valerian said, nodding a greeting to each of them. So that was a zerg evolution master. There had been rumors of creatures like that, but they'd never been fully confirmed. "Thank you for your invitation."

Thank you for accepting it, Zagara said. *Please, come closer. Sit. Partake of refreshments, if you desire.*

Her mandibles clacked twice. *And then let us discuss how we may usher in a new era of peace among our peoples.*

Erin had heard any number of horror stories about the general craziness of the Dominion Reaper Corps. It was with a certain degree of surprise, and a high degree of relief, that she watched Lieutenant Halkman bring them to a smooth landing on Gystt's surface.

Of course, the fact that Halkman had insisted they call him Dizz hadn't helped her confidence level any. Especially when she asked if it was short for Dizzy and he told her it was short for Disaster.

"Okay, we're here," Dizz announced as the whine of the engines faded away. "Whist, Tanya? You're up."

"Right," Sergeant Cray—Whist, as he'd insisted everyone call him—confirmed as he popped his restraints. "The rest of you relax while we check things out."

There are no zerg near the dropship.

Erin's body twitched hard against her restraints as Ulavu's words echoed through her brain. As a xenobiologist, she'd naturally read a lot about the protoss, and she'd thought she understood them pretty well.

But reading about psionic communication and actually experiencing it were two very different things.

"Glad you think so," Whist growled as he walked to the back and started climbing into his armor. Clearly, he wasn't thrown by having alien thoughts bouncing around the inside of *his* skull. "You don't mind if we check it out for ourselves, do you?"

Not at all, Ulavu assured him.

"Shouldn't the rest of us at least suit up?" Erin asked hesitantly, watching with secret envy as Whist climbed with quick efficiency into his CMC combat suit. Her own attempts at getting into the armor aboard the *Hyperion* had been utter embarrassments. Her attempts to get out of it before the dropship launched hadn't been much better.

"Nope," Whist called over his shoulder. "If there's trouble and Dizz has to do a quick dustoff, you don't want to be halfway into your suit. Trust me." He paused long enough to give her a pointed look. "Besides, can you even get into it alone?"

Erin felt her face redden. "Probably not."

"So there's that." He finished sealing his suit, pausing with his visor open. "Tanya?"

"Ready."

Erin looked at the other side of the dropship, a shiver running up her back. She hadn't read nearly as much about ghosts as she had about protoss and zerg, mainly because there wasn't a lot about the program that wasn't classified. Still, as with the reapers, there were plenty of disturbing rumors about them.

"Let's do it," Whist said, sealing his faceplate. He pulled a pair of gauss rifles from the rack by the aft drop ramp, then slung one over his shoulder and cradled the other in ready position. "Dizz?"

In response, the ramp dropped down, its far edge slamming against the ground with a *thud* that Erin felt straight through her seat. A second later Whist and Tanya were outside, one breaking left, the other breaking right. Erin stared at the greenery at the foot of the ramp, her mind spinning in a dozen different directions—

"Clear." Whist's crisp voice came over the dropship speakers. "Olly olly oxen free."

"That means we're cleared to go," Dizz translated, popping his straps. "Erin, you need help getting into your CMC?"

I will assist her, Ulavu said before Erin could answer.

"Really?" Dizz asked. "Okay, sure. Let me know if you need help."

"Uh . . ." Erin said, taking a step backward before she could stop herself.

Dizz noticed. "Trouble?" he asked.

Erin gazed at the alien, who had stopped at her reaction. "No," she lied.

"Good," Dizz said, turning back to his own armor.

Do not be afraid, Ulavu said, starting toward her again. *I will not harm you.*

Erin bit back the reply that wanted to come out. Maybe he wouldn't hurt her . . . but his race had hurt a lot of other people. Despite their claims of honor, the protoss had the blood of millions of terrans on their hands.

Had they ever acknowledged their crimes? Or even admitted that they'd made mistakes, if they still claimed the destruction was necessary?

There was no denying the protoss were an ancient race. But without a better sense of ethics, Erin would never call them an honorable one.

Still, this wasn't the time and place for a philosophical or moral discussion. Their job was to figure out what the Swarm was up to. If that meant working with a protoss, so be it.

Even if it meant letting him close enough to help her get dressed.

To her mild surprise, Ulavu had no problem at all getting the various pieces of her armor to fit together in the right places and in the correct order. But then, he *had* just seen Whist get into the same type of suit.

Protoss were supposed to be quick, strong, and graceful. Apparently, they also had excellent visual memories.

Four minutes later, they were all outside. Ten seconds after that, Dizz had sealed the drop ramp back into place.

And the five of them were alone. On an impossibly lush planet.

Almost certainly surrounded by zerg.

"Okay, Erin, this is your show," Dizz said. "Which way?"

Erin keyed in her heads-up display, rather pleased that she remembered how to do it without any false starts. "That way," she said, pointing between a pair of small hills. "About thirty kilometers." Carefully, she began walking—*left leg, right leg, left leg.* She was getting the hang of this. She started up the saddle point between the hills—

"Hold it!" Tanya snapped.

Erin did her best. But she was already halfway into her step; she was on a slope, and she didn't have her balance reflexes yet. For a fraction of a second she teetered, then slammed straight down onto her faceplate.

The inside of the armor was padded, and there was strategically placed crash webbing to protect her head and torso. But the impact still knocked the air out of her. Cursing silently, she pushed against the ground with one hand, levering herself up onto her side.

And froze. Staring down at her from no more than ten meters away was a full-grown hydralisk.

The field manual said that hydralisks were the Swarm's shock troops of choice. Lying in front of one, Erin had no trouble believing that. The creature was an armor-plated serpent, its torso permanently reared like a cobra or rattlesnake, the whole thing rising to nearly twice the height of an armored marine. From Erin's position, it looked a lot bigger. Its long head stretched back nearly half the standing height of its torso, lowering its mouth to within easy reach of its victim. Its long arms ended in tri-bladed scythes backed by twitching striated muscles that could easily slice through a marine combat suit.

Dimly, she was aware that Dizz, Whist, and Tanya all had their weapons up and trained on the massive zerg. But in that splintered moment, all she could see were the dead eyes and serrated mandibles pointed in her direction. All she could hear was the coldly analytic note in the manual—*hydralisks have hundreds of poison-tipped needle spines that their unique musculature can throw at near-hypersonic speed.* All she could feel was the thudding of her heart, and the low throbbing of her armor. The splintered moment passed; another took its place . . .

And with a small shake of its head, the hydralisk turned and slithered away. It moved around a pair of bushes and disappeared behind a line of trees.

"I'll be damned," Whist muttered, lowering his gun. "I guess these psi block gizmos work."

"Or else Zagara was telling the truth about a truce," Tanya said. "You all right, Erin?"

Erin nodded, frowning. The thudding of her heart was starting to fade, leaving the gentle throbbing of her armor as the only sensation through her skin.

Only the throbbing wasn't coming from the armor. She could tell that now. It was coming from *outside* the armor.

"Personally, I believe in magic tech more than I believe in magic zerg," Whist said. "Erin? *Say* something, kid."

"I'm okay," Erin said, belatedly remembering they couldn't see her nod her head inside her helmet.

"Well, then, get up and let's get going," Whist said. "So did Cruikshank mention why we're the only two who got these block things, Dizz? Sounds like something that would be damn handy for all of us."

"It was probably so that when you and I get stomped, everyone else can call for help," Dizz said. "Seems the blocks do a real number on long-range comms."

"What do you mean?"

"I mean they knock them out completely," Dizz said. "I haven't been able to raise the *Hyperion* since we turned them on."

"Oh, well, that's just great," Whist growled. "Cruikshank could have at least mentioned that."

"He could have if he'd known about it," Dizz said. "We're the field test, remember? Erin, you need a hand?"

"No, wait. I'm listening to something," Erin said. "Can everyone be quiet a minute?"

The others fell silent. Erin strained her ears, trying to get a handle on the elusive sound. It was unlike anything she'd heard before, but it reminded her of . . . machinery? Voices? Impulsively, she rolled onto her back and pressed her helmet against the ground.

And there it was.

"So what is it?" Whist prompted. "Nap time?"

"It's coming from the ground," Erin said, listening hard. "Or *through* the ground. It's like a combination of machinery, voices, and . . . singing."

"You sure you're not hearing something in your cooling system?" Dizz asked. "Maybe the turbines? All of that's right there on your back."

"It's not that," Erin assured him. "It's . . . well, it's like I said. Machinery, voices, and singing."

"Zerg don't use machinery," Dizz said. "And as far as I know, they don't sing."

"It's not something psionic, either," Tanya put in. "Ulavu's not getting anything."

"Yeah, well, he also didn't spot that hydralisk sneaking up on us," Whist pointed out. "Psi block messing with you, Ulavu?"

There is a small effect, Ulavu admitted. *But I continue to be capable of sensing notable zerg presence.*

"*Notable?*" Whist echoed. "You mean, like more than one at a time? Great. Let's hope Zagara doesn't figure out she can send them in single file. So where is this zerg dance party of yours going on, Erin?"

"I don't know how far away it is," Erin said, fighting back her frustration. They didn't believe her. None of them did. "Can you help me get this off?" she added, fumbling with her helmet. "Maybe it'll be clearer that way."

"Yeah, hang on," Whist said. "There's a trick to it."

It took a minute, but he got it off. "Now what?"

"Now I try again," Erin said, pressing the back of her head against the ground. The grass felt prickly, but not painfully so.

"Let me try, too," Tanya offered, pulling off her visor. She lay down on the grass beside Erin.

And for the first time since they'd left the *Hyperion,* the two women were off the group comm circuit.

"Can I ask you a question?" Erin said in a low voice. "A personal question?"

There was a moment of silence. "All right," Tanya said, her own voice studiously neutral.

"Ulavu," Erin said, nodding her head microscopically toward the protoss. "What's his story?"

"It's not a secret," Tanya said. "Some ghosts found him wandering around the edge of a battlefield after all the shooting was over. He told them he was a researcher, and that he'd gotten lost. They took him back to Ursa, cleaned him up, and contacted the protoss. Who didn't want him back."

Erin frowned. "Why not?"

"We don't know," Tanya said. "Or at least, *I* don't know. Maybe someone higher up the ladder knows. Why do you ask?"

Erin hesitated. This was probably going to sound extremely racist. But Tanya had asked. "I just wonder if we can trust him, that's all," she said. "I mean, they *did* burn off Chau Sara, and—"

"Point one: that was over a decade ago," Tanya cut in. "Point two: they've paid for their actions. Point three: Ulavu isn't a warrior, he was nowhere near Chau Sara, and I would be grateful if you wouldn't pin your prejudices against his race on his back. Clear?"

Mentally, Erin shook her head. She *knew* Tanya would take it wrong. "I'm sorry," she said. "I just—"

"Well, don't." Abruptly, Tanya pushed off the ground and rose back to her feet.

"Well?" Whist asked.

"I hear it, too," Tanya said, her voice calm and back to normal. "I'm not sure I'd call it *singing* or *machinery*, but I get the voices and mechanical noises."

"So we know something's there," Dizz said. "I don't suppose you can figure out where it's coming from?"

"It's a little hard to pin down," Erin said. After rolling back onto her stomach, she pushed herself up to kneeling and then to standing, not nearly as smoothly as Tanya had managed. Still, her balance seemed better this time. "But as near as I can tell, the direction's the same as the focal point we're heading for."

"I guess we'd better get there, then," Dizz said. "And I don't want to be here all day, so here's what we're going to do. We'll start off at a walk, and as you get used to the suit, we'll work our way up to a double-time jog. That's about twenty klicks an hour." He looked at Ulavu. "Can you handle twenty klicks an hour?"

Yes, Ulavu's voice echoed inside of Erin's head.

"If you can't, we're going to leave you behind," Dizz warned. "Okay, Erin, let's get your helmet back on and then go. Oh, and we'll let Whist take point instead of you. That way he gets to the nasties before you do. Okay?"

Erin looked at the group of trees where the hydralisk had disappeared. "Oh, yes," she said, a shiver running up her back. "Yes, indeed."

"There," Cruikshank said, pointing to the ground display. "You see it, sir?"

"I see it," Admiral Horner confirmed, his voice giving nothing away. "I'm not sure it's cause for immediate alarm."

Cruikshank ground his teeth. *Vac heads.* Put 'em in space, and everything they ever knew about ground combat leaked straight out their ears. "Sir, those are all the ingredients for a classic Juno layered defense," he said as calmly as he could. "It's a favorite zerg counterploy to armored columns."

"I'm familiar with Juno lines, Colonel, thank you," Horner said, just as calmly. "I also know a typical Juno includes one to two hundred zerg. I'm only counting ten down there."

"Which should be more than enough for two soldiers, a ghost, and two civilians," Cruikshank countered. "If the comms don't come up, and we can't warn them to go around that cluster, I strongly recommend we get part of my force ready to go down as backup."

Horner rubbed a finger across his lower lip. Cruikshank held his breath . . .

"I don't want to entangle more forces down there than we need to," the admiral said at last. "Not with all these leviathans up here that could suddenly decide to pounce on us. *Especially* not with Emperor Valerian elsewhere on the planet where he might need immediate extraction."

Which was why I only said part *of my force,* Cruikshank grumbled to himself. "Understood, sir. And speaking of the emperor, shouldn't we warn him that the truce might be failing?"

"I don't want to interrupt his meeting until we have more data," Horner said. "For all we know, this could just be a bunch of random zerg gathering around a water spring or something." His lips compressed briefly. "But you're right; we can't simply abandon them. Go ahead and load thirty percent of your force—thirty percent only— for a possible rescue mission."

"Yes, sir." Cruikshank lifted his datapad and punched a single key.

An efficiency of movement that wasn't lost on Horner. "I gather you already had the order logged?" the admiral asked.

"Old habits, sir," Cruikshank admitted cautiously. Some command officers hated when line officers did that, believing that it usurped their authority and made them little more than useless rubber-stamps in the military machine. Which, in some cases, was all to the good.

"Yes, I remember the days before long chains of command." Horner looked back at the display. "When the stakes weren't quite as high as they are now."

"Yes, sir." Though Cruikshank was pretty sure that the stakes always *seemed* high when you were in the middle of fighting for them. Did that say something about perception? Or did it say more about human nature in general?

And did he really care?

"But this is the hand we've been given," Horner continued. "So get down to the bay and prepare our cards. And hope like hell we don't need to play them."

CHAPTER SEVEN

I do not believe our situations are so very different, Zagara said, her psionic voice a growl. *Even now, Emperor Valerian, you strive to bring splintered terran factions together to one mind and purpose. You also, Hierarch Artanis, struggle with unity among the protoss. In that same way, I and the broodmothers under my authority wish to create a unified zerg.*

"You *had* a unified zerg once," Valerian reminded her. "The result was the slaughter of terrans and protoss and the devastation of entire planets."

Do you accept responsibility for the evils of your father, Emperor Arcturus Mengsk? Zagara asked pointedly. *It was he who established the psi emitter on the terran planet of Tarsonis that lured the Swarm and drove it to destroy all who dwelled there. Or do you, Hierarch Artanis, take accountability for the excesses of the Conclave in past years? None of us can change that which was. We can only accept that mistakes were made and that evil was often the result, and pledge ourselves to avoid both the mistakes and the evil.*

And we are to believe that the essence of the zerg has truly changed? Artanis demanded. *Because despite the evils of our forebears, the definitions of protoss and terran remain the same as always.*

I understand your skepticism, Zagara said. *But the zerg are truly not as we once were. The gift of the Queen of Blades has raised us to heights we could never have imagined. She who was once terran, then zerg, and now xel'naga has through her mercy and grace—*

Enough discussion for now, Artanis cut in, standing up abruptly. *I wish to examine the plants you have presented.*

Zagara seemed taken aback. *Of course, Hierarch,* she called after him as he strode off toward the nearest of the display cases. His high templar and dark templar guards joined him, keeping a respectful but watchful distance. *I will explain each in turn, both its function and its origin—*

There will be a time later for explanation, Artanis again cut in. *I will first examine them alone.*

Valerian looked at him, then back at Zagara. Zerg faces being what they were, it was impossible for him to tell whether she was confused, embarrassed, angry, or something else. But it *was* the first time since their arrival that she'd been rendered speechless.

As for Abathur, the evolution master remained silent, as he had since the meeting began. For that matter, Valerian wasn't even certain he *could* speak.

But right now, Artanis and his reaction were Valerian's first priority. Something was clearly going on beneath the surface, and he needed to find out what it was. "If you'll excuse me, Overqueen," he said, standing up. He headed in Artanis's wake, his own bodyguards moving to accompany him.

He caught up to the group of protoss at the first of the display cases. "Hierarch Artanis," he greeted the protoss quietly.

Emperor Valerian Mengsk, Artanis responded. *You do not need to be here.*

"It's clear that you're troubled," Valerian said.

My thoughts and troubles are private, Artanis said, his tone making it clear that further inquiry was unwelcome. *They are not your concern.*

"With all due respect, Hierarch, I believe they are," Valerian said. "This meeting may well map out the future of our peoples, with life and death, war and peace, hanging in the balance. Anything that clouds our thoughts or judgment must be addressed."

For a long moment Artanis was silent. *You will consider it a small and foolish thing.*

"Nothing that is important to even a single individual is small or foolish," Valerian assured him.

Another long pause. *Untold thousands of years ago, the protoss of Aiur were visited by a race of overbeings whom we named the xel'naga,* he said at last. *More than just visited. One of them, the one named Amon, stepped forward to nurture us—or so we believed—raising us over the centuries from our animal origins to the beings we are today. But even as this period came to its full glory, tribal passions arose within us. Slowly they eroded our unity, threatening our culture and our very existence. In our blind vanity we did the unthinkable: we attacked our benefactor. His response, and the response of his people, was to leave us.*

Valerian remained silent, resisting the impulse to point out that he knew all this. Whatever Artanis wanted or needed to say, he needed to tell it in his own way.

The xel'naga's departure drove us to despair and anger, guilt and violence, Artanis continued, the tone of his thoughts going darker. *The protoss as a race nearly died then, swallowed up by the Aeon of Strife. It was only through the strength and wisdom of Khas and his discovery of the Khala, our communal telepathic link, that we were able to at last overcome our differences and begin to heal the bonds among us.*

Valerian felt his throat tighten. Bonds that the battle against

Amon had shattered by denying the protoss the use of the Khala. Artanis stood atop a branch point in protoss history, with the hope of unity on one side and the threat of chaos and a return to self-destruction on the other.

We were the first, Emperor Valerian Mengsk, Artanis said. *The first among many others, or so we were told. Our path of honor would have one day led to our ascension to xel'naga. But Amon's manipulation tore us from that path. It robbed us of our honor and our destiny. It nearly destroyed us. It most certainly drove us from our proper and rightful future.* He hunched his shoulders. *It is both a blessing and a curse to forge one's own path. As you, too, know so well.*

Abruptly, he turned to Valerian, his skin mottling violently with emotion. *It is we who should have received the glory of being raised to the status of xel'naga. Sarah Kerrigan—Queen of Blades—perhaps she was worthy. I cannot judge. But what about us? We fought beside her against Amon. We died beside her. The victory was ours as well as hers. Why then was she permitted an honor that has been denied to all protoss?*

"I don't know," Valerian said, his voice reflexively going into soothing political-negotiation mode even as the universe seemed to tilt a little around him. *That* was what had Artanis tied up in figure-eight knots? A one-of-a-kind creature had managed to ascend to xel'naga while the protoss had been left behind?

It seemed absurd. Petty, even. But Artanis was clearly taking it very seriously.

And really, why not? In Artanis's mind, Kerrigan's ascension had given both terrans and zerg some kind of vague, otherworldly stamp of approval.

It didn't make much sense to Valerian. Kerrigan had been a unique case: unique among terrans for her extraordinary psionic ability, unique among the zerg for her free will and creativity. Given all that, he couldn't see how her ascension reflected on either of the two peoples in general.

But Artanis didn't see it that way. And for a race as proud as the protoss, that might well feel like the ultimate humiliation.

"Whatever happened to Kerrigan was a single, isolated event that has nothing to do with the protoss," Valerian told him firmly. "You are a noble race, a race that has spent much of its existence serving as guardians for many other species. You have nothing to be ashamed of."

Artanis emitted an odd sound, vaguely like a snort, though how he had managed it without a nose or mouth Valerian couldn't guess. *It was easy to stand above others when the Khala bound us together,* he said. *Now, with that unity diminished, what are we to do?*

"You'll find a new path," Valerian said. "You've been beaten down countless times throughout your history, and have always risen from the ashes. You'll do so this time, too."

Perhaps, Artanis said. *But you are wrong about the xel'naga. A single ascension may indeed be an isolated event. But there is also that.* He jabbed a finger at the case they were standing beside. *Explain to me, if you can, why the gift of xel'naga essence was given to the zerg but denied us.*

"The—*what*?" Valerian interrupted himself, his brain suddenly skidding again. "What are you talking about? Where is there xel'naga essence?"

There, Artanis said, pointing again at the plant. *Do you not see it?*

Valerian peered through the transparent organic casing. There were three plants inside, each made up of four distinct shades of green with orange and red highlights. The plants were of slightly different heights, but all three had thick, woody-looking stalks tapering to a flowered tip, with a couple dozen leaf-bearing twigs along each stem. The leaves themselves were broad and pointed, with seven spread out on each twig. "I don't see anything," he said. "But then, I don't know what I'm looking for."

The number of leaves on each branch, Artanis said. *The pattern of the branches as they spiral upward. The arrangement of veins and the pattern of margins in the leaves. Just as many terran flora and fauna echo numbers of the Fibonacci series, so, too, does the xel'naga essence manifest itself in numbers of the Cuccodujo series.* He pointed again. *They are not fully xel'naga. But they certainly contain xel'naga essence.*

"Interesting," Valerian said, his heartbeat picking up as he eyed the plants with new interest. "You're sure?"

You doubt my word?

"Not at all," Valerian said hastily. "I'm simply pointing out that the essence you recovered from the xel'naga bodies during the battle with Amon could have been corrupted, either by age or something else."

It was not corrupted, Artanis said. *And the conclusions and analyses are firm enough that I may state with certainty that these plants have incorporated xel'naga essence.*

"I see," Valerian murmured. As far as he knew, no one in the Dominion had even scored a sample of xel'naga tissue, let alone figured out how to properly analyze it. Making a deal to get access to the protoss data was definitely going on his list of things to discuss with Artanis after all this was over. "If I may make a suggestion?"

You may.

"I think it might be wise to continue our examination of the plants," Valerian said, nodding to the rest of the cases around the edges of the room. "See if we can determine if all or only some of them include xel'naga factors. Once we know that, we can return to Zagara and ask her about it."

You do not expect that her words will merely be more lies?

"She may not actually have lied to us," Valerian pointed out. "The xel'naga connection may simply be something she hasn't yet had a chance to mention."

Artanis was silent a moment. *Very well,* he said reluctantly. *We will continue. But I firmly believe she is lying.*

"Then let's catch her at it and see what happens." Valerian gestured toward the next case in line. "And it would be helpful if you would give me the numbers or pattern of this Cuccodujo series."

When something goes to hell, one of Tanya's instructors back in the Ghost Academy had liked to say, *everything else will probably go to hell with it.* In this case, Ulavu barely had time to warn that a zerg was approaching when ten of the creatures burst through the foliage a hundred meters away and headed straight toward them.

Tanya felt the air freeze in her lungs as she reflexively ran the numbers. Five leopard-sized zerglings were ranged at the front of the pack, their sickle-bladed limbs and razor fangs poised to cut straight through CMC neosteel and tear into human flesh. A baneling anchored each end of the line, the bloated acid sacs on their backs pulsating as they strode along. That acid would take marginally longer to destroy their armor, but would be no less effective at the job. Behind the banelings were a pair of hydralisks like the one the group had encountered earlier. But these two had nothing of that first hydralisk's air of idle curiosity about them. Their eyes were fixed on the intruders, their claws twitching, the muscles that launched their poison needles rippling with anticipation.

And behind all of them, one of the nastiest heavy-ground zerg of them all: a ravager, standing even taller than the hydralisks, its broad, turtle-like shell surrounded by a crown of bone spikes. Set deep within the circle of spikes was an organic mortar capable of launching globs of acidic bile through the air, strong enough to destroy even protoss force fields.

"Combat stance," Whist said, his voice unnaturally calm as he took a wide step to the right and brought up his gauss rifle. "Hold fire until they close to seventy meters, then target the hydralisks first. When the zerglings get within fifty meters, switch targets to them—"

"Wait," Erin protested. "They may not be attacking. Shouldn't we wait to see if they are?"

"Why do you think I said to wait until they reach seventy?" Whist countered. "If they're still coming—"

"Incoming!" Dizz snapped.

Tanya caught her breath. A globule of orange slime had shot out from the ravager's back and was arcing toward them like a well-kicked football.

"Scatter!" Dizz barked, the word almost lost as he kicked power to his jump pack and leaped up into the air.

Out of the corner of her eye, Tanya saw Erin stagger as she tried to get clear of the acidic ball in her still-unfamiliar suit. She started to turn toward the scientist, wondering if she would reach her in time.

But Ulavu was already on it. Tanya had barely taken her first step when the protoss brushed past, moving faster than she'd ever seen him travel. He grabbed Erin and hauled her away from the incoming bile. Tanya checked her own motion and backpedaled hard, taking another quick look at the arcing globule. It would be close . . .

Luckily, not quite as close as it had looked. The bile splashed to the ground a solid two meters away.

Just about where she and Erin would have been if she'd tried to get the other woman out of the way.

A second later her headset erupted with the staccato crackle of Whist's gauss rifle on full auto, the sound counterpointed by the slightly higher pitch of Dizz's P-45 gauss pistol as he soared over the battlefield, firing angled shots beneath the hydralisks' armored heads into their torsos.

All right, she told herself firmly. *You've practiced for this. You can do it.*

Sure enough, even as the thought flashed through her mind, she found reflexes and muscle memory taking over, bringing her canister rifle to bear and squeezing off a round into the hydralisk on the right end. Normal C-10 ammo wasn't rated at this range against heavily armored zerg like hydralisks, but Cruikshank had assured her that the rounds he was sending down with her were the latest innovations that Dominion tech had been able to produce.

He was right. The round blew a small but significant piece off the hydralisk's exposed-rib-style torso armor. She chambered another round and fired again, taking another chunk off the enemy.

Her secret concern earlier was that she wouldn't be able to do her job as a soldier. That fear was now gone. She was indeed a soldier.

Time now to see if she was also a ghost.

Back at the academy, her instructors had originally told her to go for the brain. What no one had realized at the time was that the thick skull carapace was an amazingly good heat sink. Unless she positioned her hot spot directly in the center of the brain matter, the heat got siphoned away so quickly that it took forever to scorch enough tissue for a kill. The eyes were another good target, but with the same limitations.

Fortunately, zerg also had a lot of interior organs, and those weren't nearly so well protected. She'd studied the anatomy of every zerg variation known, most of it on mangled corpses brought in from the battlefield.

Time to see how well she'd learned her lessons.

The attack force was getting closer. She fired a pair of rounds into one of the banelings, sending it staggering with the impact. Then, shifting her attention to the ravager at the back of the formation, she focused her mind.

She'd never used her power against a live zerg before. Her instructors hadn't wanted to take the risk that even an isolated prisoner might somehow be able to use its psionic connection with the Swarm to leak information about her ability. Still, each of her experiments had ended the same way: a few seconds of effort, a careful focusing of her pyrokinetic power, and the carcass would burst into flame.

Only it wasn't working. The ravager continued on, shrugging off both her efforts and the bursts of hypersonic 8mm spikes Whist was occasionally sending into its torso when he could spare a moment from his assault on the hydralisks. Tanya leaned into the effort, wondering desperately what was wrong. Even at sixty meters the creature should be well within her range. Was its movement throwing off her aim? Was its circulatory system dissipating or diffusing the heat like the skull carapace did? She clenched her teeth harder . . .

And without even the slightest poof of flame or smoke, the ravager abruptly collapsed to the ground and lay still.

"Shift fire to zerglings!" Whist shouted over the noise.

Tanya blinked, refocusing her attention on the rest of the battlefield. The leading edge of the assault line of zerglings had passed the fifty-meter mark, and both Whist and Dizz had abandoned their attacks on the larger zerg to the rear and concentrated their fire on the closer threat. Firing a round into each of the two nearest zerglings, Tanya shifted her mental attack to one of the hydralisks.

Once again, it didn't work. Or at least, it didn't work fast enough. She kept trying, firing her C-10 on pure reflex at the charging zerglings, focusing all her power on the hydralisk.

And then it went down. She smiled in private victory—

—only to realize it was Dizz's fire that had killed it. Swearing under her breath, she took another moment for assessment.

Not too bad. Two of the zerglings were down, but the other three were still coming, fighting stubbornly against the blasts that Whist and Dizz were hammering into them. The two banelings were relatively untouched; Tanya fired a pair of rounds from her C-10 into the closest, staggering it to a momentary halt, at the same time focusing her power on it. It got a few more steps before it collapsed, though whether from the explosive rounds or her pyrokinetic attack, she couldn't tell. She shifted her attack to the remaining baneling, noting out of the corner of her eye that one more zergling was down and that Dizz was also firing at her baneling. The baneling went down, and Tanya shifted her attention to the remaining two zerglings.

Ten seconds later, it was over.

Tanya took a deep breath, let it out in a long, shuddering sigh. *So did I do it?* she wondered.

Maybe. Maybe not. She'd faced combat, and she'd lived through it. That was something. But how much of their victory had hinged on her power, she still didn't know.

But she hadn't lost control. That was the possibility that had worried her the most. She'd waded into the heat of combat, and hadn't lost control.

"And that, boys and girls," Whist said into the suddenly deafening silence, "is how it's done. Anyone hurt?"

Valerian and Artanis were about two-thirds of the way around the room when Matt alerted them to the incident.

"You're sure it was an isolated attack?" Valerian asked quietly into his comm. Zagara and Abathur were halfway across the structure, but he had no idea how good their hearing was.

"That's how it seems so far," Matt said. "There are other zerg in the area—both individuals and groups like this one—and they haven't made any move against the team."

Though that could be the psi blocks messing with their communication, Valerian knew. "Any idea what set this group off?"

"No, sir," Matt said. "The team might have some ideas, but we still can't raise them. The techs are trying to figure out how to punch a signal through the psi blocks' interference, but so far they haven't had any luck."

Valerian shook his head. Damn untested tech.

Still, as downsides went, comm silence was a relatively small price to pay for keeping masses of zerg off their backs.

They are unharmed? Artanis asked.

"It appears so," Valerian assured him. "We're not sure why this group attacked, but so far none of the other zerg nearby have made any aggressive moves."

And Ulavu? Any word of him?

Valerian eyed him closely. Was that some actual concern he was sensing in the hierarch's tone? "Nothing specific," he said. "But the sensors seem to indicate no one was hurt."

That is good, Artanis said. *Then let us continue our study, and add this incident to the matters we will discuss with Zagara.*

Valerian looked over his shoulder at Zagara, still waiting patiently like a good diplomat.

Or perhaps like a spider in her web.

"Yes," he agreed, turning back to the plant case. "We will definitely have a list."

CHAPTER EIGHT

All ten of the zerg seemed solidly dead. But Whist had long since learned the virtue of making sure.

A single spike to each carcass, either between carapace plates or at soft intersect points, made sure.

The others were waiting in a small clump near the ravager's still-smoldering acid-bile burn as Whist strode toward them, taking advantage of that handful of seconds to do a quick assessment. Dizz was behaving like a proper soldier should, slowly turning in place and keeping watch for new threats. Erin was crouched beside the burn, pretending to examine it while she worked off the adrenaline shaking that Whist could see even through her CMC. Tanya and Ulavu were standing near her, watching Whist and probably talking together via that annoying ghost–protoss psi thing.

Whist still wasn't sure about Tanya. She'd kept firing, but she'd also done a lot of staring while he and Dizz handled the bulk of the fighting. Best guess was that she was *very* new to all this combat stuff. It might even have been her first battle, which raised the question of why Cruikshank had saddled them with her to begin with.

Unless all the staring had been her using some ghost trick against the attackers. But if she had, Whist hadn't seen a lick of evidence of it. As for Ulavu, at least he'd stayed out of the way, which was about the best any of them could have hoped for.

By the time Whist rejoined the group, Erin had finished her make-believe inspection and risen from her crouch. "They're all dead?" she asked, only a slight quaver still left in her voice.

"All dead," Whist assured her.

"Thank God," she murmured. "Is it . . . always like that?"

"No, usually they move faster," Whist said calmly. "Probably the psi blocks. Dizz?"

"They're usually harder to kill, too," Dizz offered, still doing his slow sweep. "Nothing so far. Which, I've got to say, is pretty damn sloppy. Did Zagara really think ten zerg were all she'd need?"

I do not believe these zerg were sent by Zagara, Ulavu said. *I believe we have merely run afoul of a balance crossing.*

Whist frowned. "A *what?*"

It is the line or arc where the territories of two zerg queens or broodmothers are at equilibrium, Ulavu explained. *At such places the zerg are under less control and are more likely to act on individual instinct.*

Whist pursed his lips. "Dizz?"

"Never heard of it," Dizz said. "Can't say I've ever seen it, either."

The effect is less noticeable on a battlefield, where territories are continually in flux, Ulavu said. *Only in static conditions, such as on a planet, does it come into play.*

"Okay, assume that's what happened, and that it's not just the psi blocks hiding us from whoever else is out there," Whist said. "What's our next move?"

We stay on our present path, Ulavu said. *We have already cleared this part of the balance crossing. Deviating to a different path would gain us nothing. It would merely bring us to a separate group of uncontrolled zerg.*

Whist looked at Tanya. "You're his boss. You buy this?"

"I'm hardly his boss," she said, a little stiffly. "But yes, I do. Ulavu's usually right about these things."

"Well, for lack of a better theory, I guess we'll take this one," Whist said. "Let's get moving."

"One other point first," Dizz said, lifting a finger. "If you all think back carefully, you may remember that *I* was put in command here."

Whist felt his lip twist. Was Dizz *really* going to pull rank crap on them?

"We also know—or if we didn't, we should now—that Sergeant Cray has a lot more field experience than I do," Dizz continued. "Under the somewhat old-fashioned notion of the best person for the job, I hereby formally relinquish my command in his favor." He cocked his head. "Consider it a battlefield promotion, Sergeant. Congratulations."

It took Whist a second to find his voice. That was *definitely* not the kind of rank crap he was used to. "Thanks," he said.

"Wait a second," Erin said, sounding confused. "Can he *do* that?"

"Technically, probably not," Dizz said with a casual shrug. "As a practical matter, who's going to stop me?"

"It's all right, Erin," Whist added. "I used to order lieutenants around all the time."

"See?" Dizz said. "So. We're heading straight on to Erin's focal point, then?"

"Unless you have a better idea," Whist said.

"Shouldn't we call this in before we go?" Erin asked. "At least tell them what just happened?"

"They're watching from orbit," Whist reminded her. "Cruikshank and Horner will have had a grandstand view of the whole thing.

Begs the question of why no backup, but it was probably over too fast."

"They've also probably relayed a report to Emperor Valerian," Dizz added. "So don't worry. Everyone who matters is already in the loop."

"I meant should we tell them Ulavu's theory that this was an isolated incident," Erin said.

"They'll know whether it was isolated by whether or not we get attacked again," Dizz said patiently.

"Let's put it this way," Whist said. "We can't call Cruikshank unless we shut down the psi blocks, or send one of you out of their range. You think either of those is a good idea?"

Erin winced. "Not really."

"So we keep going," Whist concluded. "I'll take point, with Tanya behind me, Ulavu and Erin next, and Dizz at rear guard. I figure we're only about three klicks out, so we'll do the rest at a walk with eyes open and weapons ready." He looked at Ulavu. "Just in case that little slugfest *wasn't* some zerg turf war. Got it?"

"Got it," Dizz said. "You heard the chief. Line up, and let's get on with it."

Whist strode to the front of the new line, wondering what the hell that had been about. What kind of criminal—even a former criminal—scored himself a line command, then just handed it off at the first opportunity?

Because all the criminals Whist had ever met had one characteristic in common: they were self-centered to the point of full-blown narcissism. Almost by definition, people who defied society's laws did so because they liked doing exactly what they wanted, and to hell with everyone else. The power to order other people around was an extra bonus most of them would jump at.

Unless Dizz's goal hadn't been to give Whist power, but to load him with responsibility.

He scowled. Sure—that had to be it. Dizz had seen how their first battle had gone, figured they'd been damn lucky to get through it unscathed, and decided to slither out from under accountability for whatever happened in round two.

Was that how a criminal would think? Or was that more like a politician?

Did the reapers take disgraced government types?

"Hey, chief." Dizz's voice came through Whist's headset. "Couple of hills up ahead. You want me to do a bounce and see if there's anything on the other side?"

"Sure, go ahead," Whist said.

Behind him came the sound of a jump pack, and his rear display showed Dizz doing a quick fifty-meter vertical.

Or maybe there was something simpler behind Dizz's decision to give up his command.

Whist looked over his shoulder, ostensibly checking on Dizz's maneuver, but actually taking a good look at Tanya. She'd returned her C-10 to shoulder-slung position: accessible enough, but not as quick on the draw as it would be if she were holding it. Was she carrying it that way because she knew she wouldn't need it?

Tanya was a ghost. At the very least that meant she was a teep. That was obvious just from the way she and Ulavu held their private conversations.

What if she was more than just a teep? What if she was also packing something stronger? Telekinesis, maybe. If she'd been slowing down the zerg or even speeding up the already hypersonic gauss rifle bolts, that might explain the easy victory.

Power like that would make her very useful. It might also make her a hell of a loose cannon.

Because ghosts had even more of a reputation for craziness than reapers. They were rumored to require cybernetic implants to keep them mentally stable, and probably needed a drugstore of enhancement chemicals to keep them functioning. Whist hadn't heard any specific stories of ghosts turning on their officers, but he had no doubt that things like that sometimes happened.

Had Dizz passed over command in the hope of keeping himself out of the line of fire if Tanya went psycho?

Whist turned back to face forward, freshly aware that Tanya was now behind him. *It's fine,* he told himself firmly. *Just do your job, and trust her to do hers.*

"Looks clear ahead," Dizz reported.

"Thanks," Whist said. Trust them all to do their jobs, and hope there weren't any other nasty surprises waiting for them.

Yeah. Right.

There was no intent to deceive you, Zagara insisted, her gravelly psionic voice dark, the Overqueen hovering on the edge of being offended.

An attitude that wasn't lost on Artanis. *How could there not be?* the protoss countered. *The xel'naga were sentient beings, creatures who spoke and shaped their environment and everyone around them. They were not plants. How then can their essence be fashioned into plant life without deliberate manipulation?*

Zagara cocked her head to the side . . .

And to Valerian's mild surprise, Abathur, still standing silently beside her, drew himself up. *Of course deliberate manipulation,* he said in a deep, resonant tone. *Manipulation what zerg do. What zerg are.*

"Welcome to the conversation," Valerian said, inclining his head. So the evolution master could communicate, after all. "Did you handle the job personally? Or were you only the supervisor?"

Abathur alone made creation, Abathur said, a note of pride evident in his voice.

Of course, Artanis said, his skin mottling. *There has ever been only one evolution master. Abathur is that one.*

"I see," Valerian said, feeling his eyes narrow. "So he was the one behind all the zerg mutations during the war? All the variants that gave us—and you—so much grief?"

Abathur serves at my command, Zagara said. *He has always served the Swarm, whether under the Overmind or the Queen of Blades. If you seek to assign blame, place it upon them, or upon me. Not upon him.*

"I wasn't assigning blame, Overqueen," Valerian said. "Merely establishing cause, method, and effect. And he created the zerg–xel'naga plants we see around us?"

Have said already, Abathur said. *Does terran organism claim a lie? Too primitive to understand?*

Zagara half turned, and Valerian had the sense of a private psionic conversation taking place. Abathur ducked his head a few centimeters. *Informed being rude,* he said. *Pardon is asked.*

Yet your question carries unpleasant weight, Zagara added darkly. *You disapprove of his activities? You disapprove of the Swarm?*

"We've seen what comes of his creations," Valerian said, struggling to remain calm and civil. They'd seen, all right. It had been the pattern throughout the war: Dominion soldiers would fight and die and finally find a weakness in some zerg strain. They would begin to exploit it, and then, within weeks or days—sometimes within hours—a new strain would appear with that loophole filled in. "We've faced them in the battlefield and watched them kill our people."

Do you fear these plants as well? Zagara scoffed. *Abathur's purpose is to mold life. Is it not better for me to turn his purpose from the creation of weapons of infestation to the creation of life that is harmless and beneficial?*

Who is to say that these are harmless? Artanis put in, nodding back toward the display cases. *Perhaps they are a new infestation vector for the further devastation of our planets.*

If you believe that, why are you here? Zagara demanded. *If you believe I plan betrayal, why have you come to meet?*

In the small hope that the Swarm has indeed changed, Artanis said. *That has not yet been proven.*

Zagara drew herself up, and Valerian could see the muscles beneath her thick skin working. "A specific example, Overqueen," he said quickly. "You told us that the broodmothers are under your control."

I have already said that.

"And the broodmothers control the zerg in their territories?"

They do.

"Including the group of zerg that attacked our survey team?"

Zagara seemed taken aback. *Your survey team was attacked?*

"Yes, a short time ago," Valerian said. "I received the report as Hierarch Artanis and I were examining the plants."

Were they harmed? Zagara said, her claws twitching a little. *Were there further attacks?*

"No, to both questions," Valerian said.

For a few seconds Zagara was silent. Slowly, her twitching claws came to a rest. *It was not a deliberate assault,* she said. *I have now communicated with the broodmothers. Your survey team was passing through a balance crossing between territories, where members of the Swarm are left to their own instincts and means.*

"Sounds rather sloppy on the broodmothers' part," Valerian said.

It is more than merely sloppy, Zagara said, her tone ominous. *The broodmothers have been disciplined. Neither they nor any of the others will allow such failure again.*

That does not fully address the attack, Artanis said. *If the Swarm has truly changed, why attack the survey team at all?*

Do not all groups change from the leader downward? Zagara pointed out. *Protoss and terrans behave that way. So does the Swarm.* She waved a claw at each of them. *And protoss and terrans also have base instincts to defend themselves against threats. Should the members of the Swarm be otherwise?*

"No, I suppose that's not unreasonable," Valerian conceded.

When the survey team moves on, the other broodmothers have been instructed to allow them safe passage, Zagara continued. *We were discussing the plants.*

"Actually, I believe we were discussing Abathur," Valerian corrected, frowning. *When* the team moved on, she'd said. Not *if* they moved on. Was she expecting them to leave that area?

Was she *hoping* they'd leave?

Briefly, he wondered if he should call her on it. If it was just a slip, a small mistake in terran grammar . . . but if it wasn't, maybe there was something in the Focal Point One area she really didn't want them to see.

And tipping her off that they already knew it was an area of interest would be the absolute worst thing to do.

Very well, Zagara said. To Valerian, it didn't sound as if Abathur was a topic she really wanted to talk about. *Abathur is an ancient being, created long before my existence by the Overmind to facilitate the absorption and reconfiguration of alien essences into the Swarm. Do you know the origin of the Overmind?*

"No," Valerian said. "Mostly we have speculation."

It was an entity created in ancient times by the xel'naga Amon, Zagara said. *It embodied zerg consciousness and brought unity and command to the feral groupings. Later, it developed other agents to solidify its control.*

"And the Overmind in turn created Abathur?" Valerian asked, eyeing Abathur with a freshly awakened sense of foreboding. The Swarm was alien enough; now here was a creature who not only predated everything the Dominion knew about the zerg, but had been created by an even more alien mind.

How did Abathur think? How did he feel? Could Valerian ever begin to comprehend either?

It did, Zagara said.

You must trust him, Artanis said. *Did you not permit him to perform the modifications that altered you to become a broodmother?*

I did, Zagara said. *But the changes were not of his own volition or design. They came from the will of the Queen of Blades, under which Abathur and I were both submitted. She wished me able to understand her thoughts and ways better than I did. Better than any queen or broodmother before me ever could.*

"Because she was grooming you to take over for her?"

I do not know her thoughts beyond her stated desire for me to think more as she did.

Valerian felt his lip twitch. To think more as Kerrigan had. That could be very good, or it could be very, very bad.

The procedure was bitterness and pain, Zagara continued, her claws opening and closing restlessly. *But I underwent it willingly. It is what has allowed me to look past the endless cycle of zerg existence and see a new and better path.*

"That, plus the xel'naga essence Kerrigan left you," Valerian said, frowning as another thought struck him. "Do *you* have any xel'naga in you?"

No, Zagara said quickly. Maybe a little too quickly. *It was not yet in the hands of the Queen of Blades when I was modified.*

"Because that would certainly make it easier for someone to ascend to xel'naga," Valerian pressed. "Tell me: once the xel'naga essence *was* in your hands, did you perhaps ask Abathur for a few new modifications?"

No, Zagara said firmly. *I was left behind to command the Swarm. For that, I need no additional modification.*

Valerian looked at Artanis. But the protoss remained silent. Maybe he was satisfied.

Or maybe he just thought there was no point in asking more questions.

"All right," Valerian said, turning back to Zagara. "Earlier you said that you might be able to assist the Dominion and the protoss in rebuilding our devastated planets. Let's hear how exactly you would go about doing that."

CHAPTER NINE

Tanya was expecting to be attacked at least once more before the team reached Erin's theoretical focal point.

But the attack didn't happen. They came within sight of several more zerg, but none of them—not even the bigger, nastier ones—made any move against the intruders. Most of them, at least those more than a hundred meters away, didn't even seem to notice the survey team.

Finally, they reached the mesa Erin had marked from orbit.

"So it's not an overhang?" Erin asked.

"Nope, the sides are straight up and down," Dizz said, peering down from his high-flying vantage point. "And that tree line on the south face is actually three separate rows, close-packed and more or less parallel with one another. Nothing on top but grass and a few low bushes. The whole thing stretches back about half a klick, with a lot of erosion along the back side. Looks like basalt under the dirt, so maybe it started life as a lava bubble."

"You said the tree line was three close-packed rows," Whist said. "How close is close?"

"The lines are about two meters apart, though the branches themselves fill in a lot of that," Dizz said. "The individual trees in each of the two inner lines are packed about as close together as the ones you can see in the outer line. About a meter apart, with their branches really squashed."

"That can't be good for them," Tanya commented, eyeing the line of trees. With their trunks that close, and with their branches intertwined like wooden mesh, they formed an impenetrable tangle.

"Erin?" Whist prompted.

Tanya turned to see Erin flat on her back, her helmet off, once again pressing her head against the ground. "I can still hear the sound," she reported.

"Is it louder than it was before?"

"I don't think so. Maybe a little clearer, but no louder." She rolled over and pushed herself back to her feet. "But this doesn't make any sense," she continued, waving a gauntleted hand at the rows of trees. "These trees are way too close together. Even if they're running taproots, there's just not enough room for their secondaries and root hairs. And that doesn't even address the branch problem—those lower ones are useless. They should have withered or at least lost their leaves."

"Yeah, but these are magic zerg trees," Dizz pointed out, still floating over them. "Remember?"

"And they've only been here a few years," Tanya added.

"Doesn't matter," Erin insisted. "Even magic trees need nutrients, and they have to get them from somewhere."

Unless they do not have any roots, Ulavu suggested.

"And what, they get everything through their leaves and bark?" Tanya asked.

Protoss physiology and biochemistry have similarities, Ulavu pointed out. *True, our energy absorption is over a wider range of the electromagnetic spectrum than most plants can access. But the principle remains.*

"Okay, but if they don't have roots, what's holding them up?" Whist asked.

"Maybe not much," Dizz said. "Let me try something."

He maneuvered over the trees. Then, abruptly, he dropped out of the sky and disappeared among the branches.

"Dizz?" Tanya called tentatively, frowning.

"I'm okay," Dizz assured her. "I just wanted a closer look at the lower trunks."

"You could have done that from here," Whist said.

"I already looked at that side. Well, well."

"Well, well, what?" Whist asked.

"Do me a favor," Dizz said. "Go to the . . . sixth tree from the west and give it a shove, will you?"

"Give it a *shove*?" Whist echoed. "A shove where?"

"Toward the hill," Dizz said. "The rest of you, keep an eye on the top while he pushes."

Whist muttered something under his breath but obediently strode to the indicated tree. Planting his feet, he set his gauntlets against the trunk and pushed. "And?"

"Did the top move?" Dizz asked.

"Not that I could see," Tanya reported.

"Me neither," Erin seconded.

"Okay," Dizz said. "Take a step back, Whist, and everyone watch the top again."

And to Tanya's amazement, the top of the tree swayed. Not much, but very noticeably. "Did it move?" Dizz asked.

"Like a big bad wolf just blew at it," Whist said. "What the hell did you do?"

"Same thing you did, but without all your fancy servos," Dizz said. "These things aren't just trees. They're some kind of living pal-isade. You can see the lower edge under the trunks on this side where some of the dirt has eroded away. They're basically just rooted on that side, with this side swinging free."

"That doesn't make any sense," Whist growled. "Who designs a palisade you can just push over?"

"I think the point is that you can only push it over from the in-side," Dizz said. "That tells me it was designed to keep things out but not in."

"Out of what?" Tanya asked, frowning.

"Out of whatever's behind the inner line," Dizz said. "It's hard to tell through all the branches, but I think there's an opening into this side of the mesa."

"How big an opening?"

"I'm guessing a hydralisk could get through without bumping its head," Dizz said. "Shall we break out the grenades and see if we can clear ourselves a path?"

That would not be good right now, Ulavu warned, his eyes on something past Tanya's shoulder.

"Why not?" Dizz asked.

"Because speaking of hydralisks, there's a pack of them about two hundred meters to the west," Tanya said tightly as she followed Ulavu's line of sight. "Four, maybe five of them."

"Everyone just hold still and be cool," Whist said. "They're head-ing north. Let's see if they'll keep doing it."

To Tanya's relief, the hydralisks did indeed keep going, appar-ently oblivious to the intruders. The team watched in silence until they disappeared behind another line of low hills.

"Okay, they're gone," Whist said. "Yeah, let's pass on grenades for the moment. Last thing we want is to wake up the neighborhood."

"A good matched set of psi blades would really be handy about now," Dizz commented. "Ulavu, you wouldn't happen to have a focuser or two tucked away under those gardening gloves, would you?"

Of course not, Ulavu protested. *I am a researcher, not a Templar. I have no psi blades, nor could I even use one.*

"I thought all protoss had that Khala thing," Whist said.

"Dark templar don't," Erin told him. "Anyway, the Khala was . . . well, something happened to it in the war; I'm not sure what. Nobody knows much about it," she added, raising her eyebrows toward Ulavu in silent invitation.

Tanya felt her lip twist. If Erin was hoping for enlightenment on that point, she was wasting her breath. From the whispers she'd heard around the ghost program, it sounded like the Khala had been commandeered by the rogue xel'naga Amon, who had then used it to control the protoss who were linked together through that psionic connection. The only way to defeat him had been for all the protoss to sever their nerve cords at the critical moment, thus robbing Amon of his link and power and sending him back to the Void. Unfortunately, cutting their nerve cords had also permanently severed the protoss' own connection to one another through the Khala.

Over the years she'd occasionally asked Ulavu for more details. But he refused to talk about it. And if he wouldn't talk to Tanya, he certainly wouldn't open up on such a painful topic to a group of terran strangers.

Sure enough, Ulavu remained silent. Erin waited hopefully another moment, then turned away.

"Okay, so we can't use grenades, and we're all out of Templar," Whist concluded. "I don't suppose, Tanya, that your ghost power happens to be telekinesis?"

"Sorry," Tanya said. "How about you and Erin? A couple of servo-enhanced CMC suits pushing on the trees from Dizz's side might do something."

"It might at that," Whist said. After stepping back to the line of trees, he took hold of one of the lower branches and with a little effort snapped it off. "Let me clear away enough of these to get around to the other side."

"That'll take forever," Tanya pointed out.

"Allow me," Dizz said. There was the hiss of a jump pack, and he arced into view over the treetops. He landed beside Erin—

And before she could do more than emit a startled squeak, he grabbed her around the chest and lifted her straight up. He arced again over the trees, and a moment later reappeared, alone, this time grabbing Whist and taking him behind the tree line to join her. "Tanya, you want me back out there where I can help you watch?" he added. "This could take a while."

"No, we're good," Tanya assured him, turning her back on the trees and giving the area a quick visual sweep. "Go ahead and—"

She broke off as a sharp crackling of splintered wood suddenly filled the air. She looked over her shoulder just in time to see one of the trees tip over and slam ponderously to the ground.

"Or maybe it won't," Dizz amended. "That was easier than I thought."

"The thing's more like a drawbridge than a palisade," Whist said with a grunt. "Weird. Okay, we'll put down one more, then move inward to the next line. Clear!"

There was another crash as a second tree fell. "Good," Dizz said. "That should give us enough room to get in but still keep out the bigger nasties."

"Okay," Whist said. "We'll knock down two in the next line, then figure out how we're going to get inside the last one."

The middle line of trees proved equally easy to topple, though instead of falling flat to the ground, the newly downed trees ended up angled upward toward the sky, resting precariously across the first two.

"Now for the tricky part," Whist said. "We can't get behind them from above—they're pressed too closely against the mesa for Dizz to drop us in."

"And if there's an opening back there, we won't have anything to brace ourselves against anyway," Erin pointed out. "We had to do that for the first two lines."

"Right," Whist said. "Well, like Tanya said, straight-up cutting through the branches will take a while. So—" He raised his eyebrows. "I think this time we're stuck with the grenades."

Perhaps you could use your power, Tanya Caulfield, Ulavu suggested.

Tanya tensed, her first thought being that he'd sent that comment to the entire team. But the thought flicked away as quickly as it had come. Of course that had been a private communication. Her power was still a closely kept secret, and Ulavu would never betray her that way. *It would be tricky,* she told him. *Burning the trunk will take more than enough heat to ignite the nearby leaves, twigs, and ground cover.*

But you can focus, can you not?

Yes, but creating that much heat means some is bound to escape through conduction and radiation.

Using grenades will draw attention, he warned.

So will starting a forest fire. She hesitated. *It's a question of control,* she added reluctantly. *I'm not sure if I can use my power here without igniting an inferno.*

He inclined his head. *I accept your logic. We will allow them to use grenades.*

Tanya nodded back and returned her attention to the rest of the discussion.

Which had apparently been a short one. Whist was already breaking off the lowest branches on their target tree, while Dizz made some adjustments on a slender cylinder he'd pulled from his belt pack. "We're going with grenades, then?" she asked.

Dizz shot her an odd look. "Yes, we already decided that," he said. "Try to keep up."

Tanya felt her face warming. "Sorry."

"Yeah," Dizz said. "We'll handle this. You just watch for visitors."

The intertwined branches were tougher and more tangled than anyone had realized, and it took nearly ten minutes for Whist to dig away enough of them to get the grenade in place. Twice during that time Tanya considered offering to try her pyro, despite the risks. Both times she resisted the temptation.

Finally, everything was ready. Dizz ordered everyone clear, and with a *crack* that was surprisingly loud even through the muffling of Tanya's hood, the grenade exploded. The blast lifted the tree half a meter off the ground and sent it crashing onto the rest of the freshly cut timber.

Dizz had been right: there was indeed an opening back there. Tanya couldn't see its full horizontal extent with the rest of the tree line blocking it, but it was definitely high enough for a hydralisk to get in.

"One more and we're in," Whist said, pulling out one of his own grenades.

"Or we could just make do with what we've got," Tanya said tensely, her eyes flicking across the line of zerglings, roaches, and hydralisks that had suddenly appeared through the trees. "Incoming: west and south."

"Hell in a basket," Dizz bit out. "We really *did* wake up the neighborhood, didn't we?"

"Everyone in," Whist ordered. "Everybody in *now!*"

No, Ulavu said.

"Why not?" Whist demanded.

I mean, no, the grenades did not draw them, Ulavu said, his mental voice taut. *They are being drawn by something inside.*

"How the hell can that happen with the psi blocks running?" Whist asked.

"And what kind of something is drawing them?" Erin added, her voice catching.

I have no answer to either question. I am . . . unable to focus in that direction.

"I can't, either," Tanya seconded, trying to concentrate. But it was as if something had suddenly begun buzzing in the front of her brain—buzzing, confusing, and destabilizing. Her vision wavered . . .

With an effort, she snapped herself back, pressing a finger against the side of her head near the implant. This was absolutely no time for her to lose control.

"Well, we definitely know what's out *here,*" Dizz said. "Whatever's in there, I vote we go in and take our chances."

"Especially since the hydralisks can't come in after us," Whist pointed out. "Everyone inside—same as our marching order." Turning sideways, he began forcing his way through the narrow gap. "Tanya, you got any more armor-piercing rounds in that rifle, this might be a good time to spend them."

"What about whatever's inside?" Tanya asked, unslinging her C-10. "It's got some weird buzzing going in my brain."

"You still functional?" Whist countered.

"Mostly."

"Then like Dizz said, we worry about things in order," Whist told her. "Starting with slowing down those hydralisks."

Tanya braced herself. "Got it."

Dizz was already firing, his P-45 gauss pistol blazing spikes at the incoming zerg. After thumbing off her C-10's safety, Tanya lined it up on the nearest hydralisk and fired. The creature staggered at the impact—

"I'm in!" Whist shouted from behind her. "Come on, Ulavu. Tanya, two more rounds, then get back here. Erin, you're after her. Dizz, keep firing but be ready to give Erin a push if she gets stuck."

Ten seconds later, Ulavu was through the gap. Twenty seconds after that, Tanya had joined him.

From the inside, the hidden cave was more impressive than she'd expected. It was about twelve meters high, about the same as the width of the opening behind the line of palisade trees. The cave extended about seventy meters back from the entrance, with a gently sloping ramp starting at about twenty meters and taking up most of the space on one side. At the top was a landing, though she couldn't see through the supporting wall whether a corridor headed from there off to the side or whether the landing did a switchback to another ramp heading farther up. However the cave had started out, most of the interior had been remade in the layered, acid-melted-flesh look typical of zerg biological construction.

"Watch the ramp," Whist ordered, tapping her shoulder as he slung his C-14.

Tanya raised her rifle again, watching the ramp and landing while keeping one eye on the ceiling. There could conceivably be something lurking up there, hidden by the folds and texturing. The buzzing in her mind was getting stronger, and she gave her head a quick shake to try to clear it. It didn't seem to help.

There was a sudden tearing of branches from behind her. She glanced around, tensing, to see Whist hauling Erin bodily through the narrow passage between the trees. Apparently, the other woman *had* gotten stuck. Tanya caught another glimpse of Dizz, his back to Erin as he continued to fire, then swung around again to her guard duty.

Nothing had attacked, or had even appeared, by the time Dizz finally shoved his way into the cave.

"Well, that was fun," Dizz said, breathing heavily as he jammed a fresh mag into his gauss pistol. "Nice place. Now what?"

"Watch the door," Whist ordered. "Shoot anything that gets in."

"Assuming they even try," Dizz said, peering cautiously through the gap. "The whole gang seems to have stopped. Maybe trying to figure out what to do next."

"Or whichever broodmother is running this sector is figuring it out for them," Whist said grimly. "Or are we at another, whaddaya-callit, balance crossing?"

No, Ulavu conceded. *We are well within a broodmother's territory.*

"I figured," Dizz said. "So much for Zagara's promises. Wait a second—one of the banelings has started up again. Not moving very fast, though."

"Broodmother's probably working out if it can get us with its acid even if it gets stuck in the gap," Whist said. "Keep an eye on it." He pulled out a light and flicked it across the ceiling near the edge. "Dizz, do those look like fracture lines to you?"

"Not a clue," Dizz said. "You guys spend more time in caves and hugging rock formations than we do."

"Yes, they're fracture lines," Erin said. "I did a unit on geology in college—"

"Yeah, fine, you're hired," Whist interrupted her. "Dizz, you're going to start shooting at the fractures. See if you can bring down some of that rock in front of the gap. Erin, you're going to tell him where to shoot."

But do we not thereby risk bringing down the entire mesa on top of us? Ulavu objected. *We could all die, or be trapped.*

"One: that stuff's tougher than it looks," Whist told him. "He's not going to bring down much, just enough to fill part of the gap against acid bursts and anything trying to get in. Two: as long as we've got grenades, we're not getting trapped. Three: this isn't a debate."

"Here," Dizz said, handing Erin a flashlight. "Point me a target. The rest of you going to check out the cave?"

"That's the idea," Whist confirmed. "At least up to that landing. I'll take point, Ulavu next, Tanya at rear guard. Dizz, if they start moving again and it looks like you'll have more than you can handle, whistle."

Dizz snorted. "Count on it."

The ramp, Tanya discovered as they started up, wasn't particularly steep. It also had the same texturing as the rest of the cave's interior, which offered more secure footing than smooth rock or metal.

But even so, she found herself stumbling as Whist led the way up. The buzzing in her mind was getting louder, threatening her balance and her concentration—

She started as a hand suddenly gripped her upper arm and shook it. "You okay?" Whist asked.

Tanya blinked. The last thing she remembered was the three of them approaching the top of the ramp. Now, inexplicably, they had already rounded a corner and were a few steps up what had turned out to be a switchback landing and a second section of ramp. Another fifty meters ahead the ramp again ended, possibly at another switchback. "I'm fine," she said. "What happened?"

"Ulavu said you were sleepwalking or something," Whist said. "That buzzing in your head—is it like being inside a beehive?"

"Yes," Tanya said, frowning at him. "Why, do you hear it, too?"

"I hear *something*," he said grimly. "Don't think it's as loud as yours—I'm not tripping around corners, anyway. Makes it damn hard to focus, though."

Tanya looked at Ulavu. *Are you all right?* she asked.

I am able to function, he assured her. *But I am deeply concerned for your safety and health, Tanya Caulfield. Perhaps you should return to assist the others at the entrance.*

Despite the pressure on her mind, Tanya had to smile at that one. A marine and a protoss researcher, alone with whatever was spinning boomerangs through their brains. Like she was going to let *that* happen. *It's all right,* she said. *I can do this.*

They were coming up on the second landing now. Still no sign of anything, but the buzzing was getting louder and harder to fight. They reached the landing, started around the corner toward yet another section of ramp—

She had just enough time to see the four creatures bounding down the ramp toward them when the buzzing abruptly erupted into a massive, throbbing explosion.

And the world went black.

CHAPTER TEN

Zerg urban tactics, Whist had long ago discovered, were amazingly predictable. They always waited around a corner, then charged in madly with whatever numbers the overlord or queen or whatever figured would be needed.

He'd been prepared at the blind spot around the first landing. Nothing. Too obvious, maybe, or else whatever was causing the brain buzzing wanted to work on defocusing the team a little longer. Didn't matter, really, because he was just as prepared at the second landing, where the expected attack was actually launched.

There were four zerg, charging silently down the third ramp toward them. Each was about the size of a large dog, a bit smaller than a zergling but with more of the arched-cobra look of a hydralisk. They were the usual collection of angles, fangs, and claws that marked all zerg variants, though there were subtle differences in the specific layout of the killing components.

What *was* strikingly different was their coloration. Instead of the usual dark brown that characterized most zerg, these were light brown with red highlights on their legs and claws, and with triple lines of bright red spots starting between their eyes and running all the way up their skulls and then down the centers of their backs.

It was a color scheme he'd never seen before, especially the red-dot thing. Definitely something new that Zagara had put together for whatever the hell scheme she was spinning.

He raised his C-14, setting his teeth against the suddenly violent level of buzzing in his brain. The buzzing was apparently the second part of Zagara's new one–two punch.

Let her try. Whist had been hit by fatigue, hunger, dehydration, smoke, desertion, ridiculous odds, and the whole general haze of war. He'd gotten through all of them, and he and Tanya would get through this one, too.

What he *wasn't* prepared for was Tanya suddenly collapsing on the ramp behind him. He had about a quarter second to wonder what the hell had happened, and to realize he'd just lost fifty percent of his firepower—

And then it was too late to do anything but start shooting.

For the first few seconds, he thought he could stay on top of it. His first burst caught the lead zerg squarely in the torso, just beneath the gaping mouth, knocking it back and reducing its charge to a limping crawl. Either these things were a lot wimpier than they looked, or else he'd had the luck to nail a weak spot. He lined up his C-14 on the next zerg, blinking as his vision suddenly blurred and wavered.

It was at that moment that he knew he was going to die.

He could barely focus on the second target, and without clear vision he couldn't hope to hit that sweet spot again. Even if he was lucky enough to do so, there were two more zerg behind it.

He would die, and then Ulavu would die, and then Tanya would die, probably still flat on her back. Dizz and Erin would be next, attacked from behind without warning because they were concentrating on the threat outside and were counting on Whist and Tanya to guard their backs.

They were all going to die, and no one would ever even know what had happened. The psi block that had been so brilliantly installed in his armor kept him from shouting out a warning to Cruikshank about Zagara's betrayal.

But he could at least use the short-range comm to warn Dizz and Erin before he died. Strange that he hadn't thought of doing that until just this second. Was mental slowness part of the physical confusion from all the buzzing in his mind?

No matter. The buzzing would be over soon. He squeezed off a burst into the second zerg, the impact flipping it over on its back. At least that was how it looked—his vision was so blurry now that he couldn't be sure. He blinked at the two remaining blobs coming toward him, tried to line up his C-14 on one of them—

And then, to his shock and bewilderment, a figure brushed past from behind, gently but firmly pushing the barrel of his gauss rifle to the side.

His first thought was that Tanya had somehow awakened from her sudden faint. His second thought was that Dizz had magically divined what was happening and had managed to get here in the nick of time. He blinked twice and shook his head, the movement briefly unfogging his vision.

The figure wasn't Tanya or Dizz. It was just Ulavu, striding forward with his arms stretched out to the front and sides, as if he were offering the attacking zerg a friendly bear hug. The protoss's hands knotted into fists, his thick gardening gloves stretching and splitting open across the backs. The gloves fell off, revealing thinner gloves beneath them with complex metal patterns attached to their outer wrists. Even before the gloves hit the ground, the metal patterns were in motion: popping up, unfolding, and reconfiguring themselves into flattened cylinders. They weren't like anything Whist had ever seen before, and yet seemed somehow disturbingly familiar.

He had just enough time to feel his mouth drop open when the cylinders erupted with the incandescent green flame of warp blades.

Ulavu wasn't some useless civilian scholar and researcher.

He was a dark templar.

The two remaining zerg might have tried to scramble to a stop as they recognized their new and unexpected enemy. But if that was their intent, they failed. The first zerg's momentum took it straight into the weapons, impaling itself on the shimmering blades as its body slammed into Ulavu's fists. Ulavu staggered slightly with the impact, but by the time the second zerg hurled itself at him, he'd recovered enough balance to neatly sidestep the arcing leap and slash a horizontal slice through the zerg's entire body, gutting it from chest to tail.

And as the buzzing abruptly dropped to barely background level, Whist realized it was over.

Or maybe, he amended soberly, it had just begun.

Ulavu took a moment to survey his handiwork, probably making sure both his targets were dead. He crossed in turn to each of the two Whist had wounded and made sure they also wouldn't cause any further trouble. Then, almost reluctantly, he turned back to face Whist. *Do not be alarmed,* the protoss's voice came in Whist's head as the warp blades vanished. *I am indeed your ally. I ask that you do not reveal my secret to the others.*

Whist took a careful breath. *Why not—?* he forced the thought.

Cursing, he keyed off his comm and opened his visor. Some people could do this thought-to-thought communication with protoss, but with his brain still spinning from the buzzing, it was way too much effort. "Why not?" he repeated aloud.

Ulavu's eyes flicked past Whist to Tanya. *I have deceived her these many years,* he said, sounding almost embarrassed. That was a new one for the books, at least in Whist's experience. Protoss never got embarrassed. *She will be hurt and dismayed to learn the truth.*

"You think?" Whist shot back as sarcastically as he could manage. "What the hell is going on? Who are you, anyway?"

I am Ulavu, the protoss said. *I am a researcher. But I am also more.*

"Something more, as in a dark templar?" Whist growled. His throbbing brain made a connection to that previous conversation. "Yeah. Cute. Dizz only asked about *psi* blades. The weapons you guys use are called *warp* blades. Completely different."

They are, Ulavu said.

"Not in practice," Whist said. "Fine. Whatever. Nice to know protoss can split hairs, too."

I did not wish to lie. I spoke truth without revealing my identity.

"Yeah, well, it's all academic anyway, because your bubble's about to go poof." Whist gestured to the four zerg carcasses. "Unless you've got a clever way to explain away warp blade wounds."

In answer, Ulavu reached over and plucked a grenade from Whist's belt. *This will eradicate all traces.*

The protoss started to pull his arm away. Whist caught his wrist, vaguely aware that if Ulavu activated that particular warp blade again, he'd finish his life with the nickname Lefty. "Hold it," he warned. "Not saying I don't appreciate having some extra muscle along. God knows we can use it. But if you want me to play ball on this secret-identity stuff, I need to know why."

Ulavu was silent a moment. *Hierarch Artanis is uncertain how much he can trust terrans,* he said. *The Nerazim are similarly ambivalent. We have all seen the viciousness of terran combat, and the disunity of the terran race.*

"Yeah, you protoss should talk," Whist growled. "So what, Artanis sent you to spy on us?"

He sent me to observe, Ulavu corrected. More hairsplitting. *He wished to know whether terran unity could be achieved and whether conflict among you could be eliminated. Of equal importance, he wished to know if the ferocity you had demonstrated in battle would now be turned against the protoss.*

"This may come as news to a born-and-bred warrior," Whist said, "but we terrans are pretty damn sick of war right now. Even if we weren't, we're not crazy enough to launch one against you. Trust me."

I do trust you, Sergeant Foster Cray, Ulavu said. *But I was given a mission. I must complete it.*

Whist scowled, trying to think. This conversation was a long way from being over—that much was for damn sure. But right now, they didn't have time for chitchat. The fact that the buzzing was still going on even though this batch of zerg were dead strongly implied there were more little nasties lurking around somewhere. "Fine," he said, releasing his grip on Ulavu's wrist. "I'll try to keep your secret. *But.*" He raised a warning finger. "If we get in this deep again, you'd damn well better join in the fun. Clear?"

Clear, Ulavu agreed. There was a subtle change in the tone of his thoughts, and Whist had the strangest sensation of an ironic smile. *I can hardly complete my mission if I am dead.*

"Good. Remember that." Whist nodded toward the carcasses. "Go ahead and mulch them. Make sure you're not standing too close."

Whatever else the protoss military taught its dark templar, at least it gave them basic knowledge of Dominion weaponry. Ulavu positioned himself exactly half a meter out of primary blast range before tossing Whist's grenade into the zerg dogpile. "Okay," Whist said as the echo of the blast faded away. "Let's see if there's anything we can do for Tanya."

He knelt down beside her and flipped open her armor's bio dis-play. *I believe she was the main target for the attack,* Ulavu said, crouching at Whist's side.

"Really?" Whist said, looking sideways at him. He'd never seen a protoss crouch. It looked strange with those back-jointed knees. "Well, it sure worked. She's out like a light." He nodded toward Ulavu's forearms. "Those look new."

They are experimental, Ulavu said. He looked down at the warp blade focusers, and as Whist watched they folded back into their flat forms. *Not as powerful or as sturdy as traditional focusers. But better for situations like this.*

"Like when you're playing things cool," Whist said. Gently, he tapped Tanya's cheek. "Come on, kid, wake up."

Ulavu leaned closer. *Let me try. Can you remove her visor?*

"Sure." Whist popped the catches and eased it off. Tanya's eyes were closed, but her face looked peaceful enough. He'd half expected to find a twisted expression of pain or terror. "She's all yours."

Thank you. Ulavu fell silent, his eyes focused on Tanya's face. There was a sound of footsteps behind them—

Whist spun around on his knee, bringing up his C-14. "Whoa!" Dizz called as he and Erin came around the corner, his voice faint through Whist's helmet. "It's just us."

"You should have called ahead," Whist growled, lowering his muzzle.

"We did," Dizz said. "Your comm's off."

"Oh." Making a face, Whist turned it back on. "I thought you were securing the entrance."

"Oh, it's secured, all right," Dizz assured him grimly, breaking into a jog as he spotted Tanya lying on the floor. "Whole ceiling came down in front of the gap. We're going to have to wreck some more trees to get out. What happened here?"

"Meet the brain bugs," Whist said, gesturing to the mess that had once been the four zerg. "The latest product of Lying Bitch Zagara, Incorporated."

"They got Tanya?"

With a sudden, shuddering gasp, Tanya twitched and opened her eyes. "Ulavu—?"

I am here, Tanya Caulfield, the protoss said, catching her armored hand and squeezing it. Somewhere along the line, Whist noted, he'd replaced the gardening gloves, once again concealing his gauntlets and their warp blade focusers. *Are you all right?*

"I think so." Tanya shifted her eyes to Whist, a pained expression creasing her face. "I bailed on the fight, didn't I?"

"Don't worry about it," Whist assured her. "A few shots, a grenade, and we got it done."

"What are these things?" Erin asked. She had gone over to the carcasses and was kneeling beside them, fingering a piece of dorsal carapace. "I've never seen a zerg with this coloration."

"Like I said, something new," Whist said. "We think they're what was causing the mental buzzing."

"You mean the buzzing I can still hear?" Dizz asked.

"Which means, yes, there must be more of them somewhere," Whist agreed.

Dizz huffed out a breath. "Terrific."

"Wait a minute," Erin objected. "This doesn't make any sense. Apart from group communication, the zerg have never had psionic powers before. They've certainly never had projective psionics of any kind."

"Aside from Kerrigan," Tanya said. "Not sure that counts."

"But how?" Erin persisted. "That ability simply isn't in zerg genetics."

"Well, maybe they found some new genetics somewhere," Whist said. "They're really good at doing that, you know."

"At least it explains your fancy plant pattern," Dizz commented. "Got to be connected somehow."

"No," Erin said. "The pattern was in the plants. Psionic genetics only show up in animals. No, there's something else going on here."

"So let's go get some answers," Whist said, squinting up the ramp. "Got at least one ramp to go, and then whatever else is up there."

"What about the brain bugs?" Dizz asked.

"We find them, we kill them," Whist said.

"Good," Dizz said. "Just checking. That's kind of a stupid name, you know."

"You got something better?"

"No, but lucky for us we have an expert on these things." Dizz cocked an eyebrow at Erin. "Over to you, Doc."

"Psyolisks," she said promptly. "It fits both their profile and one of the standard zerg naming conventions."

Dizz looked at Whist. "She's good," he said. "Psyolisks it is." He held a hand down to Tanya. "You feel up to moving?"

"Sure." Ignoring his proffered hand—and Ulavu's—she got back to her feet. "Don't worry. This won't happen again."

Whist looked at Ulavu. *She is correct,* the protoss confirmed privately. *Now that they know about me, I will undoubtedly be their primary target.*

Whist turned away, pursing his lips. *If* they knew about him. With the psi blocks humming away, and all the witnesses to Ulavu's attack dead, they might not.

He hoped not, anyway. Given the choice, he'd take a functioning dark templar over a ghost of undefined power any day. Especially a dark templar the enemy didn't know about. "Let me know if you start going light-headed again, Tanya," he said. "That goes for all of you. Oh, and watch out—the buzzing can blur your vision. I think you'll be okay if you know it's coming and stay on top of it."

"And if not, try a quick stim?" Dizz suggested.

"Probably," Whist said. "Erin, did Cruikshank show you how to do that?"

"Yes," Erin said, her voice grim. "I've also seen the list of stim side effects. I think I'll take my chances with the buzzing."

"Suit yourself," Whist said. "Okay. Same marching order. Let's do this."

The ramp they were on turned out to be the last one. The landing at the top opened into a wide corridor that in turn led to an archway about fifty meters farther ahead. Beyond the archway was what looked like a cavern, but their angle didn't allow them to see very far into it. Oddly enough, especially given that they seemed more or less in the middle of the mesa, there was a surprising amount of dim light filtering in from somewhere.

Dizz noticed it, too. "Wonder what the light's coming from," he commented as they all paused.

"The spectrum is the same as the sunlight," Erin said. She had crouched down a couple of steps to the side and was poking at the rough floor with her finger. "No obvious source, so it's probably coming in via several conduits from the top or sides."

"Never mind that," Tanya said. "I assume we're going to check out that chamber up ahead?"

"We should," Erin said, still poking at the floor. "That's where the pattern we've been following starts."

Whist and Dizz exchanged looks. "We doing magic now?" Dizz asked.

"No, we're doing lichens," Erin said. "They show the same pattern as what we saw from orbit in the macroflora. That pattern definitely leads to that chamber." She stood up. "Are we going?"

"In a minute," Whist said, frowning at the floor. He hadn't even noticed there were tiny plants down there. "You keep talking about this plant pattern, but you've never said what it is. What is it, some kind of giant arrow only people with science degrees can see?"

"It's a little more subtle than an arrow," Erin said. "It's . . . You know how if there's a place where the wind always comes from the same direction, the trees and bushes lean the other direction? It's sort of like that. The tree leaves, for one thing. Leaves usually have slightly different colors or textures on their tops and undersides. They're also turned mainly upward so as to catch the sunlight, but here on Gystt there's an extra vector added in. The trees themselves are noticeably taller near the focal points, too, as if they received the most intense growth spurt. There are also indications in the tree branch arrangements, the symmetry of smaller shrubs—"

"Okay, fine," Whist interrupted. "We'll take your word for it."

"It's almost like a flow pattern," Erin continued. "*Flow* isn't really the right word, but it gives you a sense."

"And you can see that in the lichens, too?" Tanya asked.

"Yes," Erin said.

"What about you?" Dizz asked, gesturing to Ulavu. "You're the other researcher in this group. Does this make any sense to you?"

I have not seen the pattern, Ulavu conceded. *But Dr. Erin Wyland has greater expertise in such matters than I do, and patterns are often apparent only to those who know what to look for. I am willing to trust her judgment.*

"Fine," Whist said, trying to forget all the times he or one of his unit had thought they saw something in the rocks or bushes that turned out not to be there. Human eyes and brains were really good at finding patterns whether they were there or not.

Still, whatever was going on with the plants, the psyolisks definitely needed to be checked out. The chamber up ahead was the next step; they might as well make it a clean sweep. "Usual order. And stay sharp. If the buzzing gets louder, for anyone, for God's sake say something."

"You think we ought to call this in first?" Tanya asked. "Just in case."

"You mean turn off the psi blocks?" Dizz asked pointedly.

"Why not?" Tanya countered. "They don't seem to be doing a lot of good in here."

"We don't know that," Dizz said. "Actually, the fact that Whist was able to take down four psyolisks by himself strongly suggests that they're doing *something* to slow down the opposition."

Whist looked sideways at Ulavu, to find the protoss gazing back at him. He wasn't saying anything, but the reminder of Whist's promise lay heavy in the air.

"Or they're just weaker than the average zerg," Tanya said. "A grenade wouldn't have done that much damage against even a single zergling—"

"Enough," Whist interrupted. "The psi blocks stay on; discussion over."

He looked at Tanya, who clearly had more to say. "Discussion over," he repeated flatly.

She wrinkled her nose but turned away without comment.

"Okay," he said, hefting his C-14 and touching his elbow to his spare mags in his belt, just to make sure they were there. "Let's go."

CHAPTER ELEVEN

The corridor, Tanya quickly discovered, wasn't nearly as smooth-walled as it had looked from the top of the ramp. It had indentations, some of them large enough for a small zerg, others extending far enough back that Whist had to shine a light into them to make sure they were empty. It made for slow and rather nerve-racking progress.

But wherever the rest of the psyolisks were hiding, they apparently had decided not to bother with piecemeal ambush. Nothing attacked or even showed itself.

But the buzzing in her brain was definitely getting louder. Whatever Zagara had planned, she was a long way from being finished.

And that plan could get horrific in a hurry. During the war Sarah Kerrigan had been trapped by the Overmind and absorbed into the Swarm. If Zagara had something similar in mind for Tanya . . .

She shook her head firmly. It was *not* going to come to that. Absolutely and positively not. Whatever happened, whatever it took, she would make sure she died before the zerg turned her into something horrible like the Queen of Blades.

Finally, they reached the archway. "Here we go," Whist murmured. "Stay sharp."

How do you feel? Ulavu's thought came to Tanya through the buzzing.

I'm fine, she replied, frowning. He was trying to hide it, but she could sense an unusual level of pain in his tone. *Are you all right?*

I am fine, he assured her. *But if I should fall unconscious, I would appreciate your pledge that you will protect me.*

Absolutely, she promised, a knot forming in her gut. He hadn't asked anything like that in any of the other battles or near-battles the team had faced to this point. Was there something different about this situation, something he knew about and she didn't?

Maybe it wasn't as different as she thought. Maybe after she'd blacked out back on the ramp, he'd blacked out, too.

Of course, if they both blacked out, there wouldn't be a lot she could do to protect him. Which just meant she had damn better stay on her feet this time.

And she would. The last time, she'd been taken by surprise. Now that she knew what to expect, she was confident she could fight off the effects.

And if not, there were always the stims Dizz had suggested.

The chamber was much larger than the entryway cave three ramps below them. A hundred meters straight ahead, built into the far wall, was a three-tiered zerg-style structure with sixty milky-white pods nestled into the curves and textured material. The pods were ovate, roughly a meter long, with a translucent outer skin. Something was inside each one, but even with the vision enhancements in Tanya's visor, she couldn't make out any details. The support structure itself was unlike anything she'd ever seen, though it shared some of the characteristic features of zerg spawning pools and evolution chambers.

And, perhaps, of the structure that housed the chrysalis the Overmind had used to imprison Kerrigan during her forced transformation. "Well," she commented, keeping her voice level. "*That's new.*"

"Yeah," Whist said tightly. "And *that's* not."

Tanya turned her attention from the pods. The sides of the chamber were fifty meters away in both directions.

Lined up against both walls were more psyolisks. At least twenty on each side, all of them just standing silently.

And as her stomach knotted up, she felt the buzzing in her brain getting louder.

"Whist?" Dizz murmured. "What are we waiting for?"

"Easy," Whist cautioned. "They're up to something."

"All the more reason to start evening up the numbers right now," Dizz insisted.

"Maybe they're waiting to see if we're interested in those pods," Erin offered. "Any idea what those are?"

"Never seen them before," Whist said. "Course, we haven't seen psyolisks before, either, so we left known territory a long time ago."

"Some new kind of spawning pool or evolution chamber, I'm guessing," Tanya said, studying the psyolisks. She hadn't had a chance to try anything on the last batch, and Whist's grenade had messed up the carcasses too much for her to look for weak spots.

But they looked a lot like scaled-down hydralisks. If they shared the same organ layout as well, she should be able to take them.

They may be waiting for us to move away from the tunnel, Ulavu suggested.

"Away from a quick exit, and without a wall to put our backs to?" Whist said grimly. "Sure, that makes sense."

"Are we leaving, then?" Erin asked.

Whist snorted. "Like hell. We were given a mission, Doc, which seems to have come down to taking a look at those damn pods. So we take a look at the damn pods."

"*Then* we get the hell out?" Dizz suggested.

"Probably." Whist looked back at Erin. "Doesn't mean we have to drag you into the middle of it. You could stay back here, where you can make a run for it if the psyolisks decide they don't want us poking around the pods."

Tanya frowned. Now that Whist mentioned it, what *were* the psyolisks doing all the way at the sides of the room? If they were trying to guard the pods, shouldn't they have formed their lines across the team's path?

"Oh, absolutely," Erin said sourly. "Alone and unarmed? Thanks, but I'll take my chances with the rest of you."

"You didn't *have* to be unarmed, you know," Whist pointed out. "You passed right by the rack of C-14s on your way out of the dropship."

"None of which I know how to use," Erin said. "I barely got five minutes of instruction."

"Great—that puts you ahead of most marine recruits," Whist said. He unslung his spare gauss rifle from his shoulder and handed it over. "Here—already set for semiauto. Flip off the safety—thumb lever just over the mag release—then point and shoot. Try not to hit any of us."

"And hold on to this for me while you're at it," Tanya added, unslinging her C-10 and offering it to Erin.

"Whoa, whoa," Whist said. "We're disarming ourselves in the face of the enemy now, are we?"

"We're thinking this through," Tanya corrected, pointing to the lines of zerg. "Look at them. There's nothing on either wall that looks interesting, so they must be here to guard the pods. So why are they standing there instead of right in front of us?"

"Because—" Whist broke off. "Ah-*ha*. Because they don't want stray shots hitting the pods."

"That's what I'm thinking," Tanya agreed. "I'm also thinking that if I head over there unarmed, they might just let me get away with it."

"Because if they charge toward you, they'll eventually end up putting themselves between the rest of us and the pods," Dizz murmured. "Interesting. You may be right."

"And if I am, the trick is to look as harmless as possible," Tanya concluded. "Erin?"

Reluctantly, Erin accepted the rifle. "Be careful."

"I will," Tanya promised.

She stepped forward, then stopped as Whist caught her upper arm. "You're just *looking* harmless, right?" he asked in a low voice.

Tanya nodded. "I'll be okay—"

"Because zerg have ways of messing with people's minds," Whist went on. "Usually by infesting their target—seen *way* too much of that, and it's not pretty. I'm thinking these psyolisks might be a try at bypassing the meat part of the infestation and going straight for the brain."

"And you think I might have been taken over?" Tanya asked, a shiver running up her back. If something like that had happened, she would surely know it. Wouldn't she? "In that case, shouldn't I have kept my weapon so they could make me fight the rest of you?"

"Maybe. Or maybe they first want to see how far they can mess with you."

Tanya looked at the silent lines of zerg, consciously unclenching her teeth. "Tell you what," she said. "I'm going to look at the pods. If I die really stupidly, I'll concede you may have a case. If not, we'll assume I'm still in my right mind. Deal?"

"Deal." He released her arm. "Be careful."

"Right." She looked back at Ulavu. *Watch yourself, Ulavu,* she said. *If they attack, stay behind Whist or Dizz.*

I will be fine, he assured her, a strange darkness in his mental tone that she couldn't remember ever sensing before. *Be safe.*

She gave him a reassuring smile. Then, fighting back her misgivings, she started walking.

A hundred meters, her rangefinder had put it. But now that Tanya was walking alone, with her C-10 at an ever-increasing distance behind her, the pods seemed a hell of a lot farther than that. She kept an eye on both lines of psyolisks as she walked, wondering if and when they would decide she'd gotten too close.

She was thirty meters away, and looking to her right, when she apparently tripped their invisible line.

"Left!" Whist snapped.

She spun her head in that direction even as the background buzz suddenly became a raucous hammering in her brain. The zerg were on the move, the whole line easing forward as if someone was choreographing them. They weren't charging yet, but rather slithering ahead at the pace of a fast jog. Maybe they were waiting to see what she would do, or seeing if they could knock her out again.

Or maybe waiting to see how solid a mental hold they had on her.

If that was it, they were going to be sorely disappointed. Stretching out with her mind, fighting against the buzz, she focused on the nearest psyolisk, visualizing the part of its anatomy where the heart/lung cluster should be . . .

With a violent spasm, the zerg reared up and toppled over on its side. Tanya didn't wait to see it flop to the floor, but shifted her attention and her power to the next zerg in line. From her left the chamber erupted in stuttering thunder as Whist and Dizz opened up with their gauss weapons. Her second target collapsed, and she shifted to the next. This attack was a little off-center, and the psyolisk's side erupted in a burst of black-laced yellow flame. Scowling, she blinked against the buzzing and focused again, and this time it went down. Others were going down alongside it, and she took a second to check the other side.

The zerg back there were falling as well. A quick look at her comrades showed Dizz and Whist standing back-to-back, their weapons blasting away, with Erin and Ulavu back-to-back beside them. Erin was shooting more tentatively than the soldiers but seemed to be holding her own, while Ulavu was mainly hunched over, trying to stay out of everyone's way. Tanya fried two more zerg on the right side, then shifted back to the left.

The attack front had diminished significantly, but there were still plenty of psyolisks charging doggedly toward her. And they were getting closer. She fried one, then another, then another, watching as more fell to Whist's gauss rifle bursts. The familiar red haze had settled across her vision, rage and determination and bloodlust from her power, pain and disorientation from the brain buzz. She fought on and on, killing and killing and killing—

And suddenly, it was over.

Slowly, the haze faded. Tanya realized she was panting, her skin under her armor wet with perspiration. The buzzing was gone, too—not just diminished, but completely gone. She looked around her, noting the scattered zerg carcasses. Then, almost afraid of what she would see, she turned back toward her teammates.

To her relief, all four were still on their feet, with all their extremities still attached in the original places. Whist's and Dizz's armor looked as if they'd been through a mulcher, with multiple slices and punctures from psyolisk claws—apparently the enemy attack wave had made it right up to their doorsteps. But there was no evidence of leaking blood or emergency suit lockdowns, which implied that none of the claws had made it all the way through to the soft terran flesh inside. She hadn't checked her own armor, but it probably looked just as bad. Certainly she had vague memories of psyolisks getting up into her face before she or one of the others nailed them. "Everyone all right?" she called.

Her answer was a tense silence, and three wide-eyed stares. "Are you all right?" she repeated.

"Oh my God," Erin breathed. She was standing beside Ulavu, the gauss rifle sagging in her grip. "You're a . . ." She trailed off, pointing.

Tanya looked at the line of zerg carcasses. Apparently, she'd been off-target with more than just that one early attack. No fewer than four of the carcasses were smoldering, with one of them showing little tongues of smoke-laced yellow flame still dancing around the open wound.

The proper term is pyrokeet, Ulavu said.

Dizz cocked an eyebrow. *"Pyrokeet?"*

"That's just what they called me at the academy," Tanya said, grimacing as she walked back to them. So much for the Dominion's best-kept secret. "It was mostly a joke."

"I don't know," Dizz said thoughtfully. "Kinda suits you."

Do you speak an insult? Ulavu demanded.

"It's all right, Ulavu," Tanya said quickly. The last thing she wanted was an argument on her behalf, especially over something as silly as the stupid nickname her fellow ghosts had given her.

"Yeah, no offense." Dizz snorted a sort-of laugh. "Wow."

"Something funny?" Whist asked, his voice ominous. Apparently, he didn't want any arguments, either.

"No, no, not at all," Dizz said. "It's just really great to have you aboard."

"Thanks." Tanya looked back at Erin, searching for a way to change the subject. "You seem to have come out of it all right. Nice going."

"Thank you," Erin said, blinking at the gauss rifle in her hands as if suddenly remembering she was still holding it. "But don't give me any credit, because I was lousy. It's luck they mostly left me alone. They were hitting you and Whist and Dizz pretty hard. Oh, and here's your gun." Still cradling the gauss rifle, she unslung Tanya's C-10 and handed it over. "If you, you know, really need it."

"Options are always good to have," Tanya said, frowning as she took the rifle and slung it back on her shoulder. "They left you alone? Really?"

"Well, mostly, like I said," Erin said. Her voice had picked up a small tremble, Tanya noticed. The fading adrenaline of the battle's aftermath. "I was mostly hitting what I was shooting at, I think, at least after the first couple of rounds. I couldn't have kept them all back, though, without Dizz's help."

A protection that Sergeant Foster Cray graciously offered me, as well, Ulavu said.

"I'm glad," Erin said. "I was worried about what would happen to you—I couldn't even take the time to see where you were or what you were doing."

"Yeah, well, between Tanya and me we held down our side of the room okay," Whist said, an oddly gruff edge to his voice. "Anyway, kudos on your first battle, Erin. Consider yourself graduated from recruit-level competence to officer-level."

"Present company excepted, of course," Tanya said, nodding to Dizz. It was probably just as well Erin hadn't been able to look behind her, because the psyolisks had gotten perilously close to Ulavu. There were a handful of carcasses near where the two of them had been standing, close enough that it must have taken some impressive shooting by Whist to take them down in time. "Anyway. Shall we go see what all the fuss was about?"

"What, you think we haven't all figured it out?" Whist said, his voice tight. "But sure, let's go take a look."

The walk across the cavern was much quieter this time. With the mental buzzing gone, even their echoing footsteps seemed extra loud.

And in the end, they did indeed find what everyone was probably thinking.

"There," Whist said, pointing through the translucent dome on one of the pods. "Right there, where it's close to the surface. Same red three-line dorsal dotting."

Tanya nodded silently. The creature was moving slightly inside what they now could see was some kind of fluid, and when one of its limbs drifted close to the surface they could see it had the same red-highlighted light-brown outer shell as the psyolisks.

"Only they're smaller," Erin murmured. "They're babies."

"Who grow up to be *those*," Dizz said, jerking a thumb over his shoulder. "So don't go all maternal on us."

"I'm not going maternal," Erin insisted stiffly. "I'm just saying there's a difference between killing them in here and killing them out there."

"Sure is," Dizz agreed. "Out there they try to kill you back. So we take them out?"

"We take them out," Whist confirmed. "And then we call Cruikshank, tell him what Zagara's up to, and let the fleet take care of it while we get the hell off this rock."

If you expect the fleet and Emperor Valerian Mengsk to destroy this place, why do we need to do so ourselves? Ulavu asked.

"Call it insurance," Whist said, eyeing him closely. "Why? *You* feeling all maternal or something?"

"Whist, he's just a—" Tanya began.

Whist cut her off with a gesture. "I asked if you had a problem."

Not with the decision, but with the execution, Ulavu said. *I question our ability to destroy this many pods with the resources available.*

Whist pursed his lips. "Dizz, what's your ammo look like?"

"I'm on my last mag," Dizz said. "He's got a point—that pod material's pretty thick. It may take a couple of shots per."

Whist looked at Tanya. "How about you?"

Tanya wrinkled her nose. "It would be a stretch," she said. "If I use my power too much, it takes time to regenerate."

We do not want her helpless, Ulavu said firmly.

"Absolutely not," Whist agreed.

For a moment, the marine and the protoss locked eyes. Tanya frowned, wondering what was going on. But then Whist simply turned away. "I guess we'll have to leave them to the fleet, then," he said. "Let's get outside—we probably won't get a good transmission in here."

"Whoa, whoa," Dizz said. "I just said I was low on ammo. We've still got options."

"Such as?"

"We've got grenades; we've got dead zerg bodies, and we've got fire." Dizz grinned suddenly. "You wondered why I laughed earlier when we found out about Tanya? It was at the irony of it all."

"What irony?" Erin asked.

"The fact that we've got a fancy ghost who gets praise and comfy beds because of what she can do." Dizz looked at Whist. "You've been trying ever since we met to figure out what crime I committed that got me tossed into the Reaper Corps. The irony? I was a—well, let's just say I was the old-fashioned type of pyrokeet. I just used gadgets and liquids instead of brain waves."

"You're kidding," Erin said, sounding stunned. "You were an—?"

"Yep," Dizz said, a slight edge of bitterness in his tone. "Just like Tanya. Only I didn't get any medals for it. I got put in the reapers."

There was a moment of awkward silence. "Okay," Whist said at last. "So what do we do?"

"We start by lining up the carcasses along the edge," Dizz said. The brief hint of bitterness had vanished, Tanya noted, and he was all business again. A man doing what he loved . . . "Zerg actually burn quite well, and quite hot, with the right encouragement and the proper catalysts."

"Do I want to know how you figured that out?" Whist asked.

"Probably not," Dizz said. "But didn't you ever wonder why protoss took out zerg-infested planets by burning them off instead of using tectonics or sunset viruses? It's because once a bunch of zerg gets hot enough to burn—I mean, *really* burn—the fire becomes self-sustaining. Way more efficient than blasting fault lines."

"Kind of hard on the surrounding landscape, though," Tanya pointed out.

"Extremely hard on the landscape," Dizz agreed. "In here, though, it should be fine." He looked at the pods, tapping his finger thoughtfully against his lips. "Some of the tree branches from the entrance would probably be useful, too. Maybe grab whatever broken ones are down there."

"Or break new ones," Whist said, pulling out his combat knife. "Ulavu, you heard the man. Go get some branches."

As you request, Ulavu said. He hesitated a moment, then took the knife and headed back across the chamber.

"Shouldn't someone go with him?" Tanya asked, frowning at the protoss's back.

"He'll be fine," Whist said shortly. "Now what?"

"We make up some of that catalytic encouragement I mentioned," Dizz said. "Starting by taking apart a few grenades and switching them from *boom* to *sizzle*. I'll do that. The rest of you get busy hauling carcasses."

Tanya carried the still-smoldering ones first, on the grounds that if anyone should get fetid smoke in their face, it was her. Then, while Whist and Erin continued clearing out the zerg from the main charge, she headed over for the ones near where Ulavu had been standing.

There were five of them, she discovered as she sorted them out, two of them lying practically on top of each other. That must have been a particularly tricky shot, and she wondered briefly how Whist had managed it. She took the two carcasses by the base of their claws, making sure not to grab the claws themselves, and started to pull them across the rough floor.

She paused. Pulling on their limbs that way exposed their torsos and the rib-cage-like outer bone structure. Right in the center, just to the side of the layered sternum, was a gaping wound. Not a puncture wound, like a gauss rifle spike would leave, but a slash like that from a wide-bladed knife.

And both carcasses had the exact same wound.

She frowned, leaning forward for a closer look. A knife wound, definitely. But who in the Dominion made knives that could cut through zerg bone in a single thrust? Had someone come up with something new since the war ended?

She looked over at Whist, hauling carcasses, and Dizz, carefully turning grenades inside out. Both men had field knives—well, Dizz did; Whist had given his to Ulavu to cut tree branches—but those weapons didn't have blades that were wide enough to make this kind of wound. Some new breed of vibrating or chain-cut blade, maybe? A vibroblade could theoretically make the wound look wider as it dug through zerg bone.

But even if something like that existed, the weapon at Dizz's waist didn't have nearly the size and bulk that would be needed to house that kind of mechanism, not to mention the necessary power supply. Neither had the knife Whist had given Ulavu.

Could one of the gauss bolts have somehow picked up a spin halfway to the target? No—that was even more unlikely than a vibroblade she'd somehow failed to hear about. Not only would that probably have wrecked whatever gun it had been fired from, but it typically took half a dozen bolts to break through zerg bone armor even when they were going straight and delivered all their momentum and kinetic energy to a single fifty-square-millimeter spot. A spinning bolt would almost certainly just bounce off instead of cutting through the bone like—

Like a protoss psi blade.

She stared at the wound, a sudden icy feeling wrapping around her heart. No. It wasn't possible. It *couldn't* be possible.

But there was no other explanation. Nothing else that made sense.

Ulavu was a Templar. A hard, cold, exquisitely deadly protoss warrior. Who had been hanging out in the ghost program, masquerading as a harmless researcher.

Pretending to be Tanya's friend.

"Tanya?" Whist called. "Trouble?"

Tanya blinked away sudden tears. "No trouble," she called back. Straightening up, she started pulling the carcasses across to where the others were working.

Feeling her heart crumbling within her.

She'd thought Ulavu was her friend. She'd wrapped herself in that relationship. Even when he went off and did crazy things like that midnight visit to Dante's Circle, all of her thoughts and responses had been predicated on the certain knowledge that he would also be there for her if the situation were reversed. She had his back, and he had hers.

Only he didn't. And probably never had.

He'd lied to Commandant Schmidt about who he was. He'd lied to the rest of the ghosts. There was no reason to think he hadn't lied to Tanya, too.

She looked at each of the others as she walked mechanically across the room. Did everyone else on the team already know? Had Ulavu revealed his true identity in battle? Erin's back had been to him, but Whist might have seen him in action.

Or maybe Ulavu had told all of them. Maybe they were all secretly amused by Tanya's naïve ignorance.

She could ask them. But she didn't dare. Besides, whether they knew or not didn't really matter.

She'd had something special. Now she didn't.

She'd never had friends. Not really. As a child, she'd blamed it on her power, and people's fear of it. Later, at the Ghost Academy, she'd blamed it on the implant they'd put into her brain, and the way it sometimes messed with her mind and emotions. During the war she'd blamed it on the stresses of combat that were tearing at the whole of terran society. After the war, she'd blamed it on people's PTSD or the struggle to adjust to peacetime life.

But it was none of those. She knew that now.

It was her. She could get along with people for a while. But sooner or later, usually just when everything was going smoothly, she would say something wrong, or do something wrong, and they would be gone, never to return.

Ulavu had been the sole exception. Unlike any of her fellow terrans, he always had been there, always willing to forgive an unintended slight or an unexpected outburst. He'd been her rock. Her anchor. Her friend.

Only now she knew it had all been a lie.

So let Whist know. What did she care? Let Erin know, and Dizz, and Emperor Valerian, and the whole damn Dominion if it came to that. She didn't care. Nothing mattered anymore.

For that matter, there was really no reason for Dizz to fiddle with those grenades. Tanya could just as easily stand over the pods and ignite everything, taking the whole place down in a sort of Old Earth Viking funeral pyre. The mission was over. There was no reason not to go out right here and now and put an end to her misery.

She clenched her teeth. No. This part of the mission was over, but Erin had said there were two other focal points. Valerian might decide to nuke the planet from orbit, but he might also decide that a more surgical strike was needed. A strike that might include their team.

Ulavu had forfeited her trust and her loyalty. But Whist and the others hadn't. Not even if they were all secretly laughing behind her back.

She would stay with them. She would do whatever was necessary to complete the mission. She owed the Dominion that much for the time and effort it had put into her over the years.

But if it came down to the need for someone to make the ultimate sacrifice, as had happened with so many missions during the war . . . well, at least Whist wouldn't have to send out a call for volunteers.

Ulavu returned with more branches than he should have been able to scavenge, or even to cut with Whist's knife. Tanya pretended not to notice. At one point the protoss inquired about her health and her strength. She answered him civilly, burying her anger and anguish deep where he wouldn't see them.

And when the preparations were finished, she watched with the others from the end of the tunnel, with malevolent satisfaction, as the pods and zerg carcasses consumed themselves in white-hot flame.

It took their last three grenades to blow open a new path through the tree palisade blocking the cavern entrance. Fortunately, the group of zerg that had driven them inside earlier was nowhere to be seen.

"What now?" Erin asked.

"Dizz goes and gets the dropship," Whist said. "Once he's on his way, I'll turn off my psi block and call in our report."

"Okay." Erin shivered. "I just hope turning it off doesn't bring a new batch."

"If it does, we'll kill them," Tanya said calmly.

Whist threw her an odd look, but nodded. "Exactly," he said. "Hit the sky, Dizz. The sooner we're out of here, the better."

CHAPTER TWELVE

Midway through Valerian's presentation of the survey team's report, Abathur's arms had started twitching. By the time he reached the part about the pods, the evolution master's clawed hands were working as if he were trying to strangle an invisible opponent.

And by the time he finished—

Terran organisms destroyed adostra? Abathur snarled. *Terran organisms* destroyed *adostra? Work of Abathur's hands—future of Swarm—burned to ash?*

"The team was attacked," Valerian said, watching Zagara out of the corner of his eye. So far the Overqueen hadn't spoken, nor had she moved a muscle. But throughout his report Valerian had felt an ever-deepening sense of danger and foreboding from her.

And right now she looked as alien as any zerg had ever looked.

Impossible, Abathur bit out. *Adostra harmless. Dreaming. Cannot attack.*

"I'm not talking about the ones in the pods," Valerian said. "I'm talking about the other ones, the ones we're calling psyolisks."

And yet you destroyed the adostra in their pods, Zagara said quietly.

A shiver ran up Valerian's back. Very alien . . . and *very* angry.

Artanis, at least, wasn't moved so easily. *You knew of these creatures,* he said. *Yet you said nothing. Why?*

You dare to ask that? Zagara countered. *After all your sentiment against the Swarm and against the evolution master's attempts to create and mold and extend life? You dare to ask why we would not trust you with the knowledge of the adostra?*

So you admit you lied to us?

I allowed you to go anywhere, Emperor Valerian, Zagara said, ignoring Artanis's question. *You repaid that graciousness with wanton slaughter.*

"It wasn't wanton, Overqueen," Valerian said. A movement caught his eye: a pair of ravagers had appeared just outside the entrance to the chamber. So far they hadn't entered, but it was clear they were ready to do so at a moment's notice.

Artanis had noticed them, too. *Do you now bring a direct attack?* he demanded.

Would I not be justified in doing so? Zagara shot back. *You have attempted to destroy the future of the zerg. Shall I have no right to fight back in the Swarm's defense?*

The survey team was attacked, Artanis said.

The zerg you speak of do not exist, Zagara said. *Yet I do not attack. Despite deadly provocation, I stand ready to continue our discussion.*

But I do not. Artanis stood and lifted a hand. *We will leave now. And we will then deliver to you the penalty for your actions.*

The high templar and dark templar escort shifted positions, forming a cordon back to the shuttle. Zagara drew herself up, and Valerian sensed her making a supreme effort to rein in her anger. *I ask you to reconsider, Hierarch Artanis,* she said. *I ask most strongly and urgently. This conversation is vital to the future of our civilizations.*

I will hear nothing more. Artanis turned to Valerian. *Come, Emperor Valerian Mengsk. It is time we leave this place.*

Valerian hesitated. Artanis was undoubtedly right. In all of Zagara's talk about xel'naga-influenced plants and grandiose plans for feeding starving terrans, she'd never said a word about new zerg strains.

Yet they clearly existed. And it was absolutely certain that zerg with the kind of psionic abilities Sergeant Cray had described could not be permitted to leave Gystt.

But there was something wrong here. Something that didn't make sense.

Why would Zagara invite them to Gystt and allow him to send a survey team anywhere on the planet, knowing full well what that team might run into? Not only *might*, but *had*. Even more telling, she'd known since the team's run-in with zerg at the balance crossing that they were heading toward the mesa. She'd suggested at the time that she thought the team would be moving on, but she hadn't explicitly said so. She certainly hadn't insisted on it.

So why hadn't she? Why hadn't she made some excuse to Valerian and found a reason for him to withdraw the team or send it elsewhere?

Emperor Valerian Mengsk?

"Emperor Valerian?" one of Valerian's bodyguards murmured, his eyes on the waiting ravagers. "Hierarch Artanis is right. We need to go."

Valerian pursed his lips, trying to see through Zagara's armored skin and face and get to her soul. She was still angry, still agitated. Yet she was making no move to stop her guests from leaving.

Unless that move wasn't going to come from in here.

"Signal the *Hyperion*," he murmured to the guard. "See if there are mutalisks or other zerg heading in this direction."

"Already done, Emperor," the guard said. "Sensors show nothing in the air near us. The only large zerg nearby is Mukav's leviathan—the one we followed in from Korhal—and it's still on the ground."

Valerian chewed the inside of his cheek. Zagara's deepest secret had supposedly been laid bare, bringing her and the entire planet to the brink of annihilation. Yet she was doing nothing.

Emperor Valerian Mengsk? Artanis repeated his call, this time with an edge of impatience.

Valerian wanted to go. He and Artanis had been lied to, and the implied threat underlying their agreement to attend this meeting had to be carried out. Not following up on threats and promises was the worst thing a leader could do.

But something was wrong. And if he didn't get to the bottom of it, he knew he would always look back on this moment and wonder what might have been.

"Thank you, Hierarch Artanis," he said. "But I'd like to stay a little longer. We need to offer Overqueen Zagara the chance to give us an explanation."

We need offer her nothing, Artanis said flatly. *We made an agreement. That agreement has been abrogated.*

"Perhaps," Valerian said. "Nevertheless, I'm staying."

Then you do so alone, Artanis said. *I take my leave.*

Valerian nodded. "Understood."

He watched as Artanis strode into the shuttle, followed by his guards. The hatch was sealed, and a moment later the vehicle rose from the floor and disappeared through the cone and into the sky, the phoenixes rising as well in escort formation.

And now, Valerian knew, he was truly committed.

He gestured to the marine. "Call the *Hyperion* and have Admiral Horner send a dropship," he said. "And now, Overqueen, let us continue our discussion."

"They're still ignoring our requests for information," Cruikshank growled. "But whatever they're planning, they're serious as hell about it. Energy profiles indicate all their hangar bays are at full operation, probably prepping warp prisms. Best guess is that they're massing troops."

"Plus sentries and whatever other gear they packed aboard," Admiral Horner agreed grimly. "At least they're not going for a full burn-off."

"Not yet, anyway, sir," Cruikshank warned. Horner could whistle in the dark all he wanted, but to anyone with half a brain, it was obvious what Artanis was up to. Sergeant Cray had reported zerg with psionic powers, which as far as Cruikshank was concerned, already put Gystt on the nuke-it-from-orbit list.

But rather than take the terrans' word for it, Artanis had apparently decided to send some protoss down to check it out for themselves. "They may not have enough firepower assembled for a burn-off," he added. "But I'll bet they're gearing up for it."

"Probably," Horner said. "They'd just better not try it until Emperor Valerian and our team are back."

"Colonel?" the tech at the comm station called. "Sergeant Cray, sir."

Cruikshank nodded, keying his comm for relay. That was another thing: what in hell was a sergeant doing making reports and acting like he was in charge instead of Lieutenant Halkman? "Cruikshank."

"Sergeant Cray, sir," the marine's voice came. "Lieutenant Halkman's back with the dropship. Do you want us to return to the *Hyperion*?"

Cruikshank wrinkled his nose. Horner could wish and hope and make as many private threats as he wanted. But the dirty fact was that if Artanis decided to burn off Gystt while there were still terrans on the surface, he would damn well do so. And there was nothing Horner or the Dominion could do about it.

The emperor was still in harm's way by his own decision. He could do that. And while Cruikshank didn't like it, he had zero say in the matter.

Halkman and his team were different. Those four men and women were Cruikshank's responsibility, and he had no desire to leave them on that deathtrap planet a single tick longer than necessary.

Still, while Valerian was down there, the survey team's presence might conceivably be necessary. Cruikshank wasn't sure how or why, but he'd seen enough situations where victory had hinged on a single person being in the right place at the right time.

"Negative," he said. "Remain where you are and await further orders. And leave the psi blocks off unless you see zerg on the way."

There might have been the slightest hesitation. But Cray's voice was solid enough. "Yes, sir."

"And watch yourselves," Cruikshank added. "Cruikshank out."

He keyed off the comm, glaring at the protoss gathering their forces for whatever the hell they were up to. Yes, sometimes the right person at the right place made all the difference.

But more often than not, that person got killed right along with everyone else.

He hoped that wouldn't be the case here. But he wouldn't bet money on it.

You and Hierarch Artanis were correct about the xel'naga essence, Zagara said. *But I note to you that Abathur did not create the plants. He created the adostra. The adostra created the plants.*

She was still angry, Valerian could tell. But at least she was still talking.

Maybe she was sincere. Maybe she simply knew this was her absolute last chance before fire began raining down on her and the

Swarm. *The essence was something that we could not incorporate into plants—only into animal species.*

"And so you created a species that could do that."

We modified one, Zagara corrected. *It was the Queen of Blades who pointed the way and encouraged us along the proper path. She identified a species that could be used, a nonviolent, not fully sentient species. We took only those we needed, leaving the others on their planet in peace. Abathur then melded the xel'naga strands salvaged from Ulnar into them, and with his skill we were able in the end to achieve her dream.*

"Yes, the survey team saw the results of that dream," Valerian said grimly.

No, Abathur bit out. *Impossible. Terran describes creatures. Do not exist.*

I do not say your soldiers are lying, Emperor Valerian, Zagara added. *But these are not the creatures of Abathur's hands who lie dreaming within their cocooning.*

"Fine," Valerian said. *So* damn sincere . . . but Cray had been equally sincere in his report about what had just happened at Focal Point One.

Unfortunately, all Valerian had was Cray's word against Zagara's. The CMC recorders, which should have made a clear record of the battle, had apparently fallen victim to the same psi-block-induced failure that was affecting the long-range comms. The audio had been completely scrambled, and all the video showed were vague blurs that could be anything. "Tell me about these new creatures. What were they like? Or let's start with what they were *supposed* to be like."

As was said, we call them adostra, Zagara said. *We believe the word means* dreamer *in the language of the xel'naga. But their dreams are not like yours or mine. Their dreams reach deep into the psionic power of their species. They call out to life wherever it lies, whether in fields, in streams, or even deep within stone. That life is stirred, and encouraged, and nurtured, until it is finally and fully awake.*

"Wait a minute," Valerian said, frowning. "Are you saying Gystt's new plant life is the result of some animals thinking or dreaming about it?"

Animals whose very cores are composed of xel'naga essence, Zagara reminded him. *The legends speak of the xel'naga seeding the galaxy with life. Is it so hard to believe this ability was innate within them and not something merely learned over millennia of study?*

Valerian rubbed his cheek. Certainly it fit with the protoss' own legends of their interactions with the xel'naga. And the idea that adostra dreams were responsible for Gystt's explosion of life— however the hell that worked—could also explain the pattern that Dr. Wyland had first spotted. Not a wind pattern, but simply the plants in some strange way reflecting the direction of their inspiration source. "So what went wrong? Did they go rogue somehow?"

That cannot be what happened, Zagara insisted. *The adostra are not in any way hostile.*

"Are you sure?" Valerian countered, shifting his gaze to Abathur. "Did you watch everything Abathur did as he worked?"

He was monitored at all times.

"By zerg who knew as much about genetic manipulation as he did?"

No such zerg exist, Abathur said with clear pride.

He is correct, Zagara said. *But he is loyal to me.*

"Then maybe he made a mistake," Valerian suggested. "Could there have been some genetic time bomb in the adostra that no one expected, something that caused them to transform into psyolisks?"

Zagara tilted her head. *Yet what could cause such a transformation?*

"He's the evolution master," Valerian said, gesturing to Abathur. "Ask *him.*"

No, Abathur said flatly. *No possibility. Far easier to believe terrans are lying.*

Valerian pursed his lips. Stalemate. "All right, let's try it from another direction. You said all the broodmothers were loyal to you, Overqueen. Are you sure about that?"

You refer to the attack on your survey team before their entrance into the adostra cocooning structure.

"Yes," Valerian said. "According to Ulavu, they were well within the local broodmother's territory by then."

The broodmother insists she neither ordered nor condoned any such attack.

"Let's assume she's right," Valerian said, wondering briefly just how truthful the broodmothers had to be to their Overqueen, and whether Zagara would even know if they were lying. "You said the adostra had psionic powers. Could *they* have taken over the zerg outside their cocoons and made them attack the survey team?"

No, Zagara said. *The adostra are nonviolent. They would not have been part of an attack.*

"But it *is* possible?"

No.

Valerian scowled. Again, stalemate. "All right," he said. "What we need—what we're missing—are facts and evidence. Let me call the survey team and see if they can pull tissue samples from whatever's left in the cocooning area."

He'd had the sense that Zagara was finally letting go of some of her anger. Now the flow pattern reversed itself. The Overqueen's body stiffened, once again filling Valerian's senses with that stifling feeling of alienness. *From the ashes of their own destruction.*

Which the team had deemed both necessary and prudent. But Valerian had no intention of bringing that up. It was easy to second-guess a commander's on-the-ground decision, especially when Zagara had been so furious and horrified to hear about the cocooning's destruction. But defending the decision—or even agreeing with Zagara's judgment—would again get them nowhere. "I'll call them now," he said instead. "We've got a mystery here. Let's see if we can make a start at unraveling it."

"Understood, Colonel," Dizz said, his nose wrinkling a little.

Which was, Erin suspected, not a good sign. Her experience with the Dominion military was admittedly sparse, but she was pretty sure junior officers were supposed to show more respect than that to their seniors. Given the circumstances, she suspected that whatever orders Cruikshank was passing on, she wasn't going to like them.

She was right.

"Orders from the, quote, 'highest level,' unquote," Dizz said sourly. "By which I assume Cruikshank means Valerian himself. We need to go back inside and look—"

"We need to *what*?" Whist interrupted.

"Go back inside and look for tissue samples," Dizz finished. "By which I mean pieces of the psyolisks. By which I mean not a chance in hell."

Erin felt her stomach tighten. Watching the funeral pyre Dizz had set up had been bad enough. Even though she knew the creatures had tried to kill them—even though she knew that zerg at that level were little more than animals—it had felt eerie and primal and as uncivilized as anything she'd ever been part of.

Was this the sort of thing that happened in war? Probably. She'd missed most of the uglier parts of the war years, safely ensconced in her lab with nothing but tissue samples, chemical samples, and occasionally partial carcasses to remind her of what was happening out there. Now, suddenly, she was getting all of it at once: the combat, the fear, the adrenaline rush, the carnage, and, yes, the bitter-edged psychological aftermath of everything else.

And now they wanted her to dig tissue samples out of the ashes?

"What's the problem?" Tanya asked. "Is it still too hot in there?"

"Oh, it's plenty hot," Dizz assured her. "My armor won't handle it—too light, and many open places—and you and Ulavu are definitely out. But those CMC-400s are pretty good, even with the damage Whist took, so he and Erin should be fine. My point is that there isn't going to be anything left worth digging out."

"I suppose we should at least try," Whist said. He looked at Erin and raised his eyebrows. "You game?"

Not really, Erin wanted to say. But he was right. "Sure," she said, trying to put some heartiness into her voice.

"We'll keep watch out here," Dizz said as the two of them headed toward the gap in the tree palisade. "If anything goes wrong, give us a holler."

"And what, you'll send Tanya in?" Whist asked pointedly.

"Mm. Point. So just make sure nothing goes wrong."

"Right. Thanks for the tip."

"You're welcome," Dizz said. "And watch yourselves—Cruikshank wants real-time, so we need to leave the psi blocks off."

"Yeah, you watch *yourselves,*" Whist said. "All the zerg in there are already dead. Not so much out here."

There were still a few pockets of fire blazing away where the pods had once been. But for the most part, the pyre had died down to smoke. Keeping one eye on Whist and the other on her footing, Erin picked her way across the floor, glad that her air system kept her from having to smell any of it.

They reached the pods to discover that, as Dizz had predicted, there was very little left. "What a mess," Whist commented. He leaned over the nearest pod, peering past the shattered top and into the bits of smoldering material inside. "How do you want to do this?"

Erin looked down the entire line of pods, or at least as many of them as she could see through the drifting smoke. "We go to each one and look for something that's not completely blackened."

"And if we don't find anything?"

"I'll take a few samples of anything that's not ash," Erin said.

"Okay." He pointed to the top tier. "I'll start up there; you start down here, and we'll meet in the middle. Let's get this over with."

Swallowing her discomfort, Erin got to work.

The first eight pods were identical to the one she'd looked into earlier: bits of blackened flesh amid the broken debris of the chitin structure the pods had been encased in, all spattered with stains from whatever liquid had been inside. A little poking into the carbonized remains revealed occasional bones, the sight of which added an extra edge to her general queasiness.

She was about to suggest to Whist that they just give up when she reached the ninth pod.

"Whist?" she called, staring through the broken casing. "Would you come here a minute?"

"Find something?" the marine called back, picking his way carefully down from the top tier.

"No, just the opposite." She waited until he landed on the floor beside her, and then she pointed. "Nothing."

"Damn," he muttered, craning his neck to look. "One of 'em got out?"

"I don't think so," Erin said. "There's no flesh or bone, but there's also no discoloration from the liquid on either the insides of the pod or the insides of the organic plumbing. I don't think there was ever anything here."

"That's crazy," Dizz's puzzled voice said in her earphone. "All the pods were . . . I'm pretty sure they were all sealed."

"They were," Tanya confirmed tightly. "That was the first thing I checked after the battle. They all looked exactly alike."

"So why was one empty?" Dizz asked.

"And are we sure it was just *one*?" Tanya added.

"Let's find out," Whist said.

The survey was quick. The final number was—

"*Six?*" Dizz said, sounding floored. "You're saying a full ten percent of the pods were empty?"

"And were never occupied," Erin reminded him. Somehow, that fact was the one that dug the deepest into her brain.

"Or at least had been empty for a while," Whist added. "Like Erin said, no liquid residue."

"But there *was* liquid in all of them," Tanya insisted. "I looked."

"Maybe it just *looked* like there was," Erin said. "Or—no, wait. If the baby psyolisks were being fed or otherwise supported by the liquid, it was probably mostly organics, or at least it had some complex-molecule components. *That's* what would have charred and stained the pods when Dizz started the fire."

"So the empty pods could have just been filled with water?" Whist asked.

"That, or something else simple and inorganic," Erin said.

"You're suggesting they were decoys?" a new voice put in.

Erin frowned. New . . . but she had a strong feeling she'd heard it before. "Excuse me?" she asked. "Who is this?"

"Emperor Valerian," the voice came again. "I thought your discovery was important enough for Colonel Cruikshank to patch me into the conversation."

"My apologies, Emperor," Erin stammered, feeling her face redden as she silently cursed herself. Preoccupied or not, she should have instantly recognized the Dominion leader's voice.

"Never mind that," Valerian said. At least he was being gracious about it. "I need to know whether the empty pods might have been decoys."

"You mean decoys for us, Emperor?" Whist asked. "I suppose

they could have been. But what would be the point? Who even knew we were coming here?"

"That is indeed the question," Valerian said. "Lieutenant Halkman, what's the status of your team and resources?"

"We're good to go, Emperor," Dizz assured him. "What do you need us to do?"

"You have the locations of Dr. Wyland's Focal Points Two and Three?"

"Yes, Emperor."

"Good. I want you to go directly to Focal Point Three. If you find the same sort of pods there, we need a good, solid look and analysis of what's inside."

"With all due respect, Emperor, there's every indication the pods are growing the things that attacked us," Whist pointed out.

"I agree," Valerian said, his voice going grim. "In which case we will want to burn every one of them down to their component atoms. But the first step is to make sure we know precisely what we're dealing with. *And* to be sure that, if we get them, we get all of them."

"Understood, Emperor," Dizz said. "Whist, Erin—back here on the double. We'll leave as soon as you're aboard."

Five minutes later, Erin once again found herself being pressed into her seat as Dizz blasted the dropship into the sky.

"You all might as well settle in," Dizz said as he reached altitude and leveled off. "Unsuit if you want to. Or not—your choice. Just remember that even at top speed, it'll be about a seven-hour flight. There are mealbars, juices, and some colas in the survival kit if anyone's hungry or thirsty. I think I saw some skalet jerky in there, too, if your jaw wants a challenge."

"Maybe later," Whist said, peering at the map he'd pulled up on his display. "You know, Point Two was a hell of a lot closer than Three. Any idea why Valerian didn't send us there?"

"Yeah," Dizz said grimly. "We got our hourly data drop before I turned the psi block back on. It seems Hierarch Artanis has sent a force of his own to take a look at that one." He paused, and Erin saw his eyes flick to Ulavu. "And," he added, "they're under attack."

CHAPTER THIRTEEN

The warning klaxons were still hooting away in the *Hyperion*'s hangar. But inside the heavy armor and claustrophobic confines of a Warhound combat mech, the noise was reduced to a dull roar. Keeping one eye on the status pre-check and the other on the real-time orbital view of Focal Point Two, Cruikshank finished strapping into the cockpit and wondered when the orders would come.

Wondered, too, what exactly those orders would consist of.

The pre-check had turned green, and the klaxons had finally turned the hell off, when Horner's image popped up on the comm display. "Okay, Emperor Valerian was finally able to get through to Artanis," the admiral said. "The good news is that Artanis has agreed not to demolish Point Two without getting a good look and some decent samples."

Mentally, Cruikshank shook his head. The whole rationale behind getting Dominion boots on the ground had been that Valerian needed the protoss to hold back while he worked things out with

Artanis. Cruikshank's force was supposed to make sure they did exactly that, whether they liked it or not.

He'd been looking forward to kicking some protoss butt. Now, apparently, that wasn't going to happen.

"The bad news," Horner continued, "is that Artanis can't get through to his troops. Their shuttle was hit by a couple of mutalisks on its way down, which apparently took out both its psionic boosters."

"You're joking," Cruikshank said, frowning. "Is that even possible?"

"Well, it's either that or Cray's psyolisks are mucking with them," Horner said. "Something seems to be mucking with their warp fields, too—they couldn't get the warp prisms to work, which is why they used a shuttle. Doesn't matter. What matters is that Artanis can't get through to them, so you're going down to deliver his message. Artanis has recorded it, and I've downloaded it to your Warhound."

"And if the protoss refuse to listen?" Cruikshank asked hopefully. Maybe there would be at least a *little* butt-kicking.

"They shouldn't," Horner said. "Artanis put enough ID and clearance codes in his message to choke a leviathan."

"Understood, sir," Cruikshank said. So if all they were doing was delivering a message, why was a third of his force heading to the surface? "So is the rest of the force standing down?"

"You're not seeing the big picture, Colonel," Horner said grimly. "If for some reason the protoss *do* refuse to accept these new orders, we need to make sure they leave the chamber intact until our people can examine it." He raised his eyebrows. "However we have to do that."

"Understood, sir," Cruikshank said again, feeling his heart rate pick up. "Don't worry. We'll make sure we get to that chamber first."

"Good," Horner said. "Get down there. And good luck."

"Yes, sir."

Cruikshank turned and got the Warhound striding toward the dropship, a tight smile creasing his face. Protoss being the stubborn SOBs that they were, there was a good chance they wouldn't believe he was really carrying their hierarch's orders.

In which case, he was going to get to do some butt-kicking after all.

He could hardly wait.

They are creatures of beauty, Emperor Valerian Mengsk, Zagara said, her gravelly psionic voice sounding almost wistful. *They have an awareness and sentience, but not in the way of terrans or zerg. They see to the core of existence, to the deepest level of life. Their purpose is to find and nurture that life.* She seemed to grow a little taller. *Your destruction of so many of them was a crime against the entire universe.*

"The lives of my people were at risk," Valerian reminded her, trying to hold his temper. Zagara simply would not accept even the possibility that her adostra might have turned into killers. "Besides, you created this group. You surely still remember how to do that."

Our knowledge is of no use without xel'naga strands, she said. *All were used. There is no more.*

"You can't get the adostra to breed?"

We do not yet know whether they can do so, she said. *Abathur believes that, someday, they may develop that ability.*

"Your spawning pools and hatcheries don't work?"

They are designed for zerg and zerg variants, Zagara said. *As yet, they have proved unable to re-create or generate xel'naga essence. The xel'naga had a depth of molecular and quantum complexity that we still do not understand.*

"I see," Valerian murmured. So in theory, if the Dominion and the protoss could destroy all the adostra and psyolisks, that would be the end of it.

Provided that someone could prove to his satisfaction that Zagara's adostra were indeed the creatures that had attacked Halkman's survey team. Whether Valerian could then prove that to *Zagara's* satisfaction was an entirely different question.

If not, it could make the logistics of getting off Gystt extremely problematic.

But he had no choice. Artanis hadn't said it in so many words, but Valerian had the strong suspicion that his presence on the surface might be the only thing that was keeping the hierarch from ordering a full incineration.

Furthermore, if Artanis was right—if Zagara was indeed playing them with an eye toward using the psyolisks in a new war— then Valerian would not only stand back and not interfere, but might feel morally obligated to assist the protoss in their rain of destruction.

But only if he was absolutely certain that annihilation was necessary.

So he would stay, and talk, and listen. At least until Cruikshank's team had examined the Point Two chamber and taken some samples. Maybe until Halkman's team did the same at Point Three. Maybe even longer than that if necessary.

And if Zagara refused to believe and Artanis refused to wait . . . he would cross that bridge when he arrived.

Cruikshank's dropships were halfway to the surface when the word came that the protoss were under attack.

"Where the hell did they all come from?" Cruikshank asked, glaring at the image from the dropship's lower scope. The foliage on the rolling hills outside Point Two was pretty heavy, but it wasn't *that* heavy. How had all those damn zerg suddenly appeared? "Were they all inside the mesa?"

"Near as we can tell, the only ones that came out after the protoss knocked down the trees were a few of the new species Halkman's team identified," Horner said grimly. "Their so-called psyolisks. The rest apparently sneaked in from the trees around the protoss."

Cruikshank felt his lip twist. *Sneak* wasn't a word he was accustomed to using with zerg. There were a few sneaky species, but most lower-level types just charged in like brainless bulldozers.

Like they were doing right now, in fact, with the zerglings, roaches, and hydralisks doing their damnedest to overwhelm the small protoss force. "How bad is it?" he asked. "I'm losing details to the trees and acid-burn smoke."

"It's bad," Horner said. "Artanis is as much in the dark as we are, but it looks like a slaughter in progress. We started off picking up the electromagnetic signatures of ten Templar psi blades and ten Nerazim warp blades. Now we're down to six and seven."

Cruikshank squeezed his hand into a fist. The battle had been under way for maybe three minutes, and the protoss had already lost four Templar and three Nerazim? Unbelievable. "What the hell is Zagara throwing at them?"

"Zagara claims it's not her," Horner said. "She says it's not the local broodmother, either."

"Right," Cruikshank growled. "The local zerglings just happened to pick today to declare independence. *And* sentience."

"I don't believe it, either," Horner said. "But right now, the *who* doesn't matter. What matters is that the protoss are in trouble, and you're the only ones who can do anything to help."

"Don't worry, sir," Cruikshank promised darkly. So instead of kicking protoss butt, he'd now been tasked with pulling their butts out of the frying pan. Damn, and damn again. "We'll get there as fast as we can, and do whatever we can."

"I know you will," Horner said. "Good luck, Colonel. And watch yourselves. The protoss are important, but your ultimate responsibility is to the Dominion and its people."

"Understood, sir," Cruikshank said. "I'll contact you again when this is over."

He keyed off the comm and switched to short-range. "All right, troopers, you all heard the admiral. This is now a rescue mission. We hit the ground running; we pull out any protoss who are still alive, and we pan-fry every damn zerg in sight."

Four minutes later, the dropships slammed into the ground, their landing legs howling in protest at the impact. Cruikshank made sure he and his Warhound led the way from his dropship, with the three goliaths the first ones out of theirs.

To find that they were too late.

It was like a scene straight out of hell. The whole area was crawling with zerg—banelings, roaches, zerglings, hydralisks—their claws slicing at the handful of remaining high templar and dark templar, poison darts shredding flesh and clothing, acid blasts eating into grass and trees and filling the air with choking smoke. There were dead zerg everywhere, sprawled on top of one another or intermixed with dead protoss. Two robotic protoss sentries hovered over the carnage, their automated systems trying futilely to protect the warriors. Near the mesa, lying shattered on its side among the downed trees that had once blocked the cavern entrance, was a stalker.

But just because the rescue mission had gone to hell didn't mean the Dominion was just going to pack up and leave. "Attack at will!" Cruikshank shouted to his troops. "Find any pockets of resistance and reinforce them. I'm checking out that stalker—reapers, cover me. And watch the sky—we could have mutalisks show up anytime."

His Warhound strode toward the downed stalker, sweeping away zerglings that got too close and firing bursts from its rail guns at every hydralisk in range. A baneling scuttled toward him; another burst from his rail guns blew it to acid-spewing shreds.

"Watch it, Colonel," one of the reapers snapped. "You got acid on your left leg."

Cruikshank cursed under his breath as he glanced at his status display. The neutralizer spray had caught most of it in time, but the edges of the splash were still sizzling. Another shot of neutralizer took care of it. There was probably some residual corrosion going on in grooves and cracks where the spray couldn't reach, which would eventually collapse the leg if it wasn't dealt with.

But there was no time for that. The leg would last the rest of the mission, and right now that was all Cruikshank cared about.

"Mutalisks!" someone shouted. "Four-beta-high."

Cruikshank looked at the location. Two of the nasties were arrowing down from the sky, clearly intent on taking out one of the remaining protoss sentries. After glancing target locks on both of them, he sent a pair of Haywire missiles screaming into the air. A third mutalisk, swooping in at the edge of his vision, fell to a burst of Hellfire scatter missiles from one of the goliaths.

Another pair of zerglings had emerged from the pack and were slicing at Cruikshank's damaged leg. Blasting them with his rail guns, he kept going.

From the stalker's lack of motion, he had guessed that the dark templar who was melded into the machinery was as dead as the machinery itself. But as he reached it, the Nerazim's eyes opened to slits and the head turned a little to look up at the Warhound's cockpit. *You came,* a weak protoss voice said in Cruikshank's head.

"Yeah, we're here," Cruikshank said, wincing at the banality of the words. Yes, the Dominion forces had arrived. For all the damn good that was going to do most of the protoss. "Hang on—you've got a tree across one of your legs. I'll get it off and take you back to our dropship."

There is no time, the dark templar said. *You must destroy the chamber, or you and your terrans will die alongside us.*

"I can't do that," Cruikshank said, glancing at the status reports coming in on his tac display. Three Templar and four Nerazim still alive, and more zerg pouring into the area. The corrosion problem in his Warhound's leg was getting worse, with the computer estimating he had ten more minutes before it became useless. A slaughter, all right, and it was far from over. "Sorry, but I have orders to take it intact."

You cannot, the dark templar said. *Even now they are abandoning it.*

Cruikshank frowned at the cavern entrance, keying in the Warhound's telescopics. There wasn't much light in there, but there was enough to show a line of red-spotted psyolisks coming down the ramp, each pair manhandling a milky-white pod between them.

I did not believe the terran report that this new zerg could attack with psionic power, the dark templar continued, his voice starting to fade. *But it is true. They draw other zerg to the battlefield and to the attack. They then focus their power on us, one by one, with a force that overwhelms even dark templar, opening us to destruction.*

Cruikshank hissed between his teeth. And if the psyolisks were able to get those pods out of there while he and his team were otherwise engaged, God only knew where they would turn up next.

Emperor Valerian wanted the chamber taken intact. But even emperors didn't always get what they wanted. "All right," he said. "I'll—what's your name, soldier?"

I am Sagaya.

"All right, Sagaya," Cruikshank said. "You stay here and keep alive. I'll be back as soon as I can." He straightened up, wondering how many of the damn psyolisks were in there. Wondering, too, whether his rail guns and missile launchers would run out of ammo—and his leg run out of function—before he found out.

There is no need to go inside, Sagaya said. *Their destruction already awaits. I have sent in a disruptor. Any perceived attack upon it will cause its detonation.*

"Ah," Cruikshank said. Nasty weapons, disruptors. But in this case, exactly what he needed. "I think I can accommodate it. Attention, all units. I'm about to trigger a protoss disruptor inside the mesa. Watch out for flying rock."

After locking onto a spot as far up the ramp as he could see, he fired off a Haywire. It blasted its way inside, nearly taking out a pair of psyolisks and their pod along the way. It reached the first switchback and blew, lighting up the entire inside. Cruikshank held his breath . . .

The mesa didn't exactly split apart, as Cruikshank had thought it might. But it was close. The disruptor's blast blew a dozen massive holes in the top, throwing dirt and rock and vegetation high into the air and shaking the ground under the Warhound's feet. An instant later a fireburst roared out of the cave opening, blasting every bush and tree in its path and knocking Cruikshank's Warhound onto its back.

For a long moment he just lay there, aching where he'd been thrown against his webbing, wincing as the wind and fire blasted and swirled outside his cockpit's steelglass canopy. Slowly, the maelstrom faded away, and the swirling storm of leaves and dirt and branches subsided. Carefully, he got the Warhound's arms under it and levered the mech back to its feet. There was a slight lurch as the outer plating of its damaged left leg cracked, but the main support structure held. Moving slowly, mindful of his balance amid the piles of debris, he turned and surveyed the battlefield.

It was a mess. Everyone in sight—terran, protoss, and zerg—had been thrown flat onto the ground. Two of Cruikshank's three goliaths were slowly getting back to their feet, both showing signs of serious damage. The third lay motionless, its legs torn apart, its

Hellfire launcher crushed, one of its autocannons half melted from heat buildup. Cruikshank's med readout on the pilot indicated he was alive, but just barely. Elsewhere on the field, some of the marines were also picking themselves up off the ground. None of the five reapers were visible, and only two of their med readouts indicated life.

The zerg were slowly starting to move as well. But not to attack. For the most part, they were standing up, shaking their massive heads as if dazed and confused, and just looking around. Cruikshank kept his finger on the Warhound's rail-gun trigger, but none of the creatures made any hostile move. They all simply stood still for a moment as if deciding what to do, then turned and wandered or staggered away.

And as they cleared the field, Cruikshank saw three protoss slowly regain their feet.

Three.

He ran his displays through another 360, just to be sure. Then, huffing out a sigh, he keyed his long-range comm. "This is Cruikshank," he said. "Victory achieved. Enemy is yielding the field. Rescue mission . . ." He swallowed hard. "Not so much."

Zagara lashed her arms through the air in front of her as if trying to crush someone. *I do not understand.*

"Twelve terrans dead," Valerian bit out, for once not even trying to fake a diplomatic bearing. "Nineteen protoss dead. Do you still claim these psyolisks aren't hostile?"

These cannot be the adostra, Zagara insisted. *They are completely and inherently peaceful.*

"Zergling-sized creatures with semi-hydralisk form, light brown with red highlights, triple dorsal patterns of bright-red spots?"

Adostra are not of that form.

"Are you sure?" Valerian pressed. "Have you looked into the pods recently?"

Zagara's claws were still working. *No one has looked inside,* she said. *Not since they were encased in the nutrients. They are still maturing.*

"Then you really don't know *what* they might have become?"

Will not listen further, Abathur said suddenly. *Terran organism lies for destruction of Swarm. Will not listen further.* After turning his back, he strode toward the chamber entrance.

Valerian looked at Zagara, expecting her to order him back. Apparently not. Abathur passed the ravagers, still waiting in ominous silence, and disappeared elsewhere in the structure.

Maybe Zagara had decided he had nothing further to add to the conversation. Maybe she'd decided that the entire conversation was coming to a close.

Maybe she was right.

"I'm going to leave now," Valerian said, standing up. "I trust you won't try to stop me."

For a long second he thought Zagara was going to do exactly that. Her head drew back, her eyes glittering at him. Then some of the tension seemed to flow out of her. *What would such action accomplish?* she pointed out. *I seek to avoid war. Unless I can persuade you to the truth, that effort will come to nothing.*

"You can't persuade me, Overqueen, just as I can't persuade you," Valerian said. "Only the truth itself can do that. I will continue to seek out that truth as long as I can. But in the end . . ." He left the sentence unfinished.

Then go, Zagara said. *Seek the truth.*

"I will," Valerian said, some of his resolve slipping. She was so unlike any zerg he'd ever met. That alone had been worth investigating. That alone gave him pause.

And she seemed *so* sincere.

But he'd given her a fair chance. More of a chance than Artanis had given her. Certainly more than Valerian's father, Arcturus, would have. Emperor Arcturus would have declared war and begun his assault hours ago. No, whatever happened from this point on, Valerian's conscience was clear.

And you will find it, Zagara promised. *I hope that you will find it while there is still time.*

Somewhat to Valerian's surprise, no attack came as his dropship lifted through the cone and headed away from the surface. He'd barely reached the thousand-meter mark when a full squadron of Wraiths swooped in and escorted him the rest of the way to the *Hyperion.*

He arrived on the bridge to find Matt on the comm with Artanis. "I understand your position, Hierarch Artanis," the admiral was saying as Valerian entered. He caught Valerian's eye and waved him over. "I'll relay your comments and suggestions to Emperor Valerian as soon as he arrives."

"Very well, Admiral Matthew Horner," Artanis's voice came from the speaker. "Be certain he also understands that my patience is not unlimited."

"I will, Hierarch," Matt promised. "Admiral Horner out."

He keyed off the comm. "Emperor Valerian," he said, turning to Valerian. "I'm glad to see you alive and unharmed."

"I'm a bit surprised by it myself." Valerian gestured toward the comm. "What news from the protoss?"

"They've got their front toes right on the line and are leaning over it," Matt said darkly. "Artanis is about half a damn away from ordering a full-bore assault on Gystt."

Valerian curled his hand into a fist. "With our people still down there."

"Well, the survey team, anyway," Matt said. "Cruikshank's force was able to make some running repairs on their dropships before our replacements arrived. They're on their way up." His lip twisted. "What's left of them, anyway."

"Yes," Valerian murmured. "At least we made out better than the protoss."

"Only because we weren't on the ground as long," Matt said bluntly. "You saw Cruikshank's report?"

"I got the basics."

"Then you saw his take on the psyolisks' strategy."

Valerian nodded. "Gang up on the Templar and the Nerazim one at a time, break their combat concentration, then slice and dice."

"Or let the rest of the zerg do it for them," Matt said. "And that doesn't even count the effect the psionic attacks had on our people. Relatively minimal, at least compared with the effect on protoss. But still a potentially serious game-changer."

"It is indeed," Valerian agreed. "Zagara still claims that neither she nor the local broodmother was in charge of that attack."

"She claimed that about the survey team's little fracas, too," Matt reminded him. "Either she's lying or . . . You suppose the psyolisks themselves could be orchestrating the attacks?"

"That's about the only other explanation," Valerian said. "Problem is, it's pretty much impossible to prove one way or another. Not without a tap into basic zerg-to-zerg communications."

"Which neither we nor the protoss have. So what's our next move?"

"Same as before," Valerian said. "We get the survey team to Focal Point Three and hope they can finally get us some real samples."

"Ah." Matt paused. "You realize that, whatever game is being played, and whoever's playing it, Point Three is the obvious choice for our next move. If they want Halkman's team out of the way, it'll take *very* little effort."

"Yes, and I've been thinking about that," Valerian said. "I know we've got some psi disruptors aboard—you gave those psi block variants to Halkman and Cray. Do we by any chance have any psi emitters?"

Matt blinked. "I would think that drawing zerg to us would be an extraordinarily bad idea right now."

Despite the tension, Valerian had to smile at the admiral's carefully official tone. The experts still didn't know whether psi emitters induced a queen or broodmother to send her zerg in that direction, or whether they worked directly on the nearest batch of lower-level zerg. But the results were the same: a mass of nasty aliens converging on the emitter's location.

The devices had occasionally been useful during the war. They'd also been used by Valerian's father to destroy the Confederate capital planet of Tarsonis, which had paved the way for Arcturus's takeover and his creation of the Terran Dominion. Highly dangerous devices, and not to be taken lightly.

"Relax—I haven't gone *that* crazy," he assured Matt. "I was thinking of landing one a hundred klicks or so from Point Three and seeing if we can divert the local zerg away from the survey team."

"Ah," Matt said, his face clearing. "Hmm. Well, I doubt there's anything like that aboard any of our ships. But I'll bet the techs could cobble something together before the team gets there."

"Which is in . . . ?"

Matt glanced at the bridge chrono. "About five hours."

"Call the techs and get them started," Valerian said. "And get an estimate of when they'll have something up and running."

"Admiral?" the tactical officer called tensely from his seat in his sensor wraparound. "You'll want to see this, sir."

Valerian crossed to the wraparound, Matt right beside him. "Those leviathans, sir," the tac officer said, pointing to several of the displays. "The ones that've been keeping an eye on us and the protoss ships. They're all heading to the surface."

"All to different spots, looks like," Matt murmured. "The brood-mothers, you think?"

"That would make sense," Valerian said grimly. "Zagara has probably warned them all by now that negotiations have broken down. They want to be ready to evacuate if necessary."

"Taking who knows what with them," Matt said. "If Zagara wants to sneak out some psyolisks, there's no way we can intercept and search six leviathans."

"Seven, sir," the tac officer corrected. "Including the one we followed in from Korhal."

"I'd forgotten that one," Matt said, leaning closer. "Is it doing anything?"

"No, sir. Still just sitting there."

"Not surprising," Valerian said. "The situation's unstable enough as it is. Hopefully, Zagara's not going to rock the boat by running to her leviathan and taking off."

"She might if she thought it was worth the gamble," Matt pointed out. "Say, if she had some psyolisks and a captured ghost she could turn Abathur loose on."

Valerian's eyes flicked to one of the other displays. The survey team's dropship was still cutting atmosphere toward Point Three, with no imminent threats in sight. "We'll keep a close eye on her," he said.

"And speaking of rocking the boat, one more little tidbit." Matt indicated the display that showed the various hot spots in the protoss ships. "Looks like Artanis is starting to power up his purifier beam."

Valerian mouthed a curse. "Getting ready to incinerate Gystt."

"Shall I call and ask him to stand down?" Matt asked. "At least until we get the survey team out of there?"

Valerian looked back at the leviathans moving across the star-scape. Matt was right: if one—or more—of the huge creatures was tasked with taking off with a group of psyolisks, there was no way the Dominion and protoss forces could stop all of them.

And that couldn't be allowed to happen. Not after such a graphic demonstration of the devastation the new zerg could deliver to both terrans and protoss.

They had to be defeated.

"No," he told Matt. "Just remind him about our people on the ground, and ask that he keep us informed of any planned action." He hesitated. "And then begin prepping all our own space-to-ground weaponry."

Matt's eyes widened. "Valerian—sir—"

"That's an order, Admiral," Valerian cut in, putting the full weight of his position into his voice.

Matt stiffened to attention. "Understood, Your Excellency," he said, matching Valerian's formal tone.

Valerian frowned. Matt never called him Your Excellency any-more, not since Valerian had flatly told him—and everyone else—not to. Was the admiral's use of his father's favored honorific some kind of not-so-subtle hint? A deliberate reference to Emperor Arc-turus's coldly violent way of doing things?

If it was, the admiral was going to love Valerian's next order. "You will also prep the Yamato cannon," he continued. "Its target, should it prove necessary, will be Focal Point Three. You'll prep a small evac force to get the team out of there if required."

"If necessary, and if there's time?" Matt asked pointedly.

"If there's time," Valerian agreed.

"Understood, Your Excellency."

Deliberately, Valerian turned away from the admiral's gaze. Defi-nitely a reference to Emperor Arcturus.

On one level, Valerian had to agree. Wholesale slaughter, wanton collateral damage—those had been the hallmarks of his father's reign. They'd been the very things Valerian had pledged to change about the Dominion.

And now he was following squarely in his father's bloodstained footsteps. He could only hope that this was just an aberration, a momentary bump on the high road he had promised to take.

Because the alternative was that he'd been fooling himself all along. Maybe there was simply no way to make war into something civilized. Maybe warfare was always going to be a matter of *us* versus *them*. Maybe survival would always be winner take all, loser be annihilated.

Valerian had always denounced that philosophy: loudly, publicly, and sincerely. Some people had praised him for his decency. Others had criticized his naïveté.

Which of those people, he wondered, were right?

Once, he'd thought he knew. Now he wasn't nearly so certain.

Today, perhaps, he would find out.

CHAPTER FOURTEEN

Among its other duties, the implant in Tanya's brain was supposed to help smooth out her emotions. Lowering the peaks, as it were, and raising the valleys.

It wasn't doing that job very well today.

There was also a whole pharmacy of drugs available for her to take, everything from alcohol to hab to secret military cocktails that didn't even have official names. Those also promised to get her on an even keel and keep her there.

She had no interest in touching any of them.

Besides, even if she wanted to, she wouldn't know which class of drug to take. Her emotions were running a full hill-hugger ride from white-hot fury at being lied to straight down to a black depression at being lied to and back up to fury again.

The only constant in her mood was the fact that she'd been lied to.

How could Ulavu *do* that to her?

Out of the corner of her eye, she caught someone approaching. She tensed—

But it was only Erin. "Can I talk to you a minute?" the other woman asked, her forehead wrinkled in thought.

Tanya's first instinct was to say no. Her heart and soul were aching, and all she wanted was to curl up within herself—alone—until the ache went away.

But Erin's expression wasn't that of a woman who just felt like a casual chat. It was something important. Maybe even important enough to provide some mental distraction. "Sure," Tanya said, suppressing a sigh. "What's up?"

"It's this report," Erin said, pulling out her datapad and dropping into the next seat. Sometime in the past couple of hours, she'd taken off her armor, probably with Whist's help, and looked a lot fresher and more comfortable than Tanya currently felt. "This transcription of Emperor Valerian's conversation with Overqueen Zagara. Did you read it?"

"Not yet," Tanya said. "Is there a problem?"

"I don't know," Erin said, calling up a section of the report and handing her datapad to Tanya. "Zagara claims that these adostra things—they're supposedly what we saw in the pods—can't go rogue and crazy and attack people like the psyolisks did."

"People claim all sorts of things are impossible," Tanya said, skimming the section. "Someone once told me friends don't lie to each other."

Erin blinked. "Ah . . . my point is that I got to thinking about the psyolisks and what we saw in the pods. You've studied zerg anatomy, right?"

"I've looked inside a few," Tanya said. Actually, she'd seen way more than her fair share of zerg guts during her training. Marines only needed to know where the weakest part of a zerg's exterior was; she needed to know which of their innards would burn best. "There wasn't a lot left to see after Dizz finished with the pods, if that's where you're going."

"I know that," Erin said. "And Zagara says that the adostra use xel'naga essence rather than zerg varieties, so their ontogeny might be different from the normal spawning-pool version of—"

"Their *what*?"

"Their ontogeny," Erin repeated. "Their life cycle from fertilization to full adult. Zerg normally don't go through a metamorphosis stage, while the adostra almost have to if—"

"You're losing me," Tanya said, fighting back a surge of anger. She *really* wasn't in the mood for a technical discussion. "Why does it need a metamorphosis?"

"Because what we saw in the pods didn't look like the final psyolisks," Erin said. "But that's my point. The psyolisks *do* look like zerg, or at least some sort of midway point between zerglings and hydralisks. What are the odds that would happen with an unknown creature melded with non-zerg genetics?"

Tanya shook her head. "Sorry, but this is way over my head. I don't know anything about onto-whatever. All I know is that the pod things and the psyolisks both had that red-dot pattern down their backs. As far as I know, no other zerg strain has anything even close to that. And remember that six of the pods were empty, like your metamorphosis had finished and those were the ones that had gotten out."

"We ran into a lot more than just six psyolisks," Erin pointed out. "And I didn't see any trace of nutrient fluids in the empty pods."

"Because Dizz torched the place," Tanya reminded her patiently. "Look, I don't know what Zagara is claiming, and I don't care. The psyolisks are killing machines, and they need to be exterminated. Period." She gestured at Erin's untouched jumpsuit. "You're just lucky you had Ulavu at your back in there."

"I don't know what Ulavu had to do with it," Erin said, sounding puzzled. "It was Whist and Dizz who kept them off us." She made a face. "Off me, anyway. Ulavu didn't make it through nearly as well."

Tanya frowned, craning her neck to look around the cabin. Ulavu was nowhere to be seen. "Where'd he go?" she asked.

"Medical bay," Erin said, nodding to the sectioned-off compartment in the dropship's stern. "Probably changing his dressings. Well, thanks anyway." She stood up.

"Wait a minute," Tanya said, still trying to process all this. "You say Ulavu got hurt in the battle, but you didn't?"

"That's right," Erin said. "Like I said, Whist and Dizz were really good at shooting them when they got too close."

"Too close to *you*. Not too close to Ulavu."

Erin wrinkled her nose. "Yes. I already said that."

"Yeah," Tanya said. "Thanks."

For another moment Erin just stood there, probably wondering if Tanya was going unstable. Then, with a silent farewell nod, she walked away.

Leaving Tanya with a seriously confusing puzzle.

She turned it over in her mind for a few minutes. But it was quickly clear that she wasn't going to solve it without more information.

And there was, unfortunately, only one place to get what she needed.

She resisted a few minutes more. But in the end, she sighed, unstrapped, and headed back to the medical bay.

Ulavu was there, just as Erin had said. He had removed his tunic and was carefully placing a bandage across his lower torso. More bandages were visible elsewhere across his upper body. Lying at his feet were five discarded bandages, each coated with dark-purple protoss blood. He'd been torn up, all right.

Tanya hadn't even noticed.

The protoss looked up as she entered, and for a moment they locked eyes. *You have shunned me since the battles at Focal Point One,* he said at last. *Your mind has also been closed to me, as it is even now. Please tell me how I have failed you.*

Bluntness, Tanya had always felt, deserved to be answered in kind. *Sure,* she said. *But we should start with proper introductions. Am I addressing a Templar or a Nerazim?*

She had the sense of a mental sigh. *How many know?*

Tanya frowned. *I assumed everyone except me.*

No. Only Sergeant Foster Cray knows, for only he was aware when we first met the psyolisks. He ducked his head in an almost embarrassed-looking sort of half bow. *And now you also know.*

Yes, Tanya said, determined not to let her anger get sidetracked by remorse. He'd betrayed her trust, and she was furious at him, and she was going to damn well stay that way. *You haven't answered my question.*

I am Nerazim. With the loss of the Khala wrought by the war, the Nerazim ability to access Void energies makes us more versatile than most Templar.

Why do you need to be more versatile?

Is that what you wish to know, Tanya Caulfield? he asked. *Or do you wish to know why you were lied to?*

Why I was lied to? Tanya shook her head. *No—you don't get to phrase it that way. The question is why* you *lied to me. And yes, I want to know.*

I had orders, Ulavu said, and again Tanya sensed a mental sigh. *I had a mission. I was honor-bound to accomplish it. You surely understand honor and duty.*

Don't change the subject, Tanya growled. *What kind of mission was it? I assumed you protoss already knew about the ghost program.*

Hierarch Artanis needed no information, Ulavu agreed. *What he wished was for me to find and identify a Dominion ghost of a specific psionic power.*

Tanya clenched her teeth. So she hadn't been a friend to him, or even an unknowing information source. All she'd been was some sort of high-stakes door prize. *Let me guess. Something that had rarely been seen before, maybe? Like pyrokinesis?*

Ulavu inclined his head to the side. *No.*

For a second Tanya thought she'd misunderstood. *No?*

No, he said reluctantly. *I was sent to locate and befriend a teleki-netic.*

Tanya felt as if the floor had just been pulled out from under her. She hadn't even been a door prize? *What are you talking about? There are two teeks in the program right now. What was wrong with them?*

He was silent so long that she started to wonder if she'd lost contact. *I did not wish them as friends,* he said at last. *They are not . . . good souls.*

And now he was going to presume to judge all of humanity? This just got better and better. *They are perfectly acceptable souls,* she shot back.

Are they?

She scowled. No, damn it all, they really weren't. Glistrup was manic depressive and a compulsive liar, while Mai was just an all-around mean person. No one liked them.

Still, they were competent enough teeks, if somewhat low-power. *So what did you want with them?*

The protoss have developed a new weapon, Ulavu said evasively. *Of only minor tactical use, but of interest to a number of us. It was hoped a terran telekinetic would be useful in its deployment, as the human version of that ability carries unique characteristics not found in protoss. We wished to explore what could be achieved through a partnership with such a terran. I can say no more.*

Okay, Tanya said, frowning. *But the history of warfare isn't exactly choking with nice, upstanding people. You wanted a teek, and you had Glistrup and Mai to choose from. Why didn't you pick one of them?*

Because I knew neither would be satisfied sharing my attention and my friendship with another.

So what? You only needed one of them, right?

Yes. He hesitated. *But I then would not have been able to befriend you.*

Tanya glared at him. *Oh no,* she insisted. *You aren't going to put this on me. I had nothing to do with messing up your plans or your mission.*

I make no such allegation, he protested. *It was my choice. My decision. My failure.*

Tanya gazed at him, bits and pieces of the puzzle that was Ulavu finally coming together. His abandonment by the protoss, his rumored estrangement from Hierarch Artanis himself, his continuing but seemingly dead-end position at the ghost program—

That night in Dante's Circle, she said. *You said you were doing research. You were looking for a teek, weren't you?*

I had recently uncovered rumors that one of those who perished on Chau Sara had the gift, Ulavu said. *It is thought by some that such powers may follow bloodlines. I had hoped I might locate a family member in that place.*

Instead, you nearly got your head taken off. Tanya winced as the true situation in Dante's belatedly clicked. *Rather,* they *nearly got their* heads taken off.

I would not have harmed them, Ulavu assured her. *I was on Korhal IV as a guest. I would never abuse that responsibility.*

Yeah. Tanya took a deep breath. *This conversation isn't over, Ulavu. We* will *get back to it. But right now we have more immediate worries. Tell me about the main battle in Point One, the one in the upstairs chamber. What happened to you and Erin?*

We were attacked, as were you, Sergeant Foster Cray, and Lieutenant Dennis Halkman. He indicated the bandages across his torso. *As you see,* he added ruefully, *my abilities were not up to Nerazim standards.*

The psyolisks?

Yes. I found myself distracted and was often unable to focus. If not for your ability to quickly kill the enemy, we would all have perished.

Enough reason right there to make friends with me, I guess. Tanya frowned to herself. Had she just made a *joke* about it?

There were more reasons than that, Ulavu said firmly.

Yes, I know. Apparently, he hadn't caught the humor. Not the first time that had happened. *The problem is—*

"Hello?" a tentative voice came.

Tanya turned to find Whist standing in the hatchway, his eyes flicking back and forth between her and Ulavu. "Yes?" she said.

"Erin said you were acting a little twitchy," he said, taking a careful step inside. "I thought as long as I was up I'd check on Ulavu's injuries, too."

I am healing, Ulavu assured him.

"Good." Whist cocked an eyebrow at Tanya. "How about you?"

"I'm fine," Tanya said. A lie, of course, but not as much of one as she'd expected. Ulavu's betrayal still hurt terribly, but at least they'd started talking again. "I'm glad you're here, though. We were just about to tackle a serious question."

"Which is . . . ?"

"Why Erin is still alive."

"Okay, that's *not* the question I was expecting," Whist said. "You want to elaborate?"

Tanya waved at his armor. "The psyolisks got within a hair of taking you out, right?"

"More than once." Whist shrugged. "You get used to it."

"They nearly took out Dizz, too. *And,* I find out now," she added, feeling a twinge of guilt, "they took a solid crack at Ulavu, as well. So how did Erin get out without a scratch?"

Whist opened his mouth . . . closed it again. "Well . . . Ulavu was right there. I assume you were protecting her, right?"

To the best of my ability. Ulavu gestured at his bandages. *But my ability in that battle was sorely diminished.*

"Exactly my point," Tanya said. "Erin had a gauss rifle and was doing a fair amount of damage with it. But with Ulavu running at only half speed behind her, they must have had several opportunities to take her down."

"But they didn't," Whist said slowly. "In fact, it looks like they didn't even try. So why not?"

They wanted her to survive the battle, Ulavu said. *To return to Korhal IV.*

"But *why*?" Tanya persisted. "They didn't care about the rest of us. Why her?"

Perhaps she has been infested, Ulavu suggested grimly. *She lay on the open ground several times, some of those times with her helmet off. Could spores have infested her?*

"Not likely," Whist said, stroking his lower lip. "Infestations aren't that fast or quite that easy. And she'd certainly be put through the full grid of tests and micro-scans before they let her anywhere near Korhal again. Could it be something to do with her job? She's the only xenobiologist among us."

"Wouldn't that make her the first one they'd *want* to kill?" Tanya countered. "If Zagara's hiding something, Erin's the one who would spot it first."

"Unless they're *not* hiding something and want her alive to confirm that." Whist snorted. "But in that case, why try to kill *any* of us?"

"Exactly," Tanya said. "We're getting played here, and we need to figure out what the game is."

"Yeah." Whist gestured. "Come on."

Where are we going? Ulavu asked.

"We're grabbing Erin and heading to the cockpit," Whist said. "If we're going to have a skull session, we might as well gather all the skulls we have."

———

"There goes another one, Emperor," the tactical officer said tautly. "It's angling in . . . veering off now."

With a conscious effort, Valerian unclenched his teeth. That was the fourth devourer to fly near the survey team's dropship in the past two hours.

Fortunately, it was also the fourth devourer to ignore them. "You're sure it didn't get any acid on them?" he asked.

"It never got within range, Emperor," the officer assured him.

"I guess those psi blocks are still working," Matt said, coming up behind Valerian. "Handy gadgets. We may need to make them standard issue."

"Assuming no one ever wants to talk to anyone," Valerian pointed out sourly. "Which could be very handy right now."

"Yes," Matt agreed. "Ironic that we can tell when it's safe for them to shut the blocks off, but we can't tell them *unless* they shut the blocks off."

Valerian glanced at the chrono. And it would be another forty minutes before the next of the on-the-hour communications Matt had set up with Halkman's team. Until that time, Halkman's psi blocks would stay up.

And maybe they'd stay up for a long time after that, too. The number of flying zerg that had approached the dropship had gone up dramatically in the past couple of hours. Halkman would hardly shut off the blocks, even on schedule, if there was a mutalisk paralleling him at the time.

For that matter, even without a visual he was taking a risk every time he shut them off. No one knew how flying zerg hunted or what their internal sensory range was, which meant there was no way for Halkman to truly know how far away was safe enough.

Which, boiled down to its essence, meant there was a good chance the survey team would remain incommunicado until it arrived at Focal Point Three.

"At least they got the transcription and Cruikshank's battle report," Valerian said. "They've got all the information we do."

"Except for the tiny little fact that the protoss are gearing up to incinerate the planet," Matt murmured.

Valerian grimaced. And the even more ominous fact that the Dominion fleet was preparing to join in that attack.

One of the most terrible duties of a commander was the job of choosing which soldiers or units to send to certain death. As emperor, Valerian held a similar responsibility.

He'd long since accepted that burden. But he would never, ever get used to it.

Matt took a step closer to him. "I just came over to inform you, Your Excellency, that the Yamato cannon ramp-up is proceeding as scheduled. It should be ready by the time the survey team reaches Point Three."

So he was still pushing the whole Emperor Arcturus the Second thing? Fine. At this point all Valerian could do was ignore it. "Thank you, Admiral," he said. "What's the status of the evac team?"

"They'll be ready before the Yamato cannon is," Matt said. "Also, the psi emitter is ready. If you still want to use it."

Valerian eyed him. "You don't think we should?"

"There are some definite risks involved," Matt said. "The techs say it should have a range of fifty klicks, so if we put it that distance from Point Three, it should draw all the zerg away."

"But?" Valerian prompted.

"But we don't *know* it'll only project to fifty klicks," Matt said. "If the range is longer, it could draw one batch of zerg straight to Point Three even while it's drawing another batch away. Furthermore, we've never used one on a zerg-owned planet before. There may be side effects we won't know about until we try it."

"Understood," Valerian said. "But the alternative is to leave the survey team on its own or to send down Cruikshank and another set of troops. We already saw how well that worked."

"Yes, we did," Matt conceded. "So we deploy the emitter?"

"Yes," Valerian said. "There's a good spot northeast of Point Three, at right angles to the dropship's current vector."

"I'll give the orders," Matt said. Pulling out his comm, he strode away.

"Two mutalisks on scope, Emperor," the tactical officer put in. "Angling across the vector. Projection is they'll miss the dropship by about half a klick." He looked up at Valerian. "It'll work, sir," he added quietly. "I've seen emitters in action. It'll work."

"Thank you, Commander," Valerian said. "I hope you're right." He nodded toward the displays. "In the meantime, keep an eye on those mutalisks. A *very* close eye."

The group standing in the cockpit's hatchway remained silent as Erin read the transcript of Valerian's conversation with Zagara, followed by Cruikshank's report of the action at Focal Point Two. Whist, who'd made sure to grab the copilot seat when they first entered, listened with half his attention while he peered through the canopy with the other half. The landscape below looked peaceful enough, but he didn't trust it for a minute.

He didn't trust the sky, either. Twice during Erin's recital Dizz tapped his arm and pointed at a devourer or a group of mutalisks off toward the horizon.

Fortunately, none of the creatures approached the dropship, and they were usually visible for only a minute or two before they headed off on other business. But the whole thing left Whist with an acid taste in his mouth and a twisted knot in his gut. There was no way to know whether any of those encounters were coincidental or the result of someone keeping an eye on them. Either way, being caught in midair was not the kind of situation he wanted to find himself in.

"Okay, so that's everything we've got," he said when Erin had finished. "The question—the same one we've had from the start—is what the *hell* is going on. Starting with what the psyolisks are and what the things in the pods are."

"It seems obvious that the psyolisks are there to guard the pods," Dizz said. "It also strikes me that they're pretty damn rotten at their jobs."

"I beg to differ," Tanya countered. "They nearly took us down *and* did a number on the protoss and Cruikshank's force."

"While still losing all the pods both times," Dizz said. "I'm not saying they're not seriously nasty. I'm saying that as bodyguards, they're running zero-for-two."

"I'm still stuck on whether they're the same species," Whist said. "*And* I want to know what happened to the ones in the empty pods. Or if the pods were always empty," he added, to forestall Erin's inevitable objection, "why they were in the cavern in the first place."

Zagara stated that all the xel'naga essence had been used, Ulavu pointed out. *Perhaps the extra pods were meant for additional adostra they were unable to create.*

"Because they ran out of essence first?" Whist pursed his lips. "Seems like poor planning, but I guess it's possible."

"There's still Erin's question about the psyolisks," Tanya said. "If they're a matured form of adostra, and the adostra are from some non-zerg species plus xel'naga essence—"

"Hold it," Dizz interrupted. "Check this out." He nodded at the canopy.

Whist frowned. Half a dozen flying zerg were cutting across their path straight ahead, heading northeast. "Yeah, they're flying. So?"

"Right, they're flying," Dizz said. "They're flying *northeast*."

"Again, so?"

"So every zerg I've seen flying for the past hour and a half has been heading that direction," Dizz said. "You think there's a sale on premium creep or something over there?"

"These zerg don't eat creep," Erin said. "The plants exude nutrients—"

"Yeah, yeah, I know," Dizz said. "Whist? What do you think?"

"I don't know," Whist said, frowning at the zerg flapping their way across the dropship's path. "An hour and a half, you say?"

"That's when I first noticed it," Dizz said. "It could have been going on longer."

"And always northeast?"

"Always northeast."

"What in the Dominion could they be running from?" Erin murmured. "The psyolisks? Something else over there?"

Whist hissed through his teeth as it hit him. "Oh, hell," he muttered. "They're not running *from*, Erin. They're running *to*."

"To—?" Dizz looked over at Whist, and Whist saw the sudden dawning of the light. "Oh, no. They can't be serious."

"What is it?" Erin asked. "What's going on?"

"I think Cruikshank's landed a psi emitter," Whist told her. "How wonderfully stupid of him."

But those devices are not safe, Ulavu protested.

"Yeah, no kidding," Whist bit out. "When did safety matter to the top brass?"

"*Or* common sense," Dizz added.

"Okay, now you're scaring me," Erin said. "What's the problem? I thought they were used on the battlefield all the time."

"They were," Whist said. "And the brass loved 'em, because they were terrific at drawing zerg away from civilian areas."

"They were also hell in a boxcar for those of us in the field," Dizz said. "Not only do they concentrate the enemy into a massive wall of teeth and claws, but they also erase the last bit of battle caution in those tiny little zerg brains."

"I didn't think zerg *had* any battle caution," Tanya said.

It is not so much caution as positional awareness, Ulavu said.

During normal combat zerg do not wish to run into one another, so they space themselves out somewhat. A psi emitter suppresses that awareness.

"The professor's got it," Dizz confirmed. "And whatever we might have gained by letting them run all over one another wasn't worth it. Trust me."

"Yeah." Whist raised his eyebrows at Ulavu. He'd made the protoss a conditional promise, but if they were going into combat again, everyone needed to be on the same page. "Speaking of professors and all, Ulavu has something he needs to tell everyone."

"He does?" Erin asked, turning toward him.

I do, Ulavu admitted. *You have known me as a researcher. I am something more.* He drew himself up to his full height. *I am a warrior. To be specific, I am a Nerazim, a dark templar.*

For a moment no one spoke. Whist threw a surreptitious glance at each of them in turn, trying to read their reactions. Erin was dumbfounded, with a growing tinge of awe and fear. Dizz had the look of a man who'd already had suspicions and was merely having those suspicions confirmed. Tanya was nursing a quiet pain, but not a fresh one. Apparently, Ulavu had already confessed his secret to her.

Whist let the silence stretch out, wondering who would break it first. Predictably, it was Dizz. "Okay," he said briskly. "I wondered how you and Erin survived back there. I knew *I* hadn't shot those psyolisks off you and it would have taken some really fancy over-the-shoulder work for Whist to have done it. Welcome aboard. Next time it'll be your turn to take point."

Tanya cleared her throat. "Actually, we *haven't* solved the question of how Erin survived. That's one of the things—"

And without warning, the dropship slammed to a near-halt and twisted halfway up onto its right side.

Whist grabbed his armrests, dimly aware that the three standing behind him were scrambling for whatever handholds they could get as they were thrown off-balance. "Dizz?" he snapped.

"Damn," Dizz breathed, sounding almost more awed than alarmed. "We've been grabbed."

"We've *what*?"

"We've got eight mutalisks hanging from the hull," Dizz said tightly. "Make that ten. And—damn it all—two more have just jammed themselves into the main thrusters."

"They're bringing us down?" Erin asked, her voice trembling.

"Worse." Dizz pointed at the canopy as the horizon skated sideways. "They're taking us where all the rest of the damn zerg are going.

"They're taking us to the psi emitter."

CHAPTER FIFTEEN

"*Damn* it all," Matt was snarling toward the sensor station's intercom as Valerian hurried across the bridge toward him. "What the hell is the holdup with those Wraiths?"

"What's happened?" Valerian asked as he reached Matt's side.

"A swarm of mutalisks has hijacked the dropship," the admiral said tartly. "Hangar Control, I asked you a question."

Valerian felt his throat tighten as he found the proper display on the wraparound. He'd assumed Matt's explanation had been some sort of strange metaphor.

It wasn't. A group of mutalisks had literally grabbed the survey team's dropship and hauled it off-course. They appeared to be taking it—

He swallowed a curse. Of course. They were taking it to the psi emitter. Where every other zerg within a fifty-klick radius was also gathering.

"There's a glitch in the docking-bay hatch," Matt gritted out. "They can't get anything out."

"What about the Wraith squadrons on patrol?"

"They're all out of position," Matt said. "Either too far out or on the far side of the planet. They can't get to the dropship fast enough."

"Any idea how or why this happened?"

Matt shook his head. "Best guess is that it has something to do with either the emitter or whoever's running the psyolisks. Or both."

And there was only one of those factors that the Dominion had any control over. "Bluff stated; bluff called," Valerian said sourly. "Fine. Shut down the emitter."

"See, that's the problem," Matt growled. "We can't."

"You *can't*?"

"Because we didn't want the zerg to be able to shut it down, either," Matt said. "So it's locked down solid. And just for good measure, the techs also encased it in a standard field bunker before dropping it." He hissed between his teeth. "Seemed like a good idea at the time."

"I'm sure it did." Valerian stared at the display. In that case, there was only one option left. "What's the smallest nuke we can deliver from orbit?"

Matt's eyes widened. "You want to *nuke* the planet?"

"Just that one small section of it," Valerian assured him. He turned and caught the comm officer's eye. "Inform Hierarch Artanis that we're going to launch a nuke," he ordered. "One only, and as part of a rescue mission. It is *not* to be seen as the opening of full-scale operations against the planet. Make sure he understands that."

"Yes, Emperor," the officer said, clearly caught off-guard but taking the order in stride.

"Then contact Overqueen Zagara," Valerian added. "Give her the same message, and tell her I'll speak directly to her in a few minutes."

"Yes, Emperor."

He turned back to Matt. "Admiral?"

"We've got a ten-kiloton tactical weapon," Matt said. "Usually ground-based or ship-to-ship, but it should survive entry."

Valerian ran a quick calculation in his head. Assuming they could get it to the target fast enough, the dropship should still be out of range of even the peripheral wind blast. "Get it ready," he said. "Launch on my command."

"Yes, sir."

Valerian turned back to the comm officer. "Any responses?"

"Hierarch Artanis acknowledges, and expresses reservations about this action, Emperor," the officer called. "But he agrees to stand by and not interfere." His lip twitched. "Overqueen Zagara is not responding to the signal."

Valerian frowned. "She's refusing to acknowledge?"

"No, Emperor—there's no response at all," the officer said. "The transceiver she was using earlier still registers as functioning, but no one's answering our call."

"Not good," Matt murmured. "You suppose she got wind of our plans and is getting ready to run?"

"Pull up the images on those seven leviathans," Valerian ordered the tactical officer. "Are they still on the ground?"

"Yes, Emperor," the officer confirmed.

"And we haven't seen anyone boarding them?"

"No, Emperor. But there are clouds and mist down there, and the visual isn't always perfect."

"There could also be tunnels," Matt murmured.

"Yes," Valerian murmured back. And if Zagara and her brood-mothers were about to bolt . . . "One thing at a time. Is the missile ready?"

The tactical officer pulled up a status display. "Yes, Emperor."

Valerian looked at Matt. The admiral's face was rigid, giving nothing away. Did he disapprove?

Probably. In fact, he probably saw this as the sort of ham-fisted thing Valerian's father would have done.

But it didn't matter what he thought. Halkman's team was still the Dominion's best hope of figuring out what was going on before they were forced to destroy the planet. Valerian wasn't going to give up the team without a fight.

"Thank you." He braced himself, wondering distantly whether he would live to regret this. "Admiral Horner, launch missile."

The dropship's sudden lurch threw Tanya completely off-balance, sending both her and Erin tumbling helplessly toward a bank of switches and knobs on the cockpit's starboard wall. Erin was half a meter in front of Tanya, her hands scrabbling frantically for some kind of handhold, probably unaware that no matter what she did or didn't grab, Tanya would be slamming into her a fraction of a second later.

And then, even as Erin's fingers caught the edge of Whist's headrest and Tanya braced herself for impact, Ulavu's hand closed on Tanya's forearm, bringing her to a twisting and arm-wrenching halt.

Are you all right?

I'm fine, Tanya assured him, listening with half an ear as Dizz and Whist shouted out the situation. The whole dropship was rocking and shaking now as Dizz tried to regain control.

But it was a losing battle. There were too many mutalisks, they had too much combined mass, and their grips were solid. And with the main thrusters jammed Dizz didn't have enough power available to wrench the dropship free.

Ulavu had come to the same conclusion. *I will deal with them,* he said, pulling Tanya toward him and guiding her to a handhold. *Your jump pack is prepared, Lieutenant Dennis Halkman?*

"Yeah, it's prepared," Dizz shouted over the roaring whine of the afterburners as he tried to blast the mutalisks out of the thrusters. "And no, you're not taking it. Whist, see this control here?"

There is no choice, Ulavu insisted. *I can reach the mutalisks and kill them.*

"Not with a jump pack designed for reaper armor, you can't," Dizz insisted right back. "Whist, this is the autopilot. When the mutalisks are gone, key it on."

"How will I know when they're gone?" Whist asked.

"We'll probably start falling out of the sky," Dizz said, punching off the afterburners and unstrapping from his seat. "When that happens, don't waste time admiring the scenery. Erin, get your butt over here and strap in." He caught Tanya's eye and gave her a brisk nod. "Come on, pyrokeet. Visor on, and let's burn us some zerg."

The dropship had mostly stopped shaking by the time Dizz had his armor and jump pack on. But a glance out the stern as he lowered the ramp showed they were still heading toward the distant psi emitter. "Okay," Dizz's voice came through Tanya's headset over the shrieking of the wind. "We don't have time to rig a harness, so I'll have to carry you the old-fashioned way."

"Okay," Tanya said, wincing. She wasn't *exactly* afraid of heights, but being lugged around a thousand meters above the ground by someone she barely knew was not a scenario she could be happy about.

"And since you don't need to hold a weapon, and I don't trust my own strength," Dizz continued, "we'll do it face-to-face so that we can hold on to each other. That okay?"

"Sure," Tanya said, feeling marginally better. At least this way she'd have some control of the situation. "I haven't had a good hug for weeks."

"Doubt this really qualifies." Stepping in front of her, he stooped a little, offering her his upper torso armor. Tanya wrapped her arms around his shoulders, and he wrapped his around her lower ribs. "Ready? Let's go."

And with a roar from his jump pack's turbines, he launched them out the back of the dropship and into the open air.

Mutalisks were bat-winged flying zerg, as big as a medium-sized Dominion mech, with a curved posture that always reminded Tanya of giant hornets leading with their stingers as they swooped to battle. They were normally also among the fastest of the zerg flyers, and Tanya had been concerned they might be able to outrun a reaper jump pack.

She needn't have worried. Burdened with the dropship's weight, and with the psi blocks probably also interfering with their speed, the mutalisks were plodding along at a greatly reduced pace, barely above that of a normal terran jog. Dizz maneuvered them into position above and behind the dropship, rotating to give Tanya a clear view of her targets.

And the carnage began.

She took out the two blocking the thrusters first, watching with grim satisfaction as their bodies tensed, then relaxed, then dropped silently into the forest below as she burned out their hearts and lungs. After that she began working her way forward from the stern, hoping the psi block interference to their communication would keep them from immediately noticing their diminishing numbers.

She'd killed five of the twelve when the others finally woke up to the threat. Two of them detached from the hull, leaving the dropship hanging precariously in the others' grip, and swooped back toward their attackers.

Tanya set her teeth, concentrating her power on the one on the left. Something behind it caught her eye. "Dizz, *drop!*" she snapped.

Dizz obeyed instantly, shutting down his turbines and sending them plummeting toward the ground. The two mutalisks shifted course in response, angling down toward their prey—

And lurched violently in midair as Ulavu—crouched precariously in the dropship's open stern with Tanya's canister rifle gripped awkwardly in his large, nonhuman hands—blasted both zerg from behind with armor-piercing rounds. Even as the mutalisks flapped furiously, trying to regain altitude, Tanya finished them off. There was an earsplitting screech, and two of the other mutalisks let go of the dropship and swung to the attack.

That proved to be a mistake. The dropship canted sideways, its weight now too much for the remaining zerg to carry. Even as the mutalisks tried to regain control, the thrusters suddenly kicked out a massive blast and the ship broke free.

"No, no, no," Dizz groaned. "Damn it, Whist—don't fiddle with the controls. Just set the autopilot."

"Trying," Whist's tense voice came back. "No response—they must have cut something. I don't suppose you'd like to get your butt back in here?"

Dizz cursed and leaned over, and Tanya tightened her grip as he threw power to his turbines. "Yeah, we're on our way. Watch it— your nose is dipping. Grab the yoke and ease it back a couple of millimeters. I said *back* a couple of millimeters."

"I did," Whist said. "It's not responding, either."

"Must have injected glave wurms," Dizz muttered. "They've gotten into the gravs and the thruster controls." Abruptly, he shot straight up into the air. The move nearly broke Tanya's grip, but Dizz tightened his arms around her until she got her own arms resettled. "Okay, I'm looking down-course," he said. "Looks like you've got a small clearing almost dead ahead. You're going to aim for that."

There was another burst from the thrusters, sending the dropship leaping ahead. "And turn the damn thrusters *off*," he added tartly. "The master throttle's between the seats—"

"Yeah, yeah, got it," Whist said. "Any thoughts on how to slow down without thrusters or gravs?"

"You're about to make friends with the trees," Dizz said. "You've still got some grav, so you start by hitting the very tops—no more than three or four meters down. As you slow down, start edging a little deeper, into the heavier branches—use the pedals to change your pitch. With luck, the grav will hold out until you're slow enough to ease down into the clearing."

"And if it doesn't?"

"Then you're about to become a bulldozer," Dizz said bluntly. "Strap in tight, and hope like crazy the rivetheads who built the thing took pride in their work. Oh, and tell Ulavu to—" He paused. "Where'd Ulavu go?"

"Back inside," Tanya told him. "He left after I took out the rest of the mutalisks."

"Oh. Right. I missed that. Anyway, tell Ulavu to strap down, too."

"Already done," Whist said. "Anything else?"

"Nothing any of us have time for," Dizz said. "Good luck."

"Isn't there anything we can do?" Tanya murmured.

"Like I said, not enough time," Dizz said, his voice tense. "Even if we could catch them, I'd never make it to the cockpit." He paused. "Nice work with the mutalisks, by the way."

"Thanks," Tanya said. Considering that the dropship was teetering on the edge of destruction, all their heroics seemed to have been for nothing.

And then, off to her right, a sudden flicker caught her eye. She turned her head to see a fading spot of light just at the horizon. Frowning, she keyed in her visor's optical enhancement.

Rising just above the fading light was a small mushroom-shaped cloud.

"Whoa!" Dizz said. "The sale must be over."

"What sale?" Tanya asked, her mind trying to sort through the flash and the cloud. A nuke, obviously. But when did zerg start using nukes?

"That sale on premium creep I mentioned earlier," Dizz said. "They're not all flying thataway anymore."

Tanya looked around. There were three flying zerg between them and the horizon, but none of them was flying northeast.

And then it clicked. "They nuked the psi emitter," she said.

"They—whoa, *what*?"

"A nuke just went off right about where we were guessing the emitter was," Tanya said, nodding in the direction of the blast. "The question is, who took it out? Us or the zerg?"

"Must have been us," Dizz said. "Zerg don't use tech. Well, us or the protoss. Come on, Whist. Come *on* . . ."

Tanya looked back to the drama taking place below. The dropship was plowing through the trees, just as Dizz had instructed. It was visibly slowing, to the point that Dizz and Tanya were finally starting to close the distance.

She caught her breath. It was slowing, but not slowing enough. "Dizz?"

"You're still too hot, Whist," Dizz warned. "You've got to get deeper. Don't worry about scratching the paint."

"Can't," Whist said. "Gravs are twitching at me."

Dizz hissed out a curse. "Then shut them down."

"Say again?"

"Shut down the gravs," Dizz repeated. "Master lever's forward of the throttle—twist the handle ninety clockwise, then pull back."

"Dizz—"

"You're going to pancake anyway," Dizz cut him off. "You need to be in the clearing when you do it."

"Great. Okay, here goes."

The dropship sank abruptly, and even over the wind noise, Tanya could hear the much louder crunching of wood as the ship tore through larger branches. But it was still five meters up as it passed the last line and shot into the clearing. Tanya bit her lip as it fell like a rock, slammed to the ground, and skidded over the rough surface. She held her breath . . .

The dropship was nearly to the next line of trees when it finally bounced and swerved to a halt. "Whist?" Dizz called tentatively.

"Yeah, we're okay," Whist said. "Erin? Ulavu? Yeah, everyone's okay. I don't think this thing's going to fly again, though."

"No kidding," Dizz said, and Tanya could hear the relief in his voice. "Okay, start pulling out everything we might need. Those glave wurms are still wandering around in there, and we don't want them chewing on the spare C-14s."

"Right. We're on it."

High on the list of things every colonel knew not to do was interrupt an admiral's conversation. That went double when the admiral in question was conversing with an old friend.

It went triple when the old friend was the emperor.

And so Cruikshank waited as patiently as he could while the two men had their little chat by the tactical officer's display wraparound.

Of course, considering they were discussing the possible consequences of a technically unprovoked nuking of a technically noncombatant planet, he was more than willing to give them whatever time and space they needed.

Their dialogue began winding down, and Cruikshank took the last two steps necessary to put him into conversational range. "Admiral?"

Admiral Horner looked up. "Yes, Colonel, what is it?"

"When you have a moment, sir," Cruikshank said, "I'd like to discuss my group's next mission."

The admiral and the emperor glanced at each other. Probably wondering which of them had authorized even the planning stage for a new ground mission. "Go ahead," Horner said.

"I've been talking to Commander Rahas on the protoss mothership," Cruikshank said. "Our conclusion was—"

"Who authorized you to talk to the protoss?" Valerian interrupted.

"No one, Emperor," Cruikshank said, tensing reflexively. "It was on my own initiative. There was nothing official about the conversation—we were simply two soldiers comparing notes."

"And Commander Rahas is . . . ?"

"Hierarch Artanis's chief ground-force commander," Cruikshank said. "He was Sagaya's second-in-command before the Point Two fiasco."

Valerian's lip might have twitched at the word *fiasco*. But he merely nodded. "Continue."

"Yes, Emperor." At least the emperor didn't randomly cannonball into the shallow end the way his father sometimes had. "Our conclusion was that, as you anticipated, the psi emitter will have drawn a lot of the zerg away from Point Three. Since flying zerg are faster than groundies, most of the flyers should have gotten there first, which further suggests that the nuke we just dropped will have taken out a fair percentage of them."

"That was our conclusion, as well," Horner agreed. "Is there more?"

"Yes, sir," Cruikshank said. "Now that the emitter's gone, we expect that whoever's controlling those zerg will send them back to protect Point Three. If the dropship hadn't been attacked, the team would have gotten there well ahead of most of the returning zerg. With the team now on foot, it's going to be a race." He pursed his lips. "Enough reason right there for them to be attacked."

"It won't be a race if we send another dropship down to carry them that last thirty klicks," Valerian said.

"We could do that, Emperor, yes," Cruikshank said. "The problem I see is twofold. First, sending anything down will immediately pinpoint the team's location, which will allow the enemy to prepare ambushes along the way. Right now, with their psi blocks running, they're a lot less noticeable. Second, we've already seen how vulnerable a dropship is to aerial attack."

"We could send some Wraiths down to escort them," Horner said.

"Except that Gystt has a lot more mutalisks than we have Wraiths,"

Valerian murmured. "And not all of them will have been taken out by the nuke. So you're suggesting, Colonel, that we leave Halkman's team on foot?"

"Yes, Emperor," Cruikshank said. "The trip will take longer, but they've got powered suits, and the images we're getting don't indicate any major injuries. And again, right now they're more or less invisible to local zerg."

"Or at least harder to spot," Valerian said. "As you say, though, they're now racing the returning zerg. I assume you have a suggestion to offer?"

"We give them a buffer," Cruikshank said. "By that I mean we put a line of troops, mechs, and protoss on the ground, about fifteen klicks out from Point Three, angled against the direction the zerg will come from. We'll hopefully be able to hold them long enough for Halkman to get inside and pull the samples we need."

"You just said the zerg would see any dropships we sent in," Valerian reminded him.

"Yes, but we won't care," Cruikshank said. "It doesn't matter if they know where we are, since we're there to fight anyway. And we won't be doing any horizontal flying, so they'll have less time to gather enough flyers to mess with us."

"There were a lot of zerg heading for the emitter," Horner warned. "If they're all under enemy control, that'll be a damn big plateful for your force to handle."

Cruikshank gave a small shrug. "That's what we're paid for, sir."

"What's the terrain look like?" Valerian asked.

"Here's the spot, Emperor." Cruikshank pulled out his datapad and keyed for the aerial view. "It's a section of rolling grassland between two forested areas. Nice visibility—the enemy has to come at us over open ground, and we can't be sneaked up on. It's situated between a fast-moving river and marshland on the southeast and this cliff line on the north."

"The scale says the area's about eight hundred meters wide," Horner pointed out. "That's a lot of territory for forty marines to cover."

"I'd also be taking the second Warhound and however many goliaths you can spare from shipboard defense," Cruikshank said. "Plus Rahas says they still have ten Templar and ten Nerazim they can deploy, plus a sentry or two for close-in support. He also says they could probably bring a pair of phoenixes, which would then be available for air support."

"That still leaves thirteen meters for each marine or protoss warrior," Horner persisted. "Worse, really, since protoss infantry usually don't use ranged weapons and will probably have to bunch closer together to hold their section of the line. Either way, if you get swarmed, I don't see how you'll keep from being overwhelmed."

"We can handle it, sir," Cruikshank insisted. "Anyway, there's no other suitable spot for ten klicks either way. Most of the rest of that area is forested, which limits our fields of fire. And once the river bends due south, there would be too long a battle line for us to cover."

"What if you set up right at Point Three?" Valerian asked.

"I'm worried that would cut things a little too close," Cruikshank said. "If Halkman's team gets delayed, they could find their way blocked by a battle. And we *need* to get them inside Point Three, because unless you want to send Dr. Cogan down with us, there's no one except Dr. Wyland who knows how to take the samples you want."

He tapped the datapad screen. "This is our best bet to slow down the zerg long enough for the survey team to do that."

Valerian and Horner exchanged looks, and Cruikshank could sense a nonverbal conversation going on. "This protoss force," Valerian said, turning back to Cruikshank. "Is that still you and Rahas talking theory, or has Hierarch Artanis given the green light for them to join in?"

"Rahas is waiting for your approval before approaching the hierarch, Emperor," Cruikshank said. "But he assures me there's no question that he'll authorize the action."

Again, Horner and Valerian looked at each other. "You make a good case, Colonel," Valerian said. "Just one question: why?"

Cruikshank frowned. "As I said before, Emperor. It's our job."

"Not why you're willing to risk your life for the survey team's mission," Valerian said. "Why you're asking for the protoss to be in on the operation. I was under the impression you didn't like the protoss."

"And that you certainly don't trust them," Horner added.

Cruikshank felt his lip twitch. "Permission to speak freely, sir?"

Valerian nodded. "Go ahead."

"You're right; I don't like or trust protoss," Cruikshank said. "But what I saw at Point Two—what the psyolisks did to them and how fast they did it—scared the hell out of me. This has to be stopped, and it has to be stopped here, or the war's going to start all over again. We can't afford that. I don't have enough soldiers and mechs to do it alone. Neither do the protoss. That's just how the battle logic works out."

"Very well put, Colonel," Valerian said. "All right. Give Rahas a call and let him know we're sending you and everyone we can spare from basic shipboard security. Then get your team together and report back when you're ready."

"Yes, Emperor." Cruikshank nodded to Horner. "Admiral." He started to turn away—

"One more thing, Colonel," Valerian said. "You asked for permission to speak freely, but I didn't hear anything that could be construed as improper or inappropriate. Why that specific request?"

Cruikshank grimaced. "I admitted I was frightened, Emperor. Official Dominion military policy is that we're *never* frightened."

"Ah," Valerian said, a small smile touching his lips. "Welcome to the real world, Colonel."

"Thank you, Emperor," Cruikshank said soberly. "Actually, I've been living here for quite a while. Excuse me, please—I have orders to carry out."

CHAPTER SIXTEEN

Erin didn't notice the ache in her side until she tried to lift the flamethrower's fuel tank and something seemed to go *pop*. She managed to lug the thing outside anyway, but from that point the pain got progressively worse.

Eventually, Whist noticed. "Trouble?" he asked as he set a rack of gauss rifles beside the fuel tank.

"I'm fine."

He raised his eyebrows. "In marine talk, *I'm fine* usually means *like hell I am*," he said. "Come on, we don't have time for games."

"It's nothing," she said. "Just some pain in my side."

"Where?" He touched her armor below her arm. "Here?"

"A little lower."

"Yeah." Whist looked around. "Dizz? We've got a cracked rib over here."

"How bad?" Dizz called back. "Can you travel?"

"Yes, of course," Erin said. "I'm okay. Really."

"Good to hear it." Whist pointed to a large tree at the edge of the clearing. "Over there—sit down. We'll get the rest of the stuff out."

"I can help."

"You can help by sitting down," Whist said firmly. "We don't have time for a closer look, and probably don't have anything aboard that'll do better than the CMC's compression suit anyway."

"Yes, sir," Erin said with a sigh. To be honest, a short break *would* probably do her good.

She eased herself down by the tree he'd indicated. It was more than a little embarrassing to sit idly by while everyone else worked. Still, Whist was in charge, and he'd given her an order.

Though the relaxation would come to a quick and violent end if some wandering zerg spotted her. Was she still inside the magic zone of sort-of invisibility from the two psi blocks?

She hoped so. She hadn't carried a weapon since the Point One cavern and her attempts to use Whist's spare gauss rifle. As Tanya had said earlier, she was lucky to have come out of that alive.

So why *had* she come out of it alive?

They'd really never answered that question. Erin herself had certainly avoided thinking about it. Luckily, there'd been plenty of other things to keep her mind busy over the past hour or so.

But all those excuses were gone now that she was just sitting here.

Why was she still alive? Had the attacking zerg sized them up, realized she was the most harmless, and decided to concentrate on the others first?

No—that made no sense. Not when a couple of quick swings of razor-sharp claws could have cut through her armor and killed her on the spot. Or at least, those claws could have taken off the arm that held the rifle and *really* made sure she was harmless. Surely one of the zerg could have spared the half second that would have taken.

Because she was a xenobiologist? Whist had suggested that. But Tanya had promptly shot that one down. Unless there was something about the adostra in their pods that was designed to fool a trained xenobiologist and no one else . . .

She snorted, the movement giving her ribs a fresh twinge. Right. *No* one set traps *that* subtle.

Besides, she was the one who had first raised the question of how the psyolisks and the adostra were connected. If that was the big secret, it was already out of the hat, and should have been grounds for her being the *first* of the survey team to be targeted.

Something caught her eye, and she looked up to see another pair of mutalisks flapping their way across the sky. She tensed, wondering if they'd been sent to finish the job the first pack had started. She watched them, ready to shout out a warning if they turned and dived.

To her relief, they continued on without even pausing. Maybe objects on the ground weren't of any real interest to them, at least not when they themselves were that high. It was only when intruders were in their territory that they'd taken enough interest to attack.

Only when intruders were in their territory.

For a long moment she thought about it, her spinning brain trying to work through the logic. She called up the reports Cruikshank had sent and read them through again. She thought about it some more.

Then, after levering herself carefully to her feet, she crossed the clearing to where the others were working.

Whist looked up as she approached. "I thought I told you to sit down," he said.

"Yes, you did," she confirmed. "I have a question."

There must have been something in her tone, because all four of them paused in their work. "Is it important?" Whist asked.

"Very important," Erin assured him. "You remember what Dizz said about the psyolisks being terrible bodyguards for the pods?"

"Sure," Whist said.

"And Tanya pointed out that they only lost because of bad luck and unexpected circumstances?"

"Again, sure."

"She was wrong," Erin said softly. "It wasn't bad luck. It was deliberate."

Explain, Ulavu said.

Erin swallowed. "The battle at Focal Point Two. The psyolisks had taken down most of the protoss and were trying to move the pods out of the cavern. The only thing that stopped them was the arrival of Colonel Cruikshank's team."

"According to Cruikshank, anyway," Whist said. "Was he wrong?"

"Not from his point of view," Erin said. "But we know better. See, there were mutalisks at the battle. I checked. They attacked while the Dominion force was trying to save the protoss. Mutalisks like the ones that attacked us and knocked us out of the sky."

She pointed at the sky. "So why didn't they do the same thing to the Dominion force on its way down?"

Whist and Dizz looked at each other. "We were traveling horizontally," Dizz said, a little uncertainly. "The Dominion ships would have been coming in vertically. That would have made them harder to hit."

"They hit the protoss shuttle on its way down just fine," Tanya reminded them. "Took out its psionic boosters, remember?"

"And they didn't even try to stop the dropships," Erin said. "There's nothing in the report about any attack until the troops and mechs were already deployed."

"They were moving the pods," Tanya murmured. "Disassembling them from the nutrient base structure couldn't have been easy to do. They must have started long before Cruikshank even landed."

"While they were already beating the snot out of the protoss," Whist said. "So why move them?"

"That's not something that makes sense?" Erin asked.

No, Ulavu told her. *The interior ramps and turns provide effective choke points. The far better strategy would have been for the psyolisks to contain and surround their attackers.*

"Especially since they were winning," Whist said. "Wait a minute. The protoss disruptor. It was already inside, ready to go off. Could that have been why they were moving the pods?"

The disruptor should never have been allowed into the cavern to begin with, Ulavu said. *Even if the mutalisks were unable to block the terran dropships, they should certainly have been able to intercept the disruptor and keep it outside.*

"Damn," Dizz muttered. "Are we saying what I *think* we're saying?"

"We're saying you were right," Whist said. "The psyolisks aren't guarding the pods. They're trying to get them destroyed."

"Not just get them destroyed," Tanya said grimly, "but get them destroyed by *us.*" She nodded toward the sky. "That's why the mutalisks didn't come back and finish the job here. They *want* us to get to Point Three so that we can destroy the pods there for them."

"Or they want us to go to Point Three and get ourselves killed, thereby goading the Dominion into destroying the pods," Whist said. "Probably doesn't make much difference to them."

"*And* furthermore to destroy them without anyone getting the samples that would show adostra and psyolisks aren't forms of the same species," Tanya said. "That's why they were moving the pods at Point Two, and why they let the disruptor in. They figured that they had to make it look to Cruikshank like he was going to lose containment. Otherwise, they couldn't push him into blasting the cavern."

"And that's why I'm alive," Erin said, an unpleasant shiver running through her. She'd hoped desperately that there was a flaw in her reasoning, something the others would find. Only they hadn't. "After they killed the rest of you in Point One, they needed someone to go running back to the Dominion and tell them how horrible the psyolisks are. That was going to be me."

"Because you were the most harmless," Dizz murmured.

"And because you'd have seen the same markings on the backs of the psyolisks and the adostra and would hopefully draw the conclusion they wanted you to draw," Tanya said. "They probably assumed you were more observant with that sort of thing than the rest of us would be."

"I wonder how they managed to get the same markings on both," Dizz said.

He who created the psyolisks would have manipulated the genetics to bring about that precise result, Ulavu said.

"He?" Whist asked.

"He means Abathur," Erin said. "He has to be the one behind this. Even Zagara credited him with creating the adostra."

"But she also said he was loyal to the Swarm," Whist reminded her. "This doesn't exactly sound like loyalty to me."

"Unless Zagara herself is the one behind it," Tanya said.

"I hope to hell not," Dizz said. "Because if she is, she's got the whole planet behind her."

"In which case, we're totally screwed," Whist said.

"Or *she* is," Tanya offered. "Between the Dominion and the protoss, there's enough firepower up there to turn this place back into an orbiting cinder."

"Maybe that's exactly what someone's going for," Erin said.

But that makes no sense, Ulavu objected. *Who stands to gain by the destruction of Gystt?*

"Who knows?" Whist said. "Some other group of zerg, some rogue protoss faction, maybe Sarah damn Kerrigan herself. And by the way, just *having* firepower doesn't mean you get to deliver it. Don't forget that Zagara's got seven leviathans to call on, not to mention however many scourge and devourers she could send against us."

"Doesn't matter," Tanya said firmly. "Not that part. Not to us, anyway. What happens up there is someone else's problem. Our problem is to reach Point Three and get the samples that'll hopefully prove whether we're right or just spitting in the wind." She looked at Ulavu, and Erin had the sense that the two of them were sharing something deep and private. "And we're all we've got," she added. "So let's get this stuff on our backs and get moving."

"And by *our backs*, you mostly mean *mine*," Whist said sourly.

"Not our fault you and Erin are the two with the heavy-duty CMCs," Dizz said. "Do you think we should let Cruikshank know about this?"

"Shutting down the psi blocks isn't a terrific idea," Whist said reluctantly, looking around. "But yeah, this is probably the time and place to do it."

"Couldn't you or Dizz go off a ways and shut down just that one?" Tanya suggested. "That way not everyone will be exposed."

"No point," Whist told her. "The zerg probably have a good bead on the crash site, so they already know we're here."

"That means that, for once, shutting off the blocks doesn't tell them anything new," Dizz added. "So the plan is to shut off both blocks, make a quick report, then turn them back on and make tracks for Point Three?"

"Right," Whist said. "Once we're gone, they can pound on the dropship to their little hearts' content." He fiddled with something inside his armor. "Okay, mine's off. You want to talk, or should I?"

"I'll do it," Dizz said. He did something with his armor. "Halkman to *Hyperion*. Halkman to *Hyperion*."

"Is there trouble?" Tanya asked.

"Not getting through," Dizz said. "Ah. Damn."

"What?" Whist demanded.

"The dropship's signal booster has glitched," Dizz said. "Probably the glave wurms again."

"I thought our suits had enough power by themselves," Erin said.

"They do," Dizz said. "Unfortunately, some tech genius set things up so that if our comms are in range of the dropship, they automatically relay through its booster. No booster, no signal."

"Can't you switch it over?"

"I'm sure *somebody* can," Dizz said sourly. "Unfortunately, they didn't teach us the subtle tech stuff in zerg-shooting school."

"So we need either distance or a shredded booster," Whist said. "And since we don't want to wake up the neighbors with a grenade, I vote for distance."

"Agreed," Dizz said reluctantly. "And at this point, we might as well just wait until we're nearly there. That way, if we attract company, we'll have someplace to duck in out of the rain."

"I don't think Cruikshank will like being left hanging that long," Erin warned.

"He'll get over it," Dizz said. "So what are we bringing?"

"Less than I thought," Whist said. "A couple of spare gauss rifles, lots of extra mags. Leave the flamethrower—"

"I'll carry the flamethrower," Erin interrupted. "And anything else you need me to."

"I thought you were hurt," Tanya said.

"I just need to learn to let my suit's servos do most of the work," Erin said.

"But the *flamethrower*?"

"You've proved the psyolisks don't like heat," Erin pointed out. "Dizz proved they burn if you get them hot enough. Besides, walls of flame can sometimes come in handy."

"You're awfully soldierly all of a sudden," Dizz said, frowning at her. "Any reason in particular?"

"I'm just trying to be part of the team."

Dizz and Whist exchanged glances. "Fine," Whist said. "Grab whatever you think you can carry, and let's go. Tanya, her CMC has some anchor points for gear attachment—give her a hand, will you?"

They didn't believe her, of course. Erin knew that. But how could she tell them the truth?

She couldn't tell them that during the war and its aftermath, she'd nurtured a private but enduring contempt for the protoss for the burning of Chau Sara. Never mind that they thought they had a good reason. Never mind that they thought they were halting the spread of zerg infestation. The cold, grim, bottom line was that they'd killed innocents for nothing, and intelligent beings ought to be better than that.

Now she, Dr. Erin Wyland, so high and mighty and incomparably moral, had done exactly the same thing to the adostra.

She winced, her ribs twinging with the sudden shift in weight as Tanya attached the fuel tank to her armor. She couldn't bring back the innocent lives she'd helped destroy. But she had one final chance to preserve this last group.

And she would do whatever she had to.

"I make it about thirty klicks to Point Three," Whist said when they were ready. "That's two hours at a decent jog."

"I think we can do better than that," Dizz said.

"I think we damn well *better* do better than that," Whist said. "Move it out. And watch each other's backs. Remember, they don't need *all* of us to get to Point Three alive."

The shuttle dropped to the hangar deck with a dull *thud*. Its hatch opened, and a single protoss emerged. He looked around, spotted Cruikshank standing with his troops and mechs, and strode toward them.

"Great," Cruikshank muttered to no one in particular, for about the fourth time in the past hour. Bad enough that he was about to take on a whole planet full of zerg with forty marines, three reapers, five goliaths, and his last remaining Warhound. Bad enough that fielding even that minuscule force had all but stripped the *Hyperion* of any internal security.

But to order him to ride in a protoss shuttle instead of loading everyone aboard good, solid Dominion dropships was just plain over the line.

The protoss stopped. *I am Alikka,* his voice came in Cruikshank's brain. *I am a Nerazim, a dark templar. I speak for Rahas. You are Colonel Abram Cruikshank?*

"I am," Cruikshank confirmed, clamping a lid hard on his sudden surge of extra annoyance. Typical arrogant protoss, deliberately using short sentences as if his listener were a child struggling his way through a first-reader book. "I command the Dominion ground forces."

Alikka's eyes flicked over the marines, reapers, and mechs standing silently behind Cruikshank. *I would think a major would be a more appropriate commander for such a small force. Were you not informed of the agreement regarding security for your ships?*

Cruikshank ground his teeth. "You mean the one about your ships guaranteeing our ships' safety in case of a zerg attack?"

That is the agreement I refer to, yes, Alikka said. *There is thus no need to leave any of your war force aboard your ships.*

"Sure," Cruikshank said. "You'll forgive me if I don't simply take your word for it."

The irritating part was that he *had* been ordered to do just that: to trust that the protoss would beat off any zerg that tried to attack and board the Dominion ships, and to take everything he had left to the surface.

He'd done it, albeit under protest. But there was no way he was going to tell Alikka that. Protoss thought too highly of themselves as it was. "But don't worry about our numbers," he added. "We'll do just fine." He hesitated, but it was too good an opportunity to pass up. "Better than your people did at Point Two, anyway."

Alikka bristled, his eyes flickering with blue light. Cruikshank tensed, but the eyes went back to normal as the protoss regained control of his emotions. Apparently, he and the deck crew weren't going to be treated to the sight of a dark templar flashing some psionic energy around the hangar. *We were taken by surprise,* he insisted stiffly. *It will not happen that way again.*

"I'm sure it won't," Cruikshank said. "But enough chitchat. We're ready to board whenever you've got space cleared out for us."

You may come now, Alikka said. *You will take care not to get in our way. Either aboard ship or when we reach the planetary surface.*

Without waiting for a response—probably not really wanting one, either—he turned and strode back toward the shuttle.

"And people wonder why I hate protoss," Cruikshank muttered. "All right, you heard him," he went on, raising his volume to drill-sergeant level. "Mount up. Mind you don't step on anyone's toes along the way."

The marines set off in brisk double time, the reapers behind them, the goliaths clumping along at the rear. Grabbing the handholds on his Warhound, Cruikshank started climbing to the cockpit.

Still, at least Alikka was an honestly arrogant SOB protoss. Cruikshank didn't like them, but he knew how to work with them. Not like that wimpy, waste-of-space researcher Ulavu, whom Valerian had insisted on sending with the survey team.

He snorted. *You will take care not to get in our way,* Alikka had warned. Better he should warn Ulavu not to get in Halkman's way.

Bad enough that the team was saddled with a human civilian. But to have *two* civilians was just pushing the hell out of the numbers.

And protoss or not, the bottom line was that Ulavu *was* a civilian.

If his lack of military competence got someone killed, he would damn well answer for it.

Cruikshank would personally guarantee that would be an experience the protoss would never forget. No matter how hard or how long he tried.

CHAPTER SEVENTEEN

The team had covered barely five kilometers when they hit the ambush.

Whist, in front, took the brunt of the attack. Four zerglings appeared without warning over a rocky rise and hurled themselves at him. He barely got his C-14 up before the first slammed into him, knocking him backward off his feet. A second later two of them were swarming on top of him while the other two hit the ground, changed direction, and charged straight at Tanya.

Which was, Tanya reflected, their first and last mistake. The team was traveling in its usual order, with Whist in front, Tanya and Ulavu behind him, Erin behind them, and Dizz bringing up the rear. Even as Tanya fell back a couple of quick steps, Ulavu darted between her and the charging zerg, the focusers on the backs of his wrists blazing as he activated his warp blades. Tanya waited just long enough to see him slice open the first zergling, and then she did a quick one-eighty, putting her back to the second attacker. A small frontal assault was often a diversion, which suggested something nasty might be sneaking up from the rear.

It was. Slipping through the woods behind Dizz were two more zerglings, with a baneling behind them, trying to keep up. Even as Dizz skidded to a halt and leveled his P-45 at the zerglings pinning down Whist, Tanya stretched out with her power and sent a pair of quick one–two blasts to the new attackers' interiors, dropping them with crackling *thud*s into the undergrowth. Dizz spun around at the sound and blasted a couple of bursts into the baneling.

The baneling slowed, and Tanya finished it off with a blast to its lungs. A second blast to its heart, just to make sure, and she turned back to Whist, wondering if he'd made it through the attack alive.

To her relief, he was already getting to his feet, the carcasses of the four zerglings scattered around him. Ulavu was standing over him, looking back and forth as he scanned the area for more trouble.

"Never a dull moment around here; that's for sure," Dizz commented as he and Erin hurried forward to join the rest of the group. "We should market this place as an adventurer's paradise. You okay, Whist?"

"Yeah," Whist said with a grunt. "Luckily, the damn things weren't really going for me." He eyed the multiple lacerations in the bag over his shoulder, then reached down and picked up what was left of a C-14 magazine. "They wanted the ammo and the spare guns. I guess even psyolisks don't like getting shot at."

"So they'd rather have a marine alive and kicking and disarmed than no marine at all?" Dizz asked. "Interesting. Also kind of stupid."

"Oh, they'd have gotten around to me sooner or later if Ulavu hadn't been so quick on the uptake," Whist assured him. "For a wimpy little researcher type, Ulavu, you're a damn good fighter. Thanks."

You are welcome, Ulavu said. Gingerly, he pressed a hand against his side. *But they were not merely attempting to disarm you. I fear that this was also a reconnaissance mission. The master of our opponents wished to learn whether we had sustained injuries during the attack and forced landing.*

"Yeah, we usually just call that a *crash*," Dizz said.

"How are *you* doing?" Tanya asked, running a critical eye over Ulavu's tunic. There were no fresh bloodstains, but with his injuries fully bandaged, that might not mean much.

The strain of fresh battle appears to have reopened one of my wounds, Ulavu admitted. *Possibly two of them. But I do not believe my combat skills will be seriously affected.*

"Yeah, we'll see how you do when the psyolisks get started on you," Whist said grimly. "How'd you get hit, anyway? I thought you dark templar could turn invisible or something."

"He was trying to be incognito, remember?" Tanya said, giving Whist a warning glare. Criticizing protoss battle tactics was not a smart thing to do.

Either Whist missed the look or he just didn't care. "Yeah, keeping your fighting skill a secret is great until it gets you killed," he said. "So?"

I agree, Ulavu said calmly. *In this case, that was not my intent. The psyolisks' psionic attack at Point One was sufficiently enervating that I found myself unable to achieve light-bending at the same time that I was wielding Void energy offensively. Under the circumstances, it seemed best to choose attack over defense.*

"Terrific," Whist said. "So you're saying we've got only about *half* a dark templar."

"That's enough, Whist," Tanya said stiffly.

"I'm just running the numbers," Whist said, glaring back at her. "We're short on ammo. We're short on portage capacity, and now we're short half a protoss. Not exactly something to cheer about. Especially since what we're *not* running short of is psyolisks."

"Actually," Erin put in, "we might be."

"Come again?" Dizz asked, frowning.

"We may be running low on psyolisks," Erin said. "I've been thinking about them, and about their connection with the adostra."

"I thought we decided there *wasn't* a connection," Whist said, crouching and sifting through the scattered debris of his ammo bag.

"Of course there is: xel'naga essence," Erin said. "I don't know anything about xel'naga, but I *do* know a fair amount about zerg genetics and how they're incorporated into the various species they conquer and adapt. If we assume Abathur used similar percentages to create the psyolisks, we have a baseline for how much xel'naga essence he would have needed to sneak out from his adostra assembly line."

"I see where you're going," Dizz said. "Those six empty pods at Point One?"

"Exactly," Erin said. "He would have told Zagara how many adostra he could make from the xel'naga essence they had on hand."

"Or she might have been able to confirm the number independently," Tanya said.

"Right," Erin said, nodding. "Either way, he tells her he can make, say, a hundred eighty adostra, or sixty for each focal point. But he then only creates a hundred sixty-two, leaving himself ten percent of the xel'naga essence to play with."

"Which he then uses to make psyolisks," Tanya said. "Presumably he needs less of it since all he wants is to add projective psionic power to an existing zerg base."

"Right," Erin said again. "From their overall looks, I'm guessing he took the hydralisk baseline and made them smaller. He probably took out the poisoned needle spines, too—they didn't use anything like that at Point One, and they surely would have done so if they'd been available."

"Designed for close-in combat," Whist murmured. "Buzz the target's brain and just go for the slash attack, and you don't need needle spines."

In addition, psionic attacks are most effective at close range, Ulavu pointed out. *Retaining needle-attack capability would be of little use to their primary attack strategy.*

"And making them zergling size lets them get into places hydralisks can't," Whist said. "Oh yeah, these were designed by a master, all right."

"I just hope he hasn't figured out a way for them to breed," Dizz said darkly.

"Zagara said they couldn't use normal spawning pools," Tanya reminded him.

"She only said they couldn't use them for adostra," Dizz corrected. "She never mentioned the psyolisks."

"Because she doesn't know about them," Tanya said.

"So we assume," Dizz said. "That hasn't yet been proved."

"A standard spawning pool would certainly require some serious modifications," Erin said. "I'm guessing Abathur will eventually figure out a way, though it might depend on how much xel'naga essence is in the psyolisks." She lifted a finger for emphasis. "*But* that also assumes he'll have enough psyolisks left at the end of this to experiment with. Which brings us back to what I said about us running short of psyolisks."

"You really think he's running out?" Tanya asked.

"Think about it," Erin said. "At Point One he probably figured we'd kill a couple of them at the most before they killed us." She made a face. "Or rather, you. Only it didn't work out that way, and he lost all forty, plus the four Whist and Ulavu took out on the way in. At Point Two, he was probably figuring the disruptor would destroy the adostra cavern but leave most of his psyolisks alive."

"He doesn't know much about disruptors, then," Whist said.

"Hey, *we* barely know about them," Dizz pointed out. "They're pretty new, aren't they, Ulavu?"

They are, Ulavu confirmed. *I was not even aware the Dominion knew their full capabilities.*

"Considering Cruikshank didn't bother with a defensive crouch and got knocked flat on his butt, I'm guessing we don't," Whist said.

"That would also fit with the overall personality profile we've always assumed for the evolution masters," Erin said. "Abathur would know a lot about terrans and protoss as species, certainly enough to know how to tune the psyolisks' psionics against us. But he would have far less interest in our tech, except where it impinges on his efforts to advance the zerg."

"And don't forget, he's been pretty busy lately," Tanya said. "First there was Kerrigan; then there was the intelligence and comprehension upgrade she ordered for Zagara, and then the whole Amon thing. Reading protoss tech manuals is probably low on his priority list."

"So if he *is* running short of psyolisks," Dizz said, "it makes perfect sense to aim for our weapons instead of us. He still wants us to invade Point Three and destroy the adostra, but he doesn't want to lose any more of his shock troops than he has to."

"Which begs the question of whether he knows about Tanya," Whist said thoughtfully. "Maybe he hasn't figured out yet what she can do."

Tanya frowned. That one hadn't occurred to her. "Why wouldn't he?"

"Why *would* he?" Whist countered. "Except for the times you start a fire on the outer carapace, what you're doing is pretty invisible."

"But the zerg have a psionic connection with each other," Erin said. "That's why we need the psi blocks. Wouldn't he find out that way?"

You have forgotten that the psyolisks are a radical departure from other zerg forms, Ulavu said. *Their psionic communication may be on an entirely different level.*

"Though they're close enough to normal zerg that they can order them around," Tanya pointed out. "They *are* the ones ordering the normal zerg, right?"

"Well, they're the ones on the scene, so I assume so," Whist said. "But that's not what I'm talking about. That kind of control is local. I'm talking about detailed information going from psyolisks to the zerg hive-mind network to Abathur. *That* may not be possible, in which case he still might not know about our pyrokinetic."

"And of course, there's no reason he has to be communicating with them in real time, either," Dizz said. "That's a point in our favor. Standard orders in this case would be pretty simple: kill half the humans and protoss, let the survivors destroy the adostra pods, then kill them, too."

Erin shivered. "You have such a way with words."

"Comes with the territory," Dizz told her. "Be thankful you're just slumming today."

"I'll never complain about a nice quiet lab again," Erin agreed. "Too bad we didn't save one of the psyolisks. An autopsy could have told us a lot."

"Given that we burned all of ours and Cruikshank sent his to the four winds, that would have been a little tricky," Whist said.

"If you'd like, we can try to save you one from Point Three," Dizz offered. "Is that everything, Whist?"

"Everything useful," Whist said sourly as he got back to his feet, three intact C-14 magazines stretched across his palms. "They left us a grand total of three mags. Whoop."

"Plus the spikes still left in the ruined ones," Tanya pointed out. "We could bring them along for reloading."

"What, in the middle of battle?" Whist shook his head. "Not a chance." He hefted the slashed bag. "Besides, this thing's also on the casualty list."

He crumpled the bag and tossed it to the side. "We'll just have to count on Abathur still wanting to leave us alive long enough to torch Point Three." He inclined his head to Tanya. "Come on—we've wasted enough time. Move it out."

"And stay sharp," Dizz added. "Like Whist said, they don't need all of us to get there alive."

Valerian was in his cabin, trying to grab an hour of sleep, when the urgent call came.

Matt was waiting for him at the bridge hatchway. "We spotted it about ten minutes ago," he said as the two men hurried toward the sensor station. "It's moving slowly—almost drifting—but definitely coming this way."

"And you're sure it's a devourer?"

"There's no doubt," Matt said grimly. "I've put our fleet on Red Alert, and Artanis has done the same with his."

Valerian nodded. Devourers were one of the zerg's preeminent space-superiority weapons: a flying monstrosity that could spit globs of acid spores that would rapidly eat at a warship's hull, with devastating results. If Zagara was sending devourers against them . . .

"The thing is," Matt continued, "there seems to be only the one of them out there."

"Just one?" Valerian asked, frowning. Usually devourers attacked in packs. "You're sure?"

"Unless they've figured out how to cloak," Matt said. "And as I said, it's not moving anywhere near their usual attack speed."

"So what *is* it doing?"

"Not a clue," Matt said as they reached the sensor station. "Commander?"

"It's still on intercept course, sir," the tactical officer said. "Seems to be slowing . . . Wait a minute." Abruptly, he stiffened, and his hand darted out to slap a button. "Alert!" he shouted as the flashing red lights of Red Alert went to the solid red of Imminent Attack. "Missile released—on intercept course!"

"Stand by point defenses!" Matt called.

Valerian leaned closer to the displays, his pulse thudding in his ears. The devourer had released something, all right. And that something was headed directly toward the *Hyperion*.

But slowly. Very slowly. In fact, not much faster than the devourer's own leisurely pace. "That doesn't look like an acid-spore glob," he said.

"I agree, Emperor," the tactical officer said, frowning at his displays. "It appears to be another zerg."

"A zerg?" Matt echoed. "What species?"

"I don't know, sir," the officer said, still frowning. "It's bigger than a broodling or a bile swarm. Certainly not glave wurms."

Valerian exchanged looks with Matt. And devourers didn't launch any of those types of biological weapons anyway. At least not the devourers they were accustomed to fighting. "You're sure it's not just a strangely shaped acid-spore glob?" Valerian asked.

"No, Emperor," the officer said firmly. "*That* I'm sure of. It's holding its shape too well. But it's still too far out for me to tell what kind of zerg it is."

"Admiral?" the officer at the point-defense station called. "Should we take it down, sir?"

Matt rubbed at his cheek. "Not yet," he said. "Let's let it get a little closer."

"The devourer's veering off, sir," the tactical officer said. "Changed course to . . . It appears to be heading for the protoss mothership."

"Comm, send an alert on the bogey to Hierarch Artanis," Matt ordered. "He's probably already on it, but let's make sure."

"Unidentified missile resolving, sir," the tactical officer added. "By configuration, I'd say it's a hydralisk. But the size doesn't fit."

Matt sucked in an audible breath. "I'll be damned," he murmured. "You thinking what I'm thinking?"

"I do believe so," Valerian agreed, the knot that had formed in his stomach dissolving. "Commander, can we track where on the planet that devourer came from?"

"Not all the way, Emperor," the tactical officer said, keying his board. "Here's what we've got."

The track appeared on the display, and Valerian smiled. "Admiral?"

"I see it, sir," Matt agreed. "Point defenses? Stand down. Hangar Control, I want a tug sent out to retrieve that object. Be careful not to damage it."

"I don't understand, sir," the tactical officer said. "What *is* it?"

"A present from Overqueen Zagara, perhaps," Matt told him. "She evidently had her zerg sift through the debris around Point Two and dig up a dead psyolisk for us to examine."

The officer huffed out a snort. "She might have told us."

"I'm guessing she wanted to go to Point Two personally, or at least get close enough to supervise the operation," Valerian said. "Maybe the transmitter she was using was permanently installed in the conference structure and couldn't be easily moved."

"Though she could have told Abathur to call it in," Matt added. "Unless he was already out of the area. Would have saved us a lot of misunderstanding and potential gunfire."

"Maybe she *did* tell him to contact us," Valerian said, gazing at the display. "Maybe creating that exact effect was why he ignored her."

He felt Matt's eyes on him. "You're thinking he's the one pulling the strings here?"

"I don't see it being anyone except him or Zagara," Valerian said.

"I also can't see how anyone but a zerg with an Overqueen's level of control could get a devourer to deliver the psyolisk to us—devourers aren't usually transports, and we're way too far out for any zerg with only local reach. If this is a goodwill gesture, it has to be coming from Zagara, which leaves Abathur as the likely candidate to be the enemy."

"If it *is* a goodwill gesture," Matt warned. "That hasn't yet been proven. I'm also a little vague on what Abathur's motive would be."

"Same here," Valerian admitted. "But I think we need to let it play out." He pointed at the display. "Actually, I'm thinking she dug up *two* dead psyolisks. We should probably let Artanis know he's about to get a delivery of his own."

"I'll handle it personally." Matt tapped the tactical officer's shoulder. "And be sure to keep a close eye on everything else, Commander. If this gift isn't from Zagara, it could be someone's idea of a diversion."

"Yes, sir."

Matt headed off toward the comm station. "And while you're doing all that," Valerian said to the tactical officer, "signal the med section. Tell them to wake up Dr. Talise Cogan and prep the biolab.

"Tell them they're about to perform the most important autopsy of their lives."

After what had happened to the survey team's dropship, Cruikshank had fully expected that the protoss would have to beat off an attack or two themselves on their way through the atmosphere.

They didn't. But it was probably simply a matter of the zerg not being sufficiently quick on the uptake. The shuttle and its twin-phoenix escort had reached the five-hundred-meter mark and were starting their final deceleration when a dozen mutalisks appeared over the craggy mountains to the north and came screaming toward them. But they were too far away, and the ships were too low, and even as the phoenix pilots rotated to bring their ion cannons to bear, the mutalisks veered away.

Which was a shame. Cruikshank had seen what protoss ion cannons could do to flying zerg, and watching this lot get shredded would have been highly entertaining.

Of course, maybe that was *why* they were leaving. Maybe whoever was running the show also remembered what ion-cannon fire did to pretty little zerg carapaces.

Not that retreating now meant they wouldn't be back. They could have done a one-eighty, headed straight back over the mountains, and just kept going. But instead they'd done a ninety and headed northeast toward where the big mass of returning zerg were clawing, rolling, and lumbering toward Focal Point Three.

Clawing, rolling, and lumbering straight at him.

The phoenix pilots obviously didn't believe the mutalisks were giving up, either. They continued to rotate their ships as the shuttle settled to the ground, keeping their weapons trained on the retreating zerg in case they had second thoughts.

Cruikshank glowered at his display with a few second thoughts of his own. Up in high orbit, this had seemed like a good idea. Now, at ground level, he wasn't nearly so sure.

We will deploy here, Rahas ordered as the shuttle's starboard hatch opened. The two sentries floated out, with the line of Templar and Nerazim following close behind. *We will take the center of the line. You and your terrans, Colonel Abram Cruikshank, will guard our flanks.*

"Understood," Cruikshank said, clamping down on his temper. So he and the rest of the Dominion forces were to be relegated to support positions while Rahas and the protoss took the brunt of the upcoming action?

Typical. *Big egotistical glory hounds.*

But Admiral Horner had told him to play nice, and he would do his best to comply. This was war, and egos didn't enter into it.

Besides, as he'd already noted, neither force could do this alone. Rahas could push the Dominion forces to the sidelines if that soothed protoss pride, but he couldn't win without them.

Cruikshank took another look at the outside display, running his eyes over the terrain. He'd already studied it as best he could from orbit, but there was no substitute for looking over a battlefield at ground level. If he anchored his goliaths at the ends, two at the edge of the marshland and three by the cliffs, and put the marines inside to screen them and take out anything small—

He froze, feeling his eyes widening. Across the compartment, the line of protoss heading out of the hatch suddenly staggered, two of them nearly falling over. For a fraction of a second he just gaped—

And then it clicked. Protoss—staggering—

"Alert!" he shouted into his comm, turning the Warhound toward the hatchway and kicking it to speed. And all the terrans were still inside, damn it, waiting for the protoss who'd insisted on going out first. "We're under attack. Get the hell outside and—"

But it was already too late. He'd barely made it two steps, and was wondering if he could even get past the protoss still slumped in the hatchway without crushing any of them, when there was a sudden, violent crack like overhead thunder, and the deck canted beneath him, throwing his Warhound sideways across the compartment.

He slammed full-bore into the bulkhead, the impact shoving him painfully into the Warhound's safety harness. A second later, as a scattering of curses filled his headset, he was thrown back again as the deck righted itself.

"What the *hell*?" someone bit out.

"I said *outside*," Cruikshank snarled. At least whatever had thrown the shuttle around had also scattered the protoss clear of the hatchway. He got his balance back and clumped the Warhound outside.

A quick scan showed no zerg closing in on them from the east, south, or west. That was something, anyway. He took a few more steps away from the hatch, double-checking, then turned around to look at the shuttle.

It didn't take much to rock a shuttle that way, the dumbfounded thought occurred to him as he took in the situation. All you needed was a devourer, flying in low from the exact opposite direction the pack of mutalisks had taken earlier when they retreated, ramming into the ship at full speed. Probably had timed the attack for the moment the protoss pilot and crew were all dazed and confused. The fact that the phoenixes' ion cannons were pointed the wrong direction had probably been a factor, too.

The phoenixes.

Cursing under his breath, he hurried around the shuttle's stern.

He expected the worst, and he got it. Both protoss fighter craft were also down, with a devourer lying across each one. Both were still uselessly facing the direction of the departing mutalisks, one of them with its nose buried halfway into the ground.

And then that final bit of Cruikshank's assessment sank in. *The moment the protoss pilot and crew were all dazed . . .*

He cursed and kicked the Warhound into motion, continuing his run around the shuttle's stern and past the phoenixes. Everything they'd gleaned so far about the psyolisks indicated that they had to be relatively close in order to wrest control of normal zerg away from the sector's more powerful but far more distant broodmother.

Sure enough, there they were, slithering through the tall grass as fast as they could go. A pair of the familiar red-spot-backed mini hydralisks.

Briefly, he wondered if they'd been lurking in the grass while they guided the devourers to their crash-landings or whether they'd ridden one of the monsters in, suicide-attack style. Not that it mattered to the end result. After lining up his rail guns, he fired a round at each of them.

The Warhound's plasma-field-charged slugs didn't carry the same momentum as a gauss rifle's spikes, so the impacts didn't send the psyolisks flying across the terrain the way a C-14 burst would have. Still, blasting the psyolisks into fine mists of carapace dust and purple blood was equally satisfying. "Everyone okay?" he called, lowering the weapons. "Sound off."

One by one, in good order, the marines, reapers, and goliaths checked in. Midway through the count a yellow light winked on in the comm section of Cruikshank's board: the *Hyperion* calling.

Well, Horner would just have to wait. Cruikshank had more urgent matters on his plate right now. The Dominion force finished checking in. "Rahas, what about your people?" he called. "Rahas? Hey, protoss—somebody—talk to me. Is everyone all right?"

This is Alikka, the dark templar's voice came in his mind. *Rahas has been injured.*

Cruikshank snarled a curse. The battle hadn't even started, and already they had casualties. "What happened?"

He was partially crushed when the devourer's attack moved the shuttle.

"How bad is it? Will he be able to direct your part of the battle line?"

He is unconscious, and cannot participate in the battle. I have ordered for him to be taken back aboard the shuttle.

The ship that currently had a dead devourer lying across the top. "You want us to get that devourer off? Between the goliaths and me, I think we can shift it."

There is no time, Alikka said grimly. *Battle will soon be upon us. There is also no point to moving any of the devourer carcasses. The hulls were breached by the impacts of the attack, and neither the shut-tle nor the phoenixes will return home without repairs.*

"What about warp fields?" Cruikshank asked. "Can't you use one of those to get Rahas back?"

They are not functioning correctly, Alikka said.

"The psyolisks?"

So we have concluded, Alikka said. *But do not be concerned, Colonel Abram Cruikshank. The medical pod will begin the healing process immediately. Rahas will recover.*

"Got it," Cruikshank said. Assuming any of them lived through the battle, which was starting to look less and less likely. "Are any other protoss hurt?"

The remainder of my force is unharmed. I will now take command.

"Yeah, I figured that," Cruikshank said, eyeing the yellow light. "Better start deploying your people. Goliaths One and Two, head to the edge of the marshland—twenty-meter separation. Goliaths Three, Four, and Five, you're by the mountains. Platoon One, you're supporting the marshland group; Platoon Two, you're at the mountains. Got it? Double-time it to your positions. I'll stay here by the ships; reapers, you hang back here with me."

He waited to make sure everyone was heading to their proper positions. Then, finally, he tapped the long-range comm switch over the yellow light. "Cruikshank."

"Where the hell have you *been*?" Horner's frustrated voice burst into his headset. "We tried to warn you about those devourers. Now it's too late."

"With all due respect, Admiral, it was always too late," Cruikshank ground out. "Turns out psyolisk power is just as good at knocking out our long-range comms as those psi blocks Halkman's tearm is carrying."

There was a brief pause. "I see," Horner said, sounding marginally less angry. "What's your situation?"

"Not good," Cruikshank conceded, shifting his gaze to the far end of the grassland. Any minute now, the zerg horde would come charging out of the forested area over there. "The shuttle and phoenixes are all down, so scratch whatever air support we were counting on. Rahas is down—not dead, but out of the fight—and Alikka has taken over the protoss contingent. Protoss warp fields are inoperable. No Dominion casualties yet, but that's more from luck than anything else. Rahas could just as easily have sent us out first, and some of us might have been under the shuttle's edge when the devourer knocked it up on its side."

"Do you want me to try to get you some air support?" Horner asked. "We could get some Wraiths to you in about forty minutes."

"Thanks for the thought, sir, but forty minutes is way too long," Cruikshank said. "What we've got is what we've got."

There was a moment of silence. "There *is* one other option," Horner said, lowering his voice. "You could pull back right now, and we could hit the zerg force with another nuke."

Cruikshank stared in disbelief at the yellow comm light. Was Admiral Matt Horner, a man who'd so loudly and publicly stated his contempt for Emperor Arcturus Mengsk's ruthlessness, actually advocating dropping a second nuke on Gystt? "I don't think that would be a good idea, sir," he said carefully. "It would take out the protoss ships, along with Commander Rahas, who's currently undergoing treatment in one of the medical pods."

"You can't get him out?"

"Once treatment has started?" Cruikshank shook his head. "I doubt it. Not safely. He would be a sitting duck." He peered at the protoss ships. "And from the position of the impacts, it's probable the devourers took out the psionic boosters, too. So Alikka and his people are also on their own."

"And you don't think Alikka would be willing to leave Rahas behind as collateral damage without direct orders?"

Cruikshank drew himself up as much as he could while strapped into a Warhound's safety harness. "*I* won't leave him behind," he bit out. "I don't mind watching protoss die in battle. To tell you the truth, I kind of enjoy it. I don't even mind killing one in combat, if it comes to that. But this particular protoss is part of my force, and he was injured in the line of duty, and I'll be damned if I'll abandon him. *Sir.*"

"At ease, Colonel," Horner said. Cruikshank couldn't tell from his voice whether he was angry or just surprised. Right now, he didn't really care. "You're the man on the ground. It's your call."

"Thank you, sir," Cruikshank said stiffly. "Now if you'll excuse me, I have a battle to prep for."

He keyed off. *And a battle to lose,* he added silently to himself.

Because that, realistically, was where this was going. It had been marginal even before the devourers took out their air support. Without the phoenixes and their firepower, they simply didn't have the numbers to hold against the expected horde of zerg. Especially not with psyolisks messing up everyone's focus and attention.

But as he'd told Emperor Valerian, fighting was their job. Sometimes it was to fight a war. Sometimes it was to fight to keep a war from happening.

Whether that was still possible was another question. Personally, Cruikshank was convinced that Zagara had betrayed them, and that treachery had in fact always been her plan. He had no idea what she'd hoped to get out of this scheme, but he had no doubt that the end result was going to be a brand-new war.

But none of that was his concern. Maybe Valerian was being played for a fool; maybe he knew something Cruikshank didn't. No matter. Cruikshank's job was to fight where and when he was ordered, and to leave policy to his emperor.

He rather hoped he and some of his force would live at least long enough to see the end of today's events. But if emperors didn't always get what they wanted, colonels could hardly expect to, either.

"Colonel, we're in position," Goliath Four reported. "Also, I'm picking up some treetop movement about a klick into the forested area. I think that's probably our zerg."

"Roger that," Cruikshank said. "Okay, everyone, this is it. Dig in, lock and load. And if we don't see another sunset, let's at least see this field soaked in zerg blood."

CHAPTER EIGHTEEN

They were about a kilometer from Point Three, and had slowed their mad dash to a more controlled and hopefully quieter jog, when out of the corner of her eye Tanya saw Ulavu suddenly break step. *Are you all right?* she asked. *What is it?*

A second later a distant buzz appeared at the back of her brain. *Never mind,* she added. "Whist, we've got psyolisks."

"Yeah, I got that," Whist said, his eyes on Ulavu as he slowed to a halt. "How bad is it?"

"Not very," Tanya said. "Just a hint. They're probably all inside Point Three. You're not feeling anything at all?"

"Nope," Whist said. "Nice to see that there's *something* that isn't dumped in double helpings on marines. So either they know we're here or they're about to. Guess it's time to break radio silence and see if Cruikshank's come up with any other little chores he wants us to do."

"We're going to turn off the psi blocks?" Erin asked, looking around uneasily.

"*We're* not," Whist corrected. "*I* am. They're supposed to have a range of fifty to one fifty meters, so I'll go about forty, shut it off, and keep going until I'm far enough from Dizz's to get a signal."

You should not go alone, Ulavu said, and Tanya could sense the pain beneath his voice. *It is not safe.*

"I agree," Dizz said.

"So do I," Tanya seconded. "The psyolisks might not be close, but there could be other nasties around."

"Point," Whist conceded. "Fine—we make it a twosome. Dizz, you have the other block, so you're out. Ulavu's in no shape for a stroll, and anyway needs to conserve his strength." He cocked an eyebrow at Tanya. "That leaves you and me. Care for a stroll in the garden?"

"I thought you'd never ask," Tanya said. "Lead on."

"The rest of you, sit tight," Whist said, checking the mag and safety on his C-14. "You see anything that isn't us, shoot it."

The psi blocks turned out to be better engineered than even their creators had realized. Whist and Tanya had to go nearly fifty meters past the theoretical cutoff point before Tanya's heads-up display indicated a call from the *Hyperion.*

But it wasn't Colonel Cruikshank who was waiting at the other end. "Are you all right?" Admiral Horner asked.

"Mostly, sir," Whist said. "Dr. Wyland's got a cracked rib, and we're low on ammo. Other than that, we're ready to tackle Point Three. Any new orders?"

"No new orders, but new information," Horner said. "About three and a half hours ago, we dropped a psi emitter fifty klicks east of you to try to draw off the zerg around Point Three."

"And then someone nuked it," Whist said. "Yeah, we noticed."

"*We* nuked it," Horner said. "We saw your dropship get grabbed by those mutalisks and thought taking out the emitter would at least keep them from dragging you any closer to it."

"It mostly worked," Whist said. "Thanks for the thought."

"You're welcome, Sergeant," Horner said with just a touch of sarcasm. "The upside is that a lot of zerg were pulled away from Point Three. The downside is that a sizable number of them appear to be coming back at a high rate of speed."

Tanya frowned. "Why would they do that?" she asked.

"Because we think some of the psyolisks got drawn away with them," Horner said. "At Points One and Two they used normal zerg as a screen against attack. The psi emitter pulled the screen away from Point Three, and they're rushing to get it back in place."

"Terrific," Whist growled, craning his neck and peering through the trees to the east. "How long have we got?"

"More than you think, less than we'd like," Horner said. "Colonel Cruikshank has set up a Dominion–protoss battle line in a choke point about fifteen klicks east of you to try to slow them down."

Tanya looked at Whist, saw her own surprise mirrored in his expression. "Did we have that many marines and mechs aboard?" she asked.

"Not even close," Horner said heavily. "On top of that, all three of their ships were hit on the ground and put out of action. We couldn't warn them about the attack because the psyolisks can apparently knock out long-range comms. The protoss' warp fields are also down—probably another psyolisk effect—so that particular route in or out is gone. Unless the zerg numbers are a lot lower than we're expecting, Cruikshank's force is going to be overrun within . . . well, not long."

"I see," Whist said, his voice deceptively calm. "So our job is to get in, get your samples, and get the hell out before everyone gets killed?"

"Basically," Horner said. "Provided you don't go rushing in like maniacs and get you and your team killed along with Cruikshank's. That won't help anyone."

"I think I can guarantee there'll be at least one survivor," Whist assured him grimly. "Let me give you a quick rundown."

Tanya listened as Whist summarized the team's data, conclusions, and speculations. "Interesting," Horner said when he'd finished. "Seems a long way to go just to get the adostra pods destroyed, but it doesn't contradict anything we've heard up here. Any thoughts as to who's behind it?"

"Well, the pool of zerg who can think for themselves is pretty shallow," Whist said. "We're thinking Abathur, with Zagara as close runner-up."

"That's about where we're sitting," Horner said. "Except that it appears Zagara sent us a devourer with a pair of psyolisk corpses to examine, so we're thinking she's a more distant runner-up."

"Handy," Whist said. "Learn anything interesting?"

"Cogan and her team are still digging," Horner said. "I've sent you a data drop with everything they've found so far. It could be a diversion, of course. But since it's not a trap, and we can't figure out how Abathur could force a devourer to obey him this far off the planet, that leaves Zagara as gift-giver and Abathur as manipulative bastard."

"Sounds logical," Whist said. "We'll keep that in mind."

"But we still need adostra samples," Horner added. "So I'd better let you get to that. Good luck, Sergeant, to all of you."

"Thank you, sir. We'll check in again when we're finished."

Whist keyed off the comm. "Okay, psi block's on," he said. "Let's collect the others and get this show back on the road."

They retraced their steps, moving as quickly as the trees and undergrowth allowed. "I assume you realize the psyolisks *don't* have to keep any of us alive anymore," Tanya said. "Slaughtering us and Colonel Cruikshank's team will probably be enough reason for Hierarch Artanis to destroy Point Three."

"Yeah, I know," Whist said. "That's why I said we were going to get this done before everyone gets killed. That includes Cruikshank."

"I thought you didn't like him."

"Of course I don't like him," Whist said. "He's an officer. What does that have to do with anything? Listen, I've got a question for you. Remember how the tree palisade was set up at Point One?"

"Of course," Tanya said. The tension of upcoming battle was starting to dig into her. She forced it back. "Designed to be pushed out from the inside."

"Right," Whist said. "But who was supposed to do the pushing? The psyolisks?"

Tanya frowned. The psyolisks were lethal enough, but they didn't have nearly the body mass it would take to knock over trees that size. "I don't know. The adostra, maybe?"

"They're even smaller than the psyolisks."

"Maybe they get bigger."

"*That* much bigger?" Whist countered. "Remember the size of the trees, and the size of the pods. Unless adostra eat lead bricks, they're never going to have the mass to push them over and get out."

"Maybe they aren't meant to get out."

"Then why did Zagara design the palisade the way she did?"

"I don't *know,*" Tanya snapped, feeling the tension trying to turn into the red haze of anger. Why was he *arguing* with her at a time like this?

"Yeah, well, I think maybe I do," Whist said. "Remember Zagara talking about how the adostra can stimulate life and growth and all that? What if they can also go the other way?"

Tanya shook her head, still fighting the haze. "You lost me."

"Say you can help a tree grow big and strong," Whist said. "Say you can also make it wilt or go all puny and withered."

"Okay. Scary thought, but okay. And?"

"Now suppose you can make it grow or wither *on just one side.*"

Tanya caught her breath, the haze and frustration fading as she finally saw where Whist was going. "You make the leaves and branches on the cavern side wither," she said. "That puts all the weight on the other side. Enough weight, and the whole thing snaps off at the base."

"Opening the way into the big wild world," Whist said with satisfaction. "So it makes sense to you, too?"

"I suppose," Tanya said, still trying to work it all through. "But what's the point? What do the adostra do once they're out?"

"How should I know?" Whist said. "Head out into Gystt to plant apple seeds or burp out unicorns or something. My point is, if that's their exit strategy, they can kill, or at least choke off life. And if they can do *that*, we might just be able to grab ourselves a new set of allies."

"Oh my God," Tanya breathed. "If that works . . . but do we really want to go down that path?"

"If it keeps us alive?" Whist retorted. "Hell yes."

"I mean do we want to introduce the adostra to the idea of killing?" Tanya persisted. "Do we even dare do that?"

"Again: hell, yes," Whist said. "Besides, they have to kill the trees to get out anyway. Right?"

"They have to wither them on one side," Tanya corrected. "Not the same thing. In fact, now that I think about it, that could be more a test of control than it is of power."

"Fine," Whist said. "Power, control—whatever. The point is that their lives are on the line, too. If we can clue them in, they might be able to help us."

"Any idea how we might do that?"

"My money's on Ulavu," Whist said. "If the psyolisks and adostra all work off xel'naga psi, and Ulavu's the one the psyolisks hit the hardest, I figure he's got the best chance of talking to them."

"And persuading them to kill," Tanya said. "*And* to kill only the psyolisks and not us. This is a very dangerous can of worms, Whist."

"Well, we don't have to decide yet," Whist said. "Matter of fact, if the psyolisks are on top of their game, we may not ever have to decide." He looked sideways at her. "They still thumping around your brain?"

"Some," Tanya said. "Not so bad that I can't control it. You may be wrong about them hitting Ulavu the hardest, though. I get the feeling that they're spreading it out more or less evenly among the five of us. It's just that you, Dizz, and Erin aren't affected as much because you don't have psionic capability."

"I don't know," Whist said doubtfully. "They gave you a pretty good wallop back there at the beginning."

"Probably because I'm the only one wearing ghost armor and they figured I was the biggest threat," Tanya said. "After that first battle Abathur might have decided I wasn't any more dangerous than anyone else, so he started spreading out the attack to try to slow all of us down equally."

"So you're thinking he doesn't know about you or Ulavu?"

"I'm hoping that he doesn't," Tanya said. "I guess we'll find out in a few minutes when we see if he's changed his strategy any."

"I guess," Whist said. "Gotta say, it's sure a nice change to surprise every new batch of zerg we run into. Dizz? We're coming in. Hold your fire."

A minute later they'd rejoined the others. "Any problems?" Whist asked.

"No, it's been quiet," Dizz said. "You get through to Cruikshank?"

"I got through to Horner," Whist corrected. "Cruikshank's doing a Horatius at the bridge fifteen klicks from here to hold off the zerg that the psyolisks are bringing back from the psi emitter crater."

"Great," Dizz said. "I don't suppose you had time to give Horner a summary of our thoughts about psyolisks and Abathur and all?"

"I gave him the high points," Whist said. "We'll see what he and Valerian can make of it. Everyone ready to do this?"

"As ready as we're going to be," Tanya said.

Yes, Ulavu confirmed.

"Probably not," Erin admitted.

"Well, look at it this way," Dizz offered. "They're probably not ready for us, either."

"That's the spirit," Whist said. "Let's get in there and wrap this up."

"And if you've always wanted to go out with memorable last words," Dizz added drily, "this would be a good time to come up with them."

"Here they come," Goliath Four reported tensely. "Looks like . . . Seems to be all zerglings."

"Got a couple of ravagers hanging back at the tree line on this side," Goliath One added. "Not moving."

"I see them," Cruikshank confirmed, checking the range. The bile globs that ravagers could launch were nasty weapons, but at the moment those particular zerg were theoretically out of range of the battle line. He thought briefly about spending a Haywire missile to see if he could take out one of them anyway, but he decided to wait until they were closer.

Especially since this first wave looked like it was designed to test the battle line and make the Dominion forces spend ammo. Better to hold off until he could get an assured kill.

He frowned as he studied the enemy configuration. Perhaps more specifically, the wave seemed designed to test the protoss section of the battle line. While the flanks certainly weren't being ignored, the majority of the charging zerglings were headed for the Templar and the Nerazim in the center. "Alikka, I don't suppose you happened to bring another of those disruptors with you?" he asked.

There is one, Alikka answered. *But we are already too close to the enemy for its use. In the open, this one would devastate all within a three-kilometer radius.*

Cruikshank nodded. He'd guessed from the blast at Point Two that the protoss had improved the yield on the things since the Dominion had seen them in the war. Nice to have it confirmed, though.

"Understood," he said. "We'll save it for our endgame. Last protoss standing, and all that. What about those sentries?"

The impact from the devourer warped the casings for their disruption beam projectors and damaged their zero-g engines. The crew is working to repair them.

Great. "Tell them to hurry," he said. "Marines, keep your fronts clear. Goliaths, support the marines, but send whatever you can spare into the center. Reapers, support the center. Stay behind the protoss and out of my line of fire, and hammer the zerg in front of them. The last thing we want is them turning one of our flanks."

He got a quick string of acknowledgments, and as the reapers took to the air and everyone else opened fire, he sent a careful look along the tree line at the far end. Somewhere back there were the psyolisks that were driving the attack.

But wherever they were lurking, they were staying out of sight. Luckily for them. He turned his attention back to the battle, picked a spot where the zerglings seemed particularly clumped, and sent a couple of plasma slugs into their midst. A handful of the beasts exploded into blood and shards, joining the scattering of other zerglings lying dead with gauss rifle spikes in them. "Ease back your center fire," Cruikshank ordered as the zerglings closed on the line. He didn't want a misplaced shot or shattered pieces of zerg hitting the protoss. "Clear flanks and watch for the second wave."

In front of him, the center of the line erupted in a blaze of shimmering fire as the Templar activated their psi blades and the Nerazim ignited their warp blades. Cruikshank held his breath . . .

And with a cacophony of screeches from the zerg and an answering chorus of psionic war cries from the protoss, the battle was joined.

Cruikshank had seen protoss in battle before, but the sight never failed to fill him with grudging awe. The Templar and the Nerazim spun and writhed like dancers trapped in an insane choreography, their blades flashing and circling, sometimes blazing extra bright as the wielder's battle fury surged, sometimes vanishing briefly as the focused energy disappeared deep inside an enemy's body. Each protoss had become an island now, surrounded by swinging sickle limbs and waving clawed tails and ever-growing piles of carcasses at their feet.

But there was a subtle difference between this battle and the others Cruikshank had seen. The protoss here seemed to be moving slower than usual, and their movements weren't quite as clean or graceful. The piles of slaughtered zerglings around them were impeding their footwork, slowly narrowing their maneuverability. One of the Templar stumbled and disappeared instantly beneath a mound of flailing claws. A second protoss went down, this one a Nerazim.

And then, across the field, a second wave of zerglings emerged from the trees and charged across the grassland.

"Reapers, move in!" Cruikshank snapped, kicking his Warhound into motion. The protoss were already in serious trouble. If that second wave reached them, they'd be done for.

And if the center of the line went, the two Dominion flanks wouldn't be far behind.

"All units, take out that second wave," he ordered. "Spend missiles if you have to, but take it out."

He was almost to the nearest of the beleaguered Templar—this one a power-suited zealot—when Goliaths One and Four sent a pair of Hellfire anti-air missiles into the center of the oncoming zerg.

Cruikshank cursed under his breath. Using heavy arms against zerglings was a criminal waste of resources when there were larger, tougher zerg undoubtedly waiting their turn to attack. But he didn't have a choice. The psyolisks' psionic assault had put the protoss in a critical position, and if the second wave was allowed to reach them, there would be nothing the Dominion force could do to help. The wave had to be stopped, period.

As for the remnants of the first wave, it was time to get creative.

A Warhound's feet were wide and flat, with gimbaled toes designed for traversing many different types of terrain. They were certainly not designed to kick or step on zerg. Which wasn't to say that in the hands of a skilled operator they couldn't do both.

And Cruikshank was a *very* skilled operator.

He'd disposed of probably four of the crowd of zerglings before the zealot in the center of the mob seemed to notice him. For a second the Templar's defense faltered with sheer surprise at the sight of the mech looming over him—

One of the zerglings lunged to the attack, its sickle limbs cutting instead into the Warhound's neosteel lower leg as Cruikshank kicked it away. "You—protoss—knee joint!" he called, planting his feet to either side of the protoss. "Up up *up!*"

For a split second he thought the zealot either had missed the idea or was still too stunned or brain-buzzed to understand. Then, with a final slash from his psi blades, he leaped up onto the Warhound's right knee joint.

He was still slower than Cruikshank had seen protoss in other battles, and his bladework was still decidedly sloppy. But with his feet and legs no longer entangled by the bodies of dead enemies, the renowned protoss agility was once again in play. Even as the zerglings tried to reach up to him, the zealot was slashing downward, stabbing his psi blades through skulls and carapaces and slicing off limbs.

Some of the zerglings switched to attacking the Warhound's legs, probably hoping to bring down both the mech and the protoss now riding it. But the zealot was on it. He leaped back and forth between the mech's knees, slashing some of the zerglings and driving the rest back. Cruikshank, with no way to assist him, turned his attention back to the still-incoming second wave, sending plasma slugs sizzling across the open ground with his rail gun. Between attacks he kept an eye on the woods for signs of the third wave or, even better, a glimpse of an unwary psyolisk. The zerglings dropped and staggered and fell . . .

And then, to Cruikshank's surprise, it was over.

He looked around the battlefield, his stomach churning. Eight of his forty marines were down. Goliath Five was canted at a nearly unworkable angle with a broken leg. On the protoss side, it looked like five of the twenty warriors were dead. Bracing himself, he turned his attention back inward to his cockpit displays and checked the med readouts.

To his relief, only two of the eight downed marines were dead, though a third was in bad condition. The other five had merely been knocked down, their CMCs taking varying amounts of damage. "Alikka?" he called. "What's your status?"

Five are dead, the protoss's bitter words came in his head. *The honor of the Nerazim is shaken.*

"Never mind the honor," Cruikshank growled. "Let's put our heads together and figure out a new strategy before the next wave rolls us up like a blanket."

There was a short pause. *Very well. I will hear your suggestions.*

Cruikshank felt his lip twist. Damn generous of him, considering that the protoss were the ones who were mostly getting massacred at the moment. "Okay, listen up," he said. "New formation. Goliaths, you're holding the ends of the line—two each. G-Five, what's with your leg?"

"It's a mess, but I can still limp," Goliath Five's pilot reported. "Battle maneuvering's going to be really limited."

"Can you straighten up at all?"

"No. Firing's a little funky from this angle, but I can do it."

"Let's see what we can do about that," Cruikshank said. He tapped a point on his battle display about a third of the way in from the mountains. "Get yourself to the spot I marked and turn to face up-battle. Alikka, get the nearest protoss over to him and cut the damaged leg off clean. Then cut the other leg to match so that he can fire level. Congratulations, G-Five: you've been promoted from mech to pillbox."

"Great. Thanks a lot, Colonel."

"No problem," Cruikshank said. "Marines, forget the flanks—you're going to spread out along the whole line, with at least two of you to each protoss. Your job will be to flank them, one on each side, and thin out incoming zerg so the protoss won't be so overwhelmed when the enemy reaches the line. And remember that they're under heavy psionic attack and won't be as accurate as usual, so make sure you keep your distance. Getting your head sliced off by accident is embarrassing."

"Colonel, we've got incoming," Goliath Three reported. "Third wave on the way."

Cruikshank looked across the field. Another line of zerg had appeared, all right, and was crossing the open area toward them.

Only instead of zerglings, this wave was made up of banelings and ravagers. As he watched, the banelings pulled out in front, their bulging acid sacs jostling as they moved. The ravagers, in contrast, were moving almost leisurely, clearly looking for the point where the terrans and protoss would be in range of their plasma discharge.

And in the woods behind them, Cruikshank caught a glimpse of hydralisks waiting in the wings.

"Move it, everyone," he ordered, raising his rail guns to target two of the distant ravagers. "Looks like they've decided this round will be acid, bile, and plasma. Kill them as far back as you can and be ready to dodge projectiles. Alikka, what's the word on those sentries? We could really use them on this one."

Agreed, Alikka said. *The disruption beams are still inoperable, but they are able to fly and to lay out force fields. I will warn you: the power is unreliable, so they may not be able to replace the barriers as they dissipate.*

"Anything they can do will be useful," Cruikshank assured him. "Get them moving."

A moment later the two flying robots shot past Cruikshank from the direction of the shuttle. They passed the line of marines and protoss and continued on a hundred meters, then switched direction to travel crossways to the zerg vector. As they flew, they laid down force-field barriers across the zerg path.

"Okay, everyone: breather time," Cruikshank called. "Remember the barriers don't last very long, and be advised the sentries may not be able to replace them. So when the barriers pop, be ready to fire before the zerg can get up to speed again."

He got acknowledgments from his team, then ran a quick check on his weapons levels. Whenever the force-field barriers vanished, he would be ready.

"Bring it on, you bastards," he murmured to himself. "Bring it on."

CHAPTER NINETEEN

Whist had expected the group to be ambushed before they reached the mesa. To his surprise, they weren't.

To his even bigger surprise, they reached the small clearing in front of the mesa to find that someone had left the door open.

"Well, *that's* different," Dizz commented uneasily as the group gathered at the edge of the clearing.

Whist nodded silently. One of the trees in the outer row had been toppled and was lying across the clearing. The tree behind it in the middle row had fallen on top of it, and the next tree back in the inner row had likewise been felled.

Beyond the fallen trees was the entryway cavern. Beckoning invitingly.

"I don't like it," Erin murmured. "Why would they open a path for us? *How* did they do it, even?"

"The *how* is simple enough," Whist said. "You can see the hack marks at the bases from here. The psyolisks just had a bunch of hydralisks do some pruning."

As to why, perhaps Abathur has conceded the fact that we will enter regardless, Ulavu suggested.

"More likely he's got a trap laid out in there," Tanya said.

"Yeah, that's my guess," Whist agreed. "Well, no point in putting it off. I'll let you know what I find." Resettling his grip on his C-14, he started forward.

"Whoa," Dizz said, taking a long step and catching Whist's shoulder. "Where do you think you're going?"

"You want to wait for an engraved invitation?" Whist countered, more harshly than he'd intended. The thought of going into the darkness alone wasn't exactly a pleasant one. "There's a mass of zerg on the way, and Cruikshank can't hold them forever. Someone has to go in there, and I'm the one with the armor, the weapons, and the training. So all of you just shut up, hang back, and get ready to come running if I yell for you."

"I hate running," Tanya said calmly, stepping to Whist's side. "I'll just walk behind you, okay? Don't worry—you and your armor are welcome to take the first brunt of the attack if you insist."

She is right, Ulavu seconded. *You must not enter alone. She or I must accompany you.*

"If those are my choices, I'll take her," Whist said. Ghosts were ghosts, and he still didn't entirely trust her not to go all crazy and amok on him.

Still, up to now she'd stayed pretty cool in combat. And with her, at least, he wouldn't have to worry about getting accidentally stabbed in the back by a warp blade if the psyolisks threw Ulavu a sudden dizzy spell. "Shake a leg, Tanya."

As Whist had already noted, the tree takedown hadn't exactly been precision quality. The trunks were lying on top of one another, angled upward and pressing against the ones to either side. He and Tanya had to scramble up and over them, then force their way through the narrow gap to get to the cavern entrance.

To find the entry area deserted.

"Strange," Tanya murmured as they played their lights around the walls, floor, and ceiling. Even the ramp and the switchback landing at the top were empty. "You think Ulavu was right about Abathur giving up?"

"I think *I* was right about it being a trap," Whist countered. "The hook's just farther in, that's all. Dizz? Bring everyone in. And watch your backs—this could be a trick to hit us while we're split up."

Fortunately, it wasn't. Two minutes later, they were all inside.

"Yeah, this is not at all creepy," Dizz said, looking around. "Ulavu? How you doing?"

The pressure is intense, Ulavu admitted. *But I am able to withstand it.*

"Tanya?"

"No problem," she said. "I think they're still spreading out their attack."

"Let's do this before they get around to fine-tuning it," Dizz said. "You want me to stay and watch the entryway?"

"Not this time," Whist said. "I'm more concerned about what's inside than what's outside. We'll hear anything that tries to force its way in."

"You're the boss," Dizz said. "Standard marching order?"

"Standard order," Whist confirmed. "Let's go."

He approached the first landing cautiously, keeping one eye on the area above them and watching for any trouble that might be lurking out of sight. But again, there was nothing. He rounded the landing corner and came into full view of the next ramp section. Still nothing.

"Awfully quiet," Erin commented uneasily.

"Agreed," Dizz said. "Did we ever figure out how the psyolisks got in these caverns in the first place?"

There is light, Ulavu pointed out. *That implies the existence of ceiling ducts. If they are large enough, the psyolisks could traverse them.*

"I suppose," Dizz said. "And come to think of it, if Zagara wasn't in on the plan, they'd have to have been moved in after she'd buttoned everything up."

"So where are they?" Whist asked. "I expected at least a reception committee."

The words were barely out of his mouth when, at the top of the ramp, a pair of zerglings suddenly appeared around the corner of the landing and charged.

Whist's C-14 shuddered in his grip as he put a burst of spikes into each of them. He'd put a second burst in the one on the left, sprawling it to the floor, when the one on the right abruptly collapsed. "Tanya?" he asked.

"Yes," she confirmed.

"Thanks." He half turned to look at Dizz. "Happy now?"

"Oh, yes," Dizz said drily. "Thanks for asking."

"No problem." Whist turned back forward and started up—

"A moment, please?" Erin said. "May I make a suggestion?"

"Sure," Whist said.

"We've got a gap in the tree palisade behind us." She pointed at the dead zerglings. "We have two carcasses we can stuff into it. Should we?"

"Absolutely," Whist said, slightly annoyed that he hadn't thought of that himself. Plugging the gap wouldn't completely prevent an attack from behind, but it would make it slower and noisier. "Dizz, Tanya, keep an eye on the ramp. Erin, grab yourself a carcass."

The zergling Whist got was the one Tanya had torched. He couldn't feel the heat through his gauntlets or smell the burnt odor through his helmet, but all the way down the ramp he could vividly imagine both. He wedged his carcass in the middle part of the gap, put Erin's in the inner part, and then led the way back up to the others. He resumed point position, and they continued their climb.

They reached the top without further incident. Through the

archway leading into the main cavern, Whist could see the familiar expanse of rough floor and the tiers of adostra pods at the far end. As with the Point One cavern, there was nothing standing between them and the pods.

"I've changed my mind," Dizz muttered as they gathered outside the archway. "I'm not happy again."

"Suck it up, buttercup," Whist advised. Not that he was exactly thrilled, either. Back at Point One, they'd been greeted by a double row of psyolisks waiting along the sides. Here, with their ammo low and everyone except Erin sporting damaged armor, that would be an unpleasant scenario to deal with. "Okay. Tanya and I'll go in, back-to-back, and see what's waiting in the wings. If we come running out again, move to the far wall and get ready to fire. This archway's pretty wide, but it's the closest thing we've got to a choke point."

"Especially since we've effectively blocked our exit," Dizz said. "Seemed like a good idea at the time."

"Still seems like one," Whist bit out. "We've got ammo, a dark templar, and a pyro. Whatever the psyolisks brought to the party, we can match them. Come on, Tanya."

He started forward, his torso and C-14 half turned to the right. Tanya walked at his side, her attention half turned to the left. They eased through the archway . . .

"Well?" Dizz prompted. "What have we got?"

Whist swallowed hard. "The reception committee I wanted," he said, eyeing the double line of zerg standing motionless at the far side of the chamber. "More zerglings. About . . . got to be thirty just on this side."

"Same number over here," Tanya said, her voice taut. "Also drawn up in two lines. There are three psyolisks skulking in the back trying not to be seen."

Whist peered closer at his lineup. "Yeah, there are four on this side," he said. "Missed them before."

"So what are you waiting for?" Dizz said. "Take them out."

No. Ulavu spoke up urgently. *You must not harm the psyolisks.*

"But they're hurting you," Erin said.

They are also surely keeping the zerglings in check, Ulavu said. *If they are killed, Tanya Caulfield and Sergeant Foster Cray will be immediately attacked.*

Whist scowled. He was right. There was no reason why the zerglings should still be sitting there unless the psyolisks were forcing them to do so.

"I don't think so," Erin said. "Remember what happened at Point One. We were attacked outside and driven in, but once we killed the psyolisks all the rest of the zerg outside dispersed. Probably went back under the control of the local broodmother."

"Who'd been ordered not to attack us," Dizz added. "She may be right."

She may also be only partially correct, Ulavu warned. *We were within the chamber for several minutes after the psyolisks died. Similarly, at Focal Point Two, the protoss and terrans were incapacitated for a time after the disruptor blast. The broodmother may require that time to reassert her control once the psyolisks are gone.*

"We don't know that," Erin pointed out.

"Doesn't matter," Whist said. "Even if it only took a minute for the broodmother to take control, we'd still be toast. There's no way we can take sixty zerglings in a mad rush."

"I'm just wondering if Ulavu's judgment might be a little clouded," Erin muttered. "They've been talking in his head all this time—"

There has been no speech, Ulavu insisted. *It is pressure and a loss of combat focus. Nothing more.*

"Loss of focus means they're getting to your intellect," Erin persisted. "If they are—"

"I said it doesn't matter," Whist said tartly. "We're not killing the psyolisks—*yet*—and that's that. The rest of you, get in here. Help us figure out what the hell they want."

"You think they want something?" Dizz asked as he and the other two eased into the chamber.

"Well, they're not posing for pictures," Whist growled. "Tanya? Any ideas?"

"No," she said. "Well . . . maybe. So far, what they've mostly wanted was for us to kill the adostra and then die. If this is really the last group of adostra . . . ?"

"Then maybe if we kill them, we get to live?" Whist suggested.

"That's all I can think of," Tanya said.

"Yes, but why do *we* have to be the ones?" Erin asked. "Why can't Abathur kill them himself?"

Perhaps if he took direct action, Zagara would know, Ulavu said. *Even an evolution master is still a zerg. He is thus linked to all other zerg and under the command of the Swarm leader.*

"I don't know," Dizz muttered. "Seems like splitting hairs to claim you're not doing something while at the same time pushing someone else to do it."

"That's where lawyers come from," Whist said sourly. "So what do we do?"

Tanya cleared her throat. "I think we ought to at least go over to the pods," she said, her voice just a shade too casual. "Just to take a look." She paused a fraction of a second. "*All* of us."

Whist felt a tight smile twitch the corners of his mouth, his private conversation with Tanya in the woods belatedly coming back. Right—*all* of them. Specifically, Ulavu. If they could get him close enough to the adostra to touch minds with them . . . "Yeah, that's a good idea," he agreed.

"You want anyone to guard the entry?" Dizz asked. He seemed a little puzzled by the decision, but he was willing to go along.

"No point," Whist said. "If they want us, they've got us."

"I suppose," Dizz said. "You're right; taking on sixty zerglings would be a tall order. I suppose we could handle thirty, though. Right?"

"Probably," Whist said, frowning. Now it was *Dizz* who was sounding a little too casual.

But he couldn't worry about that now. Everything hinged on getting Ulavu to the adostra, and hoping they could understand him. Preferably before the psyolisks launched their attack.

It was a crazy idea. But he was fresh out of better ones. "Okay," he said. "Weapons ready. Let's go take a look."

The advantage of the protoss' force fields was that they could block anything but the biggest zerg. The disadvantage was that they were short-lived and required undamaged sentries to replace them.

Which meant this was a temporary solution at best. Still, whatever time they could buy would help both the survey team and Cruikshank's own force.

He was mulling over the possibilities when, across the field, the force-field barriers began to wink out.

Cruikshank swore under his breath as the line of banelings surged forward again. Still, they were starting from a standstill instead of coming at them full bore. That was worth something.

In fact, with good, solid Dominion troops like his, it was worth a hell of a lot.

The first barrage was devastating. Most of the marines managed at least two bursts from their gauss rifles before the first line of banelings made it back up to speed. Some of the more experienced fighters got off three or even four bursts.

"Keep firing," Cruikshank called, peering at his displays as the second line of banelings surged forward. Back near the tree line, two of the ravagers were scuttling forward, clearly trying to get into range to launch their acidic bile. He targeted both and fired his rail guns. Both ravagers staggered as the plasma slugs blasted massive holes in their carapaces and sent them thudding to the ground.

Behind them, yet another line of banelings and ravagers appeared through the trees and started across the field. "Alikka, we've got another wave coming," he warned. "Another line of force-field barriers might be handy."

Agreed, Alikka said. *I will so order. Be wary of launched acidic spheres.*

Cruikshank rolled his eyes. As if he hadn't already been doing that. "I'm on it," he growled, looking back at the tree line. The sentries were heading away from the battle line, moving closer to the ravagers. That would put the next line of force-field barriers out farther, giving the Dominion fighters more time to fire once the barriers dissipated and the zerg resumed their charge.

But it also meant that, as the sentries laid down the barriers, they were closer to the lurking ravagers. Even as Cruikshank looked along the line, two more of the bile-spitters moved out of the trees toward the sentries. He targeted both and sent another pair of slugs blasting through their carapaces.

He was making sure they were down for good when, out of the corner of his eye, he saw the two sentries suddenly begin to twitch and wobble violently. He jerked his eyes back to them just as they both gave final shudders and disintegrated.

"What the *hell*?" he breathed as the shards scattered to the ground. "Alikka—what the hell just happened?"

But even before the protoss could reply, the reality belatedly hit him. There were hydralisks in the woods—he'd seen them earlier as they awaited their turn to attack. They'd stayed within the tree line, and he hadn't paid them much thought since then. Their poisoned needle spines, after all, only started becoming effective against Dominion armor and mechs at much closer ranges.

The sentries, laying out their new line, were unfortunately within that critical distance.

The robots didn't give a damn about the poison, of course. But the sheer mass of material moving at near-hypersonic speeds, digging into and through their outer shells, had been enough to take them down.

It was the hydralisks, Alikka said, his voice dark, his words confirming Cruikshank's deduction.

"Yeah, yeah, I got it," Cruikshank said.

And the worst part was that it was his fault. He'd told Alikka to send the sentries farther down the field, smugly secure in the knowledge that the ravagers couldn't get into range to launch their acidic bile blobs before he could take them down. He and the other Dominion forces were the only ones on the line with heavy ranged weapons, the only ones who could deal with that kind of threat. He should have remembered the hydralisks, located them, and dealt with them.

He'd failed. And that failure might have doomed them all.

In the distance, the line of force-field barriers the sentries had laid began winking out. "Get ready," Cruikshank said. "Here they come again."

"Colonel?" Goliath One called. "Sir, check your six. A couple of the banelings got through."

Cruikshank looked at his rear display, adding another seething curse to his mental collection. Of course some of the banelings had gotten through. There were too few soldiers trying to hold too much ground.

At least the zerg hadn't turned and attacked the troops from the rear. That was something, anyway.

But then, the psyolisks' ultimate goal wasn't to destroy Cruikshank's force. Their goal was to get to Point Three and take down Halkman's team. "What do you want me to do, blow them up?" he growled.

"No, sir, I want you to *look* at them," Goliath One said. "Do they seem confused to you?"

Cruikshank frowned. Goliath One was right. Instead of continuing their single-minded charge toward the woods and Point Three fifteen klicks away, the banelings had made it about fifty meters past the grounded protoss ships and then slowed to a halt. Now they were just looking around, rather like marines on leave wondering where the hell they were and what the hell they'd been drinking.

He blinked. Not *like* marines on leave. *Exactly* marines on leave. Somewhere along their mad rush, they'd reached the limit of the psyolisks' leash, and the broodmother of this section of the continent was trying to reestablish her control.

And with that, the solution to this whole mess was obvious. All he and Alikka had to do was pull the battle line back beyond that point, and every subsequent wave of zerg would break on the invisible boundary and become harmless. The only counter the psyolisks would have would be to also move forward, and if the terrans and the protoss pulled back far enough, the psyolisks would have to leave the cover of the woods. Once they did *that,* the goliaths and the Warhound would make quick work of them.

So really, the battle was won. And all it would cost was one more life.

Because the wrecked shuttle was still within the psyolisks' current range. Once the Dominion and protoss forces pulled back, there would be nothing to stop the zerg from tearing up the ship and the injured Rahas in his medical pod.

One protoss life, in trade for the lives of everyone else.

For a long moment Cruikshank stared at the shuttle and phoenixes, lying there with dead devourers draped across them, his conversation with Admiral Horner flicking across his memory. Cruikshank had talked a good talk about not leaving a member of his team behind, and at the time he'd meant every word of it.

But now, with his troops under pressure by an enemy that would never run out of zerg to throw at him, things weren't nearly so clear. If he could carry out his mission without losing any more of his people, at the cost of just one life—and a protoss life, at that—shouldn't he at least consider it?

Behind the ships, the banelings had ceased their confused wandering and were heading toward the river and marshland on the battlefield's south flank. They passed the phoenix on that side and disappeared.

Cruikshank focused on the phoenix. It would have been nice, he thought darkly, to have retained at least one functioning fighter craft to use against the enemy.

A functioning fighter . . .

He turned back to the battle. While he'd been preoccupied, the second line of banelings had mostly dissipated, because either they'd been killed or slipped successfully through the line and were on their way to breaking free of the psyolisks' grip. One more marine was down, he noted grimly, and two more protoss.

In the distance, more ravagers were moving forward. "Alikka?" Cruikshank called, sending a few more plasma slugs sizzling across the battlefield at the ravagers. "I've got a suggestion. A way to remake the line that should save us a lot of lives." He hesitated. "But you may not like my conditions."

Speak your idea and your conditions, Alikka said.

"Right." Cruikshank braced himself. "Here it is . . ."

CHAPTER TWENTY

"There's another wave gathering in the woods," the tactical officer reported. "This one seems to be mostly hydralisks, with more banelings as mortar backup."

"There may be some zerglings, too," Matt said, pointing to the infrared overlay. "Probably to lead the way and make Cruikshank's force spend more ammunition."

Valerian nodded heavily. "I'm starting to wish we'd nuked it," he muttered. "The whole forest."

"That end can still be achieved if you so desire it," Artanis's emotionless voice came over the speaker. "The Nerazim Alikka possesses a disruptor he can deploy. Its effects would be cleaner than a Dominion tactical nuclear weapon, but no less devastating."

"Too risky, Hierarch. We've pushed Zagara hard enough already, with the psi emitter, the nuke, and all the adostra we've killed. It's still in her best interest to come to terms with us, but at some point she might very well say to hell with it. We can't afford to let her reach that point."

"Unless she is in fact orchestrating these events," Artanis countered.

"I don't think so," Valerian said. "Did you see the survey team's report?"

"I saw it. I do not entirely follow your logic."

With an effort, Valerian disconnected his focus from the urgency of the battle below him. "We were sent a pair of psyolisk corpses," he said. "I don't believe anyone but Zagara could have controlled the devourer that far from the surface. If the corpses had been booby-trapped or part of a diversion, then I would agree that she was playing us, or at least buying time for some scheme. But the corpses were neither. I conclude, therefore, that Zagara is still acting in good faith."

"And your similar indictment of Abathur?"

"It seems reasonable that once Zagara came up with the plan to find and deliver the psyolisks, she would let us know her intentions," Valerian said. "She didn't take her transmitter with her, but presumably left orders for someone to send us a message. Abathur would be the logical candidate—he can communicate with us, and he was already on the scene."

"But if he was the manipulator," Artanis said slowly, "it would be in his best interests to disobey that order."

"Right," Valerian said. "To make us believe instead that Zagara had run out on us without explanation."

"And his purpose?"

"I'm hoping that once we settle things with Zagara we'll be able to ask him."

"Your argument is logical, Emperor Valerian," Artanis said. "But logic is not always reality. I will withhold final judgment, but I will not yet accept Zagara as innocent."

"Withholding judgment is all I ask," Valerian assured him. "Thank you."

"But be advised that we are watching the leviathans closely," Artanis added. "Any attempt by them to leave Gystt will be met with force."

Valerian grimaced. But he had a point. If Zagara or another broodmother decided to make a run for it, they could pack enough zerg inside just one of the massive creatures to keep a new war going for years. "Understood," he said.

"New battle line drawing up," Matt murmured from beside him.

Valerian shifted his attention back to that display. "Can they handle another assault?"

"I don't know," Matt said heavily. "I hope so. Looks like this one is taking longer to set up than the last couple. Maybe hydralisks are harder for the psyolisks to corral than zerglings or roaches."

"Larger brains and higher intelligence?"

"Or just bigger and nastier," Matt said. "Which reminds me." He pulled out his comm and punched in a connection. "Biolab, this is Admiral Horner," he said. "How's the autopsy going?"

"We've barely started, Admiral." Dr. Cogan's voice came from the comm's speaker. "This thing is exceptional. We're running data feeds back and forth with the protoss, but even working together, we'll be months digging out all the details."

"We haven't got months, Doctor," Valerian said shortly. "Give us something we can use."

"Yes, Emperor," Cogan said. "The bad news: we haven't been able to pinpoint the part of the brain that controls the psionic power. That means we have no idea how to destroy or jam or confuse it."

"Keep looking," Valerian said.

"We are, Emperor," Cogan said. "But here's something interesting. We know zerg can hear—we see that on the battlefield all the time—but we've always assumed most of them rely on the psionic network for orders and communication in general. We also know that higher-level zerg like queens and overseers *can* understand terran speech."

"And?" Valerian prompted.

"According to the protoss' data, there's a direct correlation be-tween speech-center development and zerg hierarchy level," Cogan said. "And as near as we can tell, this psyolisk has a *very* well-developed speech center."

"Interesting," Artanis said. "Yet they have psionic power. Why would they need to understand speech?"

"Because without it Abathur can't talk to them," Valerian said as it suddenly clicked. "With their psionic power coming from xel'naga essence, the psyolisks probably work on a different level from the zerg. Perhaps Abathur guessed that he wouldn't be able to get through to them the traditional way, so he built in speech centers that would let him just talk to them."

"Can he *do* actual speech?" Matt asked. "I didn't think even queens could do that."

"In a sense," Cogan said. "He just needs a psi-to-speech translator like the ones the zerg have on their long-range transmitters."

"He probably didn't even have to guess about the psionics," Matt offered. "If he'd already worked on the adostra, he'd have known that zerg and xel'naga psionics run on different levels."

"Higher-level zerg like Zagara and Mukav also seem to have be-come more comfortable with verbal communication since the end of the war," Valerian said.

"Then the situation is one of great urgency," Artanis said. "Since the onset of the attack against Alikka's force, I have pondered the strategy being used by the enemy. It is inconceivable to me that psyolisks alone could be directing the battle. It follows that some other zerg must be there with them."

"You mean Abathur is *there*?" Valerian asked, looking at the dis-play with sudden fresh interest.

"I do not know," Artanis said. "For that question raises yet an-other. We know little about Abathur, but what knowledge we possess suggests that he was not created for warfare. There is no reason for him to have the skill of tactics."

"That's disturbing," Valerian said, frowning at the display. "Because *someone* down there seems to have that skill."

"Overqueen Zagara would have such abilities," Artanis reminded him.

"Yes, she would," Valerian conceded. Artanis's earlier comment about logic and reality flicked through his mind. "Again, all we can do is see it through. It looks like the survey team's made it into Point Three. Let's see what they find."

"And let's hope they don't say anything they don't want the psyolisks to hear," Matt added.

According to the rangefinder in Tanya's visor, the main chamber in Point Three was exactly the same size as the one in Point One.

So why, she wondered distantly, did it feel like it was taking so much longer to walk across it to the adostra pods?

I do not believe there is any possibility that this can work, Ulavu warned. *To place all our hopes on this plan threatens to bring destruction upon us all.*

Tanya glared across the chamber. It was one thing to give something a shot and fail. It was another to simply dismiss it out of hand. *I don't see why it can't work,* she said. *It's xel'naga essence, and your people had a long history with the xel'naga. Besides, the psyolisks' attack is especially hard on you, so we know their psionics are able to link with yours.*

He gave a mental sigh. *That is not the point, Tanya Caulfield. We are told that adostra stimulate growth in plant life. By its very nature and expression, plant life is different from animal life.*

I understand that, Tanya said, fighting hard for patience. This was really not the time for a philosophical discussion. *But the adostra themselves are animals, right? So you should be able to contact them.*

And if that indeed proves to be the case, what shall I say to them? Would they, who celebrate and nurture life, understand the concept of nurturing death? Even if they do, how then would they embrace such an idea?

Tanya winced. She'd made much the same argument with Whist earlier, and still wasn't convinced she was wrong.

But that was before they found themselves facing sixty zerglings under psyolisk control. *Will you at least try?*

I will try. Ulavu paused, and she sensed him opening up his private communication with her to include the rest of the group. *I cannot promise I will succeed. I cannot promise even that I will be able to communicate with them. The adostra are far more alien than anything the protoss have ever encountered.*

Which was, Tanya knew, an impressively high bar. Throughout their long history the protoss had been everywhere and seen everything. If a bunch of dreaming creatures in nutrient pods were that intimidating, this plan might rapidly hit a dead end.

"Just do your best," Erin said encouragingly. "That's all anyone asks."

"Sure, don't worry about it," Dizz added. "You know us terrans. We never say die. Well, except to zerg," he amended. "Occasionally to protoss. But mostly to zerg. You get the point."

"You can quit babbling anytime," Whist told him.

"Sorry," Dizz said. "I just get nervous in enclosed spaces. Low ceilings and all. Most reapers do."

Tanya glanced upward. The ceiling wasn't *that* low, really. It was a good five meters above the floor, more than enough room for even Ulavu to walk without any risk of bumping his head. Still, for someone used to soaring over hills and battlefields, she supposed even five meters could get claustrophobic.

"No," Dizz said quietly. "*Look* at the ceiling."

Frowning, Tanya went back for a closer look. The ceiling was rocky, with the usual bumps and hollows a cave might have. She couldn't tell if they had been carved out by zerg claws or zerg acid or a combination of both. Ahead, just this side of the first tier of adostra pods, was a particularly lumpy indentation, looking rather like a giant protoss had slammed a fist into it. Beside the indentation was an especially large protrusion that looked like an embryonic stalactite.

And right between the two of them was a hole.

Not just a deeper pit, she saw as they approached it, but an actual hole, angling upward through the rock. She couldn't tell how far it went, but there was faint light inside, so some part must make it all the way to the surface. Possibly the route, or one of the routes, that the psyolisks had used to get in.

She looked at Dizz. He was looking back, his eyebrows raised as if she was missing something.

She looked at the hole again, trying vainly to reach out to his mind and at least get a clue as to what he was going for. But her teep power was too limited. The hole was there; it evidently reached to the top of the mesa . . .

And it was big enough for a person to squeeze into.

Not someone in CMC armor, like Whist or Erin. Not someone wearing the shoulder-mounted turbines of a reaper jump pack. Certainly not someone with the wide shoulders of a protoss.

But a human in the more compact armor of a Dominion ghost might just make it.

Was Dizz suggesting that she escape?

Her first reaction was revulsion at the very idea. How *dare* he think that she might run out on them?

But following on that reflexive anger was the sobering thought that they very well might all die in the next few minutes. If that occurred, with psyolisks blocking long-range communications, the only way Emperor Valerian and Hierarch Artanis would ever know what had happened was if someone got out before it was too late. And the only someone who could do that was her.

Even worse, if she was trapped here, Abathur might well carry her off somewhere to try to add her pyrokinesis to the zerg arsenal.

Maybe Dizz was right. Maybe, for all those very good reasons, she should make a break for it.

She squared her shoulders. *No,* she told herself flatly. She'd waited a long time for a chance to use her power for the Dominion. There was no way in hell she was going to abandon her team. Not like this.

As for Abathur, if she and the others were going to die, she would make sure there wasn't enough left of her for even an evolution master to use.

What did you mean, no?

Tanya made a face. That was supposed to have been a private thought, not a message she was sending to Ulavu. Apparently, she'd leaned a little too hard on the word. *Dizz is trying to get me to do something,* she told him. *But I can't—*

"Here we go," Whist said, coming to a halt by the first tier of pods. "Ulavu, do your stuff. Everyone else, spread out—not too far—and start poking around like you're looking for the best ways to get into the pods."

"And to destroy them," Tanya added.

"And to destroy them, right," Whist said. "Whoever finds a way in first, get everyone else over there so that we can block the psyolisks' view while Erin takes her samples. Got it? Go."

They spread out, Dizz going a couple of pods to the left, Whist going the same distance to the right. Ulavu picked one of the pods in the center between them, and Tanya stepped up to one beside his. *You can do this,* she said. *Take your time. Start by just trying to say hello.*

I am trying, he replied, his mental voice unusually stressed. *They are . . . very alien. I cannot . . . understand. Nor do I believe they understand me.*

"Uh-oh," Erin murmured from Ulavu's other side.

"What is it?" Whist asked quietly.

"The zerglings," Erin said. "They're looking . . . really restless."

Tanya sent a quick look at both ends of the chamber. The zerglings weren't just restless. They were twitching and shifting their feet, their sickle limbs moving up and down, their mandibles opening and closing.

"That's not good," Dizz said. "What the hell set them off?"

"Could they have figured out what we're doing?" Erin asked.

"Of course they've figured out what we're doing," Whist said grimly. "Damn it. Or at least they've figured out that we're not here to destroy the pods. We could have done that from across the room."

"But then why—?" Erin broke off.

"You got it," Whist said. "They let us cross the room so that we'd be as far away from the exit as possible."

"Okay, first things first," Tanya said, fighting against the buzzing in her brain and the fear twisting through her stomach. She would *not* let Abathur have her. "Can we get Erin her samples before they make their move?"

"I still don't know how to get in," Erin said. "But Ulavu could cut one open."

No, Ulavu said, his voice even more strained. *I cannot understand them. But in the core of my being, I know that opening the pod will kill the adostra inside.*

"So what?" Dizz retorted. "They're all going to die anyway, right? That's what Abathur wants."

They may die. But they will not die by my hand.

"He's right," Erin said. "We've killed too many of them already. Way too many. We are *not* going to kill any more."

"Fine," Whist said. "Then I say we give Ulavu another thirty seconds to make contact, then see about beating a dignified retreat."

Tanya eyed the twitching zerglings, and the psyolisks behind them. "They'll never let us do that," she warned.

"Probably not," Dizz said. "In that case, I guess we'll just have to kill them."

And without warning, the entire mass of zerglings charged.

They were going to die, Tanya thought distantly as she turned to the double line on her left and reached out with her power to the closest attacker. The zergling got two more steps and then stumbled and fell. She turned her attention to the one beside it, hearing behind her the muffled stutter of Whist's C-14 as he opened up on his own wave of attackers. To her right, she caught the reflected light off the pods as Ulavu activated his warp blades.

She was looking almost directly at Dizz when he kicked in his turbines and leaped straight up into the air.

Aiming for the hole in the ceiling that he'd pointed out to her earlier.

Tanya's first horrified thought was that he was running away, that he was hoping somehow to get through the narrow gap and escape the certain death heading toward them. She looked up, following his path as he rose, a flash of combined anger and betrayal sending a flicker of red across her vision.

But he wasn't heading for the hole, she realized. He was instead aiming for the big fist-shaped indentation in the ceiling.

She frowned, utterly confused now, wondering if panic could have thrown him off-course. He half turned to face her and the others, almost delicately settled the high tortoise-neck collar of his jump pack against the edge of the hole, and opened up his turbines full blast.

And as Tanya watched, the sudden violent windstorm slammed full force into the converging line of zerglings, scattering them sideways and throwing them back across the chamber.

"I got these!" he shouted, his words barely audible over the labored scream from the turbines. "Work down the other side."

Tanya spun around, feeling a smile baring her teeth. She should have known he had some other plan hatching.

But even with the enemy effectively cut by half, they were still dangerously close to the edge. Whist was working methodically through the attackers with his C-14; Erin was making some progress with her own gauss rifle, and with Tanya now joining them with her pyrokinesis, they were making headway.

But zerglings were tough. They could only be killed so quickly, and there were a hell of a lot of them. Peripherally, Tanya saw that Ulavu had closed down his warp blades—the zerglings were still too far out of melee range anyway—and had pulled out a small disk the size of a drink coaster. He crouched, cocking his hand and the disk toward his chest, then hurled it at the approaching zerglings.

And as it flew, the edge of the disk erupted into a ring of blazing green warp-blade fire, becoming a meter-diameter pinwheel of destruction. It struck the first zergling in its path, cut straight through it without even slowing, did the same to the zergling behind it—

The psyolisk waiting at the far end of the chamber tried to get out of the way. But the surprise of the unexpected attack was apparently too paralyzing, and the weapon itself was traveling too fast. The psyolisk had barely started to move when the spinning blade cut through its torso, dropping it to the stone floor. The Void energy vanished as quickly as it had appeared, and the now-plain disk bounced off the back wall and onto the floor.

Whist gave a wordless war whoop. "*Nice* job!" he shouted. "You got any more?"

No, only the one, Ulavu answered. *Tanya Caulfield, can you retrieve it?*

Tanya grimaced. All the way across the chamber, on the far side of two lines of zerglings. But he was right. The zerglings and psyolisks were momentarily confused and disorganized, and the disk was way too good a weapon to abandon. "I can try!" she shouted back. "Whist, clear me a path."

"Sure." He shifted his aim, pummeling the center of the line. Erin shifted her fire as well. Tanya tensed herself for a run, painfully aware that this was still going to take exquisite timing . . .

"Never mind—I'll get it," Dizz called. "Tanya, take this side." Before Tanya could answer, the pitch from his turbines changed, and he shot past overhead. Swerving to avoid the zerglings' efforts to pluck him out of the air with their sickle claws, he flew over their lines toward the disk.

Tanya didn't wait to see any more. She spun around, hoping Dizz's close-range turbine blast had done some damage to the zerg on that side.

It had, but not as much as she would have liked. The zerglings had been scattered back, and from the looks of things, some of them had been rather violently tossed and shoved across the rough floor. But aside from a few that were still scrabbling dizzily for balance, they seemed to be mostly pulling themselves together.

Bracing herself, she focused on the one that seemed most ready to resume the charge, then stretched out. The zergling shuddered and collapsed. She turned her attention to the next one—

Throw!

Tanya risked a glance over her shoulder. At the far end of the chamber, Dizz had landed and scooped up Ulavu's disk. The other three psyolisks on that side were charging, clearly hoping to get to him before he could take off again. Dizz flipped the disk toward them and threw power to his turbos—

The disk again blazed with Void energy, slashing through the lead zerg's torso and out its back. Its claws, still raised, scraped harmlessly across Dizz's armored shins as he scrambled for altitude. The second psyolisk in line dodged as the disk shot past, dropping sideways out of its path. The pulsating blades vanished, and with unexpected dexterity the third psyolisk darted out a claw and snatched the disk out of the air.

And writhed back in pain as the warp blades again blazed out, cutting off the limb holding the disk and slicing through the bony part of the psyolisk's head.

The last psyolisk, the one that had managed to dodge the disk, spun around and lunged toward Dizz, claws slashing furiously at his feet. It dropped in a heap as Whist sent a triple burst of spikes into it.

Tanya didn't wait to see more. She turned back to find a dozen zerglings had massed together and were converging on her, sickle limbs raised to strike. She targeted one—watched it die—targeted the next—sent it wobbling to the floor—targeted a third—realized with a sinking feeling that she'd never get all of them in time—shied back as something small and dark shot past her shoulder—

And jerked as the disk spinning toward the zerglings once again came alive with Void energy. Two more of her attackers fell, cut clear through, and the others scattered out of the disk's path, their charge momentarily blunted.

Tanya focused on the next in line, determined to use the few seconds that Ulavu had bought her to their fullest. A subtle flicker of light at the far end of the chamber caught her eye as she killed the next zergling in the pack.

And then Ulavu brushed past her, warp blades blazing from his forearms. Without hesitation, he waded into the mob. Tanya shifted her attention away from the zerglings within his reach and focused on the ones standing to the side, awaiting their turn. One of them stiffened and died; then a second and a third. A pile of carcasses was starting to gather at Ulavu's feet, threatening to trap him in place.

There was a subtle movement at the back of the chamber: the three psyolisks that had been coordinating the zerglings on that side were scuttling along the wall toward the archway. Apparently, they'd judged the battle lost and were getting out.

She smiled tightly. Like hell they were.

Thirty seconds later, it was over.

"Everyone okay?" Whist called as they all lowered their weapons. "Ulavu? You okay?"

I am not incapacitated, the protoss said.

"Good," Whist said shortly. "Not what I asked. Try again. How many new wounds have you picked up?"

Three. None are life-threatening.

"Let's take a look," Whist said, pulling out his medpack and stepping over to him. "Tanya? You're looking a little shaky, too."

"I'm fine," Tanya assured him. Her skull was throbbing with the worst headache of her life, and her implant felt like it was going to catch fire and burn out the core of her brain. She hadn't realized until it was over how much sheer effort she had been putting into the battle, or how much that effort would affect her.

But it was over, and she should have plenty of time to recover before Abathur could organize anything in the way of a rematch.

Anyway, she was certainly doing better than Whist. His armor showed at least two fresh claw marks, one of them going clear through to his undersuit. He must have blasted those particular zerglings squarely in the head at point-blank range.

The men and women in the ghost program barracks made a lot of snide jokes about marines. When this was over, she told herself firmly, she would go back and set them straight on exactly what marines did, how well they did it, and the terrible risks they took on their way to doing it.

Whist glanced up at her as he pulled a bandage from a compartment in his armor. "What's that look supposed to mean?"

Tanya blinked. "Sorry," she said. "Didn't realize I was staring."

"She's good at those looks, though," Dizz offered. "You should have seen the one she gave me when I headed up to start my windstorm."

"Yeah, that was genius," Whist told him. "Also panbrained stupid. You realize that with your pack going full tilt, if your collar had slipped off that bracing rock, you'd have snapped your neck in pretty much nothing flat?"

"You're welcome," Dizz said with a bland smile. "Always glad to do my bit for the Corps. So now what?"

"I think I may have a way to get some samples," Erin put in. She had her pack open and was poking around the contents. "It occurred to me that if we can't open the pods, maybe I *can* access the tubes carrying nutrients into and out of them. Usually there are some cast-off cells mixed in, which I can pull out." She gestured across the room. "Then all I have to do is take samples from one of the psyolisks, and we should be able to prove they're not the same species."

"Valerian already has psyolisk samples," Dizz reminded her.

"Which have been blown up and then exposed to vacuum," Erin said. "A few clean ones can't hurt."

"Point," Dizz said. "While you do that, Ulavu can help me get that thing out of the hole."

Whist frowned. "What thing, and what hole?"

"The thing wedged up into the ceiling hole," Dizz said, pointing upward. "Tanya saw it. Didn't you?"

Tanya looked up at the hole. There *was* something up there, she saw now. "Huh."

"You mean you *didn't* see it?" Dizz asked.

"No," Tanya admitted. "I thought you were just pointing out an emergency bolt-hole."

"Really?" Dizz asked, peering up at it. "Yeah, like any of us would fit through there. Well, you might. Anyway, looks to me like the best way to get to it is to cut it out of there, and for that I need our friendly local dark templar and his warp blades. If you're up to it, I mean."

Of course I can assist, Ulavu said. *Tell me what you wish me to do.*

"Nothing fancy," Dizz said. "I'll carry you up, hold you in place while you cut it out of whatever brackets or supports there are, and we bring it down here."

I will be happy to assist.

"*After* I get these bandages on," Whist said. "Speaking of warp blades, that flying disk thing of yours is a damn cool weapon. How come we've never seen one before?"

They have only been recently perfected, Ulavu said. *The disk utilizes warp-blade technology, though the projections are not warp blades precisely.*

"Well, I like it," Whist said. "Anyone see where it ended up?"

"It's over there," Tanya said as she spotted the disk lying near a pair of dead zerglings. "I'll get it."

By the time she returned, Whist had finished his bandaging, Dizz and Ulavu had retrieved the object from its hidey-hole and set it on the floor, and the three of them were crouched around it. It was a small box-shaped lump of zerg bioconstruct: gray, with a flowing gratelike pattern on one side and a handful of what looked like strangely shaped switches. "Any idea what it is?" she asked as she handed the disk to Ulavu.

"Oh, yeah," Dizz said sourly. "Five'll get you ten that this is one of the transmitters they've been using. One of Cruikshank's data bursts had a slightly blurry picture of what they thought was the transmitter in Zagara's conference building thingy."

"This is a transmitter?" Tanya asked, frowning at it. To her, it just looked like another chunk of organic zerg construct. "I didn't know they used long-range comm systems."

The zerg queen Mukav also used one when she arrived at Korhal IV to ask for terran assistance, Ulavu said.

"Okay, but why *here*?" Dizz asked. "These are zerg. Can't Abathur just use their psionic connection?"

"Not with the psyolisks," Erin called from over by the pods. She had a small access panel open, Tanya saw, and was poking inside with some kind of probe. "Different level of psionics from xel'naga essence, remember?" She half turned and lifted a finger in sudden understanding. "The machinery noise I thought I heard coming from Point One," she said. "Remember? The sound mixed in with singing?"

"This thing isn't exactly mechanical," Dizz pointed out.

"Adostra psionics isn't exactly singing, either," Whist countered. "Maybe she's right. Maybe another of these things was in Point One as part of the mix."

"But there's still no way you were hearing this—*any* of this—across that much distance," Dizz persisted.

"Maybe it was coming via the adostra," Erin said. "If they're aware of everything happening in their chamber—maybe everywhere on the planet—they could have woven the biomechanics of the transmitter into their song."

"Yes, but—" Dizz began.

"Regardless, the thing is here," Tanya interrupted. "Let's focus on that. So. Abathur creates some transmitters and sets them up in the adostra chambers. They're self-contained; they can cover the whole continent, and no one's going to know he made up a few more on the side after he built the ones he gave to Zagara and Mukav."

"Which would imply the psyolisks can hear and understand language," Whist said. "Damn. No wonder they knew we were faking it. We blabbed the whole plan right in front of them."

"They'd have figured it out eventually," Dizz said. "Here's the big question—"

"Oh my God," Tanya interrupted as a horrible thought suddenly struck her.

Because if there'd been one of these same transmitters at Point One, then Abathur *had* known about her and her power. He'd known all along.

No. Ulavu's mental voice soothed her. *He did not.*

But we talked about it, Tanya protested. *We talked about my power after the battle, right out in the open.*

No, Ulavu repeated. *All he knows is that you are a pyrokeet.*

Tanya blinked, that conversation suddenly snapping into full focus. He was right. The protoss had given the others her hated ghost nickname, and that was all.

And neither Abathur nor any other zerg could possibly have the slightest idea what a *pyrokeet* was.

With a start, she realized the others were looking at her expectantly. "Sorry," she said. "Brain glitch. Go on."

"Okay," Dizz said, peering closely at her. "Anyway, as I was saying, here's the question. If Abathur designed these transmitters to work while the psyolisks are blazing away at full power, does that mean they're immune to the psyolisks' usual comm interference?"

"Good time for that question," Tanya said. The buzzing pressure in her brain was suddenly growing louder. "Because I think more of them are on the way."

I concur, Ulavu said. *Their attack has begun anew.*

"Great," Whist muttered. "Come on, Dizz, let's go check the front door for company."

"At least this group will have to come at us one at a time," Dizz said, popping a fresh mag into his P-45. "Unless they want to take the time to cut down all the rest of the trees."

And then, without warning, there was a booming *thud* from above them, a massive crash that shook the whole mesa. An instant later came a second earsplitting crash, this one a long, crunching, splintering sort of noise. "What the *hell*?" Dizz shouted through the cacophony.

Whist swore. "That, my friends," he bit out as the crunching faded away, "was the sound of a devourer, or something just as big, bouncing along the top of the mesa and tearing across the tree palisade. And knocking the whole thing the hell down.

"They're not coming in one at a time, Dizz. They're all going to come in together."

CHAPTER TWENTY-ONE

The strategy of putting all the protoss in the center of the battle line and all the terran marines, reapers, and mechs at the flanks had worked out badly the first time Cruikshank and Alikka had tried it.

So naturally, they were trying it again.

Which probably looked odd, especially since the zerg were lining up for a massive, killing blow. A group of hydralisks had been gathered opposite the protoss in a spearhead formation, with only a thin line of zerglings stretched across the rest of the choke point to keep the terrans busy.

It was a good strategy, one that the history of this battle would suggest was a winner. Once the hydralisks had cleared out all the protoss, they could turn both terran flanks and take them out.

Cruikshank could only hope that the trick he and Alikka had come up with would make the difference for the allies.

He frowned, his train of thought stumbling over the word. *Allies.* He'd never thought of the Dominion and the protoss as having that kind of relationship. Never wanted to, either. *Yes,* they'd fought together on a few occasions, but that was a far cry from being actual *allies.* At least in Cruikshank's mind. Even after Emperor Valerian declared a cease-fire, Cruikshank had insisted on thinking of the protoss less as *friends* than as *not-enemies.* Fighting shoulder to shoulder with protoss was a new and not entirely pleasant experience for him.

Still, for all their arrogance and stiff-necked sense of superiority, he had to admit that Alikka, at least, could be made to see reason. Sometimes. When there was no other choice.

It has begun, Alikka warned. *The pressure has been increased.*

Cruikshank bared his teeth. And from the Warhound's cockpit he could see the entire center of the protoss formation wavering as they took the full brunt of the psyolisks' psionic attack. Any minute now, and the hydralisks would begin their charge.

"G-Five?" he called into his comm. The man had a name, of course, but mech pilots came and went so quickly that it was easier just to think of him as Goliath Five. Even when the Goliath Five mech itself was out of commission.

"We're ready, Colonel," Goliath Five said. "Well, *I* am, anyway. The others are—well, I'm sure they're not *actually* drunk."

"That's why you're there," Cruikshank said with a touch of grim satisfaction. Alikka hadn't liked this part of the plan. Had hated it, in fact. But Cruikshank had insisted, and the protoss had eventually given in, and he should now be damn glad that he had. Not that he would likely ever admit it. "Get ready to fire on my signal. On *my* signal," he added, just to make sure. Goliath Five was no more a fan of the protoss than was Cruikshank himself.

"Roger that, Colonel."

They approach, Alikka said, his voice sounding even more strained.

Cruikshank looked across the field. The hydralisk spearhead was on the move. "Get ready, everyone," he called. He glanced at his rear display, at the phoenixes lying half crushed in the middle of the field. Was it too late, he wondered, to pull the line behind them?

Probably. "Alikka, get your people moving . . . *now.*"

For the first half second he thought that Alikka had missed his order or, worse, that the heightened buzzing in the protoss' brains was drowning out everything else. Then, to his relief, the center of the battle line wavered and began to crumple, the protoss loping or staggering to the flanks, running away to cower behind the marines, reapers, and goliaths that were still standing against the enemy. Templar and Nerazim alike, caving before the psionic attack of the psyolisks and the threat of the oncoming hydralisks.

Cruikshank held his breath. This was the make-or-break moment. If the enemy had abandoned the idea of getting more zerg to Point Three and instead decided to annihilate the terrans and protoss who had so inconveniently dedicated themselves to blocking their path, the hydralisks would mirror the protoss move and focus their attack on the flanks.

But whoever was running the psyolisks still had their priorities straight. Redoubling their speed, the hydralisks arrowed straight for the wide gap that had opened up in front of them. Cruikshank could almost imagine the zerg commander smiling at the victory, or at least coming as close to a smile as a zerg could get.

He took a deep breath. "G-Five . . . *fire.*"

And with a crackling sizzle and a blanket static charge that straightened every hair on Cruikshank's body, one of the phoenixes lying helpless on the ground behind the battle line opened up with its ion cannons.

Protoss ion cannons were designed for anti-aircraft and anti-spacecraft combat. Cruikshank had never seen one used on the ground.

It was a sight he would not soon forget. The collimated pulse of negative ions blasted through the gap where the protoss had been standing seconds earlier, the lower edge flash-charring the grass below it, the side edges tearing apart air molecules and throwing ripples of static charge across the goliaths, reapers, and marines a hundred meters away.

And the zerg running straight into the center of the pulse simply disintegrated.

It was as awesome a sight as Cruikshank had ever witnessed. The hydralisks didn't explode as with grenades, or throw off splashes of blood as with gauss rifle spikes, or die in any of the usual ways zerg did on the battlefield. They simply came apart, like pieces of dried grass in a fire. Their carapaces peeled away; their claws and teeth and faces blurred and shattered and became dust in the wind. They went neatly, and in order, the ones in front blowing back into the ones behind, which then did the same. The first pulse made it all the way to the fourth file before it dissipated, and Cruikshank wondered briefly if the zerg commander would try to pull the attackers back or at least disperse them.

They did neither. But then, they really didn't have time. The first ion pulse had barely dissipated when Goliath Five fired his next shot, taking out the remaining three files.

That second shot was the last. Alikka had warned that the damage to the phoenix extended to the power system, and that the capacitors had only limited storage capability.

But with the hydralisks bunched together for a breakthrough, two shots were all Cruikshank needed. Even as the surviving zerg reeled under the static-charge aftereffects of the pulses, the marines and the goliaths opened fire from the ground while the reapers added their own rain of hypersonic metal from above. A few of the zerg reached the battle line, only to be slaughtered by the protoss.

And in the end, the allies held the field.

The psionic attack is fading, Alikka announced into the new silence, his relief clearly evident in his mental voice. *I believe the psyolisks are pulling back.*

"You want us to go after them, Colonel?" Goliath One asked.

Cruikshank eyed the forest, now devoid of visible zerg. It was a tempting thought.

But there could be anything still lurking in there. And while goliaths were designed for maneuverability in tight quarters, even they had their limits. "Stand down," he ordered. "Marines, pull back and regroup. Goliaths, keep an eye out for surprises. Reapers, hold altitude and log any movement. Alikka, are your people all okay?"

They are, Alikka said. *But for a time they were unable to focus properly. Combat would have been disastrous.*

"Even the phoenix command crew?" Cruikshank asked, perversely wanting the protoss commander to say it out loud.

To his surprise, Alikka did. *Even the command crew,* he said. *Perhaps even especially the command crew. You were right to insist that a terran handle the final aim and activation of the ion cannons.*

And to Cruikshank's even greater surprise, Alikka's admission didn't feel nearly as satisfying as he'd expected it to. Was he actually getting too old to gloat?

No. He was tired; that was all. Just tired. "I'm glad it worked," he said.

The yellow long-range-comm light winked on, and he tapped the switch. "Cruikshank."

"Horner," the admiral's voice came back. "Report."

"The field is ours, sir," Cruikshank said. "We've won the day."

"Congratulations," Horner said. "But the day's not over. How mobile are you?"

"We have four goliaths and a Warhound in fair to decent condition."

"Any chance of repairing or freeing any of the ships?"

"No, sir, not down here," Cruikshank said. "The warp fields still aren't working, either." He frowned, suddenly realizing where Horner was going with this. "Halkman's team?"

"Yes," Horner said. "The tree palisade's been knocked completely over—Abathur sent a devourer ramming into it—and there's a mass of zerg gathering outside."

"How long?"

"Probably not more than a few minutes."

Cruikshank mouthed a curse. And he and his force were fifteen klicks away, with some serious terrain between here and there. A soldier in fully functional combat armor could handle that kind of distance with ease, but every one of his marines and reapers had sustained battle damage to either their armor, their body, or both. "I'm sorry, Admiral," Cruikshank said. "But there's no way I can get enough of my force there in time to help."

"I know," Horner said heavily. "Neither can we."

Across the field, Alikka was checking out his people. Cruikshank stared at him . . . "*My* force can't get there, anyway, sir," he said. "But there might be another option."

For a long moment no one said anything. That alone was surprising; Erin would have expected at least some swearing. But for once, Whist and Dizz were silent.

Maybe there were situations so serious that they superseded even marine and reaper vocabularies. That was a frightening thought.

"What are we going to do?" she asked.

"*You're* going to get those samples," Whist said. "The rest of us are going to see what we can do to stop the zerg."

"Or at least slow them down," Dizz added.

Erin looked at her sample tube. "What good will it do to slow them down?"

"All the good in the world," Dizz said. "For the first time since we landed on this damn planet, Abathur's missed a bet." He pointed to the transmitter. "Like I said. If he uses this thing to talk to the psyolisks, it means their psi doesn't block it."

Erin looked at the transmitter in sudden understanding. "So once I've got my readings, we can send them to the *Hyperion*?"

"Exactly," Whist said. "Ulavu, you think you can figure out how to work it?"

It is of zerg construction, he said doubtfully. *If it uses the same protocols as human Valkyrie comm systems, a terran would likely be better equipped to understand it.*

"Maybe," Whist said. "But Erin's busy, and I need Dizz and Tanya downstairs. So you're elected. Get in gear and figure it out." He nodded toward the archway. "Let's go see what they've got planned this time."

Erin turned back to her work, her stomach knotting up. Getting their data to the *Hyperion* would be good. It might be the vital piece that would stop a war.

But if it was, she would really like to be alive to see it.

Blinking away thoughts of her own death, she got back to work.

The return line from the pod was easy to spot. It was typical zerg organic construction, with a sheathing that should be capable of self-repair. Mentally crossing her fingers, she eased a syringe through the tube and extracted a few drops. She then eased the needle out, watching another drop ooze out through the hole . . .

But just one. The needle hole had indeed closed up. Puffing out a sigh of relief, she injected the drops into the compact bioanalyzer and started fastening the access panel back into place.

From down the ramp came the staccato hiss of a gauss rifle. The final battle had begun. She finished with the panel and stood up, too quickly, fighting for balance against the tank riding over her shoulder and hip—

She caught her breath. The tank.

The flamethrower.

And Whist and Dizz had completely forgotten she had it.

She glanced at Ulavu, still fiddling with the transmitter. For a second she was tempted to toss a sample tube to him and tell him to scoop out some cells from the nearest psyolisk carcass. But he was busy, and that was her job anyway. After loping across the chamber, she found one of the psyolisks Ulavu's warp disk had eviscerated, pulled a few cells and fluids from three different areas, injected them into the bioanalyzer's secondary port, and headed for the archway.

She paused at the second landing, craning her neck to peer over the barrier. Whist, Dizz, and Tanya were below her on the bottom landing, firing down the ramp toward the entrance. She headed down, rounded the barrier, and peered between Whist and Tanya.

The tree palisade had been knocked down, all right, though she couldn't see what had been thrown against it. Clambering up and over the shattered lumber were dozens of zerglings, banelings, and hydralisks, all clearly determined to get over the barricade and charge into the defenders' fire.

And the zerg were winning. Whist was no longer firing bursts with the same abandon he'd shown earlier in the mission, and he was clearly working hard to conserve his waning ammunition supply. Dizz was doing the same. Tanya's face was pinched with strain as she torched enemy after enemy after enemy.

Erin smiled tightly. Well, Abathur and the psyolisks had a surprise coming. Fumbling with the flamethrower's nozzle, she finally got it unhooked from the tank. She stepped forward and tapped Whist on the arm. "Whist?"

He glanced over his shoulder. "You finished?"

"Yes," Erin said, wincing. Even in the last couple of seconds the zerg had gained another meter of territory. The forward line of carcasses now extended two or three meters beyond the ends of the trees, and the group climbing over the blockage behind them was pressing ever closer. "I brought you a present," she said, holding out the nozzle grip. "I think you forgot we had it."

"Didn't forget," Whist grunted. "Can't use it."

Erin blinked. "Why not?"

"Because we'd be shooting downhill," Whist said, firing off another burst from his gauss rifle. "That means a lot of the heat would come straight back at us. Our armor can't handle that."

"I thought you used these things in combat."

"Firebats use 'em," Whist said. "Marines in undamaged CMCs sometimes do." He gestured to the gaping slits in his own armor. "Marines in damaged CMCs don't. Crazy as it might seem, we prefer getting sliced up by zerg to getting barbecued alive. It's faster, and it hurts less."

Erin looked at Tanya and Dizz, wincing as she spotted the slashes and cuts and openings in their armor. Ulavu, without any armor at all, was out of the question.

Which left only one possibility.

"Fine," she said. "Show me how it works."

Whist looked up again. "What?"

"Show me how it works," she repeated. "My armor isn't damaged, remember? I'll do it. Just show me how."

"You'll be alone," Whist pointed out. "Once you open up, we'll have to retreat."

She hadn't thought about that aspect. But it made sense.

It also didn't matter. However it had to work, it had to be done.

Tanya might have been reading her mind. Maybe she was. "You don't have to do this," she called over the gunfire. "Abathur has to run out of zerg sooner or later."

"Just show me how the damn thing works," Erin snarled. "I'm scared enough, all right? Just get me started before it's too late."

"I've got it," Dizz said, holstering his gauss pistol and stepping to

Erin's side. For once, Erin noted distantly, there was none of the snarky sense of humor that always seemed to be simmering beneath his surface. "I used things like this all the time. Okay, here's the flow control. Here's the igniter trigger. Full range is about thirty meters; effective flash-cooking range for a zerg is five to ten . . ."

The weapon wasn't too complicated. All too soon, she was ready. "Okay," she said, unclipping her bioanalyzer and handing it to Tanya. "Here—the preliminary analysis should be finished. You can send it to the *Hyperion* as soon as Ulavu has the transmitter working. I'll get as far down as I can before I start."

"We'll stay and back you up as long as we can," Whist said. "Good luck."

She was halfway down the ramp when a pair of zerglings managed to slip through the barrage coming from the landing and charged. Reflexively, she ducked to the side, her fingers fumbling for the controls Dizz had shown her. The nozzle grip vibrated subtly as the fuel surged through it—

And abruptly a roiling cloud of brilliant blue-white flame blasted across her vision. It washed across both of the attacking zerg, and she caught a glimpse of their carapaces charring in midair before they shot past, out of sight.

She released the trigger, shaking with adrenaline reaction. No matter how many times zerg charged at her, no matter how close they came or how far back they stayed, each time was just as terrifying as the very first attack outside Point One.

But there was no time for introspection. Even with just a single shot the temperature inside her armor had risen noticeably. Whist hadn't been kidding about that. A few more shots, and even her fully intact armor might start to break down.

More zerg were coming at her. She ignited the nozzle again, spraying fire like water from a garden hose over the whole line. Another line leaped off the inner edge of the trees, and she again swept it with fire. Most of the zerg died with a single blast, but a few had to be given a second shot in order to take them down. She continued forward: step, spray; step, spray; step, dodge, spray. Sometimes one of the creatures got past her, and she could only hope that it was too injured to bother her or that one of the others would deal with it.

If they were still there. Her helmet had a rear display, but the smoke was swirling so thickly around her that she couldn't see anything back there. Even in front, it sometimes took a quick burst of flame to blast away the smoke long enough for her to see where the latest threat was coming from.

Dizz had shown her where the fuel-level indicator was. But she didn't dare take her eyes away from the battle long enough to look at it. If she ran out . . . but she couldn't think that way. Her plan depended on her reaching the entrance with a good deal of reserves left over.

Because she *did* have a plan. It might not be a good plan, but it was all she had. In the meantime, all she could do was step, fire, step, fire, step, fire.

It was almost a shock when she reached the bottom of the ramp and started across the entry cave itself. The smoke was getting thicker now, and the inside of her armor was becoming uncomfortably hot. She wondered how hot the outer neosteel shell was, and how much insulation her undersuit could provide. The CMC's cooling system was whining with the strain, and she suspected it wouldn't last much longer.

Her mind flashed back to Whist's comment about being barbecued alive. Distantly, she wondered what that would feel like.

Then, suddenly, she was there. Around her were mounds of charred zerg carcasses, enough to make it difficult to walk. Ten meters in front of her was the entrance to the cave.

And heaped in front of the entrance was a tangled mass of

wrecked and shattered trees. The biggest stack of kindling she would ever see.

Raising her aim, kicking the flow control all the way over, she fired.

There was another line of zerg coming over the trees. They stumbled and reared back and died under her assault. A fresh wave of smoke rolled over her, and she shot off another blast to clear it away.

To find that the world's biggest mass of kindling had now become the world's biggest bonfire.

"There you go," she muttered, taking a step backward. She gave the trees one more burst of flame, just to clear away the smoke and to confirm that no zerg were going to get through that anytime soon. "Choke on it." She turned, and peering through the smoke as she tried to weave her way through the maze of stinking carcasses, she headed back for the ramp.

She had made it to the first landing, and was halfway to the second, when she realized that the acrid smell of burnt flesh wasn't coming from the charred zerg at all.

It was coming from her.

She would never remember afterward how she made it the rest of the way up. She remembered crying out for help but hearing no answer. Certainly no one loomed out of the smoke to offer aid. She remembered calling again, then realizing that the heat and fire had likely burned off her comm antenna and charred the transmitter. She remembered the fear that that might *not* be the case, that the lack of response was because her friends were already dead. She remembered putting one foot in front of the other, the stench in her nostrils bringing her to the edge of vomiting, trying desperately to pop the catches of the armor that was rapidly killing her, but not recalling how they worked. She remembered coming around one of the landings and seeing the wavering forms of Whist, Dizz, and Tanya finally appear through the smoke. She remembered a silent scream for help echoing through her mind, and falling, and the agony as new parts of her body pressed up against the burning neo-steel of her coffin-sized prison. She remembered being laid on the floor, and Ulavu's face appearing over her—

And she remembered a sudden wash of coolness, and a lungful of incredibly chilly air.

And then, for a time, she remembered nothing at all.

CHAPTER TWENTY-TWO

"Couple of second-degree burns," Whist muttered as he carefully cut off Erin's undersuit. "Mostly at joints. Bad one at the left shoulder. No third-degrees I can see."

"Thank God," Tanya said, trying to see through the smoke rapidly filling the chamber. She hadn't seen what Erin had done down there—the heat from the flamethrower had become too intense for any of the rest of them—but from the sound and smell she guessed the trees of the former palisade were now on fire.

It was a good plan, certainly a good temporary one. A barrier like that would be intimidating to even the most determined zerg, and quickly fatal to most of them.

On the downside, the cavern's entire air supply was now rapidly turning opaque and nearly unbreathable. And of course, eventually the fire would die down.

They should have brought the rest of the gauss rifle spikes from the damaged magazines, she realized. Despite Whist's deriding of the idea, it looked like they *would* have had time to reload.

"A hell of a lot of first-degree ones, though," Whist continued. "Dizz?"

"Here," Dizz said, handing over a small field tube of burn spray. "That one's Erin's. Go ahead and use it up—I've got mine ready."

Whist grunted thanks and began to apply the salve. "She's lucky we got her out of that armor in time. Another minute, and this would have been a lot worse."

"Yes," Tanya murmured. "*We.*"

"Fine, *he* got her out," Whist growled at her. "I already said thank you."

"Yes, you did," Tanya said, looking over at Erin's armor.

Or rather, at the pieces of her armor, which were all that were left after Ulavu cut the red-hot metal off her with quick and surgically precise slashes from his warp blades.

He'd probably saved her life. He'd certainly saved her from months of pain and reconstructive skin surgery. He deserved more than just a distracted thank-you.

But for now, that would have to do.

She looked up, frowning. Ulavu had cut Erin free and had helped the others get her out of the suit. But after that he'd disappeared, not staying around to help them carry her the rest of the way up the ramp and into the adostra chamber. Had the heat and smoke rising from the fire below driven him away?

Probably. Unlike the others, he wasn't wearing any barrier to their increasingly hostile environment. Moving farther into the adostra chamber would be about all he could do.

Of course, Erin wasn't wearing armor anymore, either. When she regained consciousness, her whole body would be screaming in agony as hot air pressed against burnt flesh. Maybe when Whist was done with the salve, he could give her something to make sure she stayed asleep.

So where *was* Ulavu, anyway?

Tanya peered through the smoky gloom, finally spotted him standing by the zerg transmitter. She'd given him Erin's analyzer earlier—was he sending the data to the *Hyperion*? Or was it simply that the area near the duct was the only source of cool, fresh air he could find? *Ulavu, are you all right?* she thought toward him.

I am unharmed, his reassuring thought came back.

Tanya frowned. There was reassurance in his tone, but also something more. Excitement? *What is it? What's going on?*

Come, he said. *All of you. Come and see.*

"Next," Whist said, tossing aside the empty tube of salve.

"Here," Dizz said, holding it out.

"Before you start," Tanya said, "Ulavu wants us to join him over by the transmitter."

"Whatever it is, it can wait," Whist said. "She needs this *now.*"

"I think that's his point," Tanya said. "The air underneath that vent has to be better than what's coming up from below."

"She's right, Whist," Dizz said. "Here—you can keep treating her skin while Tanya and I carry her."

Whist hissed. "Fine. Just watch that shoulder when you pick her up."

It was tricky, but they managed it. Maybe just in time, too—even asleep, Erin's breathing was becoming labored. Briefly, Tanya wondered if her CMC's air system could be salvaged, or if it was even functional anymore.

They reached the transmitter to find Ulavu standing over it. "So is the air better here?" Whist asked as Dizz and Tanya gently laid Erin on the floor.

It is better, Ulavu said. *But I did not invite you here only for that. Behold.* He pointed up toward the hole.

And right on cue, an arm-sized chunk of rock tumbled out of the opening and fell with a muted crash onto the floor.

"What the *hell*?" Dizz said as he twitched backward.

They are enlarging the opening, Ulavu said. He stretched out one foot and swept the piece of rock to the side, and Tanya saw now that there was a growing pile of similar shards over there. *Very soon we will be able to escape this chamber.*

"*Who's* enlarging it?" Whist demanded, looking cautiously up at the hole.

My people, Ulavu said, and there was no mistaking the pride in his voice. *The protoss who fought beside Colonel Abram Cruikshank to protect us from the zerg returning from the terran psi emitter trap.*

"Ah. Them," Whist said. "Not that Abathur didn't have plenty more zerg here in the neighborhood to work with."

"Quiet," Tanya admonished him. "However many zerg he had, this way he didn't have more."

"I suppose," Whist said.

When the opening is large enough, they will take Dr. Erin Wyland to the top of the mesa, Ulavu said, ignoring the exchange. *Then you will all be brought up, and we will protect you until more aid arrives.*

Tanya looked at Whist, expecting another less-than-gracious comment. But the sergeant remained silent. Maybe he was finally remembering the state their armor and weaponry were in. "Thank you, Ulavu," she said. "From all of us."

We are glad to render you aid.

More rock chunks were falling from the hole now, almost faster than Ulavu could sweep them out of the way. A bright but somewhat muted glow appeared, the same color as Ulavu's warp blades. The glow grew brighter and sharper . . .

And with a last slicing of the rock around the opening, a dark templar dropped through and landed on the floor. He gave a quick, appraising look at each of them, then turned to face Ulavu. Tanya had the sense of a private conversation taking place—

This is Alikka, Ulavu said. *He and the others have run far to render aid to us. He is prepared now to bring Dr. Erin Wyland to the top.*

"Good," Whist said. "I don't suppose they have any medical equipment with them?"

No, a new protoss voice echoed through Tanya's brain. *But fresh Dominion air vehicles are en route and will arrive within a quarter hour. Will she survive until then?*

"After all this work, she damn well better," Whist said. "Good enough. You have any rope up there?"

In answer, a coil of slender line unrolled itself through the hole. *You know terran physiology best,* Alikka said. *You will fasten the line for maximum safety to her.*

"Thanks," Whist said drily, taking the end of the line and crouching beside Erin. "I was going to do that anyway. Tanya, you don't need that visor and hood, do you?"

"Not as much as she does," Tanya said, popping her visor and handing it over. The hood was a bit trickier, but she was able to get it off. It wouldn't protect Erin's head against bumps as well as a full helmet, but at least it would be something.

The air in the chamber was even hotter and smokier than she'd realized, and she found herself blinking back tears as the smoke and ash assaulted her eyes. Whist got the visor and hood on Erin, and Tanya adjusted the air supply controls while he went back to his rope tying.

A minute later everything was ready. At a silent order from Alikka, the protoss on top of the mesa began pulling, easing Erin's unconscious form up into the hole. Tanya winced as her head brushed the edge, but as long as the bumps stayed small the hood should absorb most of the impact.

They will be careful, Ulavu assured her.

They'd better, she warned. *She doesn't need any new injuries.*

I agree. He paused, and Tanya could sense a sudden new attentiveness. *Something odd has happened.*

"Uh-oh," Dizz said. "You hear that?"

Tanya strained her ears. "No."

"Exactly," he said, drawing his P-45. "The big bonfire outside has stopped."

Tanya frowned. He was right—the distant background roar had disappeared. "We'd better check it out."

"Hang on," Whist said, watching as Erin's legs disappeared into the hole. "I'll come with you."

You stay, Ulavu said, stepping past him toward Tanya and Dizz. *Guard and protect her, and work further on the transmitter. I will go.*

The silence seemed to grow deeper as Dizz led the way along the corridor and down the ramp. Tanya fought to keep her vision clear of the smoke and her own tears, wondering how her power would work if she could barely see her target. Not very well, she suspected. Dizz had his gauss pistol ready, but Tanya had no idea how many rounds he had left. Not many. Only Ulavu, with his warp blades, had any serious hope of stopping the next wave of zerg, and he had to wait until he was in range of their claws and teeth before he could fight back.

Except for his warp disk, anyway. But even that could only be used once before someone had to go retrieve it.

And suddenly, it clicked. Someone to retrieve it . . .

The warp disk, she said to Ulavu. *Is that why you came to the ghost program to look for a teek?*

That is correct, Ulavu confirmed. *You understand now how a Nerazim's control of Void energies combined with a telekinetic's ability to maneuver the disk within a group of enemies would create a powerful combat unit. I hoped to experiment with terran telekinetics to learn what innovations they could bring to the disk's operation.*

Definitely sounds interesting, Tanya said. *But why keep it secret? This is the sort of thing military planners love to work with.*

Ulavu was silent another few steps. *Because terrans and protoss are perhaps no longer enemies, but neither are we fully allies,* he said reluctantly. *We are vastly different peoples, Tanya Caulfield, and I fear that much work must be done before we can build a truly close relationship. It was thought best that you not yet know of this weapon or of our research in this direction, lest you misunderstand our intentions or motivations.*

I understand, Tanya said. *But I don't think Emperor Valerian would take it wrong. He seems to be an honorable man.*

Yet beings of honor may still disagree. Sometimes to the point of war.

Tanya wrinkled her nose, wishing she could argue with him, knowing she couldn't. *We'll keep your secret,* was all she could think to say.

Can you speak for the others? he asked. *At any rate, such a promise is as yet premature. There is still a strong possibility that we will all die before this day is over.*

"Boy, it's a mess down here," Dizz murmured. "Can you two even see well enough to fight?"

"We're okay," Tanya assured him, hoping it wasn't a complete lie. They wouldn't know for sure until the first zerg appeared around the landing below and charged up the ramp toward them.

And the psyolisks hadn't given up, either. She could still feel a low-level buzz in the back of her brain. Presumably they were gathering whatever was left of their forces for a final surge.

But if they were, they were taking their sweet time about it. Ten steps from the bottom landing, and still nothing. "Speaking of fighting, where are they, anyway?"

"Good question," Dizz said. "Weird. Is the air out there getting clearer?"

Tanya shook her head. "I can't tell."

It is, Ulavu confirmed, seeming as puzzled as Dizz. *I hear a new sound. But I cannot identify it.*

"Me neither," Dizz said. They reached the landing, and he paused long enough to check the indicator on his gauss pistol. "Let's find out, shall we?" Visibly bracing himself, he stepped around the corner of the landing. Blinking, Tanya followed.

To find herself facing an extraordinary sight.

The bonfire Erin had ignited in the downed palisade trees was indeed out. But it had only gone out because a solid blanket of zerg was now covering it, smothering the flames and leaving only a few wisps of rising smoke to show where the conflagration had been. Inside the cave, lined up in front of the smoldering trees, were a dozen zerg of a type Tanya had never seen before. They had the same general giant-wasp form as mutalisks, but were smaller and had larger grasping claws and wider wings. The wings were apparently what was making the unfamiliar sound as the zerg beat them furiously toward the entrance, forcing out the smoke-filled air.

And standing a few meters inside their line, overseeing the operation, was a zerg broodmother.

"Well, that's something you don't see every day," Dizz murmured.

"What, a broodmother?" Tanya asked, blinking furiously. The air was definitely starting to clear, but she was still seeing the world through a layer of tears.

"I mean the zerg fanning out the cavern," Dizz said. "They're not armored."

Tanya squinted. She'd missed that part entirely.

But he was right. Unlike every other zerg she'd ever seen, these seemed to have only a rugged, leathery skin instead of the usual interlocked bony plates.

Their conversation had apparently caught the broodmother's attention. *Ah,* she said in a gravelly psionic voice as she turned to face them. *My apologies for the lateness of my arrival. I am relieved to find you alive.*

"For the moment, anyway," Dizz said. "That question's always a little up in the air. Who are you, may I ask?"

The broodmother bowed her head and torso. *I am Overqueen Zagara.*

Tanya swallowed hard, her swimming vision blurring even more. Overqueen Zagara, the heir and successor to Sarah Kerrigan, the most powerful ghost humanity had ever produced. Here was the zerg who had brought the Dominion and the protoss to this cross-roads of war and peace, and who even now held that balance and hope in her claws.

If she had come here for Tanya . . .

I feared that the unknown creatures you have been battling would overwhelm you, Zagara continued. *I thus traveled here in the hope that my presence would wrest control back from them.*

"It seems to have worked," Dizz said. "Thank you, Overqueen. Assuming those are your zerg that put out the fire and not the psyolisks' associates."

They are mine, Zagara said. *These are also my skyrlings that I have set to clear the smoke, that you may once again have clean air.*

"Skyrlings, huh?" Dizz said. "Interesting design. A new breed, I assume?"

Yes, Zagara said. *They were created by Abathur at my command, to one day carry the adostra when they are fully grown.*

"To where?" Dizz asked.

To wherever they must be. Zagara paused, and Tanya could sense the Overqueen's mix of fear and anger. *The adostra within the growth chamber. Do they yet live?*

"As far as I know," Dizz said. "*We* certainly didn't do anything to them. Let me call and . . . You know, why don't you just come up and see for yourself?"

Tanya felt Ulavu stir beside her. To deliberately invite the zerg Overqueen behind what was left of their defensive position . . .

But Ulavu said nothing, and Tanya likewise kept silent, and after a moment Zagara lifted a clawed limb. *I will,* she declared, starting across the floor. *Do not fear. My zerg will stay under my control.*

"Good," Dizz said grimly. "Because I'm guessing there are still some psyolisks hanging around. Tanya?"

"Yes, they're still there," Tanya confirmed. "Still hoping they can make us wipe out the adostra for them."

"Or hoping to kill us and pin it on the Overqueen," Dizz said. "Whist? You getting all this?"

There was a pause. Reflexively, Tanya reached for her volume control, only then remembering that her comm was currently on Erin's head. "What does he say?"

"He says he's getting it," Dizz relayed. "He doesn't believe it, but he's getting it. Anyway, we're bringing her up," he continued. "If I were you, Whist, I'd try real hard to have that transmitter up and running by the time we get there."

He smiled tightly at Tanya. "Emperor Valerian is going to love this."

"... Overqueen Zagara then confirmed that these are the adostra she created," Lieutenant Halkman said, concluding his report. "Or at least, these are the pods that Abathur said the adostra would be grown in. Without opening one of them, she can't tell for sure."

"And she refuses to open one?" Artanis's voice came over the bridge speaker.

"She doesn't *refuse*, exactly, Hierarch Artanis," Halkman said. "But she points out that appearances can be deceiving, and even with a closer look and a smell test, she might not be able to confirm these are what she asked him to make. She said our analysis would be much more definitive."

Valerian looked over at the biolab status display. "They're starting the tests now," he told Halkman. "They say both samples Dr. Wyland took look good, and should give good results." He checked another display. "Sickbay also reports that Dr. Wyland herself has arrived, and they're getting to work on her burns."

"Thank you for letting us know, Emperor," Halkman said, sounding relieved. "One last thing: Overqueen Zagara confirms that this *is* a version of the transmitter Abathur made for her. Probably why she was able to get it working so easily. She has no idea how many more he might have made on the side. And I think that brings us up to date."

"Yet the account is not complete," Artanis said darkly. "Where are the psyolisks? How did they come to exist? Are there more? Where is Evolution Master Abathur, and will Overqueen Zagara allow him to be brought to us for questioning? Most important, are the adostra truly the creatures that Overqueen Zagara claims, or are they wrapped in yet more lies and manipulations?"

"I do not lie, Hierarch Artanis." Zagara's voice came from the speaker heavy with dignity and suppressed anger. "I have acted in full good faith throughout our encounters. I can only repeat that my good-faith efforts continue. I have left the protection of my conference structure in order to aid the Dominion survey team. I have located psyolisk carcasses, confirming their existence, and sent them to you for study. I have sacrificed many of the Swarm to extinguish the fire and bring the survey team to safety. I have ordered my broodmothers to remain within their spire centers, and the leviathans that they summoned to remain on the ground."

"Such goodwill may be merely fear of our fury," Artanis said. "We will not soon forget the battle that cost the lives of Templar and Nerazim alike."

"That battle was initiated and driven by the psyolisks."

"So you say," Artanis said. "We have heard enough words. We need now to hear some evidence."

"You have the evidence of the psyolisk carcasses and the report of the survey team."

"Neither of which gives proof of the perpetrator or intent," Artanis countered. "I repeat my question. Where is Abathur?"

"I do not know," Zagara said. "I allow him to go where he will, subject to my command. Furthermore, I refuse to believe the evil you charge him with. Abathur is the evolution master, eldest of all living zerg. His loyalty is to the Swarm."

"Then whence come the psyolisks?" Artanis demanded.

"I do not know," Zagara said again.

"If I may interpose my thoughts," Valerian said quickly. To him it was obvious that Abathur was manipulating this mess, though the evolution master's motivations were still murky. But Artanis and Zagara were at a horn-locked stalemate, and nothing was going to budge either of them.

Nothing but absolute, objective proof. And the only way to get that proof was to drag Abathur out into the open and persuade him to talk.

Which might be harder than it looked. Valerian assumed he had to answer Zagara's summons, but there was a lot about the interaction between Overqueen and evolution master that he didn't understand. If Zagara refused to call him, or if Abathur refused to come when she called . . .

Valerian frowned as an odd thought suddenly struck him. *To come when called . . .*

Artanis and Zagara had gone silent. Valerian had interrupted their argument, and they were waiting for him to say his piece.

He had one shot at this. He had better make it work.

"We've had long-distance communications like this one," he said, improvising as he went, hoping his brain could stay ahead of his words. "We've had face-to-face conversations in zerg territory. I think it's time, Overqueen Zagara, for you to speak with us in Dominion territory."

"I will not travel to Korhal IV," Zagara said flatly.

"I'm not asking you to," Valerian hastened to assure her. "But I would very much like to speak with you aboard the *Hyperion*. Am I correct in assuming that your personal leviathan is the one in which Mukav came to me to deliver your plea for help?"

"It is."

"Then may I ask you to summon it to Point Three?" Valerian said. "I would humbly request that you board it in the company of the remaining members of my survey team and join me for a conversation."

There was a short silence. "Your request is strange, Emperor Valerian," Zagara said at last. "I see no purpose to it."

"The purpose is peace," Valerian said. "I believe that if you will grant me this request, we can together establish the proof that Hierarch Artanis requires."

Another silence. Valerian mentally crossed his fingers . . .

"Very well, Emperor Valerian," Zagara said. "I will summon my leviathan."

"Thank you, Overqueen Zagara," Valerian said. "One final request: a moment in private with my survey team?"

An even longer silence. "Very well, Emperor Valerian," Zagara said again. "I will return outside to await my leviathan."

Matt reached over and tapped the mute button. "With all due respect, Valerian, this plan is nuts," he said in a low voice. "Bringing her aboard the *Hyperion* is begging for trouble."

"Don't worry; she won't be coming aboard," Valerian said. "Hierarch Artanis, are you still there?"

"I am," Artanis said. "I, too, have objections. If you seek to imprison or destroy her as a way of blunting the Swarm's ability to make war, it will have only limited effect."

"Be assured I have no intention of doing either," Valerian said, tapping the mute key. "Lieutenant Halkman, has Zagara left?"

"Yes, Emperor, she has," Halkman said.

"Is the psyolisk interference gone?"

"Let me check . . . Yes, Emperor, they seem to have pulled back."

"Good. I need you to close down the zerg transmitter and shift to your suit's long-range."

"One moment." There was a brief pause, followed by the muted sound of sustained gauss pistol fire. "Okay, the zerg transmitter is off the air," Halkman said, a bit drily.

Valerian felt his lip twitch. Still, with alien constructs, that was probably the only way to be absolutely sure. "Admiral?"

"Zerg transmission off at this end," Matt confirmed.

Valerian nodded. "Lieutenant? You still there?"

"Affirmative, Emperor," Halkman said.

"And you, Hierarch Artanis?"

"I am."

"All right," Valerian said. "All of you, listen carefully. Let's assume that everything Zagara has told us is the truth, and that all the survey team's speculations are also true. That gives us the theory that Abathur created the adostra as life-nurturing beings under Zagara's orders, then siphoned off some of the xel'naga essence on his own and melded it with zerg genetics to make his new psionic-powered psyolisks."

"Perhaps at Overqueen Zagara's direction," Artanis said.

"Again, let's assume for the moment that she's not involved," Valerian said. "Let's further assume that Abathur has been manipulating the situation from the start, trying to get us to destroy the adostra so as to poison our conversations and goad Zagara into restarting the war."

"All right," Matt said. "So where do all the assumptions and logic take us?"

"To the two questions we've all been wondering about," Valerian said. "One, if Abathur is manipulating things, what's his endgame? And two, where is he now?"

"We've tried scanning, but there's just too much surface area down there," Matt said. "And given the zerg penchant for digging massive tunnel systems, he could be anywhere on the planet."

"Actually, I don't think so," Valerian said. "At least part of his endgame has to be getting safely off Gystt. He's hardly going to precipitate a war with him stuck on the planet in the center of the gunsights.

Given that these psyolisks have to be part of his long-term plan for zerg victory, he must also have held back a number of them to take off the planet with him. That means he has to be planning to commandeer a leviathan."

"Of which there are seven on the surface," Artanis said.

"Correct," Valerian said. "But I think I can narrow it down. Do you remember, Hierarch Artanis, what Zagara said when we first arrived? She greeted us and then thanked me, specifically, for coming so quickly. And she was right—we *did* arrive more quickly than we otherwise might have. Admiral Horner, do you remember why we were so prompt?"

"Because you were intrigued by Mukav's message, sir," Matt said, sounding puzzled. "Because the hope of peace was something you thought worth pursuing."

"Yes, of course," Valerian said. "But both reasons would have brought us here eventually. Why did we come so *quickly*?"

Matt looked at him sharply. "Because Mukav wouldn't give us any details about the situation," he said. "She just repeated the same bare-bones invitation over and over."

"And what would have happened if she *had* been more talkative?"

"We'd have brought her down for more detailed questioning," Matt said grimly. He was on the same page now. "And we would have taken a good, hard look at her leviathan."

"A moment," Artanis said. "Are you suggesting that Abathur and his psyolisks are aboard *that* particular leviathan?"

"It's the perfect hiding place," Valerian told him. "We've seen it; we've done a cursory flyby, and everything we've seen indicates it's harmless."

"It's a quirk of terran psychology, Hierarch Artanis," Matt explained. "If you're planning a crime, you make a point of walking past the police officer on duty, because drawing attention to yourself gives the impression that you have nothing to hide."

"Exactly," Valerian said. "That also means that if that leviathan takes off, it'll be the one we *least* suspect that he'll be aboard." He lifted a finger as another piece fell into place. "Also, we know now from the survey team's discovery that whoever controls the psyo-lisks does so via commands delivered through one of those biome-chanical transmitters. Possibly commands that are pitched too high for humans or protoss to hear—Dr. Cogan's team has already found high-frequency capability in the psyolisk carcass Zagara sent us. We also know Mukav has the same kind of transmitter aboard her levi-athan because that's how she first contacted us. That was how Abathur could listen in on the battles at the focal points and direct the psyolisks."

"Yet if he was already safely off the planet, why would he come back?" Artanis asked, still sounding unconvinced.

"I can answer that one, Hierarch Artanis," Halkman put in. "As Emperor Valerian said, he needed to be here to watch over the situ-ation, make sure we all played the parts he had planned for us, and fine-tune the script if we went off-book."

"Which still raises the question of how an evolution master be-came that good at strategy," Valerian said. "We still need to figure that one out."

"Maybe he did a little work on himself between psyolisks," Matt suggested. "Or on Mukav. He could hardly sneak his psyolisks aboard without her knowing, so she would have to be in on it with him."

"And adding enhanced tactical ability to a queen would be harder to spot than adding it to himself," Valerian said as the pieces fell together. "Anyway, Abathur was in the conference structure during the attack at Point One, so he couldn't have run that one himself."

"So Mukav is the brains, and he's the one who made her that way?" Matt asked.

"However it works, we can sort it out once we have him," Vale-rian said. "Right now, we need to draw him into the open. That's why I told Zagara to bring the leviathan to Point Three. I want to get our people aboard without arousing suspicion."

"That assumes Abathur won't simply ignore Zagara's summons and stay put," Matt warned.

"He won't," Valerian assured him. "Remember, we set all this up using a transmitter he can tap into. As far as he knows, we're handing him the perfect opportunity to get a jump start on his escape. With his leviathan already in space, he can get out from under most of our weapons without any suspicion or resistance on our part."

"And if Zagara's with him when he runs, it'll make her look equally guilty," Halkman pointed out.

"Which would fit perfectly with his overall plan," Valerian said. "So once you're aboard, Lieutenant, your mission will be to locate Abathur and detain him."

"Understood, Emperor," Halkman said. "And the same with any psyolisks we find?"

"I recommend their destruction," Artanis said.

"I agree," Valerian said, a message on one of the displays catching his eye. "Speaking of which," he added, keying the biolab into the circuit, "Dr. Cogan has just come up with some numbers for you. Dr. Cogan?"

"Thank you, Emperor." Cogan's voice came over the speaker. "Okay, these are preliminary numbers, so don't lean too hard on them. We've done an initial workup on the psyolisk, including a first-order attempt to sort out the percentages of xel'naga and non-xel'naga. It's always hard to tell with an unfamiliar species, but by comparing their genetics to the adostra sample Dr. Wyland sent, and taking into account the number of psyolisks already killed—"

"Dr. Cogan," Valerian prompted.

"Sorry, Emperor. Bottom line: we estimate Abathur could still have anywhere from three to five hundred psyolisks to play with."

"Of which most will be aboard the leviathan, I assume?" Halkman asked.

"Probably," Valerian said, wincing. That was a *lot* of psyolisks for three terrans and a protoss civilian to take on.

Artanis was obviously thinking the same thing. "You will need assistance," he said. "I will send a phalanx of warriors to accompany you."

"With all due respect, Hierarch Artanis, I don't think that would be a good idea," Halkman warned. "Zagara's supposed to be a willing passenger on a harmless leviathan. If we throw in a whole bunch of extra troops, protoss *or* Dominion, Abathur may smell a rat and take off."

"And we will shoot him out of the sky," Artanis said darkly.

"If we do that, we'll never learn the full truth," Valerian said. "Lieutenant?"

"I think we can handle it, Emperor," Halkman said. "But we're going to need new armor and weapons. A fresh jump pack would be useful, too."

"I'll switch you over to the quartermaster," Valerian said. "And if we don't speak again before you board the leviathan, Lieutenant, good luck."

"Thank you, Emperor," Halkman said.

"Transferring you now," Matt said, and keyed the control.

The indicator light from the comm winked out. "I do not agree with this plan, Emperor Valerian," Artanis said. "It is fraught with uncertainty and risk. If you are wrong, and if Overqueen Zagara's goal is to bring a leviathan into our midst, we will find ourselves embroiled in battle in a position of terrible weakness."

"I know it's dangerous, Hierarch Artanis," Valerian said carefully. Surely Artanis wasn't going to pull out of this *now*? "But I think it's the only way to know for sure."

"And if I refuse to assist? If I now draw the protoss forces away, and leave you to face Zagara and her leviathan alone?"

Matt was watching him very closely. "Then the Dominion will stand alone," Valerian said. "But before you answer, allow me to remind you of some history."

"What sort of history?"

"The only history that matters," Valerian said. "The history between the terrans and the protoss. You remember Chau Sara?"

On the display Artanis's skin was going mottled. "Yes," he said, his voice very alien.

"You remember what the protoss did to those colonists," Valerian said. The mottling was a sign of intense emotion, and the distant thought struck him that he was pushing the hierarch pretty hard.

He didn't care. "You remember that there was a faction of the Confederacy—and later the Dominion—that was all for wiping the entire protoss race out of existence," he continued. "Do you remember why that goal was abandoned?"

Artanis didn't answer.

"Because a man named Jim Raynor made a decision," Valerian said. "He decided to trust the protoss executor Tassadar, and therefore your people. That was the turning point, the start of the path that's led us here."

"And you wish me to make that same leap of trust?"

"Raynor had plenty of evidence that the protoss weren't to be trusted," Valerian said. "But he listened to Tassadar's story, and his version of the protoss' reasoning, and decided to take a chance.

"Right now, we're standing in the same place he was. We've seen the devastation the zerg can cause, and yet we hear Zagara tell us that she and the Swarm have changed. I'm willing to take that leap of trust. Are you?"

He gestured toward the planet below them. "If my plan fails and we can't resolve this, there may be war. But if we don't even try, there *will* be war."

For a moment Artanis was silent. "Do you remember what you said to me on the planet? That the protoss were a noble race that had served as guardians for many other species. Do you remember what I said in return?"

"That it was easy to stand above others when the Khala bound you together," Valerian murmured.

"I have been thinking further," Artanis said. "Perhaps nobility and honor were never meant to be easy. Perhaps there was always to be risk involved. And perhaps there can be no nobility without trust."

He drew himself up. "The protoss struck first before, Emperor Valerian, on Chau Sara. That action cost many lives across the years, and even now is a poison between our peoples. I will not again attack first. Not here, not now. I will follow your path, and trust in your judgment. And the protoss will regain our nobility."

"You never lost it," Valerian assured him quietly. "Thank you, Hierarch. Whether we rise or fall today, we will stand together."

Artanis inclined his head. "I will await your word."

His image vanished from the display. "Well," Valerian said, turning to Matt. "It's up to the team now."

"Yes, it is." Matt hesitated. "You don't expect them to survive, do you?"

Valerian sighed. "Probably not," he said. "No, they're very likely going to their deaths. Or worse—I may be sending Tanya Caulfield straight into the hands of the zerg's evolution master, with all the horrific consequences that implies. But if they can prove that Abathur is there and get him to admit his part, we may yet defuse the crisis."

"And you're going to accomplish this how?"

"By letting Abathur think he's won," Valerian said. "Get me the quartermaster. I have an order of my own for him."

CHAPTER TWENTY-THREE

Tanya had always known leviathans were big. Everyone knew that. The creatures were *huge,* in fact, bigger than Dominion battlecruisers or protoss carriers.

But it wasn't until now, walking up to one lying angled across a set of hills, that she fully appreciated how huge they really were.

And they were supposed to find a single evolution master and a bunch of psyolisks in all *that*?

As usual, Whist had had an answer.

You just need to think like a marine, he'd assured her as the four of them had prepared to leave the adostra cavern, very likely for the last time. *Don't worry about finding the enemy. Odds are, the enemy will find you.*

It had not, in Tanya's opinion, been a particularly encouraging thought.

Tanya Caulfield? Ulavu's thought came. *Are you all right?*

Just a little nervous, she assured him. Ulavu was walking on the far side of Zagara from Tanya, the two of them flanking the Over-queen while Whist took the lead and Dizz took the rear. It was probably supposed to look as if the four of them were escorting a prisoner, though from a purely tactical perspective their position-ing was incredibly stupid. Their only hope was that Zagara truly wanted peace, and was willing to go to extraordinary lengths to achieve it.

They were already seriously pushing that commitment. Valerian had forbidden them to tell Zagara the truth about what was going on, lest Abathur get wind of it through the zerg psionic connection, and the Overqueen was none too pleased with the travel arrange-ment. Even without Tanya's limited teep power, she would have been able to tell that Zagara was bristling with the indignity that had been foisted on her. Luckily, she apparently wanted to avoid war even more than she wanted to preserve her dignity.

What she would think—and do—when she learned how she'd been manipulated was anyone's guess. Tanya wasn't looking forward to that.

At least they were as well equipped as possible for the imminent meeting. A dropship had delivered a new CMC powered combat suit for Whist, replacing his battle-worn one, along with a new gauss rifle and all the ammo magazines he could carry. Dizz had similarly been brought new reaper armor and a fresh jump pack. Tanya herself had been given a full helmet to replace the ghost visor she'd left with Erin, plus a new canister rifle courtesy of Emperor Valerian himself.

The rifle was all for show. Hopefully, Abathur wouldn't realize that until it was too late.

Ulavu, as the civilian everyone aboard the *Hyperion* still thought he was, had been offered a return trip aboard the dropship. He'd refused, citing the possible need for more insight on zerg and zerg mentality.

Tanya was still not sure how she felt about him and his long deception. But for the moment, she was just happy to have him at her side.

Still, against a leviathan holding up to five hundred psyolisks, three terrans and a protoss were a pretty pathetic showing.

Hopefully, Abathur would think so, too.

There were several sphincter-type openings visible in the leviathan's thick hide, she saw as they approached, each leading into a dark, ribbed tunnel. Whist looked back at Zagara, who silently indicated one of them, and the group headed inside.

The tunnel they found themselves in had a very different feel from that of the adostra chambers. There, the general sense had been one of space, even airiness. Here, everything was much closer, verging on claustrophobic. Every surface was pockmarked with nooks and crannies, making footing difficult, and there were a multitude of smaller tunnels and ducts that headed off at random places and in random directions. The group was quickly forced into single file, with Whist and Tanya leading the way, Zagara in the middle, and Ulavu and Dizz behind her.

And unlike the adostra chambers, once they moved out of view of the sunlight outside, the tunnel had no illumination except the beams from their own lights.

Tanya kept her light tracking across the surfaces as they walked, peering tensely into each tunnel big enough to hold a psyolisk. If Abathur decided to pick them off on the way to the leviathan's control center, this tunnel was the perfect place to do it.

But no attack came. It was so quiet, in fact, that Tanya began to wonder if Emperor Valerian had been wrong about Abathur's plan. Valerian's theory was logical enough, but even logic was of limited use when some of the pieces were being filled in by guesswork. If Abathur wasn't aboard—or if he *had* been aboard but had already left—then they would be back where they'd started.

And logic and theories weren't going to keep Artanis from incinerating the planet.

They are here.

Tanya felt her breath catch in her throat. *Are you sure?*

I can feel them, Ulavu confirmed. *You cannot?*

No, Tanya said, her last wisps of doubt blowing away. If the psyolisks were here, surely Abathur was, too.

"Everyone stay sharp," Whist murmured.

They'd been walking another ten minutes, and Tanya had started to feel her share of the brain buzz, when she finally spotted a hint of dim light in the distance. The light grew stronger as they approached, and she sensed the subtle changes in Whist's mind and posture as he slipped into full combat mode.

And then, suddenly, they were there. The tunnel made one final sharp turn and opened into a chamber at least half again as big as the main adostra caverns inside the mesas.

Whist stepped inside, breaking to his right. Tanya followed, taking the cue and breaking to the left.

Visually, the chamber was like a roomier version of the tunnel they'd just left. Like the tunnel, the chamber had walls that flowed into floor and ceiling without any hard edges or sharp breaks, and there was the same sort of texturing and multitude of side tunnels. Standing motionless near the entrance, watching as the group filed in, was a zerg queen, her body shape and limb arrangement subtly different from Zagara's. Set into the wall near her was a duplicate of the transmitter they'd dug out of the Point Three ceiling.

And standing in the center of the chamber, instantly recognizable from the pictures Valerian had sent, was Abathur.

Behind Tanya, Zagara stepped into the chamber and came to an abrupt halt. *Abathur?*

The zerg—Abathur—gesticulated with his smaller, inner limbs. Tanya could feel something at the very edge of her mind—

"Hold it," Dizz said. "I know you're surprised to see him, Over-queen Zagara, but let's not forget you have guests. Let's have a conversation—"

What do you do here? Zagara's demand pounded against Tanya's mind like a winter rain, and she was barely able to get out of the way as the Overqueen strode past, her eyes blazing, her limbs stretched and poised to slash and tear, heading straight at Abathur.

The evolution master flinched once, then stood his ground. *Abathur does what is necessary for Swarm,* he replied.

You betray the Swarm, Zagara insisted. She continued toward him, and for a moment Tanya thought she was going to physically run him down. Instead she stopped just in front of him, her limbs held high, her claws twitching as if they were trying to go for the evolution master on their own.

Once again, Abathur held his ground, even in the face of the clearly furious Overqueen. Maybe, Tanya thought, he had more courage than she'd realized.

Or maybe he simply knew that he had the upper hand.

Overqueen Zagara speaks of treachery. The other queen spoke up, taking a step toward the group. *I am Mukav. I will speak their words.*

"Thanks, but we've got it," Dizz said.

Yet the nuances may escape you, Mukav said, taking another step toward them. *I will stand ready to interpret.*

No explanation owed, Abathur said to Zagara, his mental voice grating and insolent. *But explanation will give.*

Do so, Zagara ordered, and Tanya had the sudden mental picture of a tightly coiled spring. The Overqueen was just barely restraining herself.

Swarm supreme, Abathur said. *Swarm unique. Meant from beginning. Will be again.*

The Swarm will always be unique, Zagara said. *You give no justification for betrayal.*

Did not betray Swarm, Abathur insisted. *Betrayed only betrayer. Who is this betrayer?*

Abathur's claws twitched. *Overqueen. Overqueen is betrayer.*

"How can she betray the Swarm?" Dizz asked. "She's the Overqueen. Anything she does is by definition the will of the Swarm."

Both zerg ignored him. For a moment the mental confrontation degenerated from understandable words into images, emotions, and sensations that spun by too quickly for Tanya to keep up. All she could sift out of it was that Abathur was defiant and unapologetic, and Zagara was furious and ready to rip him apart with her bare claws.

What she didn't know was that Abathur had a hole card.

Slowly, Tanya sent her gaze around the room, peering into each of the darkened tunnels as best she could. Unfortunately, all of them had the same twisty curves as the one their group had entered by, which meant there could be psyolisks lurking unseen in every one of them.

"Hey—Abathur!" Dizz called, trying one more time to get in on the conversation. "We're on Overqueen Zagara's side here. How about explaining it so that the rest of us can understand?"

Abathur looked past Zagara, and it seemed to Tanya that his multiple eyes were measuring Dizz. *Terrans owed no explanation,* he said. *But Abathur will give.*

"Good," Dizz said. "Let's hear it."

Swarm supreme, Abathur said. *Swarm unique. Meant from very beginning. Will be again.*

"Yes, we got that part," Dizz said. "So what, you can't be unique without wiping out everything else?"

Inferior species cannot understand Swarm, Abathur said, his mental voice heavy with contempt. *Swarm supreme. Swarm meant to fill universe. Swarm meant to assimilate all. Discard what not needed.*

He says that the Swarm was meant to assimilate all, Mukav said.

Tanya glanced over, noting with surprise that the queen was considerably closer than she'd been when the conversation started. Apparently, she'd been moving toward the group while she acted as self-appointed translator.

Should they be letting her get that close?

Tanya looked at Dizz and Whist, but both were focused on the drama taking place across the chamber. Maybe they hadn't even noticed Mukav's approach.

"Thanks, but I'd like to hear this from Evolution Master Abathur himself," Dizz said to Mukav. "So you say the Swarm is supreme, Abathur?"

Swarm must grow. Change, Abathur said. *Without war, can do neither.*

"So are the psyolisks the zerg's next step toward starting another war?" Dizz called.

Chitha not zerg, Abathur said, his psionic voice a growl. *Swarm essence must dominate. Swarm essence not dominant in chitha. Swarm and xel'naga essence equal.*

"Ah-*ha*," Dizz said, nodding. "So *that's* your problem. Equal partnership isn't what you're used to, is it?"

No matter. Chitha not zerg, but chitha zerg weapon. Will give Swarm victory over protoss. Abathur jabbed a claw toward Ulavu.

"I don't know," Dizz said doubtfully. "Psyolisks are tricky enough to fight, but they die easier than the hydralisk that you based them on. But again, isn't it cheating to use xel'naga essence? Doesn't that make it a xel'naga victory, not a zerg victory?"

Victory not important, Abathur said. *Perfection important. Swarm on path to perfection.*

"Unless you've already left that path," Dizz said. "Or been passed by. Maybe it's the adostra that are perfection?"

Adostra. Abathur uttered the word like a curse. *Abomination.*

"How can they be an abomination?" Dizz asked. "You created them, didn't you?"

Zagara *created abomination,* Abathur retorted, this time jabbing his claw toward Zagara. *Abathur merely tool.*

"What's so wrong with them?" Dizz pressed. "How do the adostra take anything away from the zerg?"

Zerg *manipulate essence,* Abathur said stiffly. Zerg *create new life. New purpose in others.* Zerg *drive evolution. Mold into image of Swarm. Do not give that power to alien beings.*

The adostra deal only with plant life, Zagara said. She was clearly still furious, Tanya could tell, but at least she had calmed down enough to use intelligible words again. *They do not intrude upon the Swarm.*

Do not? Abathur countered. *Zagara ordered that power be given to adostra. Ordered adostra not be absorbed into Swarm.*

The power was in the xel'naga essence, Zagara insisted. *That gift was not given to us to be absorbed into the Swarm.*

Zagara's *promise to Queen of Blades,* Abathur said darkly. *Foolish promise.*

"So you wanted the adostra destroyed," Dizz said. "But not just destroyed. You wanted *us*—terrans and protoss—to destroy them. That way your own hands would be clean and Overqueen Zagara would have no one to blame but us."

Path of war out of Swarm's claws, Abathur said. *Zagara—Abathur does not name* Overqueen—*is summoned by terrans and protoss. Acceptance is further betrayal of Swarm.*

"So how does it play out from here?" Dizz pressed. "You're going to kill us all anyway, so it can't hurt to show how clever you've been."

Cleverness does not matter, Abathur ground out. *Only Swarm matters. Leviathan has left Gystt. Leviathan will flee. Terrans and protoss will name Zagara betrayer. Terrans and protoss will attack Swarm. Swarm will respond. Swarm will again be at war.*

"Good plan," Dizz said. "But not going to work. They won't attack, because they'll know that you kidnapped Overqueen Zagara."

How? Abathur scoffed. *Cannot speak truth to terrans and protoss. Inferior species will have only evidence of eyes and prejudice of thoughts.*

"See, that's where you're wrong," Dizz said. "It's true our long-range comms won't work with your psyolisks present. But there are other ways. Ulavu, for example, is a protoss, and protoss have a form of the same psionic communication as the zerg."

Protoss communication also blocked by chitha, Abathur said.

"I don't think so," Dizz said. "You see, we noticed how every time a protoss force landed on Gystt, you made sure to hit their transport in the right place to knock out the psionic boosters. The protoss may be the primary target for psyolisk psi attacks, but those attacks don't interfere with their communication. In fact, Ulavu's been relaying this entire conversation to his people."

Lies, Abathur said, his green eyes focusing on Ulavu. *Terran underestimates Abathur. Have studied full depth of protoss psionic communication. Know reach, distance covered.* He gestured. *Know size and volume of psionic booster that can reach across such distances. Protoss does not carry.*

"You're right; he doesn't," Tanya spoke up. She hefted her canister rifle.

Or rather, the psionic booster that Valerian and the protoss techs had built in the shape of a canister rifle. "But I do."

Abathur froze, his eyes on Tanya. "So you see, there's really no point in maintaining this charade," Dizz said. "Let's go back to Gystt, and we can—"

With a wordless cry, Ulavu dropped to his knees. Tanya took a step toward him and staggered back, a scream boiling up in her throat as a blaze of agony exploded through her brain.

And in that second, Mukav leaped across the remaining distance between them and attacked.

Her first slash caught Whist across the back of his helmet and cooling unit, throwing him five meters across the floor. Dizz spun around, dodged just a shade too slow, and took her second slash across his chest plate. He pinwheeled, nearly losing his balance—

And then shot up into the air, spinning and jinking like an injured bird as he tried to get some distance. Mukav slashed again, just catching the heel of his boot and nearly bringing him down. He recovered enough to keep from crashing and twisted back toward her, firing a shot from his gauss pistol that missed completely. She took one final, useless swipe at him, then turned toward Tanya and Ulavu.

There was nothing Tanya could do. Her brain was throbbing too hard to focus her power, her vision blurring too much, her armor too thin to block the claw when it came down in the killing blow. She tried to back up—knew she'd never get out of the way in time—

And twitched violently as a blaze of green cut across her field of view.

Ulavu had thrown his warp disk.

Not as accurately as he might have wanted, she realized instantly. Instead of slicing through Mukav's body, the spinning Void energy merely chopped off the limb poised above Tanya. But it was enough. Mukav screamed in agony and rage as the limb went flying. She turned reflexively toward Ulavu, raising her remaining slashing limb to strike.

And staggered as Whist, still lying on his back, opened up with his C-14. For a pair of heartbeats she jerked and twitched as the spikes hammered into her, trying to line up a shot at Ulavu but unable to regain her stability long enough to strike. From somewhere above Tanya came a new scream, this one in her ears instead of her mind, a long, piercing, mechanical sound, and Tanya felt the pressure in her brain ease a little. Whist kept firing, his spikes chipping away at Mukav's armor plating. The queen turned from Ulavu, abandoning that attack, and started toward the marine. There was a new double flash of green—

And Mukav slumped over and collapsed to the floor. Tanya blinked away some of the blurring to see Ulavu lying beside the dead queen's abdomen. Even dazed by the psyolisk attack, he'd retained enough focus and control to roll half beneath Mukav as she'd turned toward Whist and stab his warp blades into her underside.

Whist sent another two bursts into the queen, just to be sure. "Tanya?" he called, his voice strained and oddly slurred.

"We're okay," she called back, shaking her head and blinking against the mental interference still pressing against her mind. Turning from Mukav's carcass, she looked across the room.

It was as bad as she could have guessed. Worse. Zagara and Abathur were embroiled in direct personal combat, their limbs slashing at each other like ancient swordsmen in battle. Zagara was bigger and angrier, but Abathur was holding his own.

And he had allies. Boiling out of every tunnel was wave after wave of psyolisks.

It didn't matter that Abathur's scheme had been laid bare. Not to him. All that mattered was that the zerg returned to what they had once been. That they regained the power to follow their genetic imperative, to twist and mold other beings with ruthless efficiency, and then to join those beings to the Swarm. The power to grow and change and continue down the path toward perfection, even if perfection was never achieved.

The only one who stood in the way of that return to glory was Zagara. If she died, whether or not the Dominion and protoss knew what had happened, the Swarm would eventually return to its original nature and he would have achieved his goal.

He and Mukav had planned this well. They had Zagara, they had position, and they had overwhelming numbers.

What they *hadn't* counted on was that Zagara would have a few numbers of her own.

So far Dizz was the only one in action, hovering above and behind Zagara and firing methodically at the lines of psyolisks streaming toward the combatants. Firing at them, and hopefully confusing them. The long scream earlier that had shaken away some of Tanya's mental fog—a scream that had gone quieter but hadn't faded completely—was coming from the turbo microscreen in Dizz's jump pack, a special addition he'd asked for after Dr. Cogan's suggestion that Abathur might communicate with his psyolisks via ultrasonics.

It seemed to be working, too, at least to a degree. The psyolisks were moving slower than usual, slower than they had under the influence of the team's psi blocks alone. A few of the creatures paused as they came into the chamber, as if waiting for orders that never came.

But confusing them wouldn't be enough. There were just too many of them, and only one Dizz, and there was really no fine-tuning Abathur needed to do anyway. The psyolisks already knew what they were supposed to do.

Dizz would probably survive, the morbid thought drifted through the tangle that was Tanya's mind as she watched him soar up there above the conflict. She and Whist *might* survive back here by the entrance; they could make a run for it if necessary and find a choke point where they could make a stand until Valerian could send a dropship.

For Ulavu, there was no such question or distant hope. Ulavu was going to die.

Tanya had been right earlier. Abathur hadn't realized until now that Ulavu was a Nerazim warrior, and his response to that revelation had been to hit the protoss with as hard a psionic attack as the evolution master could manage.

There was no defense against that assault. Ulavu couldn't hide behind a hail of hypersonic 8mm spikes. He couldn't escape by flying to the ceiling. The pressure on Tanya's own mind was tearing away at her soul—how much more of Abathur's assault was being dumped on the hated protoss?

Maybe Ulavu's mind was tougher than Tanya knew. But she'd seen that mind. She'd been as close to Ulavu as any terran had ever been. He was strong, certainly. But he wasn't that strong.

His presence here had ruined Abathur's plan, and Abathur would have his revenge.

Ulavu had lied to Tanya. He'd betrayed her trust and their friendship.

But he'd also saved her life.

And sometimes broken friendships could be healed.

Could theirs? Tanya had no idea. The pain was still too fresh, too deep. Even if it healed, it might leave a scar that would never go away.

But ultimately, it didn't matter. This wasn't for friendship. This was because Ulavu was part of her team, and she was a ghost, a soldier of the Dominion, and her job was to protect him to the fullest of her ability.

No matter what the cost.

Ghost implants were there for a reason. Ghosts were unstable wild cards, some with known limits to their power, some without; some with known limits to their emotional stability, some without.

Tanya had no idea what her limits were. She had no idea what would happen without the implant.

Time to find out.

Stretching out with her power, aware that she was literally playing with fire, she reached inward, raising the temperature at the center of the implant just high enough to burn out its core electronics. She had the sense of nearby brain cells burning and growing dark . . . the sense of the implant failing . . . the sense of a slave whose chains had suddenly been stripped off. Through the black swirls of Abathur's psionic attack, and the red haze of her own righteous fury, she stretched out her power.

And the psyolisks began to die.

Slowly at first, just one at a time. Then more quickly, with two or three falling as she stared her rage at them.

Then, suddenly, they were falling in waves, toppling to the floor together like smoldering cordwood, their limbs flailing helplessly against the unseen attack that was destroying them from the inside. They died as they charged across the chamber; died as they emerged, ready for combat; died even while they were still inside the tunnels.

Through it all Tanya seemed to float above them, her body stretching out to fill the chamber, her mind full of alien thoughts and chatterings and agony. Distantly, she was aware that her hands were pressed against the floor, but there was no sensation of touch or smell or hearing. All was mind; all was sight; all was alien.

All was death.

It was a massacre, terrible and wonderful and horrifically satisfying. Tanya swept the room with hidden fire, burning some of the enemy even past the point of death, just because she could.

Distantly, she sensed Abathur trying desperately to call for a retreat. But his orders were unheard and unheeded through the blanketing noise from Dizz's jump pack. The buzz in Tanya's head began to fade, and the stutter from Whist's gauss rifle began to slow.

The haze faded into numbness. Vaguely, she wondered why she was staring at the arching roof of the leviathan chamber . . .

And then Dizz was kneeling over her, his expression tense. "You okay?" he asked. "Tanya? Talk to me."

"I'm okay," she breathed. Were her hands shaking?

They were. So was her entire body.

"Come on," he said, slipping a hand under her shoulders. "We've reached the *Hyperion,* and there's a dropship coming alongside. We need to get you to sickbay."

"Wait," she said as he lifted her off the floor. "Ulavu. Where's Ulavu?"

"He's fine," Dizz said, and for the first time Tanya noticed the oddness to his voice. "Just a little shaky. Whist's helping him down the tunnel."

"Okay." Tanya eased back to her feet, clutching at Dizz's arm as the compartment again swayed around her. Dead psyolisks were everywhere, she saw with a flicker of guilt. Creatures who had just been doing as they'd been ordered. "What about Zagara?" she asked as Dizz walked her toward the tunnel. "Did she win?"

"Oh, she won and a half," Dizz confirmed. "You should have seen it."

"I was a little distracted."

"Yeah," Dizz said grimly. "Well. I only saw a queen fight once during the war. It was pretty vicious. *This* fight left that one in the dust. They were going at it like they were trying to rip each other down by molecular layers. For a while Abathur was throwing psyolisks at her, too—just literally making them leap onto her back or torso and dig in."

"Is she all right?"

"Seems to be," Dizz said. "Luckily, our little jump pack modification kept him from grabbing anyone except the psyolisks closest to him, and Whist and I were able to blast enough of them off her to keep the attack at a level she could handle. It was probably distracting as hell, though.

"And then, suddenly . . ." He shook his head. "There must have been some tipping point with how many psyolisks Abathur had left to hit her with, because suddenly she was tearing into him like a mulcher on a stump."

"Did she kill him?"

"I don't think so," Dizz said. "But she came damn close. He looked like a dishrag when she dragged him out of here."

"But she didn't kill him," Tanya said, just making sure she'd heard him right. "And you and Whist didn't, either?"

"Oh, we were more than ready," Dizz said grimly. "But Zagara told us not to. She said he was one of a kind, and that the Swarm needs an evolution master to survive."

"Why?"

"She didn't say, and we didn't ask," Dizz said. "She was hauling him out, and Cruikshank had dropships and fighters on the way—" He waved a hand. "Anyway, that's *way* above my rank level. She and Valerian and probably Artanis can hash that one out."

"I suppose," Tanya said. "What happened to the rest of the psyolisks? Was Zagara able to control them?"

Dizz hesitated. "Actually . . . by the time she finished knocking the stuffing out of him, they were pretty much all dead."

Tanya swallowed hard. "Me?"

"Well, you had help," Dizz said. He was trying to be his usual flippant self, she could tell. But for once, it wasn't working. "Anyway. If you feel ready to move, we need to get you aboard the *Hyperion* and start fixing whatever happened to you."

"Yes." Tanya hesitated. "Dizz . . . did I scare you back there?"

Dizz pursed his lips. "Truthfully?"

"Truthfully."

"Yes," he conceded. "I think you scared all of us."

"That seems fair," Tanya murmured. The tunnel was starting to fade around her. "I think I'm going to need to be carried."

"No problem," Dizz assured her, shifting his grip. "Just relax. Sleep if you need to. Why does it seem fair?"

"I didn't want to be the only one," Tanya said. Her voice was fading away, even as the tunnel was going completely black. "Because I bloody well scared myself."

CHAPTER TWENTY-FOUR

"There she goes," Matt commented.

Valerian nodded, watching the leviathan pull away from its close orbit and head back toward Gystt's surface. "There *they* go," he corrected.

"Yeah." Matt muttered something under his breath. "I don't like it. Leaving him alive is *not* a good idea."

"Zagara says the Swarm needs him," Valerian reminded him.

"But she won't tell us why."

"Which doesn't mean it's not true," Valerian said. "As long as he's under her control—and she claims he is—it seems to me we need to give her the benefit of the doubt."

"Except that he hates her."

Valerian had to smile at that one. "How many years did *you* hate *me*?"

"That's different," Matt insisted. "And I never really *hated* you. I just didn't trust you."

"Of course. So much better."

"Whatever you say," Matt said. "Speaking of trust, you may have noticed that Artanis's purifier beam is still powered up."

Powered up, and no doubt still targeting the Point Three adostra chamber.

I will not again attack first, the hierarch had said earlier. Had he truly meant it? "Trust isn't an easy commodity to come by these days," Valerian murmured. "I'm hoping he's simply making sure he's ready for a quick second shot if Zagara delivers the first."

"Or making sure she knows he *can* deliver the first shot if he wants to," Matt said. "He's heard the evidence and the arguments. Now he has to make up his own mind."

"I suppose you're right," Valerian conceded. "Well, he's made the right choices up to now. All we can do is hope he keeps it up." He cocked an eye at Matt. "So how did *I* do?"

"There were moments," Matt said. "But in the end you came through okay."

"Thanks," Valerian said ruefully. "It's amazing how the proper and righteous path is so much easier to follow when you don't have the power to leave it."

"Welcome to the world of absolute power," Matt said. "Near-absolute, anyway. Luckily, you have people around who can help nudge you back on the path if you start veering off."

"I appreciate it." Valerian took a deep breath. "In the meantime, the Dominion still has serious problems to deal with. We'll give Zagara time to get back to Gystt, and Artanis time to do whatever stand-down he wants to do, and then see if either or both of them are up to another conversation."

The doctors had warned Tanya that walking might be tricky for a while as her brain tried to rewire itself around the neurons she'd destroyed when she fried her implant. But for the moment, at least, she had an arm to lean on.

For the moment.

I hear you're going back, she commented.

Yes, Ulavu said. *Hierarch Artanis believes that the events on Gystt have raised the Dominion's awareness of my presence, and that it will no longer be possible for me to remain with the ghost program in my previously unnoticed position. More urgently, my true identity will soon be made known, followed closely by recriminations and feelings of betrayal.* He hesitated. *You are yourself aware of the damage such feelings can cause.*

I am, Tanya conceded, feeling a twinge of resentment deep within her. *But it's not necessarily certain that your identity will be discovered. I've discussed it with Whist and the others, and everyone's agreed to keep your part of the mission out of their reports.*

Ulavu turned to her, and she could sense his surprise. *You* spoke *to them on my behalf? After my betrayal of your trust?*

Tanya shrugged. *We were a team. A team's supposed to look out for each other.*

I am humbled, Ulavu said. *Thank you.*

Don't thank me yet, Tanya warned. *It's still possible that someone will find a way to dig something out of those scrambled suit recorders. If they do, all bets are off.*

I nevertheless appreciate your faithfulness, Ulavu said. *I am both humbled and shamed.*

Tanya sighed. *I understand why you did it, Ulavu. I don't hold it against you.*

Thank you, Tanya Caulfield. I am more grateful for your forgiveness than you can imagine.

"Hey!" Colonel Cruikshank's voice called from behind them. "You—protoss. Hold it."

Tanya jerked, the sudden movement briefly intensifying her

chronic shaking. Ulavu was ready, catching her arm with his other hand, bringing her back on balance and sending reassurance and strength through her thoughts. They stopped in an orderly fashion and Ulavu carefully turned them around.

Cruikshank strode up to them, a controlled thundercloud of an expression on his face. "I was just in sickbay, looking at Dr. Wyland," he said. "First-degree burns over most of her body. Were you responsible for that?"

Tanya opened her mouth, closed it again as Ulavu squeezed her arm warningly. *Why do you think it was I?*

"I'll take that as a yes," Cruikshank growled. "And the answer is because you're a civilian who had no business being on a military mission in the first place. You screwed up, and Wyland paid for it. Tell me I'm wrong."

"He was with us at Emperor Valerian's request," Tanya reminded him frostily.

"Which just goes to show that even emperors shouldn't get everything they want," Cruikshank retorted. "They tell me you're leaving with Artanis and the main protoss force, so I can't do anything about this. Fine. But be *very* sure that I will never again willingly allow civilians to serve alongside my people." He focused on Tanya. "That goes for you, too."

Tanya shook her head. "I don't think so."

"Why not? Because you have your own special dispensation from the emperor?"

"Because I've applied to be reinstated into the ghost program."

"Because—" Cruikshank broke off, his eyes widening. "You're joking. I thought you just talked your way *out*."

"Well, I'm talking my way back in," Tanya said.

"Why?"

Tanya shrugged. "This was my first mission. It turns out I like them."

For a moment Cruikshank just stared at her. "Great," he growled at last. "Fine. Means someday I might have you under my command again. I can hardly wait." With a final glare at Ulavu, he turned and stalked away.

I thought you'd learned your lesson about lying to people, Tanya said reproachfully as Ulavu turned them around again and they continued on their way. *Why did you let him think you caused Erin's burns?*

I did not lie, Ulavu corrected her mildly. *In truth, Dr. Erin Wyland's first-degree burns are indeed due to my actions.*

Because without you and your warp blades, they'd have been third-degree burns?

My statement is still truthful, Ulavu said. *If Colonel Abram Cruikshank draws an incorrect conclusion, that is not my doing. You did not tell me you were returning to the ghost program.*

Tanya shrugged. *I have to,* she said. *You still want to recruit a teek to help with the protoss warp disk program, remember? You can't do it anymore, so I will.*

I appreciate your willingness, Tanya Caulfield. But it is not your responsibility.

It is if I choose it. And I choose it. Reaching up a trembling hand, she squeezed his arm. *Because helping each other is what friends do.*

The officers' bar on the *Hyperion* was strictly off-limits to marine sergeants. It was possibly off-limits to reapers, too, officers or otherwise.

As far as Whist could tell, Dizz didn't give a damn about that. Whist himself certainly didn't.

Luckily, no one else in the bar seemed inclined to challenge them on the point. Maybe it was the massive bandage on the back of Whist's head, or the equally impressive one across Dizz's chest.

"So I hear you're staying?" he asked Dizz as a stiffly silent waiter brought their drinks.

"Under some protest, yes," Dizz said. "Seems I've been summarily recalled to active duty and assigned to the *Phobos* as part of their brand-new, quote, 'Zerg Compliance Ground-Force Unit,' unquote. ZCGFU. Makes for a hell of an acronym."

"What are they complying with?"

"God only knows," Dizz admitted. "Whatever deal Valerian, Artanis, and Zagara came up with, I suppose. Plus chasing down any psyolisks that got away, plus watching over the adostra, plus keeping tabs on Abathur, et cetera, et cetera. Great fun."

"Hey, it could be worse," Whist said. "You could have been assigned as ambassador or something. You'd probably have had to live on the ground then."

"I probably will anyway," Dizz said sourly. "And I assume you're joking about the ambassador thing. I want to fly, not talk for a living. Hardly my forte."

"Oh, I don't know," Whist mused. "You put on a terrific show in there with Abathur. I'd hire you as prosecuting attorney any day."

Dizz shrugged. "Former criminal, remember? You sit through enough courtroom proceedings, you learn how it all works."

He picked up his drink and swirled it meditatively. "You gotta admit, though. No matter how you slice it, that was one hell of a day's work."

"Sure was," Whist said, frowning. It had been such a long day, he'd nearly forgotten that everything they'd done had indeed been crammed into that single sunup-to-sundown period. "So who are we drinking to this time?" he asked, picking up his glass. "The ones Cruikshank lost in his part of the One-Day War?"

"First drink is to them," Dizz agreed, nodding. "Second drink—" He gave Whist a lopsided smile. "Second drink is to all the future comrades who *won't* die because of what we all did down there today."

Whist shook his head. "And I thought reapers didn't have souls."

"*I* thought marines didn't have brains."

"Still a fair chance we're both right," Whist pointed out.

"That there is." Dizz reached over the table and tapped Whist's glass with the edge of his. "Cheers, friend."

"Cheers."

KOPRULU SECTOR TIMELINE

c. 1500 AD—A group of rogue protoss is exiled from the protoss homeworld of Aiur for refusing to join the Khala, a telepathic link shared by the entire race. These rogues, called the dark templar, cut their nerve cords to permanently sever their connection with the Khala.

2231—The government of Earth launches four supercarriers—the *Argo,* the *Sarengo,* the *Reagan,* and the *Nagglfar*—to colonize hospitable planets mapped out in a nearby star system. Tens of thousands of passengers are placed in stasis for the journey, which is estimated to last one year.

2232—The supercarriers' linked navigation systems fail. The ships travel through space blindly, without a programmed destination.

2259—The ships' warp engines finally melt down. The supercarriers emerge into an unmapped region of the galaxy that will later be known as the Koprulu sector, and they make emergency landings on three planets—Umoja, Tarsonis, and Moria.

2323—The Terran Confederacy is founded on Tarsonis.

2475—Two corporate entities on Moria form an alliance, the Kel-Morian Combine, to stand against Confederate intrusions on their territory.

2485—Tensions between the Confederacy and the Kel-Morian Combine explode into open war. This conflict will later become known as the Guild Wars.

2489—The Confederacy declares victory in the Guild Wars.

2489—Umojan colonies form a military coalition called the Umojan Protectorate to ensure independence from Confederate tyranny.

2489—Senator Angus Mengsk and members of his family are brutally murdered by assassins after Mengsk dissents from Confederate leaders. His surviving son, Arcturus, openly rebels against the Confederacy from his homeworld of Korhal IV.

2491—The Confederacy decimates Korhal IV through nuclear bombardment. Arcturus Mengsk begins sustained guerrilla operations against the Confederacy.

2491—Mengsk's forces, the Sons of Korhal, capture ghost operative Sarah Kerrigan and secure her cooperation against the Confederacy.

2499—FIRST CONTACT

- The zerg, a previously unknown alien race, invade the planets of Chau Sara and Mar Sara. Shortly thereafter, a second unknown alien race, the protoss, razes all life on Chau Sara.
- Marshal Jim Raynor, while leading the fight against the zerg on Mar Sara, rebels against the Confederacy and joins with the Sons of Korhal.
- More planets openly revolt against the Confederacy.

2500—THE DOMINION RISES

- Arcturus Mengsk uses the Confederacy's own experimental technology to draw the zerg Swarm to the capital world of Tarsonis. The planet is utterly destroyed. Mengsk also leaves his loyal operative Sarah Kerrigan behind to die, causing Jim Raynor to defect.

- Unbeknownst to terran forces, Kerrigan is captured by the zerg, not killed.
- Mengsk declares himself the ruler of a new nation—the Dominion. He consolidates the scattered forces of the Confederacy under his command.
- The protoss homeworld of Aiur is overrun by the zerg, but the Swarm's leader, the Overmind, is killed.

2500—NEW CONFLICT

- Forces from the United Earth Directorate (UED) expeditionary fleet arrive in the Koprulu sector, seeking to assert control over terran planets.
- With the Overmind dead, Sarah Kerrigan—newly infested and empowered by the zerg—seeks control of the Swarm. She allies briefly with protoss and human factions to oppose UED forces.
- After securing her position as the uncontested ruler of the zerg, Kerrigan turns on her allies. Retaliatory assaults against her stronghold on Char by protoss, UED, and Dominion forces fail.
- Surviving UED forces scatter. None return to Earth.

2502—Dominion intelligence confirms that Artanis, a young protoss military commander, is leading both the Aiur protoss and dark templar factions.

2504—CIVIL WAR

- Jim Raynor redoubles his insurgent activities against the Dominion. Valerian Mengsk, Arcturus's son, aids him in secret.
- Zerg forces begin to invade Dominion territory again.
- Civil unrest spreads across core Dominion worlds after allegations of Arcturus Mengsk's excesses are made public.
- Armies led by Valerian Mengsk and General Horace Warfield invade the zerg planet of Char (with assistance from Jim Raynor's forces). They neutralize and capture Sarah Kerrigan.

2505—THE SWARM REEMERGES

- Arcturus Mengsk launches a raid on Valerian Mengsk's stronghold in Umojan territory. Jim Raynor is captured. Sarah Kerrigan escapes.
- Arcturus Mengsk declares victory against the zerg and enacts a brutal civil suppression regime to end unrest.
- Kerrigan reclaims control of the zerg.
- The Swarm invades Korhal, cutting a direct path to Arcturus's palace and killing the emperor. Zerg forces leave the planet immediately.
- Valerian Mengsk becomes the Dominion's leader. He pledges to reform his father's policies and promote peace throughout the Koprulu sector.

2506—WAR WITH AMON

- The protoss' Golden Armada launches an attack to retake Aiur from the zerg.
- During the invasion of Aiur, the protoss discover that the zerg on the planet have been enslaved by the rogue xel'naga Amon. Amon then corrupts the Khala and gains control of all protoss within the psionic link. The dark templar Zeratul severs Hierarch Artanis's nerve cords, destroying his connection to the Khala and allowing him to escape Amon's possession, but Zeratul is killed in the battle.
- Artanis liberates as many other protoss as he can. They join up with the surviving dark templar and flee from Aiur on the arkship *Spear of Adun*.
- Artanis and his forces journey to Ulnar to learn the fate of the xel'naga, the protoss' ancient benefactors, and find that all but Amon have perished. While there, Artanis uncovers Amon's plan to use the protoss and the Overmind's remains to forge a new host body. If Amon succeeds, all life in the universe will be destroyed.

- Using an ancient xel'naga relic known as the Keystone, Artanis drives Amon from the Khala, and the formerly enslaved protoss sever their nerve cords to ensure their freedom. Artanis and his forces retake Aiur. Amon is banished to the Void.

2508—AFTERMATH

- Kerrigan, Jim Raynor, Artanis, the broodmother Zagara, and their forces enter the Void to attempt to defeat Amon once and for all. Kerrigan absorbs the remaining power of a xel'naga, becoming xel'naga herself. She gives Zagara command of the Swarm. Then, with the aid of her allies, Kerrigan destroys Amon, disappearing shortly afterward. Raynor also disappears sometime after the battle.
- The terrans, the protoss, and the zerg end hostilities with one another.
- Valerian Mengsk begins open elections in the Dominion.
- Zagara takes control of the systems near Char for the zerg Swarm.

ABOUT THE AUTHOR

TIMOTHY ZAHN has been writing science fiction since 1975 and sold his first story to *Analog* in 1978. Since then Zahn has published over a hundred short stories and novellas, numerous novels, and three short-fiction collections. Along the way he has won a Hugo Award (for the novella *Cascade Point*, in 1984) and has been nominated twice more. He is best known for his ten *Star Wars* novels (*Heir to the Empire, Dark Force Rising, The Last Command, Specter of the Past, Vision of the Future, Survivor's Quest, Outbound Flight, Allegiance, Choices of One,* and *Scoundrels*). His most recent publications have been the science fiction Cobra series and the six-part young adult Dragonback series. He has a BS in physics from Michigan State University, and an MS in physics from the University of Illinois.

Facebook.com/TimothyZahn

ABOUT THE TYPE

This book was set in Minion, a 1990 Adobe Originals typeface by Robert Slimbach (b. 1956). Minion is inspired by classical, old-style typefaces of the late Renaissance, a period of elegant, beautiful, and highly readable type designs. Created primarily for text setting, Minion combines the aesthetic and functional qualities that make text type highly readable with the versatility of digital technology.